A

JEALOUS GOD

BY THE SAME AUTHOR

Chimera
The Bitter Cross
A Place in Italy

A
JEALOUS GOD
by

Simon Mawer

ANDRE DEUTSCH

First published in Great Britain in 1996 by
André Deutsch Limited
106 Great Russell Street
London WC1B 3LJ

ISBN 0 233 98964 1

CIP data available for this title from
the British Library

Printed in Great Britain by
WBC Bridgend

For Julia

I

1

The view was remarkable, the stuff of tourist guides: the valley of Gehenna, or Hinnom – take your choice – at your feet and, on the far side, the Citadel and the Jaffa Gate and the long line of the wall draped like a curtain across the hillside. At the gate where the buses stopped was the little rabble of stalls selling kebab and felafel, while above the battlements rose the domes and towers of the Old City. The names had taken on an altogether different ring in his mind over the last year, familiarity giving him the illusion of possession: the Holy Sepulchre, the Muristan, the Dome of the Rock, Al-Aqsa, the Hurvah synagogue, the Church of the Dormition. And then behind and above them all the far hill, which really was the place itself, however much the experts might dispute the others – the Mount of Bleeding Olives, as one of the clerks had called it.

'If you don't mind my saying so, sir,' the sergeant observed after due consideration, 'you can keep it.' He was a heavy, sweating man (the ceiling fan seemed to make no more impression on him than did the view of the City), with the kind of literal mind that one had come to expect from soldiers. Not for him ancient cities or sacred shrines.

'You're not a religious man, Sergeant?'

'Religious, sir?'

Why were they always suspicious when asked a personal question? 'Yes, religious. Church, prayer, belief in God. You know what I mean.'

The sergeant sniffed. 'Well, church parade sir, naturally. And funerals. And marriage. But loving-kindness to all men, love your neighbour as yourself, love your enemies, that kind of thing? No, sir. I mean, we haven't none of us done very well in the last few years, have we?'

'Not really.'

The man pounded his typewriter with all the determination of a grave-digger. He paused. 'When did you join up, sir? If I might ask.'

'Thirty-nine'

'So you've been through it all.'

The major, who was many years younger than the sergeant, shrugged. 'I suppose so.'

'And you've got family, too, haven't you?' He pointed to the photograph on Major Harding's desk, the shot of Lorna and the little girl taken in the garden of his father-in-law's house. 'Well, I joined up right at the start, too, and it seems to me that it was bad enough fighting a war against fucking Germans, if you'll forgive my French, for six fucking years, but fighting another war here against a bunch of fucking Jews all in the name of religion, instead of going home to the wife and kids and getting back to normal is a bit of a . . . an *imposition*.'

Harding smiled at the man's restraint. 'It's not got much to do with religion,' he said. 'Politics, war, anything but religion in fact. What would you do with the Jews, Sergeant, if you had the power?'

'But I don't, sir, do I? It's not my job.' The sergeant fiddled with the paper in his typewriter. Harding stood looking towards the lacquered, turquoise box whose grey dome was like a delicate, leaden bubble blown out of the heart of the Old City – the very spot where Abraham planned to sacrifice his son Isaac at the whim of a jealous god.

'What if it were?'

'If Adolf Hitler had done *his* job better,' the sergeant decided, 'we wouldn't have all these bloody Ikeys to deal with in the first place, would we?'

There seemed no answer to that. The sergeant continued to thump on his typewriter. The major continued to look out of the window. Far below in the Hinnom Valley an armoured car of the Life Guards ground up the slope towards the Jaffa Gate. Through the open window the noise of its engine could be heard in the hot midday air. The date was the twenty-second of July 1946.

Up there in Military Headquarters on the fourth floor, and in the Government Secretariat in the south wing of the building, men and women continued to sweat out the morning, confident in the fact that it would soon be lunchtime, and at lunchtime, in the ineffable manner of colonial government, things would more or less close down. But elsewhere in the building things were different. In the foyer lounge, decorated – as Killin always said, as though Cecil B de Mille designed it for King Herod – Nubian stewards in white pantaloons and red fezzes were already waiting on a shifting population of Jew and Arab and Gentile. Customers were calling for drinks at the bar. The tables in the Grill Room and the main dining room on the ground floor and the Regence Café down in the basement, were laid and ready for the lunchtime onslaught. The kitchens were reaching their quotidian climax of hysteria. For the King David, standing on its high hill, rising above the whole city, overbearing even the Holy of Holies, was a monster of grotesque and disparate parts: at once the seat of government and a luxury hotel.

The major turned from his contemplation of the view. An ATS clerk had just come in with a file and he reached for a postcard which had being lying on his desk. 'Jenny, be a dear and go and post this for me, will you? I want it to catch the noon collection.' He glanced at it before handing it over, read it through one last time.

> *This is almost the view from my window. The building with the dome is where Jesus' Temple used to be, where He drove out the traders and stall-holders. They still haven't gone back there, but there are thousands of them in the rest of the city. They have forced me to buy lots of presents for you both.*
>
> *Much love, Daddy.*

The clerk took it. 'For the little girl, is it sir? How sweet.'

Harding watched her go, then turned back to his work. At that moment there was a noise like the sound of pistol shots, distant and muffled. 'What the devil's that?'

The sergeant paused in his typing. 'Like the bloody wild west these days,' he said.

'Didn't it come from inside the hotel?'

'Dunno, sir.'

Harding listened for moment, then rang down to Security. The line was occupied. He shrugged as he replaced the 'phone. Pistol shots in Jerusalem. It was almost the norm. He glanced at his watch. 'I've got to see someone,' he told the sergeant. 'Lock up for me, will you?'

In the corridor outside the office there were people milling around, stirred up by talk of a gun battle in the basement. A small crowd had gathered at the head of the stairs like passengers at a muster station. 'Load of balls,' someone was saying as Harding walked towards the lifts. 'Usual bloody cock-up.'

The lift took him from the bleakness of Military Headquarters down through the hushed and carpeted bedroom floors and into the main foyer of the hotel. It was a bizarre journey. It went from olive green to polychrome, from functional to theatrical, from secretive to public, from quiet to chaos. The foyer was seething. Stewards in their absurd fancy dress tried to placate the agitated. People crowded round anyone who looked as though he might be important, even plucking at Harding's sleeve as he passed. 'Have you seen the manager?' someone called, pushing through the throng. 'He's wanted on the 'phone. Have you seen the manager?'

And from the main bar a familiar voice cried out, 'Andrew, come and have a jar!'

Harding looked in at the door. Killin was perched on one of the bar stools, brandishing a glass of beer. 'What's going on?' Harding asked. 'Everyone seems in a tizz.'

Killin screwed up his face, as though at all the confusion of the Orient, the chaos, the usual bloody excitability. 'One of the Arabs went berserk in the kitchens or something. Tried to shoot the chef. I feel like shooting the chef sometimes. What'll you have?'

'Not now.' Harding gave a little wave and disappeared amongst the crowd.

The time was 12.18. That was what Killin told the military police; that was what he told Lorna as well. He happened to look at his watch at just that moment. 12.18.

Two minutes later there was an explosion in the road outside the front of the hotel followed by the sound of breaking glass. There were cries from within the foyer. Killin took his beer and went with the crowd through the main doors to look. There was a cloud of smoke over by the YMCA building and people were shouting and running around. A bus lay on its side in the road amidst a litter of broken glass while cars edged past under the frantic control of a policeman.

'Salameh's store,' someone said. 'They've blown the window in.'

'Usual bloody nonsense.'

A siren went off, rising and falling, like the air raid sirens that so many people had grown familiar with in recent years. The thing with terrorist attacks, the way they were different from air raids, was that when the sirens went off the attack was already over. There was nervous laughter from the people watching from the hotel steps, a sense of relief. Passengers had begun clambering out through the windows of the bus but no great damage seemed to have been done. You could laugh when they did no real damage. There was something absurd about a bomb that went off like that, as absurd as a firework, a catherine-wheel or a jumping-jack or something. Little more than a hoax really. A woman was being helped across the road towards the KD. She was clutching a bleeding arm but she seemed to be all right.

'Usual bloody nonsense,' said the man at Killin's side. 'One wonders what all the fuss is about half the time.' Someone seemed to agree with him, for quite soon another siren blew, this time long and constant – the all-clear – and people relaxed. Killin and the other customers took their drinks back inside. People returned to their offices, wondering whether there was really any point in going back to work at all now. Secretaries went back to their typing, committees reconvened, clerks returned to their filing cabinets, drinkers ordered another round. It was just another disturbance in the Holy City, worthy of another half-inch of column space in the British newspapers back home, another thoughtful leader in the *Palestine Post*.

Five minutes later, at 12.37, seven hundred and seventy pounds of TNT, packed into milk churns and placed in the Regence Café directly beneath the Government Secretariat, detonated. Focused by the confines of the basement the blast was directed upwards through the six stories of concrete, stone and steel. It blew through floors and collapsed walls as though they were made of cardboard. It blew a column of smoke and yellow limestone dust high into the blue Jerusalem sky, high above the Hinnom Valley and the walls of the Old City, high above the Dome of the Rock and the Western Wall of the Temple Mount, high above the Church of the Holy Sepulchre and the Al-Aqsa mosque and the Hurvah synagogue. It blew people and furniture and filing cabinets to pieces with a fine indifference.

Men and women screamed. Whistles blew and policemen shouted. People ran towards the pall of smoke and a crowd gathered at the scene of the wreckage. Pieces of paper floated down through the smoke like birds fluttering to earth. Dust shifted in the bright air. Shorn of one of its limbs, the trunk of the hotel loomed through the cloud like a great, mangled beast. Staircases were draped down exposed inner walls; corridors gaped open like surprised mouths; torn wallpaper was displayed like pallid flesh to the cruel light of day. On the heap of rubble men in knee-length khaki shorts scrabbled with concrete beams and stone blocks while blood and dust made a peculiar form of mud. A human head, blown across the road from the hotel, had stuck high on the wall of the YMCA building opposite.

Dennis Killin was one of the men clambering over the wreckage. He split his nails and tore a gash in his leg and sprained a wrist so badly that it had to be put in plaster later. 'Where's Andrew Harding?' he kept asking people. 'Have you seen Andrew Harding?'

2

It is unfortunate to begin with a death; but for Helen it was, in a sense, the beginning. It amounts to her first real memory, her first adult memory, if by adult one means the first moment when you learn about an event from the world outside, and understand that world to be malign, random and entirely indifferent.

Thinking of death, that death, she leaves the library of the School of Biblical Studies and pauses uncertainly on the pavement outside, watching the traffic streaming down towards the Euston Road: Helen Harding, fortyish, blondish; happy worrying about other people; ridden with guilt about her mother; more or less content when shut within the confines of the library; sometimes amused but often bored with Eric; often confused over the question of Miriam, her daughter, now at university; disturbingly indifferent to her son Paul, who is struggling with school and examinations and adolescence – an unequal fight that he seems in danger of losing at times. What amazes her is the fact that one can be fortyish and still be as confused as she was at his age. She had always nurtured greater expectations of maturity.

She crosses the road and enters the cold and scented gloom of the Church of Saint Edward the Confessor, a hideous confection of black and red brick which lies opposite the library. Inside there is the cold touch of remoteness, a breath of incense on the chill air, a sensation of old beliefs and past enthusiasms. Christ hangs crucified in the shadows of the far end of the nave and a sanctuary light gleams red like a single, mad eye. Helen stands for a while beside the font and the display of devotional books and says a prayer, almost in the manner of someone throwing a stone into a well to find out its depth, to find out if there is even water there at all.

'Our Father which art in heaven, hallowed be thy name. Thy kingdom come. They will be done . . .' Words from childhood, conjuring up images rather than meaning, images of her own father rather than a heavenly one, images of a man who has lurked in the shadows of her mind throughout her life, taking on different natures at different ages – a fairy-tale, pied piper quality when she was young and a saint-like nobility when she was older; sometimes the easy smile of a companion, occasionally the stern mien of a judge – but each identity fed equally by the bland studio portrait that she kept, and keeps still, like a holy picture, on her dressing table.

'And lead us not into temptation, but deliver us from evil.'

She shivers, at the cold, at the sight of the Christ pinned like an insect against the shadows, at the words themselves. In the text it is not *evil* in any abstract sense; it is του πονηρου: the Evil One. Satan.

After waiting in the silence for a few minutes – can she hear the ripples? – she goes back out into the evening light of the city, out from the cold shadows into the noise of the street, out into the stream of office workers and tourists.

> The fields from Islington to Marylebone,
> To Primrose Hill and Saint John's Wood,
> Were builded over with pillars of gold;
> And there Jerusalem's pillars stood.

But she looks in vain, seeing only red buses and hurrying crowds and an old man sitting in a cardboard box reading a newspaper upside down, and a black youth going by on a skateboard, weaving amongst the crowd. Leaves scurry across the street from one of those little patches of green that still survive amongst the concrete and tarmac, a former graveyard lying in those very fields where Blake saw his visions. The youth on the skateboard is plugged into headphones and singing to himself.

All time is not equivalent. The years Helen looks back on seem to be of a different substance than the present, made out of different material: childhood appears dense and tightly woven and obscure; adulthood evanescent and transparent.

At first she wondered whether she was to blame in some way. There was a ring on the doorbell, followed by the entry of a tall shining officer with a solemn shining face, and at his side a lady who seemed brisk and efficient, like a doctor. They brought with them a whispering, a sense of unease, a sense of the difficulty of everything. The tall officer smiled bravely at her. 'You must be Helen.'

In Helen's world there was no other possibility. 'Of course.'

'Jolly good.' The officer ruffled her hair, not knowing what else to do. His lips were tightly compressed and there was a sense of congratulation about his expression, but who exactly was being congratulated was not clear.

'You'd best go to your room and play, my dear,' the lady suggested.

'What have I done?'

'Nothing, dear. Nothing at all. Just be a good girl for a moment.'

'Do what you're told, darling,' her mother said. She wore red eyes and had adopted a whisper. 'I'll come up in a bit.'

'Mummy's got a cold,' Helen told herself. She could relate to colds. You were threatened with them if you did a whole lot of things of which adults disapproved – went out in the rain without a hat, didn't wear shoes in the house, that kind of thing. Maybe the lady *was* a doctor. So she went upstairs as she had been told and found one of her dolls and played hospitals. It was a complex game of injections and medicines and plastic anatomy, and by the end of the game the doll lay in pieces, its limbs scattered over the carpet and the head sitting grotesquely on its own on the bed. 'This is all for the best,' she explained to the head in solemn and adult tones. 'Now you are much better.'

Later, a few weeks later, her mother explained it all. 'Daddy's not going to come back to us,' she said. 'He's gone away forever. He still loves us darling, but he's gone away forever. He's gone to Jesus.'

Gone to Jesus. It seemed reasonable enough. 'If he's gone to Jesus, then that's a good thing,' Helen told her mother. You try to put your learning to work and that was what Helen had been taught in Sunday School, that it is the ambition of all good people to go to Jesus. Death is what life is all about, children; death and going to Jesus if you're good. Bad people? Well, that's a bit more complicated. But at least now she understood the red eyes and the hushed voice and, less clearly, the sense of the difficulty of things; not a cold at all. Tears. She lay in bed that night and tried to weep as her mother had wept, tried to weep for the dead father whom she had known so vaguely, and found that she couldn't. Her eyes remained dry, like her mind. Never, in all her childhood, did Helen weep for her father.

★

She decides to take a taxi home. Inside the cab, detached from the crowds on the pavement, remote from black youths on skateboards or drunks in cardboard boxes or women with push-chairs and piles of shopping, she feels vaguely guilty. The discrete guilt of the bourgeoisie, Eric calls it. She pays off the cab and lets herself into the house, calling out to her son as she opens the door. 'Paul, it's me.'

An indistinct response comes from one of the rooms upstairs.

'We're out this evening.'

He responds again, the muffled cry of adolescence, as though from a great distance and confused by layers of incomprehension: 'So what?'

'So I'm telling you, darling. Will you be okay?'

'Why not?'

She shrugs and picks up the mail from the mat. There are bills and circulars and a reminder that some subscription or other is due, and a letter from acquaintances in America. She can't quite imagine why Paul didn't pick the post up himself, but she has learned not to ask too much. Clutching the letter she goes to her bedroom, remembering a postcard lying on a different doormat in just the way those letters had – a shaft of light slanting into another hallway from a pane of glass in a different front door, the postcard lying on the mat half in the light, half in shadow. The card showed a photograph of the Old City of Jerusalem. Helen's memory gives it colour – paints the great dome gold and the walls beneath blue, gives the other buildings yellow stones and red tiled rooves, spreads over everything a sky of exactly the same peerless blue as the tiles below the dome – but that is present knowledge casting its shadow back into the past. In whatever passes for reality, the picture was black and white.

She hid the card. She knew it was not intended for her mother because she could read her own name in carefully looped letters at the top: *Darling Helen*. Most of the other words were beyond her, but not that one, and not the salutation at the bottom: *much love, Daddy*.

It was a message from beyond the grave.

Chronology is never the most powerful aspect of memory for a child. Dates mean little. It is the adult who can take a memory and catalogue it, card index it, date stamp it. She must have found the postcard sometime after the visit of the shining officer and the brisk lady, but the finding of it was – is – just one moment like so many others frozen out of the past; like one of those old photographs that you sometimes come upon in the bottom drawer of a desk: unnamed people staring out of the Edwardian era into the Elizabethan, always wearing expressions of an optimism which is hardly justified by subsequent events.

Over the weeks, maybe even months, Helen deciphered that message. She kept the card in a secret place in her room and took it out occasionally and scanned the words for meaning. It was like breaking a code, working away at the blocks of jumbled letters, gradually easing clarity out of the gibberish. She employed great cunning. 'Mummy, what's this say?' she would ask in apparent innocence, laboriously writing the word *VIEW* alongside the picture that she was drawing of a house and a child and a man and a woman.

Her mother peered over her shoulder. 'That's a difficult one to read. *Veeoo*. It's what you see when you look out of a window or something. You've drawn a *view* of the house.'

'And what's *temple*?'

'It's this part of your head.' Her mother's fingers pressed gently amongst the mass of golden hair.

'Jesus' temple?'

'Oh, that. Where did you hear about that?'

'Sunday School,' Helen answered quickly. She clutched her secret to herself with a breathless excitement. She was more cunning than any adult. She would read her father's words from beyond the grave and she would understand them. They were for her alone.

'Well, the Temple is the place where Jesus went to say his prayers,' her mother told her.

'Daddy's with Jesus now, isn't he?'

'I expect so, darling. Now let's see if you can draw a tree in the garden . . .'

So she went on with the deception, the drawing of MUMY and DADY and HELEN and the house, and now the tree, perhaps the tree of the knowledge of good and evil, but without a serpent yet. Another piece of the code had been broken. *VIEW. TEMPLE.*

The postcard still exists amongst her papers, the looped letters painfully clear to an adult eye, the ink, once black, now faded to a dark brown in the forty-odd years that have passed since it was written. What did it mean to her when she first deciphered it in its entirety? Its meaning is clear enough now, obvious and rather banal, and she cannot even identify the moment when the whole message emerged from the fog of illegibility:

This is almost the view from my window. The building with the dome is where Jesus' Temple used to be, where He drove out the traders and stall-holders. They still haven't gone back there, but there are thousands of them in the rest of the city. They have forced me to buy lots of presents for you both.

The rock beneath the dome is the place where Abraham, at the whim of a jealous god, was prepared to sacrifice his child. She knows that now. She knows a great deal now; but little about her father. Aside from that postcard and a few photographs, she owns no more of him than a vague assembly of imperfect recollections without either setting or context or chronology: walking with him to church one Sunday morning; seeing him at attention, glittering, before a mass of similarly glittering men; leaning over the wing of a car – 'that's the distributor,' he said, pointing – to examine the engine with him; waving to an aeroplane in which, she had been told, he was sitting. The aeroplane took off in the rain trailing a plume of spray, its lights glistening in the tarmac like shop windows dressed for Christmas; and she never saw him again.

She undresses and has a shower, and as she comes from the bathroom with her towel wrapped round her she catches sight of a photograph on her dressing table – a child staring out of the silver frame into the present with an expression of narrow-eyed defiance, almost as though she is about to bite. Helen smiles at the picture distractedly as though at a vague acquaintance and while drying herself she glances in the mirror to try and work out how much of what she sees now is the same as it was in that photograph. Not much, she fancies. Now she sees mottled legs and clumsy hips and loose, narrow breasts; then she possessed a slender, androgynous grace. Now, hurrying for the bus or something, she feels herself awkward and clumsy; then she could run with ease. Now she sees through a glass darkly, then face to face.

Just as she finishes drying Eric rings to say that he will be delayed at work and can she go on without him? Of course she can. She has gone on for most of her life without him, so why should a mere dinner party prove a problem? She jiggles the cradle to cut the line and rings for another taxi, then dresses (young clothes still: the final surrender to middle-age can wait) and sits down to perform that minimum of make-up (*maquillage* Eric calls it) which, according to him, makes her look like Greta Garbo. She knows that to be a complete and utter lie, but it is the kind of lie, delivered in the kind of manner, which amused her when they first met sixteen years ago. She enjoys lies of that nature. Some of the other ones she finds a bit hard to take.

Just as she is smoothing the eye-shadow with one of her long fingers – 'claws', someone once said of them – the doorbell rings. 'Paul, darling,' she calls to her son, 'I'm going. Can you find yourself something in the fridge? We might be late, so don't wait up. Be good.' And leaving the lipstick to do in the cab, she grabs her coat and runs downstairs to the hall.

Claws. Who had it been?

She remembers just as she opens the front door – Michael. She climbs into the taxi thinking of the past almost as though it has substance, as though it possesses shape. Michael. Michael and Anthony; and Tommy.

The stepfather just happened, a coming without cause and without reason, one of those tricks that fate plays. 'Would you like a new Daddy?' her mother asked one day. Helen remained non-committal on the matter, but that didn't deter her mother from going ahead with the marriage. Like her true father, Tommy was in the army; indeed he bore a striking resemblance to the shining officer who had visited the house on that strange day earlier, although he couldn't have been the same because that officer had a wife and Helen knew you were not allowed two of those. Nevertheless the vague suspicion remained.

Tommy called her Squirrel. 'For ever hiding things away,' he would explain. He was very kind and affectionate but he never broke through the shell of reserve which Helen had built round her. 'Give Tommy a smile, Squirrel,' he would say, and of course she would oblige readily enough; but the smile seemed to come from a store of polite expressions and looked as though it had been planted there with care and deliberation.

With the stepfather came two step-brothers – Anthony and Michael, forever playing with guns and toy soldiers and, later, with themselves. They were at boarding school and only appeared at holidays, and at first Helen tried as best she could to ignore them. They were an intrusion, an army that had invaded and conquered her territory and subjugated the inhabitants. Passive resistance and civil disobedience were her only weapons.

'She's a sister for you,' Lorna explained optimistically to Michael after an early quarrel. 'Isn't that nice? Isn't it a good thing to have someone else your age?'

'She's younger than me.'

21

'Almost your age.'

'And she can't do boys' things.'

Helen watched the exchange sullenly. She knew that she looked plain like that, an acid expression scarring her face, but she didn't care. 'Who wants to do boys' things?' she asked, and then instantly betrayed herself to the opposition: 'And anyway, I *can*.'

'See? Anyway you can't.'

'I can so.'

Scenes are frozen out of the past, like excerpts from a film. There are scenes in colour, scenes in black and white, scenes with voices and sounds, scenes with scent, scenes that are no more than single, static images: a crowd of people at a graveside; a cricket match at the village with Tommy walking in from the wicket; Tommy and Lorna arguing over something in the kitchen of a married quarter somewhere, sometime. Helen may be sitting now in the back of a taxi picking its way through the traffic south of the river, but she is not seeing the dreary houses, the grey-green of a common, the brilliant lights of Tescos and Pizza Hut, meretricious signals of the present. She is witnessing the past, scenes apparently picked at random from that store which, psychologists tell us, may be well-buried but is yet complete: swimming in the river at the end of the garden of Guerdon House; creeping into the boathouse pursued by Michael; building a treehouse in the orchard; cycling round the local villages; a host of incidents and images from which you can try and make some kind of sense if you please.

'Come DOWN you two; for goodness' sake, come down!'

She can hear her mother's voice calling, and she can feel the rough bark of holm oak beneath her hands. The texture of that bark has stayed with her throughout her life, the memory of it not only in her mind but there, tangibly, in her palms. Pale faces peer upwards at her through a fretwork of branches. Directly above, so close that she could touch them if only she dare let go of the branch, are the heels of Michael's plimsolls. His sharply foreshortened legs disappear into grey flannel shorts. He peers down at her.

'You're frightened.'

'So are you.'

'I'm not, so.'

'Your knee's shaking.'

'It's the wind.'

Childhood memory is a text edited by a random and capricious hand. For Helen there is no before and no after, just those moments of clinging to the rough black bark, with Michael just above her and the adult world far beneath. Wind courses through the leaves, swaying their world back and forth as though something has broken in the foundations of the earth and they are adrift on a stormy sea. The branch flexes and creaks beneath their weight and her mother's voice comes up faintly from far below. 'Oh my God,' she is saying, 'what if they fall?' The words are intended for her husband, not for the children up there in the high canopy of leaves. And then Tommy's voice reaches up to them, and it is the voice of a man who is under authority, having soldiers under him: 'COME DOWN AT ONCE!' it bellows.

The agitation of the adults down below seems very remote. Although the children don't know it, Tommy's anger is not directed at them up there in the tree but at Lorna. Lorna shouldn't have let them out of her sight. Lorna is damned irresponsible. But up there amongst the branches there is only victory and defeat. 'I did it, didn't I?' Helen insists to Michael.

'Yes.'

'So there. It's not diff at all.' She allows the words of triumph to do their work, then grants him some self-esteem. 'Let's go down, Michael,' she says, and it is the first time she has ever spoken his name. Without a further word, without any argument, they inch back towards the elephantine lower branches and the dull and horizontal adult world – a place of less tangible but much greater danger than the world up there amongst the leaves.

'Damned foolhardy!' Tommy shouted when they reached the ground. 'Could have got both of you killed.' He was not scolding Helen, of course. He was scolding Michael – and Lorna.

The great oak still stands in the garden of Guerdon House. In those distant days it was on the edge of the orchard and the kitchen garden, amidst the ruins of a greenhouse which the tree itself, with its dense, year-round shade, had rendered useless. Helen grew up with it and knew it as well as she knew the house itself. And yet in her memory there is none of that detail. In her memory there is just the seething wind all around her, and the rough edge of bark beneath her hands, and a sensation of triumph.

Dinner with Gemma and Howard. The one is Foreign Office, the other some kind of journalist specialising in economics. Gemma greets Helen at the front door with a familiarity that neither of them really feel: 'Darling, how lovely to see you.' They exchange kisses. 'Are you on your own? Where's Eric?'

'He's awfully sorry, but there's some kind of telephone deal with someone in New York. We're to start without him if he hasn't appeared. I'm not the first, am I?'

'Almost. Come on in, darling.' Gemma takes Helen's hand and leads her in, as though otherwise she might escape. 'We've got an old friend of ours here whom you *must* meet. Complete surprise. He's over from Argentina.'

Why, Helen wonders as she takes off her coat, *must* one meet someone? The talk continues as they go through into the sitting room with its French windows opening onto the area garden, its painting of the valley in the Dordogne where Gemma and Howard have a cottage, its lacquered table and other *ex*-quisite (you never hear the stress on the wrong syllable in *this* house) items which they brought back from Japan when Gemma was at the embassy there; and the figure rising from an armchair beside the vacant fireplace where coals have not burned since the Clean Air Act of nineteen fifty something, when all these people were but children.

Helen hesitates in the doorway, like an actress in an amateur play, uncertain of her cue. 'Good God.'

'Oh, go on in, Helen,' Gemma says brightly behind her. 'Don't stand on ceremony.' She calls to the kitchen, 'Helen says Eric's going to be late, Howard. A 'phone call from the States or something...'

'Bugger him!'

The guest Helen just *has* to meet smiles.

'Michael,' she says, 'how strange.'

There is an absurd hiatus in the rituals of social intercourse. What should they do? Shake hands? Kiss? In the event it is a combination of the two, Michael attempting to kiss on both cheeks in the Latin fashion, Helen proffering only the right and laughing in embarrassment when the little manoeuvre goes wrong and threatens more than it ought.

'You two know each other already? What a surprise.'

'Oh, yes,' says Helen. 'We know each other. I...' She hesitates at the absurdity of it all. 'I was just thinking of you. Just now.'

Together they stole coins from Lorna's purse and bought a packet of Woodbines from the NAAFI. 'For our mother,' Helen explained, with solemn mendacity, to the woman behind the counter.

'Are you sure, dear?'

Helen at her most insistent, proffering her coins and looking at

24

the woman with steady, cold eyes, daring her to argue: 'Of course I'm sure.'

It must have been difficult to imagine Colonel Constance's wife smoking Woodbines; but then it must have been equally difficult to imagine Colonel Constance's children telling lies: an interesting conflict of unlikelihoods. So the exchange was made, to bring in its wake complaint and inquiry and a severe reprimand from the NAAFI manager; but that is the adult perspective. For the children there was just the breathless flight to the safety of the nearby woods, clutching the packet to themselves as though by possessing it they had taken possession of a mysterious power previously possessed only by grown-ups.

'Got the matches?'

''Course.'

The woods seemed vast and empty, the floor littered with copper leaves and beech mast, the grey trunks reaching up towards the roof of leaves like the pillars of a church. That was what it reminded Helen of – a church. Birdsong echoed high up in the gothic vaulting, and guilt corroded her excitement. 'We shouldn't have done it.'

Michael shrugged, crouching down behind a massive trunk. 'We've done it now.' The heady scent of unlit tobacco came out as he opened the packet. 'Cigarette,' he said, pulling one out.

'Smoke,' she answered.

'Fire.'

'Heat.'

'Passion.'

'What's passion?'

'I've won.'

'But what is it?'

'Admit I've won. Go on, admit it.'

'You've won. What's passion?'

She struck a match for him and he lit a cigarette as he had seen *them* doing. He drew in a mouthful of acrid smoke. The glowing tip of the cigarette glared at Helen as though it was a single, angry eye. It seemed that the whole of the adult world was watching her through that eye. Birdsong echoed in the spaces overhead and she looked straight back at the glowing tip as though to try and make out what was going on there in the adult world. 'What's passion?' she repeated.

'Passion's love,' Michael told her. He held out the cigarette. 'Here, you try.'

'I don't want to.'

'Go on.'

She took the thing between thumb and forefinger, drew on it and spluttered. 'It's not nice.'

'It's not meant to be *nice*.'

Why did they do something like this that wasn't meant to be nice? It couldn't be good, either. So – not nice, not good. What other motive could there be?

Michael took the cigarette back and leant against the bole of the tree and, through a veil of blue smoke, regarded her with what he supposed were adult eyes. 'Show us your pinkie,' he said. 'That's what they do.'

She thought about it for a while. 'I bet they don't.'

'They do. Then they put their willies inside.'

'They don't.'

'They do. That's love. Anthony told me. That's passion.'

'That's disgusting.'

Michael shrugged and puffed, and felt queasy. 'You *daren't*.'

She looked at him with that expression that he had come to recognise, the one of grim determination, with her mouth clamped tight and her eyes hard. It was the expression she had worn when following him up the tree at Guerdon House. Without a word she clambered to her feet and hitched up her skirt, while he puffed at the cigarette and watched thoughtfully. 'There,' she said, pulling her pants down to her knees.

'I've seen that.'

'When?'

'In the bath.'

'You were spying.'

He shrugged again and took another puff, confident of his victory. 'You've got to show me everything. That's passion.'

She hesitated a moment. Would her father be watching? Was the calm face of her father, with its faint and enigmatic smile, watching her from some subtle vantage point? Somehow she did not think that it would matter. Perhaps he would not view the scene with the mind of a common adult. Perhaps he would understand questions of challenge and survival.

Perhaps he was not even there at all.

At that moment, standing over Michael in the shadowy wood with her skirt up round her waist and her knickers round her knees, she understood for the first time that her father both existed and didn't exist. He lived and was dead, mattered and meant nothing. You could think the two opposite things at the same time. The understanding was a small revelation. She could do this, and not do it. She could (this was a phrase which Tommy used all the time) have her cake and eat it.

Holding her skirt up with her elbows she put her hands down to the fragile little purse of flesh between her legs and pulled it open. 'There.'

Michael looked for a moment. Then he nodded and stubbed out the cigarette just as his father did. 'Now you can see my willy,' he said, getting to his feet.

'I don't *want* to see your willy.' But he showed her just the same. 'You're not putting it in,' she warned.

'How many years is it?' Helen knows the answer with a fair degree of accuracy but asks it just the same as though to gain time. 'Twenty, twenty-five?' She watches Michael like an interrogator looking for the slightest slip, the smallest betrayal – a date wrong here, a place mis-identified, a name forgotten, a confidence betrayed.

Gemma is delighted. 'That long? How amazing. Howard, have you heard this? What an extraordinary coincidence.'

'Twenty,' Michael insists, laughing. 'For heaven's sake, twenty. 'Nineteen sixty-five, six?'

Twenty years. The idea of dismissing twenty years in a single phrase would have seemed absurd once. Once upon a time twenty years had been a lifetime, and more than a lifetime – a kind of infinity, a new country stretching away into the unimaginable future: unknown, ineffable, indeterminate in its possibilities. And now? The twinkling of an eye.

'Twenty,' she agrees. 'Yes, twenty.'

When Helen was twelve they packed her off to boarding school, to a convent run by Anglican nuns. Along with a large trunk and a tuck box, she carried with her the studio portrait photograph of her father and that postcard of the Old City. 'That,' she would explain to her fellow pupils, pointing to the Dome of the Rock, 'is the Temple in Jerusalem, where they crucified Jesus. Every year the Jews celebrate the event with a carnival.'

The protestations of the small nun who taught Divinity were in vain, for the other pupils more or less believed what Helen said. 'I should know, because my father was killed in Jerusalem.' It was a powerful argument, one which no adult could gainsay, and she employed it with cunning and imagination; but it was a weapon that could cut both ways. 'At least I've still *got* a father,' Michael would point out.

'At least I've still got a mother,' Helen retorted.

'So have I but she's gone away.'

'*And* my father was a hero.' The counter-thrust was almost mortal. At Beatings of Retreats and Queen's Birthday Parades and such-like Tommy Constance wore many decorations on his breast, but to observant eyes they were all campaign medals – the Africa Star, the Defence Medal, the 1939–1945 Star, that kind of thing. In a drawer in Lorna's bureau Andrew Harding's DSO and MC put all gew-gaws to shame. Michael knew it, Helen knew it, and the taunt bit deep.

'Hero,' she repeated.

'Dead.'

'That's beastly.'

Michael gave in. 'All right then. Heroine.'

'Opium.'

'What's opium got to do with it?'

'Heroin's a drug like opium. I've won.'

'No you haven't. Sherlock Holmes.'

'I've won,' she repeated flatly. 'You couldn't follow, so I've won.'

'We were family,' Helen explains to Gemma. 'Were, are, can you cease to be?'

'Brother and sister of a kind.'

'Step,' she emphasises. 'Stepbrother and stepsister.'

'And you've not seen each other since—?'

'Oh, ages.' Helen is suddenly disturbed by those twenty years. It would be as well not to be too precise, as well to lay down a smokescreen of evasion and uncertainty, as well to hide things from the adult world. The mathematics of age can be dangerous.

'Since Cyprus,' Michael says, smiling at her discomfiture.

Helen grasps at the equivocation. 'Cyprus, yes. Years ago.'

3

Dust blows across the streets and through the memory and it is that white, limestone dust that is peculiar to the Mediterranean, laden with a whole spectrum of smell and sound and sight and taste – the smell of ordure and carobs and crushed vegetables, the tastes of honey-melon and sweet peppers and lamb grilled over charcoal, the insensate noise of Turkish and Greek shouted in the street, the sight of the Troodos mountains rising up from the Mesaoria Plain in folds of green and gold, with snow on the winter heights. All these things and more, a barrage of sensations that take years to unravel. The light was heavy and luminous, like a substance, like a liquid filling the world and giving it life.

She first came to all this one summer in a Vickers Viscount of British European Airways. London – Frankfurt – Rome – Nicosia was the route, continuing, for those who wished, to Tel-Aviv. She was sixteen. It was July.

Her neighbour, who had engaged her in desultory and faintly suggestive conversation all through the flight from Rome, packed away his newspaper and magazines, and wished her a good holiday. She stood up and shuffled ahead of him towards the front of the cabin where the air hostess opened the door onto a furnace. Helen hesitated in the doorway, feeling that blast of heat, that heavy, luminous hand which grips you once and never lets you go. She squinted against the glare, momentarily stunned.

'Come on, young lady,' said her erstwhile neighbour from over her shoulder. He touched her gently, as though to help her forward, but at the same time to sense the dimensions and fragility of her waist. 'No time to stand around. The future waits.'

So she stepped, squinting, out into the sunlight. There was white dust. A distant shadow in the haze might have been cloud, might have been mountain, might have been nothing more substantial than the weight of heat building up on the horizon and threatening to bear down and crush her. The rail burnt her hand. She stepped cautiously down the steps as though into a pool of molten metal.

On the apron soldiers in khaki shorts stood with rifles at the ready. An armoured car was parked discretely to one side. Only minutes before an Olympic Airways DC4 had landed and was now disgorging students from Athens University all over the concrete. The students shouted and cheered, while the soldiers eyed them nervously and edged them onto buses that would take them to the air terminal in the city, it being deemed by the government too dangerous to allow friends and relatives within the airfield perimeter. The students were shouting for union with Greece − *Enosis! Enosis!* − and Helen didn't understand. Politics in her boarding school were those of love and hate within the sixth form and amongst the nuns and lay teachers, the petty things of a close community. At school the very worst thing that could happen − only two terms ago it *had* happened, whisper it, to two girls of eccentric and wicked tastes − was expulsion from the community; here, on this island in the sun, the very worst thing that could happen was death, sudden and bloody.

Warily she clambered aboard one of the buses. The students pushed and shoved and grinned at her and waved out of the windows at the passing streets, shouting their slogans. 'English girls are our friends,' one of them told her. 'You want to come out with me?' She blushed and shook her head.

At the terminal her family was waiting for her: Lorna, past forty now, looking lean and bronzed and happy; stepfather Tommy, looking every inch what he was, which was a brigadier in the Middle East Defence Secretariat; the two boys, ravaged by acne and adolesence, smirking.

Lorna enveloped her daughter in strong arms and a cloud of Chanel Number 5. 'Darling, how marvellous. You're looking wonderful.' The boys laughed at the obvious lie. Everyone in the customs hall seemed to be bronzed and fit while she was pallid and sweaty. Her ears were ringing with the changes in air pressure and the insidious whine of the aero engines, and she felt remote, detached from all this excitement, from the shouting students and these clinging relatives. Tommy's moustache bristled briefly against her cheek and the boys planted dutiful kisses. Then Lorna took her arm and ushered her through the bare halls, past barbed wire and sentries, to the car. 'Come on, darling. We must get you to

30

the hotel. You can have a shower and cool down and change out of that dreadful uniform. And then . . .'

And then . . . Helen had felt something climbing down from that aircraft. She couldn't articulate it, even to herself. There had been a quickening in the chest, a sudden surge of excitement, a brief sense of her own pure existence. She was sixteen years old. Looking round at the airport in Nicosia, at the soldiers with their sub-machine guns, at the screaming students from Athens University, at the motley collection of British passengers following her down from the BEA aircraft, she had suddenly understood that she was different.

A dance at the Officers' Club, Episkopi. In the United States an oiled youth of undesirable manners and motions is announcing the beginning of a new era and, despite the best intentions of Lorna and Tommy and others, even in the backwater of Imperial Cyprus the young have taken to him with enthusiasm. Not Helen particularly, but she is willing to play the game for the moment, just as she has been willing to play many games throughout her life. Watch her swirling round in the middle of the dance floor doing the new dance, her pony tail flying out like a flag in a gale and her skirt billowing outwards to give Michael and others, a view of petticoat and pale thighs, and an occasional glimpse of knickers. Helen is changing. She is metamorphosing, blossoming beneath the implacable hand of hormones. No longer does she possess the jejune, androgynous form of a little girl. Now, conscious of people's gaze, she is something close to a woman. She has curved thighs and growing breasts and broadening hips, and another swelling whose name Michael knows only by a breathless perusal of encyclopaedia and dictionary: *mons veneris*, the mount of Venus. Poetry in the guise of anatomy.

'Mike,' she says in deliberately languid tones – they are on the beach so deliciously named Ladies' Mile – 'be an angel and do my back.' He hates Mike, but he does as he is bidden, kneeling to anoint her with oil.

'Sun,' he says, desperately.

'Tan.' She turns her head awkwardly and looks up at him. 'Do we *really* have to play? Aren't we a bit grown up for that kind of game?' She can feel his hands on the subtle corrugations of her ribs and sense his agonising tumescence as it threatens to break out and announce its presence to the whole beach. She finds the whole thing faintly disturbing.

'Oil,' he says.

31

'Chrism.' Her voice is distant and bored.

'What's chrism, for God's sake? How can I play if I've never even heard the word?'

'Then I've won.'

'Tell me.'

She shrugs her thin shoulders. 'I've won,' she repeats. What is certain is that he has lost. He finishes his task and puts the cap back on the bottle and moves away from her. All the intimacy of their childhood games appears irrelevant: she has escaped from the bonds of infancy and left him behind.

Helen had her first love affair that summer. He was a National Service subaltern in one of the Welsh regiments, a young man called Archie, with rather pallid good looks and a facial twitch which gave the lie to the impression that he wished to convey, which was of brisk and adult maturity. Unknowingly, for Archie was not practised in the art of seduction, he had a quite contrary trait which was what Helen found attractive: beneath the sharp and soldierly exterior he was a sensitive soul. While his fellow officers were interested in drink and rugby, football and women (in that order), Archie was interested in antiquities and Greek Orthodox monasteries. It is given to few to make their conquests in love in the shadow of a Greek Orthodox monastery but at Stavrovouni, perched high on its boss of rock above the eastern part of the island, that is what Archie achieved.

'Isn't it wonderful?' he asked the girl at his side (who was allowed no further than the first courtyard and the malodorous chapel because she was of the wrong sex), and she answered that yes, it was marvellous, and that it almost made one want to adopt the contemplative life. Archie twitched a bit at that, but let it pass. They admired the iconostasis, tipped the ancient and smelly patriarch by the door and went back out into the twentieth century feeling spiritually refreshed. On the road down (only Helen's insistence had got Archie to drive up in the first place, so steep and narrow and ill-made was the track) they stopped on a curve to admire the view. The wind was warm and the whole of the east of the island lay open to their view. Archie took her hand. This was the first physical contact they had made, other than during the dance. Like the intimate touch of a doctor, the intimacy of a dance is sterilised by convention – this plain holding of hands, on the road below Stavrovouni, with the curve of Larnaca Bay before them, was altogether more potent than any clinch to the crooning of Elvis Presley. Archie would have found her grasp surprisingly strong and the fingers thin and hard. Small, bird-like claws.

'Isn't it wonderful?'

Yes, it was wonderful.

Later he mentioned Tommy. Perhaps he was trying to make the decency of his intentions clear. 'He's a fine fellow, your old man. A brick.' He actually said that: a brick.

'He's not my old man.'

For a moment Archie imagined she was taking exception to the turn of phrase. 'Young, then,' he said rather idiotically. 'Young man.'

'I mean he's not my father.'

'Not—?'

She shook her head a little, feeling the breeze in her hair, feeling suddenly, excitingly free. 'He's my stepfather.'

'You're not Helen Constance, then?'

'Harding. Helen Harding.'

'Harding,' he repeated in wonder. 'No relation?' The governor at the time was a Harding, Field Marshal Sir John, to be exact.

'I don't think so. I'm the last Harding in the world.'

'The boys?'

'Both Constance. My mother is Constance now of course, Lorna Constance – but they're not hers. There's just me, Helen Harding. Mother suggested that Tommy adopt me so that I would take his name, but I refused. It's not that he isn't very sweet, but . . .' She squeezed Archie's hand and felt unique.

'Divorce, was it?' he asked with soft concern for her sensibilities.

'Death.'

'I'm sorry.'

'Daddy was in the army during the war. He was a hero, do you know that? He won the DSO and the MC in the desert. I don't know whether he would have stayed in once things settled down, but it happened before he had the chance to decide. He was killed in Palestine, in the King David.'

The name had a certain potency. The stuff of history now, then it was a symbol of some kind, a symbol for whatever you wished – the sacrifice of Empire, the hatefulness of terrorism, the dangers of irrationality, the folly of colonialism. She took a snapshot from her bag and showed it to Archie – a shot of Andrew Harding staring out with bland insouciance at a world that had moved a decade further on.

33

'Bloody Jews,' Archie said.

'It wasn't the Jews that did it. It was *some* Jews. That makes all the difference.'

Archie shook his head. 'My CSM was in Palestine. He says they were bastards, the Jews – the nastiest bunch of bastards he's ever fought. Worse than EOKA by far. Worse than the SS.'

'Maybe they were desperate,' she suggested, not really knowing.

'That's no excuse.'

'Who knows, except the desperate?'

He hadn't thought of that and wasn't really sure that he understood now. 'Let's go, shall we? Time for lunch.'

They got back into the car and drove down the remainder of the precipitous track to the foot of the mountain, and then to a beach he knew, which in those days was an empty mile of sand with dunes behind it and a few dusty palms, but is now backed by a row of ferro-concrete hotels and bears the weight of a burgeoning tourist industry. Lying on that beach they kissed, and she allowed him, with a degree of surprise and indignation, to do what she had specifically denied Michael only days before during that dance: she let Archie kiss her on the lips.

The sensation of intimacy, of contiguity, was startling. Carefully, lest her soul leap out and enter his body, she opened her mouth. At once his tongue, as dark and wet and live as an animal, invaded her. She kept her own tongue far back so that his flapped round in vain like a repulsive mollusc in the cavity of her mouth, a sea slug in a wet, pink cave. When the mollusc withdrew she closed the cave.

So Archie kissed her neck, and again her mouth, which this time remained resolutely closed, and then slipped his hand into the top of her swimsuit. She did not stop him. There was not much to feel really, nothing but a small pad of flesh and a small knot of nipple, so protest seemed superfluous; anyway it seemed to make him happy enough although she could not quite see what pleasure it could possibly give.

'Darling,' he whispered in her ear. She did not reply, not seeing what to answer. Darling seemed too big a commitment. He moved his hand from breast to thigh and nudged it against the tight rim of Lycra.

'Someone may see,' she whispered.

'There's no one around.' Fingers probed. 'Darling,' he repeated, in case she hadn't got the point the first time. But she had got the point and was simply waiting for the next move, more out of curiosity than anything. The fingers edged under the edge of stubborn and protective elastic and finally found their goal, that sparse flock of hair, those fragile folds where never yet man had been. They probed ineffectually and for a brief moment she felt a glimmer of something. Then she turned her hips slightly and the fingers were out and he was breathing 'darling' into her ear once more and it was all over.

4

One Sunday there was a loud voice in the Officers' Club. There were often loud voices in the Club: it was a place of loud voices and usually little notice was taken of them, but this voice was a new one and so more people looked round than might have otherwise.

'*Keo?*' the voice was declaiming in a tone of incredulity. '*Keo?* Give me Watneys any day.'

Lorna would not normally have been one to look. She was the kind of person who affected not to be moved by such things as loud voices, attention-seekers, all that kind of nonsense. She would normally have gone on with her meal in supreme and self-conscious indifference, but she found this voice strangely familiar.

'What we want is Watneys!' the voice was insisting. 'A touch of old England, a breath of beer from the mother country. Not something dreamed up by a bunch of Cyps.'

So Lorna glanced over her shoulder at the group that had just come in, and then looked sharply away and addressed herself once more to rice and curried chicken and mango chutney, which was what the menu always ran for Sunday lunch. But in that moment he had noticed her, even across the crowded dining room, even over the dozen tables which lay between her own table and the door, because he was exactly the kind of person who, while seeming not to, would actually take careful notice of every little wave thrown up by his disturbance. He didn't, as he would have said, miss a trick.

'Lorna!'

Heads looked this way and that. There wasn't much else to do, for heaven's sake. Sunday lunch and a game of polo down in Happy Valley afterwards, or a rather unseasonal swim at Four

36

Beach, or something run of the mill like that. Distractions were always welcome.

'Lorna! It *is* Lorna, isn't it? Lorna Harding?' He came between the tables, with people looking up from their own piles of rice to follow his progress, his big figure dominating the place, his voice booming a name that was no more. 'Good Lord, I haven't seen you in years. Must be ten. Lorna Harding.'

Finally he stopped right in front of their table and Tommy looked up and half rose from his seat, adopting an expression of polite but slightly impatient enquiry, like the landlord of a pub who is uncertain whether a noisy customer is quite drunk enough to merit being thrown out. Suspicions about Lorna – she was a lovely woman, too lovely by far in that climate – were just beginning to edge into his mind in those days, and here was a complete stranger coming over to their table to give such suspicions a gentle nudge. 'I'm sorry, I don't think—'

Lorna had looked up too, there being no option. 'Dennis,' she said. 'What a surprise.' She offered her hand and the newcomer leaned forward to take it. But he turned the neutral gesture of a mere handshake into an intimate one by stooping towards it and raising her hand, slim and strong and tanned, to his lips. She didn't quite snatch it away. With an astringent smile she turned to her husband. 'Tommy, this is Dennis—'

'Killin,' Dennis said, letting slip Lorna's hand and holding out his own towards Tommy. 'Dennis Killin. They used to call me "Deadly". "Deadly" Killin, you see?'

Tommy did see. He rose a stage further from his chair and shook the man's hand. 'Quite natural, I suppose.'

'It all depends.' Dennis smiled round at the party with an expression of ironical self-deprecation. 'I was in the RASC, as a matter of fact. Run Away, Someone's Coming. Not deadly at all.' He laughed at the old joke, and glanced from face to face, trying to put it all together. 'I guess, ah . . . not Lorna Harding any more? Lorna and I used to know one another in the old days, you see.'

'Constance,' Lorna said. 'Tommy and I were married eight years ago.'

'Right. Of course.' Momentarily he was at a loss. 'I used to know . . .'

'Andrew,' Lorna explained for Tommy's benefit. 'Dennis was a friend of Andrew's in Palestine.'

Killin nodded. 'Shared a house with him, as a matter of fact . . .' He looked down. Helen had been sitting with her back to him, but at the mention of her father's name she had turned. He looked down straight into her eyes. 'We've met before, haven't we? On the plane last July. This little lady must be . . .'

'Helen,' she said quietly. 'Helen Harding.'

'My word. My word,' he repeated as though otherwise people might doubt it. 'We spent a couple of hours chatting happily away on the aircraft and I never realised. You may consider my flabber to be well and truly gasted, as Bertie Wooster was wont to say. And as his second cousin Horace Wooster would have put it, a beautiful mother with an even more beautiful daughter, or something. Can't do it in Latin, I'm afraid. Latin never was my strong point.' He took a step back as though to get the girl in perspective. 'Do you know, the first time I saw you I dandled you on my knee. Can you imagine?'

Helen smiled at him without humour. The boys laughed at her discomfiture.

'And now look at her.' Killin turned to Lorna, as though she might not have noticed. 'A real beauty.'

In truth Helen was not. Her features were too harsh for that, too sharp cut. But there was something there which Dennis recognised, a quality of reserve and calculation which men longed to fracture. Dennis Killin looked down at her in the middle of that sun-swept dining room in the Officer's Club at Episkopi, and for a moment he dreamed.

'Well, enough of this chit-chat,' he said. 'I must be going back to my hosts. Tell you what: we must get in touch. I've taken a house in Limassol, a villa. No longer in the army, of course. Got out when the going was good. I'm in business, and doing quite a bit in this part of the world. You must come round and see me sometime.' He held out his hand. 'Here's my card. Give us a ring, any time. I'm away quite a bit but you can always leave a message. There's a swimming pool,' he added, as though that made the whole proposition more attractive. 'You'd be very welcome.'

'We'd love to,' said Lorna.

We'd love to. A curious linguistic construction of the British upper-middle-class which means precisely the opposite.

You might have expected it to come to nothing. It would have come to nothing, really. There was Lorna, the brigadier's wife, the lean and tanned woman in her forties with a certain manner, a certain way of behaving; and there on the other hand, very much on the other hand, was this Killin man, with his clichés and catch-phrases and his awful prattle, and goodness knows what else. One wondered who shared the villa with him. One imagined, oh yes, one imagined some kind of mistress: Greek perhaps; or worse, Turkish. What was it Andrew had written once? 'Killin is awful but amusing' – something like that. (The letters were all in store in England, locked away in her writing box, their ink fading, their paper yellowing and turning brittle. Souvenirs of a life that had never really happened.) Anyway, whatever Andrew's relationship had been with Killin there was absolutely *no* reason whatsoever why his widow should feel under any obligation towards the man, no *earthly* reason why she should get in touch with him at all. 'Just an acquaintance of your father's,' she explained dismissively to Helen after the encounter at the Club. 'Nothing more. And really rather common.'

And then one lunchtime Tommy came back from the office and took Lorna aside, away from the ears of the children. 'You know that fellow who introduced himself to us, the one who knew Andrew?'

'Killin? What of him?'

'You haven't been in touch with him, have you?'

'In touch? What one earth makes you think—?'

'No, nothing—'

'Why would I want to get in touch with him? What on earth do you suppose we have in common, except knowing Andrew of course. Really!' There was bluster there, naturally; bluster based on a degree of guilt.

'I wasn't suggesting anything at all, dear,' Tommy reassured her, but something in the back of his mind registered the overdone indignation, the offence taken where none had been intended. His suspicions received another little nudge. 'It's just that I've read a security report on him, that's all. It seems that he's no good.'

'What kind of no good?'

'Not sure exactly, and not sure I'd be able tell you if I was. But no good all the same.'

'Then have him arrested.'

'Oh, he's done nothing *wrong*, not here at any rate. But he's mixed up in things . . .'

'What are you blathering on about, Tommy? Really, you treat me like a child at times!'

'It was just a friendly warning, that's all.'

'Well I'm an adult. I don't need to be patronised about whom I see.'

'I'm not doing that, old thing. I was just keeping you informed.' He tried to shrug the thing off, ascribing her tetchiness to her period or something – 'women's business', he'd have put it – and trying to change the subject. But it wasn't that easy. He'd touched a nerve of some kind, that much was clear. 'Oh, by the way, there's an invitation from the Oldcastles here. Came to the office through the internal mail. Do we say yes?'

'The Oldcastles?'

'Yes, you know: that fellow you're keen on, with the dowdy wife.'

'Oh, them.' Lorna may have flushed slightly. Her friendship with Peter Oldcastle had begun with hint and innuendo and the subtle evasions of a lifelong diplomat, but it was in the process of transforming itself into a more direct one. Now she couldn't tell whether Tommy was talking in all innocence or actually probing to find out where it hurt, and in her confusion she over-reacted. 'They're really rather boring,' she decided. 'For God's sake say we've got a previous engagement.'

The upshot of that conversation was twofold. Firstly Peter Oldcastle was decidedly put out at having his invitation turned down and soon began casting round for other women to share his siesta; secondly, when Dennis Killin telephoned two days later to invite her and Helen to go with him to Kyrenia for the day – 'I shouldn't think the boys would be interested, do you? Just the two of you?' – Lorna accepted.

There was a certain amount of deception about the trip. Tommy and the boys had been led to believe that Lorna and Helen were going on a picnic somewhere along the coast towards Paphos with another of the wives (Lorna was carefully evasive about her name), but in fact they made their rendezvous with Dennis on the sea front in Limassol, climbing into his car in the manner of thieves making a getaway from the scene of the crime. The town seethed around them, a shabby, dusty port of ferro-concrete and peeling paint, with canning plant and decaying godowns and all such benefits of Empire, and Lorna felt the Levantine thrill of deceit. What if we're seen? she wondered. What if someone recognises us? Dennis had a large and flashy Opel Kapitan with a white stripe along each side and splashes of red undercoat amongst the bright yellow paintwork. It couldn't have been much more conspicuous if it had been equipped with flashing lights and a siren.

'Being in the care of an old Mandate hand means you are as safe as Fort Knox,' he told them. He was wearing a slightly crumpled light-weight suit and his left armpit bulged with an automatic pistol; the two women were suitably airy and floral, suitably helpless. 'I can assure you ladies that Cyprus is nothing, but *nothing* like Palestine was. Compared with the Stern Gang this EOKA lot are a bunch of children.'

Lorna decided that he had a certain American slant to his manner of speaking, as though he had spent some time in the States, or at least wished to give the impression that he had. She was very sensitive to such things, sensitive to every moment of the day in fact. He settled himself behind the wheel and grinned over his shoulder at Helen in the back seat, and, as though to give substance to his assertion, pulled his pistol from its holster and laid it carefully on the front seat between him and Lorna.

'I think we'd rather not hear about the Stern Gang,' Lorna replied sharply. She pointed to the pistol. 'And you may put *that* thing away.'

Suitably upbraided, Dennis did as he was told and from then on he was as good as gold (Lorna's words), so much so that when they were walking by the harbour of Kyrenia after an excellent lunch at the Dome Hotel (nobody had seen them there either, thank God) she even admitted to him things that she really ought to have kept to herself, things that were really not very loyal to poor old Tommy: 'I really only agreed to come on this trip in order to spite him,' she confided. 'He really can be very tiresome.'

Helen was lagging behind a bit at the time, watching a fisherman mend his nets or something, which allowed Lorna this moment of self-indulgence. And after all, Dennis was an old friend, one she had known, if only briefly, long before Tommy Constance had come on the scene. Why shouldn't she be there with him? Why on earth not?

'That's not a very flattering thing to say to a fellow,' Killin protested.

'But it's been lovely, that's the point. Really.' Lorna rested a reassuring hand on his wrist. 'I wouldn't have told you that if it hadn't been, would I?'

That encouraged him. He took her arm and drew her nearer and asked the kind of question he really had no right to. 'Are you happy now, Lorna? I remember the last time, just after Andrew's death. You seemed . . .'

'What did I seem?' There was a provocative lilt to her voice. 'Tell me.'

'I don't know, really. I'm not very good at reading emotions. Not my line. But you're happier now?'

She shrugged, her shoulder against his, his hand on her forearm. 'Happy enough,' she said, then added equivocally, 'Is one ever as happy as one dreams?'

'Sad thought on an afternoon like this.' He squeezed her arm and she thought, 'dear Dennis', as though he were an old friend of the family. There was something so touching about him really, his vulgarity pleasantly mollified by a gentleness possessed by few of the men whom she knew. Oldcastle was a self-satisfied prig, Tommy a sexual boor. Dennis? She looked at him and wondered. 'Will we see each other again?' he asked.

'Maybe not like this,' she replied carefully.

That was the moment when Helen made her presence known just behind them by coughing slightly and skipping as though to catch them up. 'You promised us a visit to that bar, Dennis,' she reminded him. It was the first time she had called one of her parents' friends by his first name. Dennis seemed so different from the others, unconcerned with rank and position, indifferent to what was right and what was proper. During lunch he had kept up a stream of comment about the other diners which at times had reduced the two women to helpless laughter. He seemed to know all the guests at the Dome, their names, their careers, their peccadillos. Over there was an ancient Brit – a female of the species, as Dennis put it – who, he claimed, had once been in the harem of a Turkish pasha. With her was an old boy who had, he further assured them, spent a terrifying night alone in a tent with Lawrence of Arabia. And at the next table there was a certain Colonel Davy who apparently fainted at the sight of blood, and with him a one-time colonial administrator who, at dinner with a tribal chief, had unknowingly eaten his own wife.

Dennis had laughed unproariously then, just as he laughed uproariously now, turning from Lorna to put his arm round Helen's narrow shouders and draw her towards him. The noise of his laughter was such that it disturbed the gulls from their feeding. The birds rose up into the air and circled over the harbour, crying in fright at the big man and his racket. 'Young ladies shouldn't be asking to visit bars,' he admonished her. 'They should wait for disreputable men to *invite* them.'

In truth the bar was nothing much, but Dennis enlivened it. His vulgarity was not out of place there amongst the saw-dust and the wooden barrels and the ancient mahogany counter behind which the owner perched like a small bird. They drank large glasses of *commandaria* and fancied themselves part of the life of the island rather than the intruders that they were, while Dennis regaled them with unlikely stories about EOKA.

'They tried to kidnap me once, d'you know that? Fell asleep in a taxi from the airport and when I woke up we were somewhere up in the mountains. Troodos.'

Lorna laughed and looked at him askance, a famous expression that had attracted as many as it had crushed. 'You, Dennis? What on *earth* would they want to kidnap *you* for?'

He laid a finger along the side of his nose. 'There are some things that must remain secret. Tell you what,' he added, as though to change the subject, 'I'll show you where they make their bombs.'

'What on earth are you talking about?'

'EOKA. I'll show you where they make their bombs, how'd you like that? Here in the cellar.'

Suddenly he seemed anything but amusing. Lorna tried to hush him to silence. The owner nodded and grinned, but whether he was confirming the truth of what Dennis had said or merely demonstrating his lack of English was uncertain. With a flourish Dennis bent down and opened a trap in the floor. Steps led down into a cool darkness. 'Behold, the bomb factory,' he cried.

'Dennis, what kind of joke is this?' Lorna asked anxiously. Killin suddenly seemed very daring – a mad, foolhardy adventurer compared with Tommy. Tommy would never even have entered such a bar, never mind shouting about EOKA in public; and certainly he would never have done what Dennis was doing now. 'Tommy would have a fit!' she cried.

The bar-owner had turned on a light and, with an air of ritual solemnity, Dennis was descending into the underworld. 'Tommy would, but not Andrew,' he replied. 'Andrew would have had a good laugh.'

'Dennis, what one earth are you up to?'

'Come ladies, down to perdition with me.' He reached the bottom and looked up at them from below with a comic expression on his face. His hands reached up, as though to catch them should they fall. Helen stepped willingly after him.

'Helen, be careful!'

'Don't be silly, Mother.'

She descended. Two steps from the bottom she launched herself towards him and he caught her by the waist and swung her, as light as a cat, down to the dusty floor. Lorna stood on the brink and looked down on them, refusing to follow.

'There's nothing here,' Killin assured her, defeating the whole point of the exercise in order to persuade her down. 'Just a cellar.' But she only shook her head, her expression tight and nervous at the prospect of being abandoned up there in the upper world amongst Greeks who gave shelter to EOKA. 'Hurry up,' she called.

The two adventurers looked round at the dank cave. Light came from a single bulb hanging from the centre of the ceiling. Casks of ancient wine gave off their smell of yeast and vinegar into the cool air. The shadows promised secrets that one could not foretell.

'Tell me, Dennis,' Helen asked softly, as they searched for bombs. 'What was Daddy like?'

Killin turned and looked at the girl. Their two faces would have been at the opposite ends of any spectrum of features, any system of classification or identification by physiognomy: his own big and blunt and balding, hers small and sharp and dressed with its mane of golden hair. But there was something each recognised in the other, a trait in common. Neither was, or ever would be, a happy part of any community or system. They were both outsiders.

From on high her mother's voice called: 'Come on up. We've got to be getting back.' Down in the depths, Dennis Killin stroked Helen's cheek and told her that she was a real beauty.

She shook the hand away. 'Please tell me.'

He smiled at her anger. 'He was a brave man,' he said. 'Braver than ever I was, but I suppose that doesn't mean much. Liked the Jews, which wasn't a popular line to take in those days. He was unlucky, that's all.' There was something left unsaid. A cat covering up its dirt, that's what Helen thought.

'Come ON you two!' came her mother's voice.

'What else is there?'

'He was killed. Bloody bad luck. He was killed, that's all.'

'For God's sake come on, you two! What on *earth* are you doing down there?'

'What else can I tell you, my love? That I can see you in him?' He put out his hand again, not to her cheek this time, but to her lips, which were stained purple by the *commandaria*. This time she did not stop him. With the very tip of his forefinger he wiped a little purple rime from the corner of her mouth. Then, as she watched, he put the finger in his own mouth and sucked it clean. Helen felt both repelled and excited by the gesture. For the first time she understood that a man, this man, might do anything for her.

'Helen!' Lorna called. 'Come up at once!'

They climbed back out of the underworld into the upper air, strangely silent, a most unlikely Orpheus followed by an entirely appropriate Eurydice.

5

What was the relationship between Tommy and Lorna? There was evidence to go on – her unfaithfulness, their lack of mutual children, that kind of thing – but what is evidence if it is not interpreted? And doesn't the interpretation tell you as much about the interpreter as it does about the person concerned?

Helen watched them and wondered. She added other little things to her store of evidence: that they occupied twin beds rather than sharing a double one; that they argued often, quietly and urgently, with the words bitten off as though much was being left unsaid; that they held hands never, exchanged a peck on the cheek rarely, always avoided terms of endearment that could not equally have been used between brother and sister; that they never seemed to look at one another, never exchanged a secret glance.

An incident: one morning she went, fairly innocently, into her parents' bedroom to look for a particular lipstick, one that went perfectly with Lorna's and therefore her own tanned skin. Searching for this in a drawer in her mother's dressing-table she found instead a small plastic box. It might have contained face cream or something, perhaps a little nest of face powder and a powder puff. She snapped it open. Within, sleek and potent and equivocal, was a dome of thin, tightly-sprung rubber.

Helen was a child of her time and her class. She had knowledge in abundance but little experience. She knew what this curious membrane was only because of vague and ill-informed discussion at school, but knowing what it was is not the same as knowing what it meant. In the silence of the bedroom (pink and blue, scented with Chanel) she blushed, thinking, and at the same time trying not to think, where that thing had *been*. Of one fact she was now certain: her mother *did* it. That may have been obvious, but

45

Helen's view of the sexuality of adults, more particularly of her own parent, was hazy. Sex was a thing you did to make children, certainly; the question which worried her was whether it ought to be a thing you did for anything so frivolous as sensual enjoyment. Even in the abstract she couldn't really imagine the act. No film showed even an approximation of it, no book described it, and the nuns at school, evading the issue, had brought in the school doctor to explain it in surgical and anatomical detail which seemed, quite frankly, implausible. Of course she had seen Michael as a child (memory of the incident still disturbed her), but the only thing she knew about the adult male organ was a sight of Anthony, changing on the beach – a glimpse of something that more or less resembled what she saw when she donned a mask and went snorkelling round the rocks: a marine growth, a fat, worm-like creature emerging from a mass of weed. The creature both fascinated and repelled. Or maybe – disturbing thought – fascinated *because* it repelled.

Symptomatic of all this uncertainty was what she thought of as the inadequate vocabulary for the act itself: making love? having sexual intercourse? performing the sex act? copulating? They smacked, in turn, of hypocrisy, of medicine, of the circus and of the zoo. There was, of course, another word which she was reluctant even to use to herself. The nearest she could come was 'eff'. That's what the girls at school said, giggling in the darkness of the dormitory, exchanging confidences and fantasies and lies. Eff. Have you ever effed? In the darkness you couldn't see the blushes; or the dissembling.

And now the witness of this tiny rubber timpanum allowed for no doubt – her mother effed, and with intention only to gain that mysterious pleasure which the girls at school discussed in hushed terms and attempted to emulate, some of them, with their fingers. There was no other function for that little drum of latex. Unable to imagine the act in the abstract, Helen certainly could not imagine her mother doing it, lying naked and brown with her legs open and someone – Tommy, she presumed – labouring away on top of her. Did she move with him? Did she make sounds? Did she *enjoy* it?

With Daddy, yes. Daddy, Andrew, the face that looked calmly out of a dozen old snapshots, yes. In a sudden vision which was almost as real as if it had been happening there on the bed before her, Helen saw her mother lying there naked, splayed open for her father; and she felt something herself; something not cerebral

46

at all but disturbingly organic, as when Archie's fingers had probed beneath her swimsuit.

She snapped the box shut, replaced it carefully, exactly where it had nestled amongst a froth of lace underwear, and went downstairs.

Lorna returned from her shopping expedition that morning in some kind of excitement. Beneath the tan she looked flushed. Her movements were hurried and nervous as she unpacked her purchases on the kitchen table.

'I got mixed up in a demonstration, my dear. In Limassol. You can't *imagine* what it was like. Really rather frightening, all that shouting and anger.' Lifting paper bags onto the table, handing things to the Greek maid, talking all the while in that sharp, staccato delivery she affected at times: 'And what, in God's name, have they got to be angry *about*? I mean, the British have brought them prosperity, haven't they? And the rule of law, peace, all that kind of thing. And they want to join up with Greece. Greece of all places! Anyway, it was just getting nasty, I mean the police were about to charge or something, when, what do you think?'

Helen watched her. What did she think?

Lorna went on blithely: 'Dennis appeared. Knight on white charger and all that. Rescued me from the mob.' Lorna tossed her pale hair, bleached by the sun, bleached by the careful application of peroxide into streaks of yellow and gold and cream. She laughed. 'Dear Dennis. Really rather comm., but quite sweet. Took me to his villa and gave me a refreshing drink and quite put me back on my feet . . . Now what is there for lunch? Where are the boys? Shall I put a picnic together and we'll go down to Ladies' Mile?'

Dennis Killin? Helen wondered. But of course the little box with its heavy burden of sex and guilt lay upstairs in the drawer, its presence there rather than in Lorna's handbag (rather than up Lorna's vagina in fact, but this particular understanding did not come until later) providing some kind of alibi. She watched her mother at the beach that afternoon and wondered. She saw Lorna talking rapidly and erratically, laughing at something and then forgetting all about it in an instant, looking round at the others on the beach as though expecting someone to appear, making faint mockery of Tommy when he turned up, giving Michael a smile of sly complicity which suggested that the two of them had some secret to share; Helen watched all this and wondered. At one point, reaching forward beneath Michael's gaze to pick up a bottle of orangeade, her mother's swimsuit gaped open and afforded him a sudden and surprising glimpse of one delicate breast. Helen saw it, Michael saw it. Could it have been intended? It lay there in its bed of lycra like a pale lemon in tissue paper, tipped with a tender, roseate nipple that would surely burn with its heat; and Helen sensed the boy holding his breath as he witnessed the unseeable. Then Lorna passed the bottle to Helen, sat up, and the glimpse had gone.

'Your strap's loose,' she told her mother later, adjusting it for her.

'Thank you darling,' said her mother with a distant smile. 'Difficult not to keep falling out of these things.'

So summer went, and winter, and the next year came round and each holiday involved the same journey out across Europe, away from the grey and green of England to the bleached whiteness of the eastern Mediterranean, with the surprise of finding people you knew waiting for you, and home of a kind amongst the dry slopes and the bougainvillea and the jasmine and the curiously deviant life of the British Services abroad. Did those last imperialists, those negligent people who nowadays smile out of so many snapshots, see themselves at the time for what they were – the fading embers of a whole culture? Or were they blind to the perspectives of history? Tommy remained jovial and impersonal, Lorna was, at once, both loving and distant and always an object of admiration. Object, yes. Men looked at her like that, Helen noticed. Less did she notice that they also looked at *her* like that, for she was, of course, growing and changing. Time is not equivalent at different ages. Years that for Lorna seemed to flicker past like a film shown at double speed, inched by for Helen. Lorna was the same angular, attractive woman in 1957 as in 1958 as in 1959, but in those same years Helen transformed. The young woman who left Cyprus was not the girl who had arrived.

Shortly before it all came to an end, shortly before accusation and recrimination and, finally, litigation put paid to any under-standing there may have been between Tommy and Lorna, Cyprus gave Helen one last gift. It was a momentary distraction from the ordinary matters of growing up and trying to understand the woman who was her mother and the girl who was herself and the forces which were about to wreck their makeshift family – Cyprus gave her a trip to the Holy Land. Perhaps Lorna was trying to take shelter from the storm that was about to break around them both.

Anyway, that spring she and Helen flew to Tel Aviv with a group of women from the Wives' Club of Episkopi, led by the senior chaplain.

The group stayed the first night on the coast and travelled up to Jerusalem by bus early the next morning. West Jerusalem was strangely familiar to anyone who had just come from Cyprus: there was the same white dust, the same grey vegetation, the same colonial architecture in grubby limestone, the same sounds, the same smells. The policemen on duty seemed no different from the Cypriot police they had just left behind, being as swarthy as Turks some of them and wearing a uniform that was British in all but the detail of the badges. Only the Hasidic Jews in their long coats and black hats seemed strange to the ladies, creatures from another continent, another civilisation. The sight of them made you shiver somehow. But although gratifying in its way that was hardly justification for a whole day's visit. 'For goodness' sake,' someone complained, 'there's nothing on this side. I mean, who wants to see modern synagogues and old-fashioned Jews? When do we cross over?'

But Helen looked and wondered. Would *he* have seen this? Would he have seen these streets and these people? Was this the city that her father had known? When she asked where he had lived Lorna shrugged. 'Heaven knows, darling. It was ages ago. He must have mentioned it in a letter, I suppose. Was it the German Settlement or something? Colony, maybe. Or am I muddling it with the American one?' But there was no German Colony on the map they had, no German anything. American Colony, yes, over on the other side of the thick green line which snaked its way from top to bottom of the map and severed east from west, Arab from Jew.

'What was he like, Mummy?' Helen asked, hoping that as the subject had been broached, Lorna might say something. But Lorna, as always, was evasive.

'He was a young man, darling, barely older than you are now. I've told you. For goodness' sake, I hardly knew him really, what with the war and then all that nonsense here. There were a few months when we first got married, a week or two when he was on leave from Germany, and then he was out to Palestine after it was all over. You can't get to *know* someone like that, can you? He wanted me to join him, but I had you to worry about by then. Now come on or we'll lose the others.'

'Did you love him?'

Now there's a question. They stood on a pavement in West

Jerusalem and Lorna looked up at the trees of some park or other, probably a memorial park in this blessed country which was so full of memorials, and then back at her daughter, squinting against the sun. 'Of course darling. I was very much in love with him.'

'And what does that mean?'

'Love? Good heavens!'

'*In* love. You said, *in* love with him.'

Lorna smiled impatiently, angry at being caught out. 'It means what it says, my dear. I was *in* love with him. Maybe I didn't *love* him. I think there's a difference. You'll find out one day. Maybe what you felt for Archie—'

'I was never interested in Archie. I liked him that's all.'

'Well you'll find out one day, I'm sure. One day. Now—'

'And Tommy? Do you love Tommy?'

Such questions on a sunny spring morning in Jerusalem, with the traffic going by and the indifferent crowds on the pavement, and the little flock of ladies from the Wives' Club at Episkopi disappearing towards Ben Yehuda Street.

'I am *very* fond of Tommy, despite everything. Now come along, Helen darling. Let's talk about this some other time, shall we? We'll lose the others if we don't get a move on.'

But they never did talk about it, neither then nor later. They soon caught the party up and went off to an hotel for afternoon tea, and the talk was all about the city and the museum they had visited and when would they cross over? Helen did not realise it, but part of the itinerary had been revised for her benefit – the intended stop for tea had been at the King David, one of the few places were you could get a view of the Old City from across the green line, from across the Valley of Hinnom; but that had been cancelled at Lorna's request. 'It might be too upsetting,' she had explained to the understanding chaplain.

So, no German Colony and no King David, and no discussion of Andrew Harding either. Did his ghost haunt those bright and noisy streets? It seems doubtful. Jerusalem was by then a very different city from the one he had known a decade earlier. Maybe it would have been better just to forget, but the past was all she had of him really.

After tea they climbed back into the coach and drove off to the crossing point. Going across the Mamilla Road they caught a glimpse of the green line itself, not a line and certainly not a green one: a great blank wall erected across the far end of the street and rising up to the first floor of the houses.

'The wall is constructed against Arab snipers,' said the courier into her microphone. 'They fire from the walls of the Old City at the peace-loving people of West Jerusalem.'

The ladies looked. There was an armoured car down there, and a dirty white van with the United Nations flag hanging from an aerial. And then the view had gone and they were amongst the buildings again until the bus reached the crossing point – checkpoint, border post, whatever you want to call it – the Mandelbaum Gate, so called not because an almond tree grew there (poetic thought) but because one S. Mandelbaum had lived on the spot until they blew his house to bits in 1948. The members of the Episkopi Wives' Club disembarked from the bus, a gaggle of ladies in light frocks looking around with curiosity at the dull houses, the wasteland, the coils of wire and the pre-fab shed where you actually crossed over.

'Passports ready, ladies?' the chaplain called. 'Baptismal certificates?' Oh, yes, that had been necessary. No Jews across the green line, you see, only Christians.

Two porters carried their baggage halfway across and dumped it in a pile. Others from the far side came to retrieve it; then the ladies themselves crossed over, watched by Israeli border police on the one side and Arab Legionnaires on the other. The ladies didn't turn a hair at the barbed wire and the weapons search and the baleful eyes of sub-machine guns and border policemen, for they had seen it all before, more or less. It was just like Cyprus.

Next morning the Old City welcomed them as it welcomes all tourists, with a mixture of relief, with cheap trinkets and poorly printed guide books, and complaints about the past and the present and, no doubt, the future. They haggled over crucifixes carved from olive wood from the Garden of Gethsemane and cotton shifts embroidered, so the shop-keeper assured them, by Bedouin women. They trooped through the warren of alleyways and up onto the Temple Mount where they exclaimed at the unearthly beauty of the Dome of the Rock with exclamations of delight and surprise. They examined the *lithostraton* beneath the convent of the Sisters of Sion with amazement and they followed the Via Dolorosa with a strange emotion compounded of piety and fantasy and insignificance. Some of the ladies were noticed to be in tears.

But the Holy Sepulchre they viewed with scepticism. 'You must be prepared for disappointment,' the chaplain had warned them in his wise little talk at the hotel the evening before. 'It is not the *happiest* of places. The various sects which administer it do not give the best impression of brotherly love. It is more of a Tower of Babel than a Rock of Ages.'

And how could anyone believe that there in the shadows, in that absurd stone hut, on that marble slab, amongst those flickering lamps and the dreadful smell of incense, the Body had actually laid? Absurd. They all took comfort in the fact that Anglicanism was perfectly able to get along without the embarrassing need for a real, historical Jesus and a real, historical Jerusalem. Indeed in keeping with its spirit of detachment from things oriental, the Church of England had even managed to invent an alternative site for the crucifixion and entombment, outside the Damascus Gate and conveniently near the Anglican Cathedral. The basis for such a claim was no more than a chance formation of rock and a conviction that the real place must have been a pretty garden, preferably an English one although that would have been stretching things a bit far; but it pleased the wives far more than had the awful, oriental chaos of the Holy Sepulchre.

'And of course,' the chaplain told them in authoritative tones as they stood in front of the Garden Tomb, 'the Gospels are unanimous and unequivocal in stating that He was crucified *outside* the city walls, which, as we have just seen, does not apply to the church of the Holy Sepulchre which is quite plainly *within* the walls. Quod erat demonstrandum, as the mathematicians say.' He beamed on his flock as though from a great height, and they smiled back at him with joy and admiration.

'I think you've got your walls wrong,' said Helen.

'I'm sorry, young lady?'

She smiled sweetly. 'You've got your walls wrong,' she repeated. 'The present north wall of the Old City dates from after the death of Christ.'

'Shhh,' said Lorna.

'In fact when the crucifixion took place, the actual north wall ran right through the present Old City, just to the south of what is now the Christian quarter, just south of the Holy Sepulchre in fact. So then it *was* outside the city wall.'

'You are an expert, young lady? An archaeologist, perhaps?'

She had done well enough so far, but at the last her nerve let her down. She blushed. Her smile slipped.

'A wall is a wall,' said the chaplain, seeing her weakness. 'Concrete evidence.' The ladies laughed.

But the point was not that Helen had been made to look foolish before the other members of the party, although this had happened, but that she had *felt* the Holy Sepulchre to be real. The age of it, the mysterious desperation about it, the grim determination of the different churches – Orthodox, Armenian, Catholic, Coptic

– to cling to it, to touch it, to cleave forever to the rock of ages, compelled her as no other site could possibly have done, however beautiful and peaceful and reminiscent of childhood hymns. And the idea of her father was there too, moving in the scented shadows of the place like an icon glimpsed through the fog of incense. If he is dead, she thought, then he knows everything.

'I think you're wrong, that's all,' she murmured; and of course the chaplain was, completely.

It was on the flight back to Cyprus that Lorna broke the news to Helen. 'You must have known that things weren't working out, darling. Anyway, we're going back to England, just the two of us.'

'Where will we live?' Helen asked.

'Guerdon House, of course, Grandpapa's house. It'll be lovely. And you've got such a lot to look forward to, your A'levels, university and that kind of thing.'

Helen looked away, out of the window. The aero engines shrilled in her ears. The sun flashed off the wings, dazzlingly bright. She felt alone, as though she were floating disembodied amongst the clouds.

6

Of course Lorna's memory, so precise in those days, was exact. The house that she and Helen never looked for had indeed been in the German Colony. It was the modern mapmakers, with their Jewish sensibilities, who gave her the opportunity to be confused – Emeq Refa'im is the name it had acquired by then. Christian, Arab, Jewish, the quarter's racial identity has changed as rapidly as the city's itself, but physically it remains more or less as it appeared in 1946, an area of quiet, tree-lined avenues where the bourgeois of the city like to live. With their symmetry, their four-square simplicity, their red-tiled, narrow-eaved rooves and their modest gardens, the houses of the quarter are likely to appeal to such people.

The house itself belonged to an Arab businessman who was away in Beirut most of the time. He left the place furnished, and with a servant to look after it, and an exhortation to keep the Jews out. Whether he intended this generally, out of the whole area of the German Colony, or specifically, out of his house, was not clear.

The place was a bit of a find in fact, spacious and comfortable, easily big enough for the two of them to get away from each other when necessary, indeed big enough to hold three, for they sub-let one room for much of the time to a man called Silver who had come out a few months earlier to work for some charity or other and had suffered a nameless spiritual crisis in the meantime. Now he spent much of his time shut away in his room at the back of the house, reading; a victim, so Killin claimed, of the Jerusalem Syndrome.

'I've seen it often enough, take my word for it. You come here as a more or less normal sort of fellow but soon you begin to believe all that heavenly city nonsense, and before you can say "apocalitz" you're forgetting it's just a fly-blown place full of Yids and Arabs and you're actually coming to *believe* it.' Killin in full flow, brandishing a gin and tonic at the back garden with its jasmine and hibiscus and bougainvillea and the dusty palm tree which had harboured a colony of rats until they'd called the Health Department and a man had come round with poison.

'It's *apocalypse*,' Harding corrected him.

'Whatever. They all had it round here, you know – the syndrome. That's what the German Colony was all about. Latter-day Templars, that's what they called themselves. Typical Jerusalem Syndrome. Thought they were fulfilling the prophecies of the New Testament, converting the Jews or whatever. Load of bloody nonsense. Look what happened to them.'

'I'm sure you're dying to tell me.'

'The bastards were interned in thirty-nine, that's what. Bloody Nazis, that's what. Never trust a man who believes in something, that's my motto. The trouble with this place is that everyone here seems to believe in something . . .' It was a familiar enough litany. You heard it time and again at the Club, or in the office, or anywhere where the British gathered in fact: 'What's wrong with this place is that people don't see it for what it is, just another damned Middle-Eastern city with too many flies and too many beggars and too little water. They all think it *means* something. That's why the Mandate is the best thing that has happened to the place. A bit of objectivity, for Christ's sake, and a bit less of the Promised Land rubbish. You see' – pointing with the forefinger of the same hand that held his drink, pointing straight at Harding – 'we British are the only people here who don't give a damn about the religious thing. And when we leave it's going to be chaos.'

'It's precious near chaos now.'

'Don't you believe it. I know strife compared with which this would be concord, hills compared with which this would be a valley. Book of Proverbs.'

Harding enjoyed Killin's act. Caricatures amused him. 'Sounds more like *Through the Looking-Glass*.'

'Alice in Bloody Wonderland,' Killin agreed cheerfully. 'That's exactly it. Now finish your drink and let's be getting ready.' He drained his glass and stood up decisively, and as he did so Silver appeared in the shadows of the doorway, holding a book in his hand and blinking against the sunlight like a gecko.

'Are you fellows going somewhere?'

'Dance at the Club,' Killin explained. 'Give me wine and women, song and laughter, and Alka-Seltzer the day after. There is' – he winked lasciviously – 'a bevy of nurses I happen to know . . .'

'Come with us,' Harding suggested.

Silver smiled and shook his head. 'I've got a meeting at the YMCA, a study group.'

'We can give you a lift, if you like.'

'That'd be fine. I say, listen to this.' He opened his book and began to read: ' "In the Talmud the Aramaic term *naggar*, craftsman or carpenter, is often used to denote *teacher* or *scholar*. So, for example, in the tractate *Yebamoth*—" '

'Oh, for God's sake, old fellow!'

Silver frowned. 'Don't you see? It opens up the possibility that when the Gospel refers to Joseph as a carpenter it might not have been intended *literally*. He might have been a teacher, a scholar. That would surely explain Jesus' teaching in the Temple as a child . . .'

But Killin had pushed past him into the house, calling for the Arab servant to bring another drink to the bathroom and then to lay out his clothes. The big man's voice boomed in the high-ceilinged rooms as Silver stood silently in the doorway to the garden with his book and his theories. Harding felt a certain sympathy with him. Perhaps now was the time for men like him, the studious and the thoughtful. Killin and his kind had been all right during the war when the best thing to do was not to think, or if you thought at all, to think in black and white, good and bad, fact and fiction. But now things were different, weren't they? Peace, as Killin said, had broken out like a nasty attack of the pox. The problem in Palestine (he always made the most of his jokes) was that it looked like developing into general paresis of the insane.

Now he called from the bathroom: 'For God's sake hurry up, you fellows. I manage the impossible, set up some unattached skirt, and all you do is mope around talking about the bloody Bible. If we're slow the girls will be snatched by the wolves.'

So the three men piled into Harding's Riley and set off towards the city centre. The streets were cool, bathed in that clear, honeyed light for which Jerusalem is famous. There were few pedestrians around and the army was out in force because there had been a bomb scare earlier in the day and a couple of arrests in the Old City. People were uneasy. Near the railway station a trio of policemen were standing around watching as a youth cleaned a slogan from a wall; further on, at the beginning of Julian's Way, their car was flagged down by soldiers. Harding wound down the window and leaned out.

'Anything up, Sergeant?'

'Just routine, sir.' The soldier examined their identity cards in a cursory way, then handed them back and saluted sharply. As the Riley moved past the road block beneath the baleful eye of a Sten gun, Killin began to sing in a gravelly American accent:

> 'There's barbed wire here,
> There's barbed wire there,
> My baby's got barbed wire in her hair,
> I've got the Mandate Blues.'

The song was his own composition. As ill-formed and ragged as his voice, it grew with each new incident. When they let Silver out in front of the YMCA building he added another verse:

> 'Some people go for Gentiles,
> An' some people go for Jews,
> But ma baby goes for the Bible,
> I've got the Mandate Blues.'

Climbing the steps to the main door Silver ignored him.

The party at the Club had barely begun when Harding and Killin arrived. A four-piece band was playing in a desultory fashion to an empty floor. Uniformed servants moved amongst the guests with drinks. There was a burst of laughter from a group of officers at the bar and someone called out to the newcomers in exaggerated tones: 'Over here, Andrew old chap! Come and have a peg.'

'There they are,' said Killin, pointing to a corner table where four young women were sitting. 'Just the ticket.'

One of the girls gave a smile of recognition and waved. Killin grabbed Harding's arm and led the way over, almost as though his companion might get lost negotiating his way across the room. There was a confused exchange of names. It was apparent that Killin only really knew one of the girls and had persuaded her to bring the others along. 'Mary's some kind of cousin actually. Once removed, I think. And this is Andrew Harding, our war hero. He's something in headquarters but won't say what.'

'Claims Commission,' Harding explained with a smile. 'Very boring.'

'What's the war hero part?' one of the girls asked.

He shrugged the question off but Killin answered for him. 'Long Range Desert Group, eating Germans for breakfast when you run out of bullybeef, that kind of thing. DSO, MC, gongs all over the place. Used to drive thousands of miles behind enemy lines . . .'

'I drive a desk now. A little bit safer, and a lot more boring.'

'Reluctant hero, in the great British tradition,' Killin said, clapping him on the shoulder. 'Now, who's for a drink?'

One of the girls was watching Harding with particular attention. 'Rachel,' she repeated when he asked her name. She pronounced it Ray-chl, not Rach-el, gentile, not Jew. One noticed things like that here. Her accent was American – American or Canadian, he really couldn't tell. 'Rachel Simson. From the city of brotherly love.'

'Is that Philadelphia?' Harding indicated the chair beside her. 'May I sit down?'

'Sure. I guess you're going to tell me about being a hero?'

'Only if you're going to tell me about nursing.'

'But I'm not a nurse.'

'I thought . . .'

'The other three. I'm a journalist.' She held up her hand before he could speak. 'And I promise everything's off the record.'

Harding smiled and offered her a cigarette, wondering what to talk about, thanking Killin for the whisky he brought over, smiling vaguely at the American girl with her sharp voice and her expansive smile. He felt detached from all this, remote from his colleagues at play, indifferent to the forced laughter and the awful bonhomie. He had been scorched by the Libyan sun and been dizzied by the beating wind. He had lived anyhow with men in the naked desert, and been – how did it go? – shamed into pettiness by the innumerable stars. Something like that. Whatever kind of joke you made of it, it set you apart. And then there had been a spell in the cold of northern Germany as the whole bloody shambles ground to a halt, and now here he was back in the Middle East, constrained in this dubious world of peace, wondering what the hell to do. He felt remote from it all.

'I'm freelance,' the girl was saying, in answer to a question he must have asked, 'although I came over here accredited to something called the *Quaker Review*, can you imagine?' He tried to bring his mind back to the conversation. Rachel Something. Her face was framed by a page-boy haircut and the style gave her a superficial look of innocence, but there was something about the blunt nose and the ironical turn to her mouth which betrayed a different character beneath. 'Actually,' she admitted, as though it were an embarrassing secret, 'I also do a bit of teaching to cover the gaps. At the American Episcopal School.'

'I didn't know there was one.'

She smiled wryly. 'Americans have at least one of everything, two or three of anything that matters. I'm afraid the Episcopal School doesn't come into that category. So tell me, what's an MC? Sounds like a guy with a top hat and tails. And that other thing?'

'They're medals. You win them for killing large numbers of people. You have to kill rather more to win the DSO.'

'You're kidding me.' She frowned, and almost grew angry when he laughed at her. 'But you *have* killed people,' she said. 'Why make a joke out of it?'

'What alternative do you suggest? Weeping?'

'Don't you feel guilty?'

He shrugged. 'Not really. The men I killed would have done the same for me. It was an arrangement we had.'

She looked at him with shrewd eyes. 'Peace must be very unsettling after a comfortable arrangement like that.'

'It is. War makes decisions for you. In peace you have to make your own.'

'Isn't that called growing up?'

He shook his head. 'Englishmen don't grow up. They move directly from immaturity to senility. At the age of about forty.'

'That explains a lot of what's going on here in Palestine. And what does a hero do in the Mandatory government, before he joins the ranks of the senile? Do you chase the Stern Gang and stalk the Irgun?'

'When you've been in action you learn to keep well away from dangerous people like that. I told you: I'm with the Claims Commission.'

'What's the Claims Commission?'

'We pay people off when an Army truck runs over a sheep.'

She looked sceptical. 'You expect me to believe *that*?'

'That we do it, or that it's my job?'

'Either.'

'Both.'

'From what I've seen of Army driving habits it must get quite expensive.'

At that moment the band struck up a Benny Goodman number. Rachel pushed her chair back and held out her hand. 'Shall we?

59

Someone's got to start.' And so it was she who took him by the hand and led him onto the dance floor. 'Quick work, Andrew,' Killin called as they went. 'I won't tell the wife.'

Rachel could dance. There were many things she could do. She even tried to teach him something called the Lindy Hop which was, apparently, the latest craze in the States, and he even learnt, more or less. They spent much of that evening together and he found himself amused by her, by her Americanisms and her humour, and by her refusal to be overawed or put down by her British hosts. By the time the last dance came along – early because there was another damned curfew in force that evening – they were still together. The tune was 'Moonlight Serenade', as it always seemed to be.

'You know these musicians were all in the Vienna Philharmonic until Herr Hitler came along?' she said as they danced. 'And here they are playing Glenn Miller. I wrote a piece on them recently. No one wanted it.' She leaned back in his arms so she could look straight at him. 'What Dennis said . . .'

'Dennis? Dennis wouldn't know a philharmonic orchestra from a wurlitzer.'

She laughed. 'No, what he said at the start, that he won't tell your wife. Is that true?'

'That he won't tell her?'

She laughed again. 'That you have one, stupid.'

Stoopid. He could imagine Lorna's derisive expression. 'Yes,' he said. 'And a daughter.'

'Are they in England?'

'In England, yes.'

'Waiting for the return of the hero?'

He didn't answer. The music finished and they drew apart. There was a scattering of applause. 'We'd better be going,' he said. 'I can give you a lift if you like.'

Killin was already gathering the group together, swearing there was enough room for everyone in the Riley, offering lifts to all parts of the city. 'American Colony first stop,' he called. 'Sheikh Jarrah for the dish-cloths, Mea Shearim for the beards and ringlets.'

'Maybe we'll see each other around,' Rachel said to Harding.

'Maybe.'

They were far apart really, separated by different cultures and different manners, and united only by that fickle and mendacious thing, the language. They had only been thrown together by chance, by the capricious tides of hatred which flowed through the city. You might have expected it to come to nothing.

7

A picnic. Killin had organised the whole thing. He was the kind of man who could find his way through the serpentine channels of supply, the kind who knew a man here and a man there and could conjure up delicacies which, throughout years of war, had become little more than fantasies. 'Smoked salmon!' he suggested with relish. 'I know a certain Frobisher who is not unconnected with the kitchens of Government House. Smoked salmon is no problem for Frobisher. There is also the possibility – I say possibility but I mean probability – of caviar; and the dead certainty of half a dozen bottles of a rather dubious white Bordeaux. What do you think of that, eh? And Rachel will be there,' he assured Harding. 'She particularly asked if you were coming.'

A taxi took them round to the nurses' hostel in the American Colony. It was a large machine, a pre-war Buick capable of taking eight passengers in comfort. The men – one of Killin's cronies had joined the group – sat on dickey seats while the four girls, splendid in floral dresses and wide picture hats, crowded laughing across the back seat. They brought with them the scent of roses and a sense of blithe indifference. Rachel laughed and joked with the others and barely acknowledged Harding's presence.

'Forward Jehu!' called Killin, inevitably. The Arab driver grinned and nodded approval as though he recognised the name. 'Tomb of Rachel?' he asked over his shoulder. His suggestion brought laughter from the back. 'Gee, I hope not!'

'Bethlehem? Birthplace of famous Jesus? I am Christian Arab. I come from Bethlehem. I have cousin who will sell you real souvenirs, good price.'

They swayed away from the kerb like a barge from a quayside, heading south through the city, past Jaffa Gate and the railway station and the Allenby barracks. 'What do you think an *unreal* souvenir might be?' Rachel asked. 'I badly want an unreal souvenir.' She was sitting just opposite Harding, her knees close together and touching his. 'Maybe they're things that help you forget,' she suggested.

The drive only took a few minutes. Under Killin's instructions they found a spot just off the road where they could lay out the rugs in the shade of some Aleppo pine. There was white rock and grey scrub and a blaze of spring flowers running down the hillside; over to the right, couched amongst trees, couched in barbed wire, lay Government House. But, of course, the focus of the whole place was to the north of them: the Old City cupped in its bowl of hills. You could see the long white curtain of the south wall and the small dome of the Al-Aqsa mosque and the larger one of the Dome of the Rock. At this distance, Harding thought, you really could share in the vision. A passage from the Revelation of Saint John the Divine occurred to him:

> And I saw the holy city, new Jerusalem, coming down from God out of heaven, prepared as a bride adorned for her husband.

'It's lovely,' cried the girls, drifting around in their billowing frocks. 'How *clever* you are, Dennis.'

'Reconnaissance and intelligence: the key to a successful attack,' he answered as he opened the hamper. 'Andrew'll tell you.'

'Who's attacking who?' asked someone coyly.

Dennis smirked. 'We'll know that by the end of the afternoon.' He had donned a panama hat and wore a pair of white trousers held up at his waist by a knotted regimental tie. He danced around as though he had been at the wine already. The girls laughed gratifyingly at his antics. As he unpacked the food he sang, to their applause,

> 'Oh, ya gotta have some salmon,
> And ya gotta have some booze,
> And ya gotta forget the Israelites,
> Throw *off* them Mandate Blues.'

So they strewed themselves across the ground, and the dubious Bordeaux flowed, and the smoked salmon and caviar were a great success, and by the end of the meal it appeared that Silver had drunk rather too much. Having made a chain of flowers and, with the encouragement of Mary, snatched the panama off Killin's head, he now set about trying to get the garland over the balding dome. The big man brushed him away as one might brush away a fly.

Rachel came to sit by Harding. 'And what has the Major been doing since the dance?' she asked. 'Have the cares of government been weighing on his mind? I've been waiting for the phone to ring, but no luck.'

'No time,' he said. He looked at her curiously, trying to place her within the context of the women he knew and had known. He found that he couldn't. She seemed to be of another, sharper breed.

'I'm sorry if I irritate you,' she said. 'It's being American, isn't it?'

'Don't be silly. It's being English.' The circlet was in place on Killin's head now and, to the general amusement of the audience, the wearer was performing a grotesque dance beneath the pine trees, reeling round, waving his arms. Silver watched unsmilingly, as though he had never been drunk in the first place but had merely been working to make a fool of Killin. 'What brought you out here?' Harding asked the girl. 'We just get posted wherever they decide, but you have a choice.'

'I told you at the Club. Journalism.'

'Yes, but why out here of all places? Why not a job on the Philadelphia Daily Express or something.'

She picked idly at some grass. 'The *Philadelphia Inquirer*, I guess. Learning the trade. Writing up graduation ceremonies and weddings, doing feature articles on the Amish and Valley Forge. Let's face it, Philadelphia is all right, but it's not the most exciting place.' She looked up with an awkward smile. 'And there was a man as well.'

'There often is.'

'You don't want my life history.'

'I'll tell you when to stop.'

She tossed the bits of grass into the breeze, as though tossing away that part of her past. 'We were engaged to be married. At least that was the understanding between us. I was fresh out of Bryn Mawr – do you know Bryn Mawr? – and he was in medical school and we were going steady. The war interrupted all that, but when he came back from Europe in one piece it seemed that everything would be just fine. We'd have had to wait a couple more years for him to qualify, but we'd have made a wonderful Philly couple.'

Was there sarcasm in her tone? He found her accent hard to read, her intonations and allusions just beyond his grasp. 'And?'

'I just wanted out, I suppose. I wanted something else.'

'And did you find it?'

She looked at him in that disturbing way, just as she had done during the dance at the Club: part amused, part watchful. He was, he understood, on dangerous ground: quite precisely – for the city is that kind of place and he was the kind of man who took an interest in that kind of detail – he was on the Hill of Evil Council, where Judas took his thirty pieces of silver. 'I don't know,' she said. 'The jury is still out.'

'Maybe it can be rigged.'

'How rigged?'

He shrugged as though it didn't matter. 'Let's do something together.'

She regarded him with that shrewd expression, the journalist's expression, one that surely she had practised when interviewing members of the Jewish Agency or whatever it was she did. 'Exactly what do you propose, Major Harding?'

Her words seemed to amuse him. 'Exactly, nothing. Approximately, how about the cinema?'

'The movies? Sure.'

'An unreal souvenir, maybe. Next Wednesday then. I'll pick you up at six.'

'What are we going to see?'

'I've no idea.'

That was the moment when Silver cried out 'Cheese!' and everyone turned to find that he had balanced a camera precariously on a convenient rock just up the hill from where they had camped. There were squeals from the nurses and a hasty adjusting of position and a patting of skirts and hair, until finally everyone was grinning casually at the small, black barrel of the camera. 'Leave room for me!' Silver called. He released the shutter. A curious buzzing noise came from the camera. He scuttled round and settled himself into a space between Rachel and Harding.

'All ready now!'

Momentarily imbued with a life of its own the camera clicked.

'How frightfully clever,' said Mary.

So Andrew Harding and Rachel Simson went to the cinema in Ben Yehuda Street and sat side by side amongst the usual motley Jerusalem audience while a newsreel showed recent proceedings from the Nuremburg trials. There were shots of the defendants looking stolid and indignant, like members of a town council accused of embezzlement, and extracts from film which had been presented as evidence, sequences taken after the liberation of one of the camps, with the bodies heaped in piles and British soldiers wearing masks as they drove the bulldozers. The cinema audience groaned and cried out like sleepers during a nightmare, and Rachel held Harding's hand in the desperate grip of a child. The main feature − *The Keeper of the Flame* with Katharine Hepburn and Spencer Tracy − seemed a hideous solecism after that.

At the end of the programme they struggled out with the crowd into the darkness of the city. There wasn't much of the evening left because, yet again, there was a curfew in force following an attack on a police post or something. 'A drink maybe?' Harding suggested. 'Or are you hungry?'

She shook her head. 'A drink. I had something to eat before I came out.'

They wandered up Ben Yehuda towards King George V Avenue, and found a table at the Royal where you could watch the world, such as it was, go by − a jeep patrol of the Highland Light Infantry as a matter of fact, then a couple of Hasidic Jews in their long black coats and black homburgs who reminded Rachel, so she told Harding, of the Pennsylvania Dutch, and then a group of people whom Harding knew vaguely and wished he didn't. He waved at them reluctantly, sipped his beer and glanced at the girl and wondered; while Rachel seemed uneasy, smoking nervously and stubbing out her cigarette when it was only half finished. 'Christ, those pictures,' she said, and then fell silent.

'I was there.'

The statement seemed without meaning. 'Where?'

'At Bergen-Belsen. When they liberated the place last April.'

'Oh, my Christ.'

He felt almost apologetic. 'I'm sorry . . .'

'No, go on.'

He shrugged. 'It was me and a friend. We drove down from Munster, just to have a look. It's not really the kind of thing . . .'

'I'd like to hear. If you want to tell.'

'Do you know the first thing? The first thing was the smell. A mile away. We were in a jeep and it was a fine, sunny spring day, and you could smell it before you even got there. That was when we began to realise . . .'

'Realise?'

'That words wouldn't do it justice. Nor pictures. The press was there, you see.' He shook his head. 'You can't film the smell.'

'No.' The information seemed to have shocked her, as though he had somehow been responsible for what had happened there. 'Do you . . .?'

'Do I what?'

'Want to talk about it? Do you want to talk about it?' She reached for another cigarette.

'Not really. Perhaps I should have kept quiet.'

'Hell, no. You're a witness. For crying out loud, your testimony is important.'

He shook his head. 'Let's talk about something else.'

With a visible effort, she brightened up. 'Okay. Something else.' She seemed to cast around for possibilities. 'Hey, she's good, isn't she, Katharine Hepburn? What's the line? She ran the whole gamut of emotion, from A to B.' Harding laughed. 'Not original,' she admitted. 'Dorothy Parker. She's a Bryn Mawr girl, you know that? Hepburn, not Parker. Class of '28. She came to talk to us when I was a sophomore. Good breeding.'

'Like you.'

'Oh, well-bred, sure. For a Yank.' She lit another cigarette and blew a stream of smoke upwards into the evening sky. 'So tell me about being a hero. If you don't want to tell me about Belsen, tell me about what you did before that. The girls talk about you, you know that? It seems you're quite an attraction. They say . . .'

'What do they say?'

'They say lots of things. What does your wife say, I wonder?'

'She says she wants me to come home.'

'I'll bet she does.' She turned to him. 'I tell you, I wouldn't let you out of my sight.' In the wash of light from the café windows her skin seemed almost white, her eyes much darker than he remembered them on the picnic. She wasn't, he told himself, very special. Nothing like as pretty as Lorna. He thought of good-looking girls as 'pretty', never 'beautiful'. Prettiness was something one could deal with, a mere set of physical attributes like a well-turned nose, good eyes, a nicely-curved mouth. Rachel didn't really fit the bill. Her mouth was too full, and she was wearing that bright red lipstick which made it worse. And she didn't do very much with her hair except keep it a little too short. So not particularly pretty; but striking in a way. He'd allow her that: striking.

'You like it here, don't you?' she said.

'Why do you think that?'

'At the picnic. You quoted something . . .'

He smiled. 'I didn't think I said it out loud. "And I saw the

66

holy city, new Jerusalem, coming down prepared as a bride adorned for her bridegroom."'

'There. The Book of the Apocalypse, isn't it? Dennis didn't quote anything.'

'He quotes all the time. It's just that he gets them wrong.'

She laughed. 'So what do you think of this place, Andrew?'

He shook his head. 'I really don't know. Maybe for me it's just an extension of the war, postponing decisions or something.'

'I thought you'd already made a whole lot of those.'

He smiled. 'Maybe I have. Maybe it's too late.' The curfew time was approaching and the streets were emptying. He stood up. 'I think we ought to be getting back.'

She stubbed her cigarette out. 'Maybe we should. It was fun, wasn't it?'

He nodded. 'All except for the newsreel.'

'All except for the newsreel. I guess I haven't been very good company, have I?'

'You've been fine.' They walked to the car. The streets had emptied suddenly and a police patrol drove by, a jeep with a great steel girder mounted like a beak over the bonnet that made it appear like some hideous, flightless bird. 'Christ, they look spooky like that,' Rachel said. 'What's the point?'

'The terrorists tie wires across the roads. At neck level. It takes your head off.'

'Nice.' There was a silence. He searched his pockets to find the car keys. 'Are you going to be here over Easter?' she asked.

'I've got leave. I'm going home.'

'I'm looking forward to it, the ceremony of the Holy Fire, that kind of thing. I'll be able to sell something on that.'

'It's a bit phoney, I'm afraid. I saw it in nineteen forty-two when I was on leave from the desert.'

'The Holy Fire?' She laughed that loud, transatlantic laugh. 'I don't expect to *believe* in it, for Christ's sake. I'm not that naïve.'

'People do, you know. You'd be surprised.'

'And what do you believe in, Andrew?' she asked.

'Believe in? Good God, what a question. Englishmen believe things, but they don't believe *in* things. They leave that to fanatics and foreigners. And priests.'

'And Americans?'

When he turned to open the door for her she was very close. Her expression, that much that he could see in the light from the nearest street lamp, was thoughtful. She touched the lapel of his jacket and seemed to brush something away, but she couldn't possibly have seen anything there in the shadows. It was an instinctive gesture, the kind of thing that Lorna did. But with Lorna he always made a comment, told her not to mother him or something. 'Tell me,' she repeated. 'What *do* you believe in?'

'I believe . . .' He hesitated. 'I believe that I've survived a war, but I'm not certain whether I'm going to survive the peace . . .'

And then she reached up and kissed him. There was just the faintest pressing of her body against him and a touch of her lips on his, and a sudden darting of her tongue. He tasted the sour taint of tobacco on her breath, and something more, the strange individuality of her: her uniqueness. He held her shoulders for a moment, and then gently eased her away.

'The curfew,' he said quietly. 'We could get arrested. Imagine what the hostel authorities would say about that.'

'Sure,' she said. 'Dumb of me.'

He held the car door for her and she climbed in. She didn't say anything all the way back to her hostel.

★

Dearest Lorna,

Another missive from the Unholy Land, where the Jews hate the British and the Arabs, the Arabs hate the Jews and the British, and the British hate themselves for getting into such a frightful mess. Dennis Killin makes things slightly normal by appearing pig-ignorant about the whole thing. Last Sunday he organised a picnic lunch with – can you imagine? – smoked salmon and bottles of wine. Snap-shot enclosed, and notice the sunshine even at this time of year. Killin is in the floral hat and Silver is the rather supercilious one next to me. The girls by courtesy of a nurses' hostel. Not camp-followers, despite what your father says! The spread made me feel quite guilty at the thought of you living under the burden of Mr Attlee's rationing, but really it would not be happy for you out here, and certainly not with the little girl. How is she? How are you, come to that? How I miss you both and how lovely it will be to see you over Easter. I often imagine the two of you . . .

Helen read it some forty years later, finding it amongst her mother's letters, and she thought it hypocritical. But the fact is that he tried; he tried very hard.

8

Palestine to England: Lydda to Akrotiri, Akrotiri to Malta, Malta to Gibraltar, Gibraltar to Northolt.

'A round tour of His Majesty's possessions in Europe,' was how the journalist who sat next to him described it. 'As long as they last.' The journalist was writing a series of articles on the Mandate for the *Manchester Guardian*. He propped a portable typewriter on his knees and clacked away through the racket of the flight, occasionally looking up for an opinion or a judgement. 'What do you do, then?' he shouted at one point.

'Claims Commission.'

'What's that?'

'Paying people off when an Army truck knocks over their olive tree or runs over a sheep.'

'We do *that*?' The journalist's expression was incredulous.

'As little as possible.'

The typewriter clattered on, scarcely heard above the noise of the engines. Malta appeared beneath the Dakota's wings, a small maze of lanes and fields. Red earth, just like Palestine. The journalist read out the introduction to his article, something about the seat of Pilate being as uncomfortable now as ever it was during the Roman period. 'What do you think?' he called.

Harding yelled back, 'Fine!' but he hadn't really heard. As the plane droned across the Mediterranean the whole place had become less and less real to him, just a passing experience composed of many images but with no coherence to it at all. The Damascus Gate in moonlight, the Dead Sea lying under a plain and brassy sky, the Hills of Moab over which Joshua came, the bedlam of the Holy Sepulchre, the Hasids moaning at the Wailing Wall, the Arabs prostrating themselves at the Al-Aqsa mosque, the

69

military bands at Saint George's Cathedral, the Jews demonstrating for a homeland and the refugees from Europe running the gauntlet of the blockade, while the Arabs seethed with resentment and jealousy – it just seemed a mess of history and legend, war and politics and religion. What could he make out of it all?

His companion was shouting something back but he couldn't hear. 'What d'you say?'

'What the High Commissioner said to me,' the journalist yelled. 'He said, "Sometimes I feel like washing my hands of the whole damned place." And then he looked worried and added, "For God's sake don't quote me on that."' The journalist put back his head and laughed, but the sound barely carried across the cabin. There was just his open mouth and the twin rows of teeth and the pink and glistening tongue.

In the evening they reached Gibraltar, having chased the sun for hours without catching it. The noise of the engines rang in their ears as they climbed down the steps. 'Do you realise,' the journalist remarked, 'that we've been flying a whole day and we've not got any nearer home? Here you have to run as fast as you can just to stay in the same place. Sounds like a metaphor for the Mandate.'

A night spent in the transit hotel in Gibraltar, then onwards the next morning, out over the Atlantic, over the Bay of Biscay, over Brittany, over the grey of the Channel beneath the grey of the sky. Palestine to England. The contrast was so extreme as to appear beyond comprehension or comparison. From the bright anarchy of the Holy Land to the dull resignation of a Britain that was victorious in nothing but fact: from relative plenty to rationing; from excitement to boredom and the peculiar troglodyte existence which the British seemed to live at home, as though they were a different race, a different civilization altogether from those who ruled the Empire; from freedom, a heady, personal freedom, to the strictures of a marriage he did not truly comprehend.

There was drizzle in the air, and the concrete at Northolt was slick with damp. Lorna was waiting for him as he disembarked; Lorna looking pallid and etiolated. They embraced with something like shyness.

'Helen, it's your daddy.'

The engines still roared in his ears. The journalist was ducking into the drizzle and calling something to him about reading the *Guardian*. The little girl hung behind her mother's skirts and looked at Harding with wide, animal eyes. She shook her head.

'I don't have a daddy,' she said.

They spent Easter with Harding's parents in Sussex, trying to establish that domestic life they had barely known, being fussed over by his mother and gently patronised by his father. They rediscovered personal habits and prejudices, likes and dislikes, the little rituals of existence together. And her child, his child, was a startled animal to be coaxed out of her den of suspicion and fear.

'Is it good to be back?' Lorna asked.

'It's wonderful to see you again, but . . .'

'But?' Lorna shone with a strange refulgent light, her eyes wide and blue, her skin the colour of milk. And her hair, that tent of gold.

'You're beautiful, Helen's beautiful, but England's bloody,' he told her.

'That's not very kind to your parents.'

'I wasn't referring to my parents. I mean the country, the weather, the grey people in their shabby grey clothes, with their petty worries and their tatty ration books.'

She made a little moue of distaste. 'You can't blame people for that. We won the war; now we're losing the peace. I read that somewhere.'

'The *Guardian*, I expect. Maybe we should get out.'

'What do you mean?'

'Emigrate, go to Australia or somewhere.'

She laughed at that, and touched his arm, and awoke in him a whole bleating flock of emotions which could only be silenced when Helen had been put to bed, and they had said an early good night to his parents and his father had smiled knowingly at the two of them while Lorna blushed faintly.

Oh, they were happy enough. On a fortnight's leave there isn't much time to be anything else. Lorna and he argued little because they were unfamiliar with each other and it is hard to argue with an acquaintance; and they made love often and with something approaching passion because that is easy with a stranger. And for the fortnight he felt placid and entire within the limits of their world, and he barely noticed that by the time the end of the leave came round, impatience and boredom had begun to set in.

After Easter they went to Guerdon House to stay with her father. They occupied the large room on the first floor with the windows that look out over the lawns and the water-meadows, down to the willows on the edge of the river. Her father was as remote and cynical as ever, laughing at Andrew's account of the struggles with terrorists, always expressing a contrary view, an awkward opinion.

'I should think you love it out there,' he said. 'I did in 1917. Got me away from Lorna's mother. I can tell you there was no better place to be.'

'Than Palestine?'

'Than away from Lorna's mother.' He laughed loudly, but it was a laugh with little humour. He was a sad figure, half-crippled by arthritis, shuffling from one room to another of his old, damp house. One felt that the insidious progress of rot and decay was at work in his own body just as much as in the fabric of the building. 'Do you know what *guerdon* is, eh?' he demanded. Harding affected ignorance. The question was an old one, asked of every visitor. 'Guerdon's a gift, a reward. But this place is nothing but a bane. A reward for vice, maybe.'

Did Harding think of Rachel? She was part of another continent, a fragment of another world, a secret thing in the shadows of the Levant. Only once did she step into the light of his consciousness, when they went to church on Easter Sunday and he imagined her amongst the candles and incense of the Church of the Holy Sepulchre, perhaps with some of the girls from the nurses' hostel, straining to see as the Holy Fire spread through the crowd like sparks through a field of burning stubble. There was just that image and nothing else. And a sudden sensation of the taste of tobacco on her mouth.

'Tell me about Jerusalem,' Lorna asked him more than once, and he deflected the question with ease and the city and all it contained remained inviolate: 'I've told you before. It's a tiresome place. It could be beautiful, but instead it's narrow-minded and dull and dangerous. One day it'll be worth a visit. Not now.'

'But you're going back there now, without me.'

'We've been over it all a hundred times, darling. The arguments haven't changed. In fact the way things are going it can only get worse. It's just not suitable for wives and families. They're even talking about repatriating those that are there.'

'You sound like father.'

That seemed to amuse him. 'Hardly. He loathed your mother. I love you. There's quite a difference.'

'And what do you do without me?' Her smile was provocative.

'When I'm awake I think of you, and when I'm asleep I dream of you.'

'That doesn't sound very satisfactory. I bet you have women, camp-followers or something, like father is always claiming.'

He laughed. 'The Holy Land is the land of Onan, my love. Cold showers are usually out because of water shortages, so we spend most of the time playing with ourselves. Just as we were taught at school.' She gave a shriek which was part amusement, part delight, part outrage. 'How else do you think we get by?' he protested. 'It's a hand-reared army, my dear.'

'Everyone does it?' she asked, wide-eyed.

'Everyone.'

'Even the generals?'

'Especially the generals. Generals,' he asserted with great solemnity, recalling a joke of Dennis', 'generals do it standing to attention.'

Their laughter rang through the house, stirring Helen in her sleep and waking her father in the next room, who, hearing it, supposed they were a happy couple.

II

1

Picture a street in Oxford, in April, May, the precise month is immaterial. A street, a pavement, with a background of old, dull limestone – not the bright, golden stone of Jerusalem, but a dull English limestone like the dullness of a cataracted eye. Watch Helen's figure walking, with that determined stride of hers, towards the university buildings at the far end. She doesn't conform to type: she is wearing a pale blue dress with white polka-dots and she looks far too dressy for a member of the university. Plainness is the usual image, dowdiness worn like a uniform, intending to show an impatience with the superficial things of life; but Helen's figure has a brightness about it that gives the lie to the idea that she might spend most of her time in the fusty shadows of a library reading room. You might mistake her for a tourist, or a student of one of the secretarial colleges, or a sister come up for the weekend to visit her undergraduate brother.

Coming out of a bookshop, Michael recognised her immediately. Even from behind he knew her at a glance – the cloud of pale hair, the slender waist, the shape of her legs (a shade too thin and lacking the narrowness of ankle which would have made them perfect), the particular way she moved. 'Helen,' he shouted. She didn't hear above the noise of a passing motorbike. 'Helen!' She half-turned, her expression uncertain, as though the call might not have been for her.

'Helen, it *is* you.' She stopped and turned fully and watched his approach, smiling slightly. 'Remember me?'

'Michael. Don't be silly. What on earth are you doing here?' They exchanged kisses. At least, Michael gave her a kiss while Helen merely presented a cheek, reaching up on tiptoe. Over his shoulder she could see their figures reflected in the windows of a children's bookshop, ghosts floating out of childhood, out of a world of fairy stories and monster books and a pop-up version of *The Wind in the Willows*: a young man with longish hair, dressed in the uniform of duffle coat and corduroy trousers, and a young girl in a polka-dot dress, with her left leg lifted artfully off the ground. 'Goodness, you seem to have grown taller,' she said, almost in a tone of admonishment.

She didn't know whether to be impatient with this encounter. She didn't know what to do with it at all, in fact. He seemed different, of course, apart from appearing taller: faintly amused, as though laughing at her, slightly brusque, a shade indifferent perhaps. 'What are you doing?' he asked.

'Going to a library.'

'No, here in Oxford. What are you doing in Oxford?'

'Oh, a BLitt.'

'I heard someone mention you the other day . . .'

'How come?'

He laughed and shrugged the incident off. 'Do you have time for a cup of coffee?'

'If there's one thing you have in this place, it's time.'

And so the circles touched, merged, and interlocked. They had changed. Four, five years had done their work. You may imagine the conversation, held across a grubby café table in the covered market, long before the days when the place became fashionable, subject of a preservation order and symbol of a city that the developers have long ago destroyed. A sugar dispenser stood between their mugs, one of those things like half an hour-glass, with a spout which measures the dose for you and never gives you the right amount. The sugar inside was grey. While Helen and Michael stepped cautiously towards each other over the debris of their past, her fingers held the sugar dispenser distractedly, turning it round and tilting it so that the grains tumbled and slid over one another.

'You went to Bristol, didn't you?' she said. 'What are you doing now?'

He appeared flattered by her remembering. 'A bit of teaching, waiting for something to turn up. I'm thinking of going abroad.'

'And Anthony? Where's he? And your father?'

Memory. How quickly Cyprus had fled into the past. how distant those people seemed now, occupying as they had that remote corner of a dying Empire, separated as they were from the present by the barrier of adolescence. Tommy, she learned, was now at the Ministry of Defence trying to manage expenditure cuts, merging this regiment with that, attempting to create tradition out of dissolution; Anthony had thought better of following him into the Army and was now a solicitor in the West Country. 'He's married already, poor sod, and with a child. A little boy.'

'I heard about that. Maybe mother told me.' She frowned at the idea. 'Although why she should know I can't imagine.'

'How is she?'

Helen evaded the question, making a wry face, wrinkling her nose and mouth as though at some pungent smell. 'It was bloody, wasn't it? The divorce, I mean . . . Adults are the last people you can expect to behave like adults, don't you think? Mother's never been happy since; but then I don't think she was really happy before either, do you?' She tipped the sugar dispenser and watched the grains as though trying to descry something there. 'Anyway, she's living at Guerdon House now, trying to put it into some kind of shape. She doesn't see *him* any more of course. Dennis Killin, I mean.'

'Why on earth . . .?'

She glanced up at him and wondered, wondered about the present as well as the past, tried in vain to see some kind of pattern in things, in this chance meeting. 'Why on earth what?'

Michael shook his head. 'I'd love to see her again. She was important to me.'

'Was she? She was hardly the motherly kind. Not even with me.' Her use of the past tense was deliberate, as though the Lorna who lived now was a different one from the one Michael had known only a few years before. 'Maybe you'd like to come over some time? To Guerdon House, I mean.'

'How would she take it?'

She shrugged. 'She'd be all right. She was fond of you.' Her hand flexed and turned in the space between the cups, tipping the sugar dispenser this way and that. She watched the grains run, the sands of time. 'It looks as though it could do with a good wash.'

'And your BLitt.? What's it about?'

'Oh, that.' She brightened visibly, on easier ground now. 'Actually it might be expanded into a doctorate. Can you imagine Doctor Helen? Something like The Magdalen Myth in the Life of the Early Church. My supervisor thinks it has great promise.' But she found the whole thing unlikely, that her ridiculous ideas might carry some kind of weight.

'I never thought of you as religious.'

'It's not religion, it's the *study* of religion. A very different

79

thing. If anything it encourages a healthy scepticism. Anyway you never really knew me, did you? You knew a little girl.' She looked at him with a sudden directness. 'A little too thoroughly at times perhaps,' she added. He reddened, and for a moment intimacy, the curious imposed intimacy that they had lived through, lay between them like some kind of distorting lens. They saw things in each other, knew things about each other that no one else could guess at.

'I thought the world of you,' he told her. 'Do you realise that?'

'You did?'

'You let me kiss you once. At a dance.'

'I don't remember.'

'And you just turned your head at the last moment, like that' – he moved his head sharply sideways in demonstration – 'and said we shouldn't do that kind of thing. Almost shocked, you were.'

'We were brother and sister, weren't we?'

'Were we?'

'Of a kind.' A strange kind. She felt almost naked, sitting there at the table with him.

'And then you went off with that soldier.'

'Oh, him.' She laughed awkwardly. 'Archie. Good God, it seems an aeon ago. I heard about him the other day. He's in Germany with his regiment.' She looked round for her bag and said, mendaciously, 'Look, Mike, I've got to go. Maybe we can get together some time . . .'

'And you know I always hated Mike.'

'Michael, then. Michael. I must go . . .'

'Where do you live?'

She hesitated. 'Digs in Jericho at the moment. The place is rather squalid but the landlady is quite amenable. I'm looking for a flat . . .'

'I'm in Headington. Do you have a phone?'

She shook her head. 'Not for incoming calls. I'll give you a ring. A weekend or something . . .' She stood up from the table with her bag slung over her shoulders.

'Let's fix something now,' he insisted.

They watched each other, seeing so much, knowing so much about the fragile beings that underlay the newly-hardened, adult shells. 'Why not?' she asked, as though it didn't matter. 'There's an excellent production of *The Devils* at the Playhouse. I know someone in the cast. What about that?'

★

And so they met on the pavement outside the theatre two days later, and during the second act of the play, while the leading actor was strutting the boards in soutane and biretta and the little hunchback Sister Jeanne des Anges was erupting in erotic fantasy over him, the truth began to dawn on Michael. There was something about Helen's manner as she sat in the stalls beside him, a tension in her look, a particular focus to her gaze, that gave her away. 'Isn't he brilliant?' she whispered, turning on Michael a smile that alone amongst the whole familiar armoury of her expressions, he did not recognise. 'He's having a huge success. There's talk of a professional contract . . .'

Oh, yes, she had changed, had Helen. Whichever of those several virginities she surrendered to Michael, it was not the obvious, hymenal one. That particular one mattered greatly in those days. Nowadays it is considered little more than an inconvenience, to be got out of the way as soon as decently possible — rather like having your ears pierced or one of those orthodontic contraptions fitted — but then, oh then, virginity was still imbued with a mystic significance and Hymen was still, in part, the god of marriage. Helen had kept this symbol of purity right through her schooldays, right through her first three years of university, right through the best attempts of man and beast to snatch it from her, before finally surrendering it to this budding actor, Adrian Oliver, now strutting the boards as the priest Grandier. The great climactic event had occurred in his flat in north Oxford the previous year, after a successful first night — an Edward Bond this time — and a euphoric cast party and much cheap sparkling wine. In the midst of it all he had cupped her face in his hands and quoted Marvell to her in his plangent voice:

'Now, therefore, while the youthful hue
Sits on thy skin like morning dew . . .'

and she had made the decision. So it was later that evening, in the bedroom of his flat, on his unmade bed and beneath a poster of his near namesake Sir Larry, in the role of Archie Rice, Helen surrendered the fragile barricade of her hymen to her actor — while he quoted John Donne this time, and reached his satisfactory climax with barely a pause for breath. Helen, of course, did not reach hers, did not come within a million miles of it as a matter of fact (cosmic distances seem appropriate in such matters), indeed found the whole thing rather flatly physical like having the dentist poke around inside your mouth. But she had finally done it. She had effed.

For some time after that experience she tried to convince herself of things that were not so: that she was a now a realised woman, that it was the first real emotional experience of her life, cant like that. She knew she was lying to herself and she knew that the occasion of the lie had now become a part of her life, a permanent part which could never be undone; but for the moment she was prepared to play the lie out, pretend love, pretend passion, ape affection. The pretence was good enough to convince Oliver – a fine irony – yet however much she tried she was never able to release that inner core of her being to him, never able to unleash that part of her which would have allowed her to make a fool of herself; or a lover. She was always watching.

It was weeks after that performance of *The Devils* that Michael worked out her particular smile of that evening. Certainly it contained admiration, even affection; but there was also amusement and a hint of revulsion.

'We'll go backstage afterwards and you can meet him,' she whispered. 'And maybe you'd like to have something to eat with us? The cast usually go round the corner to the Italian restaurant.'

'I'm sure you'd rather be on your own.'

'Don't be silly.'

So backstage after the final curtain, she introduced Michael as a vague friend of the family from Cyprus days, and Adrian, drunk as he was on the heady wine of success, strutting and declaiming and calling loudly over people's heads in his grand and actorly fashion, barely noticed.

Helen waited. Her habit was watching and waiting. She watched things happen as though they were children of a contingent and fortuitous universe that yet, with a subtle move, might still be influenced. She made the move two weeks later.

'We'd like you to come down to Guerdon for the weekend,' she told Michael on the phone.

'We?'

'I would. Adrian had no choice.'

'You mean he said no?'

'That,' she replied, 'would have been a choice.'

Adrian had been to Guerdon before, of course. He thought he knew the place and all its little secrets and he released them reluctantly to Michael as though it was somehow his own possession. 'Magic,' he avowed as they drove. 'A Pre-Raphaelite mansion, absolutely reeking of the blessed Damozel. It is, perhaps, an acquired taste, but . . .'

Helen reclining on the back seat of the car like the blessed Damozel herself, kept quiet. Instinctively, so too did Michael. For Guerdon House was potent, imbued more than anywhere else with their secret memories, those incidents of childhood which inform lives just as myths inform the structure of a whole culture. It was here, thrown together by chance, that they had explored that strange intimacy that had become theirs, that they had learned to be what the adults required of them: a simulacrum of brother and sister.

The car turned into the drive and faced the place. Old and grey, crowned with the turrets and steeply-pitched rooves of Victorian neo-gothic, it lay couched amongst poplar and willow, bathed in a jade-green light. Michael craned to see.

'I have been here before,' Adrian announced, bringing the car to a halt in front of the steps, 'but when or how I cannot tell.'

'A fortnight ago,' Helen said tartly.

'Rossetti, my dear, Dante Gabriel Rossetti.' Climbing out of the car he stood gazing at the place with a proprietorial air, like a leading actor in the middle of the stage. He began to quote in plangent tones:

'I have been here before,
But when or how I cannot tell.
I know the grass beyond the door,
The sweet keen smell.'

Helen ignored him. 'Do you remember?' she whispered to Michael.

'Of course I remember.'

Her eyes were bright with curiosity. It was as though she was conducting some kind of experiment, playing with chronology, trifling with the irrevocable pattern of time, trying to touch again the past. 'I can almost see it through your eyes,' she said. 'Isn't it strange? I feel I have just come back to it after a long absence.'

'I can't imagine what your mother will think when she sees me.'

'She'll be amazed.'

'Now where is the beautiful *châteleine*?' Adrian demanded.

She came out as though on cue, out through the main door onto the top of the steps, wearing an old pair of dungarees with paint marks down the front. Her hair was pulled back and tied in a scarf. Her face was grimy. Lorna. Her skin, once russet and gold, the colour of copper, was now pallid and lined. You could see the tendons of her neck and the looseness of her skin. She was in her fifties now, with the hormones dying away inside her and age looking out at her from the mirror on her dressing-table. But though much was taken, much remained – that sharp edge of beauty in her, like a weapon to use against the whole tribe of men.

'Hi!' she called. 'Just in time to help,' and then she paused and looked harder at the trio crossing the gravel towards her. 'Good God – Michael!'

He was embraced, drawn into a delicate miasma of perfume and paint thinner. 'Dear, dear Michael,' she cried, releasing him momentarily from the embrace and holding him at arms' length to look. Her face came no higher than his chest. 'Goodness, what a surprise! How many years is it now? Half a dozen? How's Tommy? You know I've written to him, but he never replies? Is he happy, poor dear? Is he? Come in, bring your things. Helen, you never told me dear Michael would be coming . . . How *wicked* you are.'

Adrian was almost ignored. Momentarily grim, powerfully suspicious, he followed them into the house, through the smell of paint stripper, under step-ladders and round rolls of wallpaper, with Lorna leading the way and talking all the time. Michael's presence had released a tidal wave of memory. Cyprus bulked large.

'My God, the sun, the light . . . and that smell, do you remember it? Heaven knows what it was – melons, orange blossom, wild thyme. And carobs. What did they do to them?'

'Kibbling,' Michael said, remembering suddenly. 'They kibbled them.'

Lorna shrieked. 'Carob kibbling! What a pong! Do you remember it? That factory outside Limassol?' She paused and looked round in disappointment, as though she had expected to see the bright Mediterranean *macchia* there on the stairs of Guerdon House. 'Here it's dark by four o'clock in the afternoon and if it's not raining the river's breaking its banks. We had a flood last December, truly. Two feet deep in the sitting room. You can still see the tide mark. Please God for the Mediterranean. Why couldn't I have been left a cottage in Kyrenia or somewhere? Do you remember Kyrenia? And Paphos. I'd even trade this place for Limassol if I had the choice.' And then, changing her tone suddenly: 'Tommy and I were happy there. We were, you know that? Whatever may have happened.'

Upstairs the carpets were all up. Since the death of Helen's grandfather the moist hand of the river had clutched the house, infiltrated it, ushered in damp and rot and all the evil river things, until the place lay in danger of ruin. Lorna was now attempting, on inadequate funds, to restore it. They came across a sullen youth peering beneath floor boards, inspecting the place for dry rot, which is just the same, Lorna informed them, as wet rot, which is simply the most malign fungus it is possible to imagine. 'You know, we found a fruiting body in the Aga when we first opened the place up? What in God's name was it doing there, if not hiding itself? In the bloody oven for heaven's sake, connected by these thick cords to the rest of the beast in the ceiling . . .'

She opened a door on a bare, bright room with twin beds, and crossed over to fling open the windows. They gave out onto the lawn and the meadow and the row of willows which stood along the riverside. 'Now you'll be fine here Michael, and' – she hesitated, wiping her forehead with the back of one hand, as though searching for his name – 'Adrian will go next door. I didn't realise you knew each other.'

'We don't,' Michael said. 'At least we didn't. Mutual friend.'

Helen stood in the centre of the room and watched. Lorna put her head on one side and looked from daughter to erstwhile stepson with bright interest. 'How delightful to discover such sisterly affection after all these years. Or is it something more than sisterly?'

'Mother, for God's sake!'

Adrian's expression had metamorphosed from mere impatience into bewilderment.

'A joke, darling, a joke. You mustn't be so sensitive.' Lorna touched her daughter's arm and smiled at Adrian. 'Now you three sort yourselves out,' she said with deliberate irony, 'and I'll just dash down and see if I can scrape some lunch together. Goodness, we have *such* a lot to talk about.'

When she had gone there was a moment of silence. Then Adrian asked, as though he were the butt of some joke, 'What the devil's going on?'

Helen looked at him with a hint of irritation. 'Isn't it obvious? I'd have thought it was obvious. Michael used to be my step-brother.' She looked at Michael, as though trying to make up her mind about something. 'Can you stop being? Maybe he still is.'

2

They had lunch in the dining room where the French windows looked out over the lawns. The talk was animated and exclusive, punctuated with references that left Adrian adrift and full of those code-words that families use without even being conscious of it. A portrait of Helen's grandfather looked down on them from the wall, scowling at the future as he had scowled at the present, at Tommy and his sons round that very table, at Helen, at Lorna.

After lunch Lorna retired to her bedroom and left the three of them, flown with wine to stroll down through the garden. The grass was ankle deep the whole garden wildly overgrown, barely kept in check by the ancient gardener and his mentally deficient grandson. Helen found that she saw things newly, as though the prism of the present had been shifted and old, familiar views had been given a new perspective. There was the holm oak they had climbed and the ruin of the greenhouse where Tommy and Lorna had trodden amongst the broken panes and called for them to come down. She shook her head when Michael asked if she remembered climbing it. 'Isn't it funny? I remember being up there, but I don't remember how we got there at all.' Her skirt trailed in the grass, grew stained with dew. She bent to pick some yellow flags which grew alongside a ditch and felt detached from the present, haunted by a past which to anyone who had been adult then was no more than a moment ago, but which to her seemed to occupy another world altogether, distant in space as well as time. 'Let's take the punt,' she suggested.

Buried amongst the willows at the end of the lawn was the mouldering wooden boat-house where Michael had once frightened her with stories of men who came for you in the night. Now Adrian led the way, ducking through the low doorway into a flickering and aqueous darkness, while she followed with Michael. The ancient punt was moored to the stage, just where it had been a dozen years ago when the two of them, breathless with excitement, had stolen it away and made an erratic progress down towards the river, paddling Indian style and finding crocodiles amongst the reed beds. They climbed in, sending the water slapping against the piles of the building and casting luminous, wobbling reflections across the roof. Michael handed Helen down, but it was Adrian who took the pole and commanded the crew. 'Push off,' he declaimed, 'and sitting well in order smite the sounding furrows!'

The punt slid out into the daylight. Willows and reed flowed past. Helen settled amongst the cushions with her armful of wild iris, like the Lady of Shallot or someone, lifting one knee to raise a tent of skirt and give her actor a glimpse of pale leg. Standing over her, Adrian wore a proprietorial smile. He was Launcelot, of course. Michael struggled with a wine-clouded memory to recall the story, to give himself some part in it. Agravain? Aggravated, certainly. Helen, Elaine stirred in his imagination. He leant forward and touched her hair where it lay spread out on the cushions. 'Straw,' he said.

She laughed. 'Golden.'

'Delicious.'

'Not a noun, delicious.'

'Neither's golden. Apple. Golden apple of the Hesperides.'

'Crab.'

'Paste.'

'Bloater.' She giggled. 'Bet you can't do that.'

The punt had emerged from the backwater into the main stream. 'You *are* tiresome,' Adrian complained.

'Straw,' said Michael triumphantly. 'I've won!'

Helen raised herself on her elbow and looked at him indignantly. 'What on earth are you talking about? How can you get to straw from bloater?'

'Straw bloater. What sardines wear on their heads.' He laughed, and she laughed with him, her eyes bright with amusement and remembrance.

'Cheat.'

'Wind.'

She sucked in her breath sharply. 'Doubtful. Fart.' She doubled up with laughter.

'Gas.'

'Bag.'

'Oh, for God's sake, do we *have* to play at being children all the time?' Adrian protested. And for the moment, a brief and thrilling moment, he might not have been there at all.

They moored amongst reeds just upstream from the lawns of Ye Olde Thames Tea Shoppe and strolled ashore, Helen holding hands between the two men, still giggling. There were tables out on the lawns. 'Lapsang Souchong,' Adrian demanded of the waitress when they had settled themselves.

The girl sucked her pencil thoughtfully. 'I can manage Earl Grey.'

'Reform Bill,' said Michael.

Helen spluttered. 'Portland Bill,' she cried through tears of laughter, and Michael felt that he owned that particular laughter, that it had only ever been his and somehow it was his still.

In the late afternoon they punted back to Guerdon House. As Michael helped Helen out of the punt she reached up and gave him a kiss on the cheek. It was a mark of recognition, an acknowledgement that for a moment he had snatched her back into childhood, away from whatever it was that the present offered. She couldn't have put it more accurately than that, of course. Michael appeared to her secretive and knowing, a disturbance in the circumscribed world that she inhabited. He occupied a part of her past in the way that a parasite occupies a secret part of its host; no one can be at ease with intimacy of that nature. Almost for comfort she held Adrian's hand as they walked up from the boathouse.

That evening over dinner Adrian explained the success of his performance in *The Devils* to Lorna, quoting verbatim the letter of congratulations from Peter Hall and the review by Kenneth Peacock Tynan. 'There is talk of something at the Royal Court,' he confided, 'but I can't say any more than that at present.'

'He's going to play the male genitals in the new Edward Bond,' Michael suggested. But only Lorna laughed. Helen watched him and watched her past, and clung to the present with a fierce desperation. That night when Adrian crept into her bedroom she was almost passionate in her response to him.

Next morning when they got downstairs Lorna was already at work stripping paint in one of the rooms. Michael left Helen and Adrian to their breakfast and went to help her.

'Your erstwhile stepson returns to the maternal bosom,' he announced awkwardly, standing at the door. She downed tools and gave him another of those embraces which had promised so much to so many different people. 'Dear Michael,' she said. 'Dear, dear Michael. I don't think I was much use to you, was I?'

'Are people meant to be of use to one another?'

'Aren't mothers?' She sat down on one of the bottom rungs of the ladder with her chin in her hands, watching him and smiling faintly. There was none of that complicity now, but rather a sadness, a sensation that things might have been different had they been within her control. She was a great fatalist, was Lorna. 'It's so lovely to see you again, do you know that? Really. They were happy times really, weren't they? Partly, anyway. Parson's egg. It only seems yesterday.'

Perhaps that was the perspective of her age. To Michael it seemed an aeon ago, but he didn't tell her that; and the happiness she referred to was an equal illusion. Adultery has a pungent smell and his memories of Cyprus stank of it.

'You know I loved him, don't you? You know I loved your father?'

He shrugged. 'I'm not sure I understand the word.'

She laughed. 'Helen once said that to me and I avoided trying to explain. Perhaps that was a mistake. What does Tommy say about me these days?'

'He refers to you as "that woman" – when he has cause to mention you, that is. Which isn't very often and usually follows a letter from the solicitor.'

'Oh dear. That doesn't sound too good.'

'He's not the kind to express remorse, if remorse is what you want to hear about.'

She shook her head. 'I thought maybe, oh I don't know – affection, perhaps. A little forgiveness . . .' She left the sentence unfinished and climbed back up the ladder to continue her work. Michael waited. For a while she worked away without speaking, trying to clean up the picture-moulding with a wire brush, trying to refurbish the past. Eventually she said, 'She needs a father, that's what the problem is. Helen, I mean. Or at least she needed one. Perhaps it's too late now. Dear Tommy tried, of course, but . . .'

'But what, for God's sake?'

She smiled down at him. 'Are you in love with her?'

'I told you I'm not sure what the term means.'

'You always were keen, weren't you? I remember the way you used to look at her. Children imagine that adults don't know what is going on, but they do, you know, they almost always do. They're not so good at knowing what's going on amongst themselves, that's the problem. It worried me sometimes the way you eyed her, as though it might be incest or something.' She laughed again, a fragile laugh that might splinter at any moment. 'Tommy used to tell me not to be silly, that a chap always looks at a gel like that' – her accent was a cruel imitation of Michael's father – 'and there was nothing in it.' She glanced down at him. 'Was there? Is there?'

It took him a moment to realise that she was waiting for a reply. He looked confused, bewildered by the vicissitudes of her mind. 'I had a ... crush on her, I suppose. When we were teenagers. Yes. It frightened me a bit.'

'Frightened you?'

'The emotion.' He tried to shrug the matter off. 'In a childish sort of way I loved her, I suppose. Maybe I still do.'

She looked at him thoughtfully and he had no means of interpreting the expression. 'What do you think of Adrian, then?'

He shrugged.

'I loathe him, you know that? I can't bear him, with his posing and his arrogance and his nauseating self-love. She deserves better.' The next words she spoke were like a blow in the stomach: 'You know he fucks her, don't you?'

The word was quite outrageous in those days. Maybe, for all our liberal-mindedness, it still is. But hearing it coming from Lorna Constance's lips in that morning sunlight, in the room where she was stripping paint in preparation for hanging hessian wallpaper, with the green lawn beyond the French windows and the poplars and willows in the distance, was an appalling shock.

She laughed at his expression. 'Does that outrage you? A rude word! Do you imagine I don't think the same way as you?' Her voice rose in pitch and there was an edge to it – anger, hysteria, he couldn't tell. 'The young don't have a monopoly on unhappiness, you know – they just have a monopoly on being allowed to show it. Who cares a damn about someone like me who's unhappy? I think of sex as often as you people do, don't you realise that? I think of sex and I wonder about love, and I don't have any more answers than you do. I'm no different, don't you understand? No different at all, except that I have a past to deal with and precious little future, which makes it a whole lot worse. I know what it *can* be like, what it *was* like. Don't you see?'

Was he meant to answer? He felt embarrassment and impatience, and a diffused sense of desire. Desire for Lorna, desire for Helen, who knows? He watched her sitting up there on the top of the step ladder like some kind of latter-day harpy, and he felt that adolescent craving that he had known years ago on the beach at Ladies' Mile when he had watched her amidst the young officers and seen their eyes on the gold of her body, and glimpsed, just that once, the sly secret of her breast.

She fumbled in the pocket of her dungarees, pulled out a packet of cigarettes and lit one with unsteady hands, blinking away the smoke and the tears. Her hands were blue-veined like old cheese.

'I'm sorry,' she said quietly. 'I'm sorry. I'm over fifty and I'm boring. Christ, I don't even need to be drunk, I can do this stone cold sober.' And quite suddenly and unexpectedly Lorna Constance, whom he hadn't seen since he was eighteen, who had been half mother to him and half Aphrodite, was weeping in front of him. 'I'm sorry,' she whispered. She shook her head and drew on her cigarette and blew smoke through the tears. 'I'm sorry. Unforgivable. I just . . .' She raised her hands as though in some kind of surrender. 'Can you help me down off this bloody thing? I don't think I can manage it by myself.' And she came unsteadily down the steps and he reached up and put his hands on her narrow waist to help her. She was impossibly light, light and tense like a dancer. As he settled her on the ground she took the cigarette from her mouth, reached up on tiptoe and kissed him on the lips. It was a feather touch, as soft as worn silk, tainted with smoke. 'I'm sorry, Michael,' she whispered. 'But I wouldn't get mixed up, if I were you. Does that sound like jealousy? Perhaps it is. But you know as well as I do what she is like. Secretive and closed. What was it Tommy used to call her? Squirrel, that was it. Always hiding things away, including her feelings. She used to keep snapshots of him, you know that don't you? I don't mean Tommy, of course: her real father. She was always imagining what he would say about things. She'd ask me, "What would Daddy have thought of that?" and she never meant Tommy. She always called Andrew "Daddy" even when I had become "Mother". Isn't that curious?'

'Revealing, I'd have thought.'

'She turned him into a kind of ideal. Tommy could never live up to that.'

'Wasn't it the same for you? Wasn't that the problem?'

'That Andrew was some kind of ideal? Good God, no.' She laughed bitterly, and the vehemence of her words were startling. 'There was nothing, absolutely nothing ideal about Mr bloody Andrew Harding. You don't know the half of it. You remind me a bit of him, can you imagine that? Certain gestures, certain mannerisms. If I'd said that a moment ago you'd have taken it as a compliment, wouldn't you? He can't have been much older than you when it happened.' She shook her head, almost as though to shake tears out of her eyes. 'I've never been able to forget him though, you know that? Never. In Christ's name, I tried hard enough, didn't I? Oh, God I tried. And ruined a few lives doing it. Oh, I take the blame for what happened with Tommy. It was my fault, all of it. I should have knuckled under and been the loving Army wife, and accepted it once or twice a month and never on Sundays. But I didn't. And I ruined it for Helen, and I guess for Tommy, and maybe for you and Anthony, although boys can take things like that well enough, can't they?' Her laugh was bitter. 'And now what?' She gestured at the chaos around her, the ladders and the planks, the rolls of wallpaper and the buckets of paint. 'This bloody ruin. Sublimation, that's what they call it. Something to occupy the body while waiting for the menopause.' Her eyes glistened. Her mind seemed random and dangerous, like a vehicle running out of control. Michael stood helplessly before her and waited for the crash. Nothing prepares you for adult hysteria. When it comes you just have to muddle through as best you can. 'You know he's still alive, don't you?'

'Who?'

'Andrew. Andrew Harding.' Her expression mingled confusion with pain, the expression of an animal that suffers and doesn't know the reason. 'He's still alive, that's the problem . . .'

'What in God's name are you talking about?'

'They didn't let me have a last look, you know that? When they brought his body back. They sent Dennis Killin with it and he had to explain. I couldn't see him.'

'Well, that's obvious . . .'

'It wasn't him—'

'Don't be ridiculous—'

'It was some other person who had been blown to smithereens by the bomb, someone they couldn't account for any other way. Or maybe just parts of someone. Maybe they didn't do their adding up right, I don't know. God knows. Anyway it wasn't Andrew. See for yourself.' She went through into the drawing room and opened the inlaid writing box that stood there on her desk. For a few moments she scrabbled through papers and then straightened up, thrusting out a letter for him. 'Read it. For God's sake read it.'

The letter was postmarked London. The address at the head was that of some religious institution.

Dear Andrew,

I'm writing this to you at the address I remember, which wasn't your house at all but your wife's old home as far as I recall. I hope it finds you there. Anyway, the reason for writing is that I caught a glimpse of you when I was in Jerusalem the other day and although I called after you, you obviously didn't hear. I must admit I heard somewhere that you had been caught up in that dreadful King David business, but obviously I was mistaken. The sight of you after all these years brought back many memories of the bad old days – remember Dennis Killin? – and I thought perhaps we might meet up again some time if you are ever in London. You may be surprised (then again you may not!) to learn that since those Jerusalem days I have been ordained to the priesthood (RC variety) which was the kind of thing Dennis always feared. How is he, I wonder? Do you see him still?

Lorna watched as he finished the letter. She seemed more relaxed now, the hysteria past, the emotion fading away. 'I've not shown it to anyone else. I've not mentioned it to anyone. I didn't know what to do with it . . .'

He shrugged, handing it back. 'Mistaken identity, I presume.'

'He shared a house with Andrew before the bomb. Silver. I remember the name.'

'A senile old priest seeing things. Did you answer him? When was it? I didn't notice the date.'

'Some months ago. I wrote back and told him, and he sent an apology. He said what you've just said, as a matter of fact: a senile old priest. But he wasn't convinced. I could tell by the tone of his reply. He wasn't convinced.'

'But that must be the explanation, mustn't it?'

She sighed and put the letter back. 'Yes, it must. Of course it must.' She looked drawn and anxious, as though frightened of what the future held. 'Of course it must.'

There was a footfall behind them and he looked round into Helen's bright and curious eyes. 'Mother dear, what's the matter?'

'She's not feeling well.'

Lorna pushed past him, touching him on the cheek as she went. 'I'm all right,' she said. 'Just a bit miz, that's all. Michael's been a dear.'

Helen took her mother's hand. 'Why don't you rest a bit? You're tired.'

There was a moment's defiance in the older woman – 'What the hell's that got to do with it?' – but she allowed herself to be lead away nevertheless. Michael watched them go, Helen leading her mother as one might lead a patient to her room, or a mourner away from the graveside, Lorna following with a kind of stubborn willingness. Nothing more was said about the incident.

Outside the weather changed and it came on to rain. They read the Sunday newspapers or flicked disconsolately through the books in the drawing room and waited for a decent time when they could dispense with each other's company. Helen was distracted, constantly going up to see her mother, fidgeting when downstairs with the two men, Michael was brooding on what had happened and only Adrian seemed to have any spirit in him. Maybe he looked upon the tensions of the day as a kind of triumph, a triumph for the forward-looking and the progressive. 'This is like a piece of bloody Chekhov,' he remarked at one point when Helen was upstairs. 'Family agonies and middle-age angst.'

'She wants you,' she told Adrian when she came down. 'She says she wants to apologise.'

'For what? Apologise for what?' he asked as he went. 'She's a dear thing. No need to apologise at all.'

When they were alone Helen eyed Michael suspiciously. 'What did she say? What was that all about?'

'Oh, for God's sake,' he snapped. 'She's unhappy at growing old, that's all. Doesn't it happen? Time of life, or something?' His father would have dismissed it as 'women's business'. He could imagine him flushing and casting around for something else to talk about. 'Doesn't she have . . . oh, I don't know . . . a boyfriend or something? That's what she needs. God, she seemed to have one all the time she was with my father.'

'Are you offering?' Helen asked.

He hovered on the edge of real anger, then seemed to find the whole thing amusing, a wry joke. 'You know the one thing we can't understand?'

'Only one thing? My goodness.'

He ignored her sarcasm. 'Ageing. You and I are still immortal. To us old age and death are just a piece of theory, like something irrelevant we learned at school. But when you get to your mother's age . . . or my father's . . .'

'Forget it,' she said. 'I'm sorry, just forget it.' She felt a sudden sense of release, as though all the emotion that her mother had spilt had somehow been hers. She was buoyed up by some absurd optimism that was quite without foundation or reason, a sensation that even if it was all beyond understanding at least it didn't matter any longer. 'Look what I found,' she said crossing the room to her mother's bureau. She opened the desk and held up a photograph album. 'Do you want to see?'

'What is it?'

'I found it the other day. Cyprus.' Michael looked over her shoulder as she leafed through the pictures. Groups of men and women in mess kit and evening dress smiled for the camera – he recognised his father and a few others. And there was a shot of Lorna dancing, leaning back out of the embrace of Archie Kesteven and laughing at the photographer, and another one of a grinning and slightly dazzled group which included Dennis Killin. Helen turned the pages. There were some faded colour shots taken on a beach, a pebble beach with sailing dinghies drawn up out of the water and men standing around in ragged shorts and plimsolls. In one of them Lorna was pulling on a halliard or something, a ridiculous pose for the benefit of the camera. She wore the bikini that he recalled so vividly. Even through the changes in fashion her beauty was plain to see.

Then Helen reached the final picture and they had jumped back a decade. It was some kind of picnic scene, in black and white.

'Where's that?'

There were barren hills in the background. The group waved glasses and smiles at the camera and one of them, a bullish young man, brandished a bottle of wine. He seemed familiar. The girls wore sling-back sandals with platform soles and summer frocks with square shoulders. One of them held a wide-brimmed hat against the breeze.

Helen pointed. 'That's Killin,' she said. And then her narrow finger touched the young man crouching at the centre of the group. 'And that's Daddy. A few months before he died. Maybe it was the last photo . . .' The man smiled amiably out of the picture while the bomb waited patiently for his coming. The photograph seemed suffused with a kind of sadness, as though the future can reach back into the past and touch with its chill hand any moment it pleases.

'Do you know something?' she asked, and for a moment it seemed that she might start one of their children's games.

'What?'

'Dennis Killin was the last man to see him alive. Did you know that? Isn't that a bloody irony?'

At that moment Adrian came back. She snapped the album shut. Somehow the thought of Adrian peering at the photos filled her with horror. 'How's Mother?'

'Oh, she's all right.' He was like a doctor who has just dealt successfully with a tricky little operation, a tracheotomy perhaps. 'Needs her morale boosting, that's all. You need to empathise, you know. An actor's trick. Empathy. What's that you've got there?'

'Nothing,' said Helen, 'nothing at all.'

3

A week or two later Helen came out of the Bodelian Library after working through lunch. It was dull and drizzling, a quintessential Oxford afternoon, leaden with the accumulated lassitude of generations of scholarship. She walked up the Broad and stood for a moment in the rain while shoppers and tourists went past and buses splashed up the Cornmarket. She decided to give her actor a ring. Perhaps they would go somewhere together that evening, out to a pub they knew on the river near Eynsham, or maybe to the Swan at Minster Lovell for dinner. It wasn't often that she took the initiative in suggesting something. Watching and waiting were her nature. Perhaps, she thought, they would spend the evening at his flat, with all that might entail.

Fiddling with the telephone and pennies cadged from the porter of Balliol – 'What's it worth, miss, eh? Pennies are like gold dust here' – she contemplated the prospect of Adrian's bed with a mixture of loathing and fascination. Fascination is a curious word and Helen knew all about it. Snakes writhe around its meaning. Eve was fascinated, fascinated no doubt by Adam's own snake, that lump of gristle which held no serpentine beauty whatever for Helen but possessed a sinister and snake-like potency as it filled her body with its spittle. Standing in the little cabin listening to the ringing on the other end, she shivered.

There was no reply to her call. Adrian was not in; nor was he at the theatre when she tried there. 'No rehearsals this afternoon, madam,' said a voice. 'There's a matinée.'

Had he said something about going up to London, something about the Royal Court? He was always arranging meetings, always going to see this producer, that agent. Perhaps he had warned her that he would be away.

She pulled the collar of her raincoat up around her neck and left the shelter of the porters' lodge for the crowds of shoppers in the Cornmarket. Walking vaguely towards Jericho brought her near to the bus station and the idea presented itself without much fuss, as an alternative to going back to her drab digs and the metred gas fire and an evening reading or listening to the radio. There was a coach to High Wycombe, from where she knew she could get a local bus to Maidenhead. The journey, begun without thought, ran on into the darkness and rain of a winter evening.

'Mind how you go, dear,' the conductor said as she got off at an unmarked stop in the middle of the countryside. 'Can't be too careful these days, you know.'

'I'm just near home,' she replied. She climbed down and stood in the rain while the bus drew away, then she set off down the lane towards Guerdon House. Perhaps the conductor had awoken a small stirring of fear in her, for she hurried through the darkness, wishing that she had phoned ahead to tell her mother that she was coming. But when she turned through the gates and saw the house at the end of the drive and lights in an upstairs window – Lorna's room, in fact – she felt a warm rush of relief and familiarity. She hurried towards the dark and comforting bulk of the house, a refugee from the groves of academe walking up the gravel drive into the groves of Aphrodite.

Nothing moved, either in the shadows round the house or behind the illuminated curtains upstairs. She climbed the steps to the front door and let herself in with her own key.

The hallway was dark. There was the smell of fresh paint, and the smell of something else which they had been using to treat woodworm or dry rot or something, something pungent and organic. 'Mother?' she called as she fumbled for the light switch. 'Mother? Are you there?' The lights came on, showing stripped oak panelling and the threadbare carpet and the large Florentine *cassone* which Lorna had bought years ago at a house sale in Devon. There was a sound from upstairs, a movement on the floor boards overhead, a shuffling and a murmuring.

'Mother!'

Helen felt a moment's disquiet. Had she thought for a moment perhaps she would not have had the courage to run up the stairs. Had she stopped to consider what the consequences might be maybe she would have picked up the telephone which stood on the side table next to the hat-stand and phoned someone – the police perhaps. But would that, in the end, have made any difference? She ran upstairs, grabbing a candlestick that happened to be standing on a table at the turn of the stairs. Light came up from the hall below but the corridor upstairs was in darkness. Only a sliver of yellow leaked out from under the door to her mother's room. There was noise within, the sound of voices.

She called, softly this time. 'Mother, are you there?'

She was going to knock. She was telling herself that there was nothing out of the ordinary, that she had only imagined things strange and frightening, that the normal thing was to knock on her mother's door before going in, and that she should do so now. She was actually raising her hand to knock when the door was flung open and Lorna stood there with a towel clutched in front of her.

'Helen, what on earth are you doing here?'

'Mother, are you all right?'

Lorna's hair was astray. She was flushed from drink, flushed in the face and across the upper part of her chest, breathing unevenly. 'Of course I'm all right. What the hell are you doing here? You're soaking wet. Why didn't you call or something? I could have met you at the station. And what's that, for God's sake?'

Helen looked down at the candlestick in her hand, as though it was a surprise to find it there. 'I thought . . .' Her voice trailed away. She looked from the candlestick to Lorna's naked legs where they emerged beneath the towel. They were uneven, blue-veined across the shins, with a sheen to the skin that comes from a lifetime's use of depilation wax. Her naked feet were strangely vulnerable, an old woman's feet pinched and distorted from being crammed for so many years into narrow, fashionable shoes.

'Go and get out of those clothes and I'll be with you in a moment,' Lorna said. 'What a fright you gave me.'

Helen looked up into her mother's eyes. 'Who's with you? You weren't talking to yourself. Who is with you?'

Lorna frowned. 'What do you mean? No one's with me.'

Helen's tone was tired. She was tired. She'd had a tiring day doing little or nothing in the library, followed by a tiring journey by bus, followed by an unpleasant fright of some kind when she arrived at the house. She *was* tired. She was tired and angry and depressed. But maybe none of those things excuse her. Maybe she should just have turned round and gone to change as her mother had suggested, and left things alone. She didn't. 'You've got someone in there, haven't you?' she said wearily. Perhaps it was the release of tension, the ebbing away of fear, which gave her the stimulus to act. 'You've got someone in there,' she repeated as she tried to push through into the room. 'You've got someone with you!' she cried. 'There's someone there!'

There was a brief and undignified struggle at the doorway. Lorna screamed and Helen tried to push her aside. 'What right have you to come barging in like this?' the older woman shouted. And of course Helen had no right, no right at all. But whatever the rights and wrongs, she pushed and kicked, and Lorna grabbed at her wrists, and then the towel slipped and she made a grab for that, and that was the moment when Helen thrust her aside and burst through into the bedroom. She stopped abruptly in front of the bed. She remembered that other bedroom, all those years ago, the empty one, also blue and pink, also smelling, like this one, of Chanel No. 5. But that bedroom had been empty, empty that is but for the bed and the dressing-table and the chest of drawers with its little plastic box containing the small timpanum of sex. This bedroom, precisely this bed, was occupied. Sitting up against the cushions, watching the intrusion with a mixture of embarrassment and amusement was Adrian Oliver himself playing his finest role.

'Helen, my dear,' he said. 'Perhaps you'd like to join us?'

Difficult. Difficult to separate the various parts of the ensuing row, particularly difficult to give them any kind of chronology. It was rather like being witness to an unpleasant car crash. The event itself is confused, and the aftermath goes on for days and weeks. Often the crash is relived by the witnesses as though to relive it might be to discover that it hasn't actually happened, that in the meantime something has slipped in the inexorable chain of cause and effect, of action and reaction, and there was no crash after all. The next time Helen will merely walk in out of the rain and go up to her mother's room and find her resting in bed with a migraine or something. A great one for migraines, was Lorna. They will exchange a few affectionate words and then she will go down to the kitchen (ancient Aga, once with dry rot fungus fruiting body in the oven) and prepare something light for their supper, which they will eat together in quiet and undemonstrative companionship (you don't *display* love) watching television in front of the fire. The next day Lorna will drive her to the bus station in High Wycombe to catch a coach back to Oxford, and all will be happy.

But of course none of that happened. It is the irreversibility of the past that is so distressing.

'How often, in God's name, *how often*?' Helen kept asking.

'You normally phone,' Lorna complained. 'Why didn't you phone?'

'You mean this has happened before? How long has it been going on then? You mean I might have come barging in at any moment and found you two fucking away? Is that it?' She had, it seemed, finally overcome one of her own inhibitions about the language of sex.

'Please don't use that word.'

'Which word should I use? Making love? Christ, you disgust me.'

'Why should I disgust you? I'm a woman, just like you, aren't I?'

'And did he tell you all about me? Did he offer comparisons about how we did it, mother and daughter? What a charming idea. Keeping it in the family.'

'You don't understand.'

'I don't *understand*? I understand only too well. Who is best then? You, I'll bet.'

'That's just disgusting.'

'*You're* disgusting: you're both disgusting. I suppose he found you less inhibited than me, is that it? What did you do for him?'

'Helen, for God's sake.'

'Did you suck him, or what? That's what he tried to get me to do. I suppose you were happy to oblige. Anything to get a bit of cock inside you.'

'Helen!'

'What I find so fantastic is that you can be outraged about it. As though you have the right to be outraged about anything.'

Difficult. Words spoken are irrevocable, that's the problem.

Weeks later she was alone in Guerdon House when the phone rang. 'Is that you Lorna?'

'It's Helen.'

'Helen? Well I never. You sound exactly like your mother.'

The subtle confusions of the telephone, that malign and deceptive instrument. 'Who is this speaking? Can I take a message?'

A silence. The hallway was still. If inanimate places can watch and wait, the hallway was watching and waiting. The past was about to take a step forward and wreak havoc in the present.

'Dear little Helen. My word, how long ago it all seems. Dear big Helen by now I suppose.'

101

'Who are you?'

'I wonder if you remember me.' A laugh, not unfamiliar. A laugh that booms round her memory, that sounds round the little, sun-bleached harbour and sends what few gulls there were crying up into the air. 'Of course you remember me. This is Dennis Killin.'

'What do you want?'

'I wanted a chat, really. I'm in England for a week or so. I wanted to look a few chums up.'

'Mother's not here.'

'You'll do, my dear.'

'I'll do for what?'

Another distant, electronic laugh. 'What are you up to nowadays? Working? You haven't got yourself hitched, have you? Not married or anything foolish like that?'

'What do you mean, *I'll do*?'

'The old Helen. You make it sound so suspicious. I was going to suggest to your mother that we meet up somewhere. Lunch or something. Lunch sounds so much less disreputable than dinner, doesn't it?'

'I told you she's not here.'

'What about you?'

Helen wondered. Her thoughts weren't clear, weren't formulated in words that can be repeated on the page. Jealousy and anger chased themselves round within her skull like children at play, malicious children, children about to wreak havoc. 'When?' she asked.

There was a silence on the other end. A distant hiss might have been mere electronic interference, might have been an indrawing of breath. The disembodied voice whispered back at her. 'Whenever you please. I'm here for a fortnight. On business. Taken a service flat for the moment, but I'm thinking of buying somewhere as a matter of fact. Tell me the time, tell me the day, I'm the poor fellow who'll always obey.'

So she took a day off from work and caught the coach up to London and met him at Victoria, Helen stepping down from the coach and finding him waiting for her on the pavement amidst a motley group of tourists with maps and guide books. Killin, one felt, would never need a map or a guide book for anywhere. He was sleek and smooth and knowing, shining as though from much use. His baldness gave him a bullet-like strength, a hardness. 'What a beauty,' he murmured as he held her fragile shoulders. 'What a beauty you've become.'

She let herself be kissed, and she felt the subtle stirrings of power and betrayal.

Days later she phoned Michael. 'What are you doing this summer?'

'This summer? What on earth are you talking about?'

'I'm talking about this summer.' She giggled. 'Now *you* say, "What on earth are you talking about?" and we go round again.'

'I haven't time to be facetious.'

His voice sounded brusque, the sound of a stranger. 'Well have you got time to tell me what you're doing this summer? Or is there another woman?'

Her words brought silence, and then a change, a lightness of tone, a wariness. 'I haven't any plans really. I was thinking of. . . Look, I can't really talk now. I'm in the middle of conversation practice with a gaggle of Spanish teenagers. If I leave them for a moment they start re-enacting the Civil War.'

'Meet me for lunch, then. Or do you have to teach table manners as well?'

'Where?'

She mentioned a pub that they both knew. 'It's just that I've got an idea, about the summer. You may be interested.'

So they met in the shadowy depths of a half-subterranean pub near Trinity. The ceiling was low and nicotine-stained, crawling with the signatures of sundry rugby fifteens and rowing eights. Hanging on the panelled walls were photographs of youth in sub-fusc, with college arms and gothic lettering – 𝔉𝔯𝔢𝔰𝔥𝔪𝔢𝔫 1963, that kind of thing. It was the sort of place American tourists love to discover, and self-conscious undergraduates love to be dis-covered in.

'What about Cyprus?' she asked as they sat at one of the exiguous tables.

He looked confused. They had done nothing more than exchange greetings and order a couple of flabby steak and kidney pies each and two halves of bitter. 'Well what about it?' she asked impatiently.

'What about what?'

'Goodness, you're slow. What about spending the summer in Cyprus? I've got the offer of a cottage. How about it?'

'Cyprus?'

'Cyprus. I just said that. You could try, oh, I don't know – Othello. And I'd say Iago and you'd say Desdemona and I'd say handkerchief . . .' She laughed at him. 'Or you could just say, yes, what a wonderful idea.'

'Yes, what a wonderful idea,' he replied, watching her suspiciously over the top of his beer. 'Who . . .?' He hesitated.

'Who does it belong to?' she prompted.

'Else. Who *else* is going to be there?'

She eyed him for a moment. That look he recognised, but it was Lorna's not Helen's: the smile of complicity. Then she looked down and began to dissect the pie on her plate. 'Do you want someone else?'

'I thought perhaps . . .'

'Well, we can always *invite* someone else if you want.' She felt the sharp, astringent taste of caprice.

'Grandier?'

She laughed out loud. 'Grandier?'

'That's how I always think of him. The randy priest.'

'And I'm . . .?'

'Not Sister Jeanne des Anges.'

'No hunchback.'

'No hunchback. The girl maybe. What was she called?'

'Philippe. I'm not pregnant either.'

And now they laughed together, suddenly a happy couple in that pokey little bar, their steak and kidney pies before them mangled but uneaten, their summer before them as yet untasted. A trio of American tourists, as wide and pale and glistening as beetle larvae, smiled as she leant towards Michael and took his hand and kissed him gently on the cheek. Just that, the touch of his skin, so familiar.

'How could you have *imagined* Adrian?' she asked, still holding his hand. 'Didn't you see him at Guerdon? My God, he was desperate. I've never seen anyone trying so hard. His real problem is that the only person he loves is himself.'

'And you?'

She ignored the question. 'So what do you think about Cyprus, then?' She shook his hand gently. 'Come on, what do you say?'

'I say yes. I've said yes. Sure. When do we go?'

'Whenever we like. I've got the place for the whole summer if I want. It's a little cottage, a couple of bedrooms, nothing much.'

'Nothing much? Whose is it? Where is it?'

'Near Kyrenia. The north coast anyway. Lapithos or somewhere.' There was something evasive about her tone.

'How did you find it?'

She paused. 'You won't be angry?'

'Angry? Why on earth should I be?'

'I don't know.' She shrugged helplessly, as though it wasn't her fault. 'It's Dennis Killin's. I'm sorry, Michael. He got in touch the other day, right out of the blue—'

'I thought all that was over.'

'Yes, it is. He hasn't seen mother in years. But he contacted me for some reason and I went up to London to meet him. Out of curiosity really. Can't say I really like him, but there it is.' She smiled a secret smile, laden with promise and subterfuge. 'You don't mind, do you? For God's sake don't mention it to her.'

'That you've seen Killin?'

She shook her head. Her tone was conspiratorial. 'Don't mention anything. That we're going, that I've seen him again, nothing. I don't want her to know a thing about it. It's mine and mine alone.'

Can you explain someone? Helen was not made of single ideas, or single, simple motives. Beneath her cool and capricious exterior she was a muddle of conflicting impulses, and love in all its manifestations – love carnal, love spiritual, love fraternal, blended with jealousy to make a heady brew.

'Michael is just like a brother to me,' she insisted to Lorna, when he came to Guerdon House once more. But whether it was fraternal love she sought she did not know herself. The semantics of love, a Greek obsession, haunted her: *eros*, *agape*, *philia*. They worried her and she worried them, like a dog with a rat.

'At least we've managed to salvage something from the mess you made,' she said acidly to her mother.

'Just be careful,' Lorna said vaguely.

'Careful of precisely what?' Helen retorted. She hadn't told Michael what had happened. By tacit agreement the two of them, mother and daughter, nursed the secret as though it were a shameful illness in the family; and like an illness its symptoms were various and subtle. Lorna had become harsh and sarcastic. Helen seemed remote and preoccupied, and took refuge in the habits of childhood now that the manners of adults had proved so damaging. And there was an occasional, unguarded glimpse of bitterness, like the sight of a spot of blood on the handkerchief.

'Who's that?' Helen whispered when Michael knocked on her door during the night. 'What do you want?'

He opened the door as stealthily as possible but it creaked on its hinges, a sound that rang through the house. The room smelt softly of her presence, a delicate amalgam of soap and scent and something that was neither of those artifical things, but was hers alone − the mammal smell of her body. He saw a faint paleness on the far side of the room, like a cloud seen in a moonlit sky. 'Michael, you shouldn't be here,' she whispered, and her tone spoke of fear. 'Don't you understand?'

The door creaked closed behind him. She turned on the bedside light and sat up in bed, pulling the pillows up behind her, watching him warily. She was surrounded by bits of her childhood, the white birds painted on the bedhead, the Victorian dolls on the dressing-table, the poster on the wall which showed a virgin sitting at the foot of a tree with a unicorn bowing down into her lap. 'What do you want?'

'I want to talk.'

'At this hour?'

Familiarity breeds contempt, babies, illusions, a whole host of things, but certainly not the boldness that is claimed for it. He sat on the edge of the bed and leant forward to kiss her gently on the mouth, but when he put out his hand to touch her breasts she took hold of his wrist and moved the hand aside. 'Don't, Michael,' she whispered. 'Please don't.'

He hesitated, on the edge of anger. The photograph of her father, her real father, looked at them from its frame on her bedside table and it was easy to ascribe a new expression to the face − a faintly sardonic smile, as though he saw through all the deceits. 'When?'

'When we're on our own, really on our own.'

'You promise?'

'You must be gentle with me, Michael,' she replied. 'It isn't that easy.'

'It isn't for me either.'

She leant back against the pillows and put her thin hand to his face, as though to smoothe away anger and frustration. 'Please be patient with me. I don't really know who you are yet, don't you see that?'

'Will you ever—?'

She hushed him to quietness. 'I've told you. Be patient.'

'Adrian was your lover.'

'Adrian's finished.'

'Why did you break up with him?'

She shook her head, as though to deny the man's existence. 'Adrian: *A drain*,' she said, smiling at him. Childhood tugged at his sleeve. It gave easy access to a Helen that was not the one he wanted. He answered reluctantly, but answered all the same, like a coward: '*An arid*. Look − '

106

'*And air.*'

'*Naiad.*'

He touched her cheek but she brushed his hand away, frowning in accusation. 'You've missed out the R.'

'All right. *An irad.*'

'What's an irad, for heaven's sake?' Her tone was petulant.

'Oh, I don't know. Some kind of law, I think. Arab. This is ridiculous.'

'I don't believe you.'

'Look it up in the dictionary. Look I want to talk . . .'

She was quiet for a moment, watching him carefully, daring him to break the game. 'Got it,' she announced with an air of triumph. '*A nadir.*'

Thus was Adrian Oliver disposed of, his name dismembered and scattered as though it were his body. And Michael laughed with her over the destruction and in the laughter he was allowed to touch his mouth onto hers again and was granted the sudden gift of her tongue, swift and lithe. But nothing more.

4

Picture a room, plastered white. A large and lumpy bed stands against one wall, with a cheap icon of the Blessed Virgin hanging over it. Opposite the bed there is a window. The window is open but the green shutters are closed and a thin afternoon light, coming through the slats, paints horizontal bars across the floor at the foot of the bed. The floor is tiled in rough, unglazed terracotta. In one corner of the room there is a chair with a rush seat and next to it a small chest of drawers in pale wood. For those who have eyes to see this item of furniture is recognisable as British Government issue. It bears, somewhere within its bowels, the familiar arrow.

Helen is standing at the window with her back to the bed where Michael lies. She is standing up to her knees in the stripes of light and dark which the shutters throw down into the room, as though standing in a pool of water. She is naked. She stands there in a little pile of discarded clothing, with her back to the bed and her face to the shutters, listening to the sounds outside, which are the sounds of a village, the incessant whistling of someone at work, a shout of anguish, the clatter of hens, the distant, agonised braying of a donkey, and behind it all, above it all – so constant that one comes to discount it – the raw scream of cicadas. But within the room there is barely the sound of a breath.

Her legs are slender and slightly curved and her narrow thighs are parted just sufficiently to disclose a small and secret tuft of hair in the cleft at the top. Her buttocks are as pale as milk. From her narrow waist her back springs up and out into the wide tent of hair. The room seems filled with the intolerable burden of her existence, a sensation of the strangeness of her, the weight of her unique being, in that small, bare room.

'You know I'm not a virgin,' she says to the shutters.

'It doesn't matter.'

'It does to me.'

Her voice is small, a part of the place. 'Adrian was the first, I've told you that.'

'It doesn't matter. Really.'

There is a silence. Somewhere in the fabric of the cottage there is a small scratching. Rodents? Insects? They are the infinitesimal scratchings which slowly and certainly reduce a place like this to dust.

Then she turns. Quaintly she is gripping her right shoulder with her left hand, so that the arm covers her breasts. Her expression is ironical, the wry look of a person who has come to accept her inadequacies. Almost with a shrug, she lets the arm drop.

'I'm nothing much, am I?'

There is anguish in her expression. She is impossibly beautiful, thin and meagre, the very quick of her exposed to his gaze along with the fact her flesh and bone. She is everything, he tells her, and her smile is reproachful as though she has just caught him out in a small lie but is prepared to let the matter pass as long as it doesn't happen again. Then suddenly she seems to make up her mind about matters. She crosses the room and reaches over his head and takes hold of the icon above the bed. She turns it to face the plaster. For that brief moment her body stretches tautly over him and light glimmers in the pale hair between her thighs, giving it a gleam of gold. Her nipples, mere inches from his face, have the colour and shape of two earthworms nosing gently out of the soil of her flesh.

She kneels back on the bed, sitting placidly on her heels to look at him. That reproachful smile is still in place. 'Should we be doing this?' she asks quietly.

'Why in heaven's name not?'

She shrugs her spare shoulders in a gesture that he knows so well, that has been part of his perception of her since they were both children. 'It's a bit diff, isn't it? Do you remember when we stole cigarettes? And then afterwards . . .'

'We were little children.'

'But it was us, wasn't it?' She shakes her head, and touches him thoughtfully on his chest, where there is a small growth of hair between his nipples. 'I know you too well,' she whispers. 'It's easier with a stranger.'

They had come on a night flight and hired a battered Opel at the airport. Helen had a vague set of directions to follow and some kind of sketch map scribbled on a piece of paper. *To Spiti Killin* was scrawled across the top. Only after lunch and getting lost near Lapithos did they finally strike the right road and began to climb through the foothills towards the limestone crest of Akromandra and the village where Killin had his cottage. The road passed through citrus and olive groves. Behind them the view opened out to display the whole scalloped northern coast running back to Kyrenia and the vanishing length of the Karpass, while all the time the curved slope of the Pentadaktylos range hung over them like a great, frozen wave. Michael drove, concentrating on the tortuous curves of the road, while Helen exclaimed the beauty of the place in small cries of delight. She felt, literally and figuratively, transported. 'Do you remember?' she kept crying out. 'Do you remember?'

The village of Ayios Ioannis was no more than a white-washed church and a few dozen houses sprawling up the hillside. The centre of the place was a narrow square with a plane tree in the middle and a shop with a few boxes of vegetables on display. There was a café with three wooden tables and a scattering of rusty metal chairs outside. The church, a few yards down the main street, was shuttered as though against a siege, perhaps the onslaught of the twentieth century which was already fighting skirmishes down on the coastal plain. The mosque further down the slope was a ruin.

'Where on earth has Dennis found to hide himself?' she exclaimed. 'He's not that kind at all.'

'What type is he?'

Michael's question went unanswered. Parking the car in the shade of a ragged oleander bush they crossed the square towards the café. There were four old men sitting at one of the tables and Helen charmed them out of their reserve by calling *kaliméra, pos iste?* which was probably more Greek than they had ever heard from the lips of a foreigner in the whole of their lives. They nodded and grinned and raised their hands in salute. '*Evkharistò,*' they replied. '*Etsi kai etsi.*'

'*Deutsch?*' one of them asked, perhaps deceived by the colour of her hair.

'English. English.'

'I got cousin in England. London. You live London?'

'Oxford.'

They shrugged, not understanding. London was the only place they had heard of. London and England were synonymous. 'You stay?'

'*Malista,*' Helen answered – certainly. 'At the Englishman's

110

house – Οικια *angliko*,' she tried, getting the word wrong by a millenium or so and evoking roars of laughter. '*Spiti*,' she corrected herself. '*Spiti angliko*. You know the Englishman? Dennis?' There seemed to be some kind of recognition. '*Kristalla*? Τας κλεις?' she asked. She turned to Michael with laughter. 'The Book of the Revelation, chapter one. Actually *Tas kleis* are the keys of death and hell, but I'm sure they'll do.'

The old boys laughed at hearing fragments of the old language from the mouth of anyone but a priest. They summoned a young boy to go and find the woman called Kristalla and he returned a few minutes later with an ancient and toothless crone who held one hand above her head as though she was bearing aloft the Olympic torch. There was a sigh of satisfaction amongst the audience. Clutched in the crone's gnarled and twisted fingers was a key-ring with three keys.

'One's for heaven,' Michael suggested, taking them as though they were a medal, 'and one's for hell. But what's the third one?'

'Purgatory,' Helen replied.

'You go with her,' one of the men said. 'She knows.' The crone bobbed and grinned, emitting little grunts through what remained of her teeth, beckoning to show the way. Cheered on by the men at the bar they followed.

The path led up a narrow alley between rubble walls. Prickly pear cactus sprouted amongst the stone. Fig branches clambered over the walls like urchins trying to get at them as they passed. Vines trailed their luminous leaves in their faces. It was beautiful, like all such places possessed of an ancient sense of peace and completeness that seems denied to northern countries. Lizards scurried across the white face of the morning and vanished into their own, silent darkness. The air seethed with bees. Someone, somewhere was whistling an aimless and repetitive tune.

The old crone stopped in front of a square cottage, an old, white-washed place with green door and shutters. '*To angliko spiti*,' she announced. In front of the cottage was a walled yard with an ancient and arthritic fig tree. On either side of the front door stood a line of rusty tins which had once held tomato paste but now grew a troop of dusty geraniums. Above the door was a balcony reached by a short flight of steps. An etiolated vine struggled up from ground level and draped itself wearily over a wooden pergola that someone had constructed up there.

'*Kallisti*,' Helen hazarded and the old woman nodded and grinned in approval. Beautiful.

The inside of Dennis Killin's cottage was dark and tainted with damp. In the kitchen they found a sink with a single tap and a rusty enamel stove. A copper pipe led from the stove out through a hole in the wall but inspection showed that there was nothing on the end.

'Dennis warned me,' Helen said. 'We'll need to get a gas cylinder from the village shop.'

A kitchen dresser yielded up its guilty secrets: a half-used bottle of olive oil; a cracked plate bearing the dried remains of some nameless food; an unused tin of tomatoes; three boxes of matches; a half bottle of Keo brandy. The matches were damp and wouldn't strike. The brandy bottle was empty. A drawer contained greasy cutlery bearing the winged eagle of the RAF. In the cupboard below there were china plates decorated with the British crown.

'All this stuff's issue,' Michael remarked. 'He's nicked it.'

Helen laughed. 'Trust Dennis.' She went round the house with that proprietary air, plumping up a few cushions, throwing open the downstairs windows. Daylight came pouring in to expel the sour smell of damp. 'We'll have to get to work in here,' she said. 'Clean the place up a bit.'

'Later, for God's sake. I'm just about all in.' Michael took her hand and she stood still for a moment, reluctantly, as though standing still meant facing difficult decisions. 'Let's get our things upstairs,' he suggested.

Narrow stone steps led from the main room on the ground floor to the upper floor. They peered into the bedrooms, at dust and more government-issue furniture. One room had twin beds and an engraving of the ruins of Salamis on the wall. The other room contained a double bed and was further blessed with an cheap icon of the Virgin Mary, as though the double bed beneath it held a sacred significance which two singles could not possess. Michael lugged their bags in and dumped them on the floor.

Helen stood at the door. 'Are we sharing a room?'

'I should think so, wouldn't you?'

'I don't know.' She stood in the doorway and watched him. 'I'll take the other one if you don't mind. I'd be happier like that.'

'Go ahead. Do what you please.'

So she picked up her bag and carried it out, while he lay on the bed and stared at the stained ceiling and felt anger seeping in to take the place of happiness, an inarticulate anger compounded of frustration and incomprehension. He knew her. He knew her, he fancied, better than anyone in the whole world, certainly differently, certainly with a more particular slant. He felt familiarity as powerful as the force of gravity.

A few minutes later she came back and stood looking at him from the doorway. He looked little changed from the boy of ten or twelve.

'Are you angry?'

He didn't offer a reply.

'It's just that I'm not used to it. Not used to sharing, I mean.' She went over to the window. 'The view is amazing, you know. You can even see the Turkish coast.' She paused with her hand on the shutters. 'I'm sorry. I don't know quite how to behave.' Then quite without fuss she slipped the straps of her dress off her shoulders and let the thing fall to her feet and stood there in a pair of plain white briefs.

Speaking to the shutters, she asked, 'There, is that what you want?'

'I want what you want.'

'No you don't. You want what you want. It's only luck when two wants coincide. Pure chance.' She bent and pulled the briefs down and stepped out of them, curving her body sideways to do so and breaking the symmetry of her figure into a momentary arabesque, before straightening up again. She remained standing with her back to him and he might have been daring her to turn round.

Some living thing scratched away in the roof above them, or in the wall itself, an insect or a bird, or maybe a bat. And she could hear the wind in the trees and feel the rough bark beneath her hands. She laughed, a small ironical laugh at nothing in particular, then kicked off her sandals and turned towards him and showed herself plainly and almost without guile, dropping her arms from across her meagre breasts to display them frankly to his gaze. The placid eyes of Mary Theotokos looked out at her from a cheap icon above the bed. They looked at her not with accusation but with compassion, but still she crossed to the bed to turn the picture round. 'Should we be doing this?' she asked, kneeling on the bed at his feet.

'Why in heaven's name not?'

She gave a little shrug. She felt naked in soul as well as body, stripped of all the trappings that she owned back in England, the earnest academic pose, the fragile porcelain looks, the air of reserve and inhibition that Adrian had tried and failed to overcome.

'Tell me,' he insisted.

'I know you too well. It's easier with a stranger.'

Her hands lay in her lap, hiding the little bush of hair. He reached out and touched her fingers and she turned them open

113

and took hold of his hand. It was an equivocal gesture that might have intended affection, might have been to keep his hand from going anywhere else. 'Why did you do that?' he asked.

'What?'

'Turn the icon.'

Another shrug. Perhaps she could shrug the whole thing off, the whole of this bodily intimacy and ascribe it all to an aberration, a kind of game that children might play, that the two of them *had* played once upon a time. 'An idea, that's all. A whim. You know I've never done this before. I've never taken my clothes off in front of a man. Can I exclude the doctor?'

'You can exclude the doctor.'

'Except you. When we were children.' She smiled, glancing away for a moment, embarrassed. 'Do you remember?'

'Of course I remember.'

'No other man has ever seen me like this, not even Adrian. It's the only thing I have left. A kind of virginity.' Then very gently she lay down against him. 'Michael, Michael,' she whispered touching his face. 'We shouldn't do this, you know.'

5

At times that summer there was only the cottage hidden amongst the alleyways, crowded round with vegetation and roofed by a silver-blue sky; and the two of them, shifting round each other in a strange dance to which only they knew the steps. It was a closed and private world into which nothing intruded that was not there by their own choice. It possessed something of a childhood game, a game of dares and challenges, of fantasy and intimacy and discovery, echoing their childhood games in the same way that an adult echoes the child itself. They were happy much of the time and occasionally assaulted by a kind of delirious joy that was as intense and fulfilling as any physical consummation, and if they did sometimes stumble over those obstructions which age and experience eventually wear away, they were also confronting an obstacle which adults, coming together for the first time, rarely have to confront – their own familiarity.

'Tell me about your other women,' she asked.

He laughed the question away. 'Too many to count.'

'You're lying. Tell me about the most beautiful one.'

'You.'

She saw the game immediately. 'The most erotic.'

'You.'

'The gentlest.'

'You.'

The litany went on, like a kind of nursery rhyme. You, you, you.

'The cruellest.'

'You.'

Yet at other times they felt themselves fade into the background of the place itself, the Levant, where past pushes against the present with a nagging insistence so that one feels that nothing is ever new, no difficulty, no love, no tragedy: the broken gothic arches of Bellapais Abbey and the dusty colonial buildings of Nicosia, the columns of Salamis and the fortifications of Famagusta, the sharp block of Kolossi Castle and the runways of the airfield beyond – all were the same, all were symbols and instruments of power and submission, of greed and hate; and they felt their insignificance beside them. On the edge of the salt lake at Akrotiri they watched jet bombers lowering in from the horizon just as the galleys of the Ottomans had once done, and she shivered, sensing the tides of history flowing mercilessly through the tideless sea, and under-standing that there is nothing new in a place like this. Clinging to Michael she murmured, 'I'm so happy, and I don't deserve it,' and her words were a kind of child's propitiation, directed at a God whose existence remained one of the uncertainties of her life. Never claim happiness, never claim success, lest they be snatched from your grasp.

It was at Petra tou Romiou, Aphrodite's beach, the very place where the goddess herself had been blown ashore on a spume of divine semen, that he caught her hand and told her that he loved her. She looked at him in that puzzled manner of hers, as though suddenly he was speaking in another dialect from the one she had learned, demotic rather than *koine* perhaps. The words were familiar to her but the constructions and the significances were slightly altered, so as to make comprehension almost impossible. 'I'm not sure what that means,' she said.

'I've always loved you,' he shouted, while the sea crashed against the rocks behind, throwing spray into the air.

'Always?' She laughed nervously at the idea of eternity and felt the stirring of fear.

'Always.' Overhead, gulls screamed derisively in the wind.

They left Aphrodite's beach to the gulls and the foam and drove on to New Paphos, which is the ancient Roman town but newer by far than Palea Paphos where the cult of Aphrodite had its home. And thus they passed from the pagan goddess to the apostle Paul himself; from love of flesh to the love of God.

She was on familiar ground here, happier with the New Testament than the pagan world, happier amongst the paradoxes and difficulties of the moral life rather than the powerful, brute emotions of the sensual life. It was a salutary contrast. 'Do you know that this is the place where Paul lost his Jewish name, Sha'ul, and took on the Latin name Paul? And the magician whom he defeated in argument in front of the governor, do you know *his* name?'

Of course he didn't.

'Bar-Jesus. That's "Son-of-Jesus". Nobody ever draws attention to it, but surely it's not just a coincidence. Sha'ul to Saul, Hebrew to Gentile, at the exact moment that Bar-Jesus is defeated. Surely it *means* something.' Walking through the decayed bones of the lower town – part classical, part Byzantine, part tattered fishing village – she wondered at the significance of it all, picked over ideas, rummaged around the anguish of Saint Paul and forgot the dangerous declarations of an hour before on Aphrodite's beach. 'I feel a paper coming on me,' she said. Her tone was only partly mocking. 'The Paphos Controversy: A Problem Of Pauline Onomastics.' She paused and searched in her memory. 'The magician's other name was Elymas. What can we make of that? *El* is obviously the Hebrew name of God . . .' It was like one of their childhood games translated into the intricacies of the biblical world.

'Elymas: *A Smely*,' Michael suggested.

'You're not taking this seriously.'

'We're on holiday.'

She surrendered. '*Am Sly*.'

'You've dropped an "e".'

'We're on holiday.'

He thought for a moment. '*Slay me*,' he said triumphantly, and won the game.

That night they made love with a peculiar intensity, and afterwards she lay awake in her own bed for a long while, trying to make sense of what had happened that day, trying to equate love with sex and finding the two things diverse, the one immediate and physical, the other as inaccessible as her soul. Maybe, had he been allowed, Michael would have been able to show her the fusion of the two, and then all would have been different. But you cannot undo the future any more than you can undo the past.

The next day Michael was on the balcony trying to repair the pergola and prune the straggling vine, while Helen was in the kitchen on the ground floor getting something together for lunch. She heard him coming down the outside steps, and then the sound of voices, just the dull percussion of men talking, not the specific words, just the tone, not the sense. But at the sound something moved inside her. She stopped whatever it was she was doing and came out into the courtyard, into the dazzling light, into the future.

'What on earth—?'

The man who had been talking to Michael turned towards her and flung open his arms, more as though to display himself than to invite an embrace. He was wearing a gaudy shirt and crumpled white trousers. He held a panama hat in one hand and there was a canvas hold-all at his feet. 'I told you to keep a bed warm for me, my love,' he said.

She allowed herself to be kissed. 'I never really imagined you'd come,' she said, detaching herself from his grasp.

'What a wonderful greeting,' he said. 'So we've got a little love nest, have we? A live-in lover?'

'Don't be tiresome, Dennis.' She turned to Michael, as though in apology. 'He mentioned something, but only in the vaguest terms. "I might pop over", or something like that. You never know when to take him seriously. You remember Michael don't you, Dennis?'

Killin looked from one to the other, recognition dawning. 'Oh, yes, of course I do. One of Tommy Constance's sons, isn't it? Michael. Of course. Little Michael. A big boy now, though, I'll bet.' He grinned at them. He was the kind of person who uses a smile as a trick, a gesture which does not signify any kind of humour. They looked suddenly as though they were his victims, a sorrowful Hansel and Gretel at the gingerbread house and he some kind of grotesque, bullish witch. 'And you've got yourselves together, have you? Made my old bolt-hole a little love nest, eh? Or are there others around?'

'We're on our own.'

'I'm sure. Does that constitute some kind of incest? Vice is nice, but incest — no, I suppose it doesn't really, not being related. But fancy a second generation of Hardings and Constances getting together. Whatever next, eh?'

'Do shut up, Dennis.'

He laughed and put his arm round her shoulders to lead her into the cottage. 'Tell me about your beautiful mother. What does she think of you two getting together like this? Or maybe she doesn't know . . .' He saw their expressions and read the truth. 'So it *is* a little secret, is it? Brother and sister playing mummies and daddies behind the potting shed, eh?' He laughed at their discomfiture. 'But I'm sure my Lorna would be delighted if you two succeeded where she and Tommy so patently failed.'

Helen felt angry, angry and frightened, as though the undercur-

118

rents in the conversation, the echoes of old suspicions, the hints of ancient jealousy, might without warning stir up the placid surface of the present. 'She's hardly yours, is she?'

Killin laughed. 'Dear Lorna. You get more and more like her as you get older, you know that? You've got her bone structure. And her eyes. And her anger.' He considered her, head on one side, as though examining a piece of sculpture or a painting. There was something dangerously possessive about the way he assessed her, as though he knew things about her that she did not know herself. It was the intimacy of the surgeon, not the lover. 'Sometimes when you smile I can see her looking out at me.'

'I'd rather not hear,' she said, and detached herself again from his grasp. He seemed undaunted by her words, merely laughing at her back and following her through to the kitchen. 'Getting something ready for lunch, are you? Don't let me get in your way, my dear. Just pretend I'm not here.'

But his injunction was impossible. Instantly he seemed to charge the small cottage with his presence. Upstairs he peered into the two bedrooms and raised his eyebrows inquisitively when he saw signs of occupation in each. 'If you're full up here I can sleep on the sofa downstairs, Helen my love. Don't worry about me.'

'Don't be silly,' she called up from below. 'I'll move my things into the other room in a sec. You make yourself at home there.' Killin tossed his bag onto one of the single beds and gave Michael a conspiratorial wink. 'Done you a favour, eh?' Then he caught sight of the photographs beside the bed. 'What's this?' The pictures were in one of those leather frames designed for travelling, two photographs facing one another across the fold: one was of Lorna, taken at some family celebration, a wedding possibly, or a baptism. She was wearing a wide picture hat, holding the thing on her head as though against a gust of wind. Her expression, one of wry amusement, suggested that the whole thing was a practical joke of some kind. She looked very beautiful, raw and sensual beneath the elegance. The opposite picture in the frame was less animated, less informal: the still soft portrait of a young man in Army uniform.

'The lovely Lorna and the tragic Andrew, is it? Oh my word, how touching.' Killin looked at Michael with an expression that was suddenly bright and knowing. 'I don't expect you think much of me, do you? But we're old friends, Helen and I.'

Michael shrugged.

'How's Tommy, then?'

'He's all right. I'll move Helen's things next door.' There were some of her clothes thrown over a chair. He picked them up and began to stuff them into her suitcase.

'Still on his own, is he?'

'Yes. Lonely, I suppose, but he doesn't show it. He believes in putting a good face on things.'

Killin nodded. 'It's natural enough to blame me, of course.'

'I blame no one. It was nothing to do with me.'

'But you'd be wrong if you imagined for one moment that Lorna was in some way innocent. Or that Tommy was, come to that.'

For the first time Michael showed a spark of anger. He straightened up and glared at Killin. 'How in God's name was *he* guilty?'

Killin moved his tongue inside his mouth almost as though tasting the question. 'By being Tommy Constance. By not being Andrew Harding. That was everyone's guilt. Tommy, me, Peter Oldcastle, half a dozen others I wouldn't be surprised. We were all at fault, all to blame.' He brandished the photograph that he had picked up from beside Helen's bed. 'None of us were Andrew Harding, you see. None of us.'

'Is that an excuse?'

He put the photographs back where he had found them. 'Excuse? I don't know. Is there ever such a thing as an excuse? Maybe there are only reasons.'

6

The next morning Killin was up before either of them, moving about the kitchen preparing breakfast. 'I'll soon be out of your hair,' he assured them when they came down. 'Don't let me cramp your style. And by the way,' he peeled some notes from a roll in his wallet, 'count me in on the house-keeping while I'm here.'

Michael tried to hand the money back – 'anyway it's far too much' – but Killin insisted.

'Take it all the same. You're my guests.'

But they were more than guests. He had a sense of ownership about him, as though possession – material, spiritual, it didn't matter – simple possession was ten-tenths of his law. So they established an uneasy *ménage à trois* in the little cottage, with intimacy the mainspring of the piece, intimacy given and withheld and hinted at, the intimacy of a glance, the intimacy of the faintest shared smile, the intimacy of a barbed comment. It was the intimacy of the subtle movements of Helen's limbs against Michael's at night, or the way she sometimes touched Killin's arm and laughed at what he said, or argued with him and grimaced at Michael in shared revulsion. A strange and paradoxical intimacy was the mainspring, and as it unwound it delivered the past. Bellapais and Buffavento, Famagusta – the city of Othello and Desdemona – and Nicosia, all these places were part of the fabric of the past that they unwove together. There was Ledra Street down which Michael and Helen had walked with Lorna and Tommy one spring day and seen a beggar with an artificial leg. 'I remember!' Helen exclaimed. 'Pink plastic. The colour of tooth-paste.' Murder Mile, the British press had dubbed the place, and Killin knew why well enough and trumped their story with his

121

own memory. 'I saw some poor bastard shot down in cold blood just over there by that pharmacy.'

In the cool of an early morning the three of them walked round the harbour of Kyrenia – crowded now with the advance flotilla of a tourist fleet – and delighted in the castle. 'Do you remember going to the Dome, that day—?'

'Do you remember Colonel Davy and the sight of blood?'

But they searched in vain for the little bar where Killin had shown Lorna and Helen the EOKA bomb factory.

'What did Mother imagine we were doing down there?' Helen wondered aloud, and they laughed together as they walked, turning to Michael to explain, but failing, of course, to catch the essence of the joke, the exquisite tensions of it. For Killin and she remembered other things as well, the hidden things, the places where danger lay – the tension of a young girl's waist as he swung her to the floor; and a blunt finger coming away from her mouth bearing a smear of purple rime.

Do you remember? It is a dangerous question, loaded with all the misapprehensions of the past.

'He claimed that he once dandled me on his knee,' Helen told Michael one evening. 'Do you remember, Dennis?'

Suddenly he seemed reluctant to play. 'It was a long, long time ago, my love.'

'Tell me.'

He shook his head, as though at the disparity of ages which could have had them together as adult and child like that. 'Too long ago to bother with.' And then, as though it really was a game, with rules, he remarked, 'if you don't remember it doesn't count.'

But she was like a moth attracted to a candle flame, fluttering nearer and nearer the small brilliance which it thinks must be the sun. The metaphor was obvious enough, for the candles which lit the cottage became graveyards for dozens of the animals. They fluttered in from the darkness round the table, searching for death as other insects search for honey. Powerless to do anything for them they watched them singe in the flame and struggle in the molten wax. 'Tell me, Dennis,' she insisted, and her expression would brook no refusal. 'Tell me.'

He shrugged. 'It was when I came back from Palestine in 1946.' He looked at the two of them sitting across the rickety table from him. 'I came back with Andrew's body.'

Helen gave a little intake of breath. Moths fluttered in the candle wax and bats flitted overhead. All around, from the prickly pears that lined the lane, from the rough stone wall round the courtyard, from the fig tree and the oleander bushes, came the soft, plangent sound of crickets. 'I had to tell Lorna that she couldn't see him. She wasn't to be allowed a last look. I had to persuade her.' Killin had a bright, sarcastic expression. He lit a cigarette and blew out a stream of smoke as though trying to blow the memory away. 'You see, there was nothing left of him that was recognisable.'

The next day they hired a boat. It was Killin's idea. He claimed he was thinking of buying the thing and wanted to take it out on trial but whether this was just a story wasn't clear. It lay at the quayside in Kyrenia harbour, a large white cabin cruiser with the name painted in florid script across the stern: *Call Girl*. It seemed entirely appropriate. Against the placid waters of the old harbour and the mouldering stone of the castle, *Call Girl* was as flagrant and meretricious as a whore.

'Dennis, it's amazing!' Helen exclaimed.

'*She*, my dear,' Killin corrected her. 'She is a she.' But he recognised the irony in her tone. 'Bit of a gin-palace, isn't she? Does forty knots, so they say. You wait and see.'

'And you can afford to buy it?'

'Can't afford not to. Not at the price they're asking.' He balanced up the short gang-plank and flung his bag onto the deck. 'Anybody at home?' A face appeared over the coaming of the flying bridge, a young Greek with bushy hair and a pair of mirrored sun-glasses propped up above his forehead. 'Costas, old chap! Everything *en daksi*?'

'Okay,' the Cypriot said. 'You come on. All okay.'

Michael and Helen followed Killin on board. As they dumped their things on the stern deck she glanced at him with the light of irony in her eyes. 'I can't really believe Dennis,' she whispered. 'Do you think he's really going to buy it?'

'Probably needs it for business.'

'Business? What business?'

'How do I know? But I can guess.'

She frowned. 'What do you mean?'

What did he mean? Dennis Killin seemed capable of anything. He had spent the last year or two somewhere in the South of France, so he claimed, amongst the shifting population of the Riviera. His business was vague – 'procurement' was all he would say, 'buying and selling' – and he seemed to deliberately foster an image of mystery and evasiveness, as though he saw himself as something of an adventurer, a player challenging the norms and the rules, laughing at society while dealing the cards from the bottom of the pack. 'I keep moving,' he had told them, 'keep on my toes, never stay anywhere long enough to get bored or to pay tax.'

Under his hand they took the boat out of the little harbour and along the coast towards the Karpass peninsula. The boat slammed into the waves. Great sheets of spray flung out sideways from her hull and the wind battered their faces as they stood up there on the bridge. Helen laughed at the speed, shook her hair in the wind, cried that it was fabulous.

'*She*, my dear,' Killin corrected her again, shouting above the racket. '*She* is fabulous. She is an expensive and beautiful woman who will probably bring ruin to me.'

Helen was like a child out on a treat. Spray dashed up as high as the bridge and she grew breathless with the speed and clutched Michael's hand. Killin looked across at her.

'Maybe I should rename her. How about *Helen of Troy*?' He gestured extravagantly. 'Is this the face that launched a thousand ships and burnt the mighty towers of Ilium?'

'Topless,' she shouted back.

He didn't hear above the noise, or pretended not to. 'What?'

'Topless!' she shouted again.

This time there was a glint of triumph in his smile. 'I bet you daren't,' he replied. She looked away in embarrassment. 'We'll see. We'll see how brave you are.'

'Don't be stupid,' she muttered; but only Michael could hear.

They went eastwards down the coast for half an hour before Killin throttled back and steered towards the coast, to a deserted bay. The silence as he cut the engines was sudden, a positive quality in the bright day, a heavy thing made up of the soft lap of water against the hull and the shriek of cicadas from the scrubby pine trees on shore.

'A swim before lunch,' he announced. 'Costas will get the food ready. And we'll take Helen at her word.' He clambered down from the bridge to the stern deck and began to undress.

'What do you mean?'

'What you said, my dear. Just now.' He looked up with a challenge in his eyes. 'The topless towers.'

'Don't be idiotic.'

'Shocked, my dear? What do you think, Michael?' Stepping out of his clothes he laughed up at the faces on the bridge. His belly was massive but somehow not flabby, a great powerful dome of muscle beneath which his penis emerged like a mushroom from the undergrowth. Helen's expression was a clumsy blend of shock and fascination. 'Do I appal you?' he called.

She reddened and looked away. 'You're showing off.'

He roared with laughter. Then with a kind of awkward pirouette he launched himself into the water. There was a flash of narrow buttocks, a massive splash and a heaving of the surface before his head appeared in the water laughing up at them once more. 'You don't dare!' he shouted.

Helen looked at Michael. 'I'm not undressing.'

He shrugged.

'Anyway there's Costas.'

'You mean you'd undress if there was just me and Dennis?'

'At least you aren't strangers.'

'I would have thought it would be easier with a stranger. Like undressing in front of the doctor.'

She pursed her lips, recognising the words. 'Are you suggesting I should?'

'It's up to you.'

'Are you going to then?'

He shrugged again. 'Will you accuse me of being disloyal?'

'Don't be ridiculous.'

So Michael went down to the lower deck, took off his clothes and jumped in. Helen looked down at the two of them treading water a few metres from the boat. 'You're to look the other way,' she called. 'And there will be no snorkel masks.'

Killin laughed. 'You've spoiled my day. I was going to hunt for sea anemones.'

'Don't you bloody well dare.' Dutifully they turned their backs, giggling like schoolboys, united for a moment in a lewd prank, until another splash signalled her arrival in the water nearby. They turned to see her face emerge, plastered across with wet hair. Her limbs moved beneath the surface, refracted by the water, distorted and broken and bent into a thousand shapes, and the patches of white were like something submarine and mysterious glimpsed tantalisingly in the depths.

'A mermaid,' Killin shouted. He splashed water at her and chased her and caught a flashing ankle so that she screamed with fright and delight like a child. But she was not a child, and the very fact of her nakedness beside them in the water seemed to charge the day with a strange energy. They played around for a while, laughing and splashing, and by the time they climbed back on board her modesty had all but fled. She slipped out of the water and sat on the little stage at the stern of the boat.

'Aphrodite risen from the waves,' Dennis said. She grabbed a towel defensively round her, but he had already seen the flock of hair and the pale breasts. He smiled at her, a direct smile like a statement of intent and, seeing the look, Michael only understood in part what it meant, only grasped the surface of its significance.

'Maybe that's what I should call the boat,' Killin suggested as he clambered up onto the boat. '*Aphrodite*. A good Cyprus name. How do you like it? Or maybe *Sea Anemone*. What do you think?' But of course he didn't want an answer.

7

They got back to the harbour in the evening, and had supper at the Dome hotel amongst the crumbling remnants of the British colonial service. One or two of the habitués of the bar acknowledged Killin's presence. Some of them appeared wary of him. 'You interested in that boat?' he was asked. 'Saw you taking her out. What's she called?'

'*Call Girl.*'

The man smirked 'You interested in buying?'

'Maybe.'

'Powerful lady.'

'Forty knots. Turkey in under two hours.' He sounded like a man in a pub boasting of how much he'd done on the Bagshot by-pass. 'I was thinking maybe of doing some chartering. You know – deep sea fishing, exploring the Panhandle, that kind of thing.'

The talk meandered round the subject, taking in Turkey and sailing and a few other themes. Helen and Michael took their drinks over to the terrace and looked out onto the darkening sea.

'What do you make of him?' Michael asked her.

'Dennis? In a way he's fun. Selfish people often are. Have you noticed that?'

'Attractive?'

She smiled. 'Are you jealous?'

'A fraction.'

She touched his hand. It was an ambivalent gesture which might have been intended to reassure, might have been an attempt at consolation. 'Why should Dennis Killin be attractive to women, do you think?'

'He is, then?'

127

'Mother always referred to him as vulgar.'

'Maybe that's part of it. Maybe women like vulgarity. Or maybe she was just trying to create an alibi.'

She nodded thoughtfully. 'I sort of knew it from the start – about Mother and Dennis, I mean. For a long while I couldn't really believe that she and your father were anything but happy together, but really I knew all the time. And now that I can add things up a little more accurately I think I understand the whole mess.' She paused uncertainly, looking out at the night and the pale line of surf along the shore. 'It was to do with my own father, my real father. Can you love someone by proxy? Maybe you can. Dennis knew Daddy, you know that. He knew him well. That had something to do with it. That's what I think.'

There was a loud voice behind them, and laughter. Killin came out onto the terrace. 'My little love birds snatching a moment together in the dark.' He put his arm round Helen's waist and drew her against him. She didn't resist. Michael thought of them chasing each other through the water that afternoon, the way he had ducked her and allowed himself to be ducked – and the brown limbs and the sudden, secret glimpses of white which were now Killin's possession as well as his own. She sensed Michael's jealousy, and she found the knowledge both frightening and fascinating, the two things blended together in a dangerous infusion.

As they walked into the dining room the older man said, 'This is where I took you and your mother for lunch. Do you remember?' But Colonel Davy and the man who ate his wife were nowhere to be seen.

They drove back to the village in the dark, talking of the Cyprus of the past, of EOKA, of the dissonant life of the British there, of the politics and the passions that had erupted all around them. 'Do you remember that riot in Limassol?' Helen asked at one point. The question was casual, off-hand, something that just grew out of the conversation, but Helen never uttered an unconsidered word. 'A government workers' demonstration or something, wasn't it? Mother got caught up in it.' She watched carefully as Killin contemplated his answer.

'I'd quite forgotten about it.' The car climbed slowly through the foothills, grinding up in low gear. He swung the vehicle into a tight bend and grated the gears as he changed down. 'I rescued her, you know that? A nasty piece of work it was too. I rescued her. The police lost their cool a bit and the army had to move in.

Tear gas and baton charges, that kind of thing. Not healthy. I remember in Jerusalem once—'

'Tell me about Limassol.'

He gestured casually, one hand on the wheel now that the road was easier. 'It wasn't a patch on Palestine, but the police were heavy at times. Johnny Turk, you know. They might have been nominally under British control but that's really what they were: Turkish bastards, plain and simple. Still are, in fact. The boys from just over the water there. No distance at all. A couple of hours.'

'Tell me,' Helen insisted. Her tone was quite easy, as though she might have been demanding an old and much-loved family story.

'Oh, nothing much really. These things happened all the time in those days. As far as I remember I was at a business meeting of some kind, and of course when the whole thing flared up we wanted to get home as quick as poss. My car was some way away, somewhere by the law courts, I think, which was where the demonstration was. Anyway, at one point I found a whole bunch of demonstrators running down the street. Took no notice of me, of course. Couldn't have given a damn. Frightened as hell, in fact.'

'Frightened?'

'Of the riot police. Felt a bit like following them myself, in fact. Except . . .'

'Except?'

He grinned round at his passengers, his face lit up from the backwash of light from the dashboard. 'I was British, wasn't I? I was on the right side, the side of the police, law and order and all that. Hooray for the Empire, salute the flag, three cheers for the Governor-General, my country cup of tea.' He gave a mock salute with his free hand and the car lurched alarmingly. 'So I didn't run away. I went on a bit and it was lucky that I did.'

'Lucky?'

'Because I found your mother. She'd got caught up in the mess as well and she hadn't run away either.' He laughed admiringly. 'Tough little cookie, Lorna.'

The first houses of the village loomed out of the darkness, the abandoned mosque with its broken minaret and a few houses that had once belonged to Turks. He parked the car in the main square and they climbed out. All the other buildings were dark, but light and laughter came from the bar.

'Mother was in trouble?' Helen was trying to picture the scene in Limassol all those years earlier, the drab houses running down to the port, the peeling paint, the debris from the riot, and fear like a substance in the air. And all this while she had been a few miles away in the house in Episkopi, looking through her mother's things, snapping open the little plastic box.

'Trouble? No, not really. It might have got nasty, but it didn't. And what might have been is what never happened, as T.S. Eliot said.' They climbed the alley towards the cottage, Dennis and Helen in front with Michael following a yard behind. 'She was just there, in a side street, with some policemen standing round her. Three or four of them; I can't remember exactly.'

'What were they doing?'

'You know the kind of thing—'

'No.'

'Oh, giving her a bit of trouble. Going through her handbag, asking her questions. Nothing more. Just policemen. But men; you understand? Men. And in a riot discipline is a shaky thing. They'd just got to touching her a bit, asking her if she was carrying any weapon or anything—'

'Touching her?'

'Just that, just that.'

'And then?'

'She caught sight of me.'

'Dennis! In Christ's name, *Dennis*!' Her face peered over uniformed shoulders, eyes wide with fear. Heads turned, moustachioed faces glowered at the intrusion from the main street as though this cul-de-sac were their own territory, their own country where they drew up the rules.

'Lorna. What the devil are you doing here?' His best accent. Linen-suited and panama-hatted, striding purposefully forward like a district officer, like a collector during the Mutiny, like all those men of empire faced with the mem-sahib in distress. 'What are these fellows up to then? What's going on, corporal?' Disembodied voices shouted in the distance. An explosion sounded somewhere, and, nearer at hand, the smash of breaking glass.

'Lady's papers not in order, sir.'

'Oh, come. Does she really need papers for you to see what she is, an English lady caught up in a bit of trouble?'

'We have to be sure. Regulations.' Tension drained away down the waste-pipe of bureaucracy.

'Well, I can vouch for her, Corporal. She's Mrs Thomas Constance. Colonel Constance is at MEDSEC. They are personal friends of mine. Really, Corporal, I think there are better things to be doing at the moment than bothering Mrs Constance.'

The policemen shifted uneasily. A dark blue Land Rover went past them down the main road, its differentials whining, dust shifting behind it. The sounds of the demonstration had moved further away now.

'Let me escort the lady to safety,' Killin suggested reasonably, holding out his hand to her. 'Perhaps you can advise us which way to go, Corporal?'

The blue uniforms moved aside and Lorna emerged from her small circle of fear and sweat to take the proffered hand. 'Oh, Dennis, thank God you came along.'

'There you are, Corporal,' he said with a careful smile. 'No harm done, no regulation broken, no damage. Right?'

The policeman nodded. 'Right, sir. You take lady to the Town Hall. Keep to main roads.'

'Excellent advice, Corporal. That's just where I left my car. Thank you.' He raised his hat. The corporal saluted. The thing was done.

'Nothing at all,' Killin said, opening the cottage door and turning on the light and handing Helen across the threshold as he once handed her onto the top of the aircraft steps. 'Nothing at all.'

They passed through the army lines at the town hall, walking through broken glass and empty gas canisters, tear gas smarting in their eyes, Lorna shivering beside him, clinging to his arm like a child. 'Oh, my God,' she kept repeating. 'Oh, my God.'

'Nothing at all, love. No harm done. You're all right.' The soldiers were wearing helmets and carrying wire netting riot shields, but they were without gas masks now. The tension had shifted to another part of the town, to run away like storm water in the maze of streets round the harbour. A voice cried out, 'Mrs Constance! Lorna Constance, isn't it?' and Archie Kesteven came over, dear, familiar Archie. 'Are you all right? Nothing wrong, is there?'

'Nothing,' she replied vaguely.

'Just a bit of a fright,' Killin assured him. 'I'll see her safely home. My car's just round the corner.'

'Helen's not here?'

'No. At home.'

'Thank God for that. Do you want us to get in touch with your husband?'

131

She smiled vaguely, as though she had not quite understood. 'No, no don't bother him. Please. I'll be fine.'

'Jolly good, then.' Kesteven saluted and watched the pair go on towards where the car was parked. Lorna began to weep as they walked, not saying anything, just letting tears run down her face.

'It's all right, my love,' Killin whispered softly. 'It's all right.'

His villa was on the outskirts of the town, a low, modern place with palm trees in the garden and a small swimming pool at the back, the kind of thing that would become commonplace in a few years, but which then had an air of luxury about it, and something raffish, something of America and Hollywood.

'You can have a rest if you like. Take a shower, have a swim, anything.' He showed her to an empty room and went off to look for a towel – 'the maid's day off' – and when he came back she was still standing in the middle of the room as though she had forgotten what to do. Her tears had stopped, leaving her cheeks streaked with mascara.

He handed her the towel. 'You look terrible.'

She bit her lower lip, like a child. 'Awful?'

'Truly awful.' He laughed. She watched him for a moment and then she laughed too. It was natural to come closer together in their laughter, to touch each other. Laughter, like alcohol, is often the way to intimacy, the breaker of barriers, the sweeper aside of inhibitions. So they came together laughing, and of course the laughter stopped and something else took its place – a touching of cheeks, a swelling desire, a touching of mouth against mouth. It was all over then, really. A kiss of that kind between adults is as good as a consummation, isn't it?

'I can't, Dennis,' she whispered. 'Oh God, I can't.'

'Why on earth not? We're here alone. It's quite safe.'

'Not that. I've left my bloody cap at home.'

'So I took her to my place,' Killin said in the most matter-of-fact voice, the voice of the rescuing hero, the perfect knight, 'for a wash and a bit of a lie-down.'

'And you, Dennis?'

'What do you mean, me?'

'Did you lie down as well? With her.'

He laughed.

'It was the first time, wasn't it?'

He shook his head, standing in the middle of the main room of the cottage where there was the broken sofa and a couple of cane chairs and the table that they used to carry out into the courtyard for meals. 'It doesn't matter, Helen. It really doesn't matter. Not any longer.'

She had that strange expression, part distant reflection, part decision. 'I knew,' she said quietly. 'Somehow I knew. Why is she like that?' she asked of neither of them in particular. Then she left the table and went upstairs to bed.

Lorna lies beside him looking up at the bare ceiling. The room is shuttered against the light. It smells of fresh plaster, an anonymous, impersonal smell, not the smell of someone's home.

'I wonder . . .'

He turns towards her and puts out his hand to touch the loose flesh of her breast. 'You wonder what?'

She eases his hand away. 'I wonder what Andrew would have said.'

'Andrew? Andrew's been dead over ten years.'

'He's not dead for me.' She looks round at him in the half light. 'Don't you see that? He's never been dead for me.'

8

'I guessed,' Helen whispered to Michael that night. 'I guessed about mother that day. I guessed and I couldn't face it . . .' And then she tried to apologise, as though it had been her own fault, her own doing, her betrayal. 'Michael, I'm so sorry . . .'

He hushed her to silence. 'Nothing to do with you. Nothing to do with me. She was unhappy in her marriage, that's all, and looking for consolation. You can sympathise with my father, but you can't condemn her.'

She shook her head in the darkness. 'I used to notice the way they watched her, the men. They knew, they all knew. They were probably taking bets.'

'That's absurd.'

'And the way she spoke to you.' Her voice was insistent, a small, live presence by his ear. 'What did she say to you?'

'What do you mean?'

'When you were at Guerdon House. When Adrian was there. You remember.'

He tried to still her words by kissing her, but she moved her head aside. 'Tell me, tell me.' She was like a moth near a candle, courting disaster. 'Tell me.'

'She said she didn't like him. Adrian. She didn't like Adrian.'

A bitter laugh. 'Grandier.'

'Grandier and Sister Jeanne des Anges.'

'Do you remember that day in the punt? What a farce.' She paused for a moment to give memory a chance, and then she was back again: 'She said more than that. Tell me.'

'Forget it, Helen. She said something about how lonely she was, that's all.'

The small voice in the darkness, the moth fluttering towards its destruction. 'Did she want you?'

'Don't be stupid.'

'I'm not being stupid.' She lay back and looked up at the ceiling. He could see her face in the faint light from the window, thin and sculptured, the cheeks hollow and the mouth hard. The half-light took her youth from her. She was very like Lorna. She spoke quietly. 'I found them in bed together? Did you know that?'

'Who?' He expected something from the past – Dennis Killin or one of the others. He vaguely remembered the man called Oldcastle. 'Who did you find in bed together?'

'Adrian and Mother,' she said. 'I found them.' And lying there beside him in the lumpy double bed in the cottage in Cyprus she told him of that visit to Guerdon House. Her voice was small and steady, like the scratchings of rodents in the wainscot, like the noise of wood-boring insects which reduce all such places, all such illusions to dust. 'I hate her,' she whispered when she had finished. 'I hate her. She'd take you from me if she knew. She'd take you. She'd take anything from me that she could.'

'That's absurd. She's an unhappy woman trying to come to terms with age, that's all.'

'Oh no.' Still staring up at the ceiling she shook her head. 'She wants revenge, that's it. Revenge on me.'

'Revenge for what?'

'Because I have something of my father in me.' She took his hand and laid it on her chest between her small breasts. 'Here inside me. In every part of my body. I'm the only person in the world who still possesses something of him.'

The next day they went down to Lambousa and swam through the heat and lay in the scented shade of a pine tree, and for a few hours forgot. But after they got back to the cottage, when they were sitting at table in the dusty little forecourt, enveloped in the strange aura of the fig tree's scent, she started again, fluttering too near the candle.

'No one has ever told me about my father,' she said. 'Not even you, Dennis. Mother claims she hardly knew him, goes on about wartime marriages and things like that. And nobody else knew him at all. Tommy once told me he met him in Cairo during the war, had a drink at Shepheard's or somewhere. But . . .' She looked at Killin. He was the flame and she fluttered helplessly around him. 'Nothing. It's as though he never existed. And yet he *did* exist. Do you know, his parent's are still alive? – my own grandparents, for God's sake, but I don't know who they are or where they live. She's kept them from me. I could try and find them, I suppose. Electoral registers or something. I don't know how you do it, but I expect I could. But for what?' Tears had started into her eyes. She gripped her hands into tight little fists as she had once held them as a child to fight for her rights against her stepbrothers, against Michael and Antony. Half the size, a third of the weight, but prepared to fight. 'You can tell me something, Dennis, you can tell me.'

'It was all a long time ago,' he replied, but she merely laughed with despite.

'That's an anodyne comment, all right. That's just what she used to say to me. It's a long time ago and all very sad, but we've got to look to the future. It's the sort of rubbish adults tell children in the vain hope that they'll give up. But adults never really understand children, do they? The only grown-ups who do are the ones who haven't grown up themselves.' She looked from one to the other of her companions, with her teeth bitten tight against some kind of anger. 'Fuck the future,' she said. 'Do you know, I cling to what memories I have of him? I cling to them.' And she held out her hands to show the desperation of her grip, like a drowning woman grasping at a plank. 'I'm afraid that as I grow older they may slip away and then I'd have nothing left of him at all. So I remember in order to keep remembering. I recall memories and I recall the memory of memories and they all go round in my head until I no longer distinguish fact from fiction, memory from fantasy. I want to know about him Dennis. I want him to live inside me. You shared a house with him. You must have known him as well as anyone.'

Dusk was hurrying on with that insistence that it has in the Mediterranean. Candles glimmered on the table and moths struggled in the wax. The liquid trilling of crickets was all around. But the village below was silent, as though waiting for whatever it was the world had in store for it. Killin considered her for a moment. Perhaps he was trying to judge whether to tell her more or not, like an adult trying to gauge how to impart the facts of life to a child, whether it should be penises and vaginas and copulation, or storks and gooseberry bushes and the caprices of God. He made up his mind.

'I never really knew him well, you know. Even if we did share the same house. He wasn't the kind you got to know well. He wasn't one of us, really . . .'

'One of who?'

'The ordinary fellows, the blokes who were just getting on with the bloody job and looking forward to going home. Andrew had some kind of cause.'

'Cause? What cause?'

For the first time Killin seemed unsure of himself. 'They were pretty grim times. Partition, United Nations resolutions, Jewish terrorists, everything. People have almost forgotten now, what with what's happened since – India, Suez, EOKA, Mao-Mao, all that kind of thing – but Palestine was as bad as anything that's come after. It was the Empire in retreat and playing dog-in-the-manger. We can't deal with these yids and no one else is going to be allowed to try, that was our motto. Oh yes, we were a disgrace all right – but then so were they. The whole bloody Holy Land was a disgrace.' He looked from her to Michael, as though seeking support or understanding or something. 'Holy, my arse! they hated us and, by and large, we hated them. Which is bloody strange when you think about it, because a good number of them *were* us; some of the most important in fact. Look at Herzog, for God's sake: bloody Guards officer! Christian name – no, that's the wrong word – first name Vivian. I ask you. Changed it to Chaim, as well he might. There were a whole lot of them like that, schizos really.'

'Who was Silver?' Michael asked.

'Silver? How do you know about Silver?'

He shrugged. 'Lorna mentioned him once.'

'Silver was the bloke who shared with us for a while. Took offence at something or other and pushed off. A bit of a pain really, a touch of the religious fanatic about him.'

'My father,' said Helen quietly.

'I'm coming to him. He had some kind of job in Headquarters. Oh, he always said it was nothing, Claims Commission or some such nonsense. But we all knew it was something more than that. He'd come on Barker's staff.'

'Barker?'

'GOC. The general in charge of the whole shambles. Andrew had been with him in Germany at the end of the war. Before that he was in the desert with some kind of private army, working behind the enemy lines, that kind of thing. A good war career, the kind that makes people sit up and take notice. When that all finished he was called home and transferred to Barker's Army Corps, and after it was all over he went with Barker to Palestine. But once he got to Palestine he was surrounded by people who were for or against, people with axes to grind, people with beliefs and creeds. On the surface it was just another bit of the Empire collapsing, but underneath there were a whole lot of mixed loyalties and mixed motives that you didn't get anywhere else. And Andrew tried to see both sides, tried to deal with people fairly.'

'What people?'

The shadows had gathered in round the little table. Candles flickered amongst the dirty plates, giving it a seductive light it did not deserve. Killin contemplated the intangible certainty of the past. 'His bosses. The Jews.' He smiled that slightly gap-toothed smile, but it was no longer confident. 'His girlfriend.'

There was a stillness at the table. Helen was looking across at him, her eyes strangely impassive.

'Why can't you shut up about this, Dennis?' Michael asked irritably. 'We're on holiday. We're not here to be upset.'

Helen ignored him. 'Girlfriend?' she repeated.

Killin nodded. 'That's what upset poor old Silver, knowing Andrew was married.'

'Who was she?'

'For goodness sake let it rest,' Michael cried. 'What's the point? It was twenty years ago.'

Killin shrugged. 'Her name was Rachel.'

'Jewish?'

'American. I forget her surname.' He frowned with the effort of remembering, but there was the powerful impression that it was all an act, that remembrance was going to be doled out with care, like ammunition to raw recruits. 'Rachel something, from Philadelphia. Led him a right dance, she did. He was in love with her, in fact. Anyone who knew him could see that. Not that there hadn't been one or two before . . .'

And Helen sat there quietly, as though watching her illusions dissolve in the caustic solvent of tears. Eventually she pushed her chair back and rose from the table unsteadily, as though she had drunk too much *ouzo*, which maybe she had. Michael put out a hand to stop her but she brushed it away.

'Attractive thing she was,' Killin called after her. 'Not as beautiful as your mother, but most attractive . . . Sexy. Oh, yes. Very sexy.'

She went into the house and up the stairs, walking with great concentration as though the steps couldn't be relied on to stay still. A door slammed.

'You're a fucking bastard, Dennis,' Michael said.

The big man pushed himself up from the table. 'I'll go,' he said. 'She doesn't need a boyfriend now, she needs a comforter.'

'What do you mean, comforter? You've just reduced her to misery, you bloody idiot!'

He shook his head. 'Not me, old fellow. Facts. Reality. Finding out what she is really like. You'll learn yourself one day. Now you just sit tight, and I'll go.'

So Michael let him. What did he imagine? Difficult to separate anticipation from what happened. Perhaps he thought that Killin would finish himself off in Helen's own eyes, finally show himself for what he really was – because of course Michael was jealous of him, consumed with jealousy of the power Killin seemed to have over her and the fascination he wielded, and the blunt self-assurance of the man. Perhaps that was Michael's motive for sitting there and watching Killin head up the stairs after her. Perhaps he expected to pick up the pieces afterwards and put them together with gentle hands, like someone restoring a piece of broken statuary or something. He heard Killin's knock on the door and her distant answer, heard him go in. He sat there in the candlelight as Killin closed the door softly behind him.

She was lying face down on the bed, weeping. There was barely any light in the room. Killin sat gently beside her and put out his hand to stroke her head.

'You just have to live with it, my love,' he said softly; and his absurd words, so banal, so prosaic, seemed to bring her comfort. So she lay there on the bed weeping, and Killin's hand stroked her hair just like a parent's might have, and his words were the soothing, crooning imprecations of a parent: 'There, there. You'll be all right. The bad dream's over,' things like that; and eventually she turned her head and kissed the hand that stroked her, and then kissed it again, into the palm. He took courage in that. He bent towards her and as he did so she remembered his body on the boat, the massive chest and strong belly, the wires of hair, the sheer blunt masculinity of it. She didn't stop him as he whispered into her ear that life was like that, that you had to take the rough with the smooth, that you had to face facts and nobody was perfect, that we all have problems that we have to come to terms with. Lying beneath the touch of his hand it seemed to her that banalities of this nature held all the secrets of life. And when he bent and kissed her ear, and then her cheek, and then the corner of her mouth with its taste of salt tears, she didn't stop him, or feel repulsion, or anything like that. And when he began to stroke her as one might a cat, with long, suave strokes, she just lay there and let him.

'You must just accept things as they are, my love. As they are.' And she found consolation in the hand that touched her and searched through her and found places where her pain could be assuaged.

'Oh, Christ,' she whispered to him. 'Oh Christ, no.'

But her prayer, if it was a prayer, went unanswered. Quite gently, for he could be a gentle man, quite gently he pulled her skirt up to her waist and slid her pants down to her knees and bent towards her.

'No,' she whispered, but still she turned and shifted her knees apart and looked up at the ceiling and the plain, cheap icon which hung, still inverted, on the wall; and she felt his mouth on her and his tongue touching her, and the pain, if it was pain, leaving her and ecstasy taking its place. Then gently and against the feeble pressure of her hands, he lay down on her. That was the moment, more or less, when Michael opened the door.

He screamed. A mindless rage burst out of him in a torrent of really rather inept abuse. What else could he do? He was hardly equipped either by education or experience for such things. The English middle class aren't very good at pure, elemental rage. So he just screamed, and then, still screaming, ran over and pushed Killin off her as though he were some kind of creature, a vampire maybe, an incubus caught feeding on her in her dreams, while Helen wept and curled up tightly as though preparing to return to the womb.

For a moment the two men faced each other across her naked, knotted form. For a moment Killin looked as he might strike Michael – he was far more powerful than the younger man. But instead he just half-laughed, and blundered past him out of the room. The door slammed. And Michael sat on the bed and wept at the absolute degradation of it all. That's what he thought, anyway, but maybe he also thought that he had won. Who knows? Who can tell anything about human behaviour, about the motives that lie beneath the actions? Maybe Helen was merely giving vent to her desires, in the manner which would become so fashionable a few years later, shortly before a retrovirus put paid to all that kind of thing. Who knows? All that is certain is that Michael had a weeping woman on his hands – oh, really weeping: great racking, hysterical, convulsive spasms, as though the life were being driven out of her – and complete confusion in his mind.

140

The moth had fluttered into the flame.

Sleep, edged with hysteria and filled with dreams that were no worse that the truth. He awoke to noises downstairs and a pallid dawn light at the windows which showed her sleeping still, sprawled across the bed in complete abandon. Her open legs disclosed that flock of fawn hair. It was a thorn-bush growing in the desert, a thorn-bush clinging to the small, life-giving source of moisture beneath. For a long time he watched her intently, as though trying to read things within her, the tides of personality which had ebbed and flowed throughout so much of his life without ever being understood. Metaphors, metaphors. We use them in order to understand and they take on a life of their own and generate confusion and bewilderment. How could he ever love her now, he wondered? How could he ever not? The word *shameless* ran through his mind; shameless as a synonym for innocent. And with it, incongruously, a sentence from the Bible that he couldn't at the time place: *Lo, I am with you always, even unto the end of the world.*

Below a door slammed. She stirred and closed her legs and turned so that her back was towards him. 'Has he gone out?' Her voice was quite calm, coming out of the silence of the room almost as though disembodied. She sat up, with her back to Michael, and shook her head so that her hair poured over her shoulders and down almost to her waist. He had witnessed this a dozen mornings now, these small, ritual gestures that were as intimate as any sexual act. As always she put up her hands and gathered the hair together and slipped it into a leather clip so that it hung down the middle of her back like the thick tail of some animal. She had bought the clip in a craft shop in Kyrenia. It had the shape of the island itself embossed on it, the shape that has been likened to the hide of an animal staked out to dry in the sun. He focused on that splayed shape and the plume of hair and waited to see what she would do. He considered the possibilities of remorse, of defiance, of misery, of plain denial. He waited.

'Leave me alone, please, Michael.' She half turned to glance at him: a twisted shoulder; the profile of her face with its acute angles, its curious curves of upper lip and chin; and the profile of a small, white, infinitely delicate breast. 'Please. I want to shower and get dressed. And then I want to go.'

'Go?'

'Leave.' She turned to look at him more directly, leaning her

141

right arm on the bed. 'I want to leave this place, this house, this island. Immediately. Will you go down to the village and telephone the airport to see if there is a flight out?' She smiled, that was the worse thing, she smiled as she might have smiled at an offical across an airline desk.

'I love you Helen,' he said quietly. 'I don't care what happened last night, I still love you.'

The smile was still there. 'Will you do that?' she asked again.

Killin returned from the village – he had been to buy bread – and she came down and told him what they were doing. Her voice was quite expressionless, as though it was all nothing, as though he was no more than a hotelier and she and Michael were going earlier than they had intended because of the state of the bathroom or something like that. She declined both the offer of breakfast and the bright connivance of his smile, and went back upstairs to pack her things.

And so they left quietly, saying nothing more to Killin, talking to one another about neutral things – the view from the village square, the little church with its red-tiled domes, the ruined mosque below, the broken houses of the old Turkish quarter. There was no longer any intimacy in what they said, no understanding that once these had been things shared. They debated which way to take, the road via Kyrenia as they had come, or the one that went eastward round the mountains, via Myrtou. Myrtou. She smiled at the prettiness of the name. 'The myrtle tree'.

That was the route they opted for. In terms of distance there was little in it and they hadn't been that way before.

Thus, after spending another night in a hotel near the airport because there wasn't a flight immediately, they flew home; and when they got to England it was grey and raining. Michael retrieved his car from the long-term park and drove her through Slough and Maidenhead to Guerdon House. The Thames valley was flat and grey and dank, and there were no mountains, neither Pentadaktylos at their backs nor Taurus before them, looming in the distance across a smokey blue sea. There was nothing very much really, just reservoirs and gravel pits and rows of semi-detached houses, and then the prettier buildings near the river.

When they drew to a halt at the gate of Guerdon House she still wore that smile. She had worn it now for about thirty-six hours and it must have been beginning to hurt. It was the polite smile of an airline official, signifying nothing.

'Do you mind if you don't come in?'

'Let me help you in with your things.'

'Better not.'

'When shall I get in touch?' he asked, and she just smiled, stood there smiling in the drizzle beside her suitcase, as though she was just about to inform him that she very much regretted the inconvenience but the flight had been cancelled.

III

1

Tennis on the dusty courts of the YMCA, half a world away from an English garden with its court hidden amongst the laurels, and tea on the lawn afterwards. Here the courts were rectangles of red earth, like small sections of the surface of Mars carefully packaged for recreational use. Cicadas rasped angrily in the dusty bushes. Other courts were in operation, with balls plucked to and fro between men and women in starched white. On the pitch beyond the cypresses a football match was in progress, two battalion teams locked in combat. Dust shifted amongst the players like the smoke from guns.

'Over here, you guys,' Rachel called. She looked like a castaway on a desert island desperately signalling to a passing ship.

'Not really my forte, old man,' Dennis complained as they made their way across to the little group. 'Not a great master of the centre court.'

'Do we need introductions?' Emily asked. 'You know Mary and Rachel of course. Have you met the Sweetfields? No? Gilbert and Angela. Gilbert's something in the Secretariat.' Sweetfield was small and sleek and resigned to an afternoon of boredom; the kind of man, one guessed immediately, who is always looking over people's shoulders to spot someone more likely to advance his career. Harding knew him vaguely as a protagonist of interminable committee meetings on the security situation. 'Political Department,' he answered to a question that had never been asked. His wife had sandy hair and a squint and, it was clear, wasn't a credit to him. From behind prominent teeth she emitted a faint spray of saliva. 'What fun it all is!' she exclaimed. Harding knew, with that certainty one has in the face of imminent disaster, that he was going to end up as her partner.

Emily called the group to order. 'How are we going to arrange things, then? Draw for partners?'

'We're short of a man,' someone remarked.

'Must be the only occasion during the whole of the Mandate.'

'Martin's meant to be coming.'

Mrs Sweetfield turned her various eyes on Harding. 'It'll make it awfully complicated being a man short. I think we ought to get another one, don't you? Shouldn't be difficult, not here.' She laughed – a little barricade of crooked white pilasters.

'I don't give Mrs Sweetbread much chance,' Harding whispered to Rachel when the woman had passed out of earshot. 'Which ball is she going to hit?'

Rachel smiled. 'Maybe she closes one eye.' She glanced at her watch. 'Look, if we don't get a move on our time on court will run out.'

So, while Dennis drew up the wicker chairs and organised a tray of drinks, a search was instituted within the neo-Byzantine depths of the YMCA building and finally an anonymous fellow from the Public Works Department was drafted in to play. He was, apparently, called Ted. 'Works and Bricks,' Mrs Sweetfield warned as he came over. 'And a Methodist to boot. But he's quite a useful player. Shall I organise the draw?'

The various names were scribbled on bits of paper, and the men's names went into someone's tennis shoe and the women's went into Mrs Sweetfield's raffia basket, the one with the camel woven on the side which she had bought, so she explained at great length, from a dear little man who had a stall just inside the Damascus Gate; and when the pairs of names were drawn out Harding's prophecy was fulfilled as certainly as if it had been by Isaiah himself.

'What super fun!' Sweetfield's wife cried. 'I'm sure we'll be a winning duo. Do tell me, who is that dear American girl with Gilbert? I don't think I've met her before and I didn't catch her name. It's so lovely to see new faces.'

Glumly he watched Rachel walking out on court with Sweetfield. 'She's called Rachel.'

'Golly, not Jewish?'

'As a matter of fact, no.'

'Not that there aren't some fine Jews,' the woman added hastily, 'but as Gilbert always says, a Jew in Golders Green is one thing and a Jew in Jerusalem is another. Actually he says something rather clever but I can't remember it exactly, something about

148

posher and *kosher*. A Jew in Jerusalem is posher, but a Jew in Golders Green is kosher, or maybe it's the other way round. Frightfully amusing, anyway.'

'Rachel's an Episcopalian.'

'Oh, is she? Well, that's all right then. Almost C of E really, I suppose. And you? You're Anthony, aren't you? I'm terrible with names.'

'Andrew. I'm not Jewish either.'

'Of course not!' She thought that ever so funny. Her laughter barked round the grounds of the YMCA, echoed off the honeyed limestone, halted tennis players in their stride and dogs in the act of urinating. 'I didn't mean what *religion*,' she protested. 'I meant, what do you *do*, dear boy? What do you *do*? You're Army, aren't you? Didn't we meet at the MacMillans'? Haven't I heard about you? Weren't you something awfully brave in the war?'

'We all showed courage in our youth,' he said.

'Did someone say that?'

'Horace.'

She frowned, trying to place the name. 'Have I met him?'

'I shouldn't think so.'

'I knew someone in Baghdad called Horace.'

'It wouldn't be him.'

'And what do you do now?' she asked.

'I'm with the Claims Commission.'

'Oh, not with a regiment?'

'Just a desk wallah.'

'Well, I suppose that's all Gilbert is really, a sort of glorified desk wallah.'

The man in question was poised at the base line to serve. Rachel crouched fetchingly up at the net, her skirt lifted to display tight curves of white cotton. 'Ready partner?' Gilbert called. One imagined that he was always checking up on things like that, and always finding people falling short of his exacting standards. He tossed the ball into the air, flashed his racquet at it, and sent it speeding into the net. 'Damn!'

'She *is* a lovely thing, isn't she?' said Mrs Sweetfield. 'Are you two together?'

'Just friends.'

The woman eyed her partner archly. 'Of course.' The match staggered on, Sweetfield losing both his service games and generally displaying a sorry lack of ability, Rachel doing her best to shore their efforts up.

'Oh, she's *useful*,' the woman decided. 'Lucky old Gilbert.'

But for all Rachel's efforts they lost the set 2–6, and came off court to the sound of Sweetfield suggesting how she might have won the vital point in the fourth game if only she had played it down the tramlines. 'I thought she showed you up, my dear,' said Mrs Sweetfield sweetly. 'Now it's up to me and Anthony to set things right.'

And they did, beating Mary and Ted 6–3. Mrs Sweetfield regarded Harding with an expression of delight. 'Wasn't that fun?'

And so the afternoon wore on beneath the deep blue of a Jerusalem sky and a staring sun that seemed an altogether different celestial body from the thing that shone down, occasionally, on Camberley or Tidworth. Faces grew florid and shiny; underarms became dark with perspiration. There was a musky smell of sweat about the hot court.

After her third match Rachel came off court and slumped into a chair beside Harding. 'It's like playing with a handicap,' she complained, just loud enough for Sweetfield to hear. 'You enjoying it?'

Her face glistened with sweat. He had, he realised, never seen Lorna sweat. Lorna was the kind of girl who calculated every move, planned every exertion in the most economical way possible – and still managed to win. 'Thank you for inviting me,' he said.

'Does that mean yes or no?'

'It means yes.' He hesitated. 'I haven't seen you around for a while. How's the writing been going?'

'Not bad, not bad at all. *The Inquirer* has started taking my stuff. And I've just landed a column in the *Palestine Post*, how about that? Haven't you seen it? An American Angle, it's called.'

'That!'

'You know it?'

'I know it. It's gaining a bit of a reputation. Can't say it's earned you many friends in the Secretariat.'

'Why, that's great!' She grinned. She was not quite as pretty as he had remembered. There were imperfections in her features which showed up in the bright light of day, a certain bluntness in her nose and mouth which was almost masculine. And yet her eyes held a strange internal light, and they still watched him with that little extra concentration as though he mattered. Nothing is more attractive than attraction reflected in the eyes of another.

A burst of applause came from a neighbouring court. 'Oh well done *you*!' a voice cried.

150

'After the cinema,' Harding said. 'I was going to get in touch, but . . .'

'But you didn't,' she said flatly.

'Pressure of work. And England, of course . . . England was bloody. I sometimes think that the whole point of the Empire is to get away from the wretched weather. How was the Holy Fire?'

'Pure circus,' she said distractedly, glancing at her watch.

'What are you doing this evening?' he asked. 'Shall we fix something with Emily and Dennis? Maybe we could all go to the Regence.'

She looked at him for a moment – 'That'd be great,' she said. 'What did I do to deserve it?' – and then looked away, out across the courts, as though there was something or somebody she was expecting over there amongst the dusty cypress trees.

'Get a move on Angel,' Sweetfield urged his wife. 'Can't hang about all day.'

Mrs Sweetfield was sitting on the other side of Harding. She patted his arm and said, in an unconvincing attempt at an American accent, 'Come on, pardner, this is the decider,' and began to stand.

That was the moment when the explosion occurred, the precise moment. All the rest, the tennis and football and swimming at the YMCA, the police patrols, the army patrols, the ordinary business of the city, the buying and the selling, the lying and the arguing, the laughter and the loving and the hating, all of that was no different from any other day of the week or week of the year. But this moment would be an instant preserved in history, a fly glued into the amber of an official report and a dozen press dispatches and two dozen minutes passed back and forth within the bowels of the British Mandatory Government. Thus are historical moments plucked out of the merely contingent. Angela Sweetfield stands halfway out of her chair with her hand on Andrew Harding's arm. Rachel Simson is looking at her watch, a plain, steel wristwatch whose only concession to femininity is its small size. Dennis Killin is, inevitably, serving Emily with a drink and wishing that he could serve her with something else. And Gilbert Sweetfield is looking round on the off-chance that someone of importance may be walking through the gardens. The moment is five-thirty in the afternoon of Saturday 4th May 1946.

The explosion was a sharp concussion on the air, a flat sound from somewhere in the south of the city. Windows rattled in the building at their backs and the report echoed round the hills before dying away into the ordinary sounds of the afternoon. That was all.

'What the devil—?' said Sweetfield, looking round as though someone there was to blame.

'What have the silly buggers done now?' Dennis asked, and then apologised for his language.

Rachel closed her eyes momentarily as though against the glare.

Angela Sweetfield sat back in her chair, saying, 'Oh dear.'

A tennis match on a neighbouring court paused for a moment with the server's hand outstretched. He let the ball fall to the ground, caught it at the first bounce, then prepared to toss it up again. 'Sorry about that,' he called to his opponent, as though somehow the explosion had been his fault. Beyond the trees the football match suffered a momentary hiccup before someone shouted 'Play on!' and the battle continued unabated.

Harding smiled round at the women on either side of him. 'I'm afraid I'll have to make a telephone call,' he said. 'Won't be a tick.'

'I'll come too,' said Rachel.

Everything in the grounds of the YMCA had returned precisely to the state of two minutes before, except for the couple now walking up the steps to the building. Nothing had happened. Life, not history, continued. Angela looked across the empty chairs to her husband. 'I can't for the life of me think why the Claims Commission should be interested in a bomb going off, can you? Claims Commission doesn't sound very important, does it?'

Gilbert sighed, as though such things ought to have been obvious. 'He's with security, my dear. GSI.'

'Sounds very grand. And what about her?'

He frowned. His lips were pinched in disapproval. 'Some kind of reporter, I believe.'

Rachel hurried to catch Harding up as he left the YMCA after telephoning. 'Can you give me a lift?'

'A lift where?'

'To wherever it is that the Claims Commission has to go . . . Where is it anyway?'

'The railway station.'

'Can you?'

'If you promise . . .'

'Promise what?'

'To be a school teacher.'

152

'I'll promise anything. I'll just go and get my things. Give me a second.'

The railway station was near the German Colony. By the time Harding and Rachel got there a crowd had gathered on the edge of the station forecourt and soldiers from Allenby Barracks were keeping them back. The crowd was mixed, Arab and Jew together in glum witness of the blast, wondering what it meant and what it would mean. A corporal let Harding through the line, but tried to hold Rachel back.

'Press,' she called, waving a card and pushing past. She hurried to catch Harding up.

'You've just broken your promise,' he accused her, but she seemed unrepentant.

'The press has a reputation to keep up.'

Inside the ticket hall was a mess of broken wood and shards of glass. Dust still hung in the air, brightly lit by shafts of sunlight. Some soldiers were picking through the rubble and a sergeant was advising them that if they cut their fingers their mummies would be cross with them. A photographer was setting up his camera on a tripod so that it pointed directly towards what had once been a ticket office. The wall just below the window had a ragged hole blown through it and in the office beyond, now exposed cruelly to public view, an Arab railway official was clambering over broken furniture trying to rescue papers. His Jewish counterpart just stood, staring miserably at the wreckage. There was an inspector of police and an army captain in charge and a coming and going of people on nameless and probably contradictory errands.

'Doesn't look too bad,' Harding said to the inspector.

The policeman glanced round and looked the two of them up and down as though that was what he had been trained to do. 'Who's the lady?'

'Rachel's a teacher. We were at a tennis party.'

'So it seems. Who the devil let her through?'

'She jumped the net.'

'Very funny.' The policeman had a strong Yorkshire accent. He sniffed at the dust and pointed over to the hole in the wall where limestone blocks showed through the plaster like teeth in a gum. 'It were over there. A couple of pounds of plastic. Of course most of the blast went outwards into the hall otherwise structural damage would have been much greater. Just wait till they learn how to focus the blast.'

'Most of them already have,' Harding said. 'We trained them.'

'Anyway, it's a bloody nuisance because that bloody Committee is due here any day now. We'll have to get it cleared up double quick.'

'Presumably that's why they did it.'

A car drew up outside and there was a shouting of orders. Harding said, 'I heard there were no casualties. That right?'

'Twenty minutes' warning.'

'Where?'

'*Palestine Post*. Agronsky got through to us straight away and we got everybody out in time.'

'The voice?'

'English, unaccented.'

'That's not difficult for them, is it?'

'Bloody traitors, half of them.'

A fresh-faced ADC approached, stepping delicately over the rubble. He saw Harding and snapped off a salute in the indefinably arrogant manner that all ADCs have, which largely comes from wielding power by proxy, but also from the more or less certain knowledge that one day they themselves will be senior officers and have their own scurrying ADCs. Towards Rachel he raised his eyebrows in a mixture of curiosity and appreciation, and inclined his head in a graceful bow. 'Major Harding, sir? The general would like a word with you.'

'The general?'

'Outside, sir.'

'Already?' He turned to Rachel. 'For God's sake keep out of sight. And this time *do* it.'

In the station forecourt the general stood with an escort of officers beside his staff car. The Union Jack drooped sadly from a little flag-staff on the car's wing. The general smiled faintly as Harding approached. 'Did you win, Harding?' he asked.

'I think we've all lost on this one, sir.'

'For the moment, Harding, just for the moment. What do you know about it?'

'Not a lot, sir. I've only just got here.'

'And a very dashing figure you cut, I must say. Just give me your impressions, that's all. I won't hold you responsible.'

Harding looked round helplessly. 'Well, sir . . . Jewish, of course. I'd say Irgun. There was a warning, you see. Lehi wouldn't have bothered with a warning.'

'Lehi?'

One of the aides leant forward. 'Stern Gang, sir.'

'Then why doesn't he *say* Stern Gang?'

'Don't know, I'm afraid, sir.'

'"Lehi" is the correct title, sir,' Harding explained.

'Don't see much correct about them. Why should they have a correct form of address, eh?'

'Quite, sir.'

'And had we been expecting anything of this kind, Major? Hasn't security been stepped up, what with that damned Anglo-American Committee on its way?'

'Of course, sir. There's been a warning out for a week or so now. There have also been straws in the wind. If you remember at the last intelligence briefing . . .'

'Something about a truce?'

'While the Committee is here. But that's the Jewish Agency line, and naturally the Irgun doesn't go along with it. It's inevitable that they try something.'

'This?' The general gestured towards the litter in the station and the working party clearing the mess up.

'I imagine this is just a foretaste, sir.'

The general grunted. 'And there's that bloody ship waiting in the wings, isn't there? Well, I daresay you'll be submitting a report.'

Harding began to protest. 'Surely the police department . . .'

'On the overall security implications, I mean. To the next meeting.'

'Certainly, sir.'

'Very good. Well, good day to you, and' – the man smiled – 'I hope the tennis isn't finished. I notice you brought your partner with you. Charming.'

Harding stood there in his absurd tennis whites and watched the general's party make its way through the arches into the station building. The general himself saluted Rachel as he passed. In the station forecourt, beyond the line of soldiers, the crowd had thinned out. Only a group of pressmen demanded to be let through. 'All in good time, gentlemen, all in good time,' a young officer was saying. 'When the general's finished his inspection.'

'Damn the goddam general,' said an American voice. 'We've got to file copy. We've got deadlines to meet. And how come *she's* here already?' he added, pointing. 'What's *The Philadelphia Inquirer* got that the *Christian Science Monitor* doesn't have? No, don't say it. I already know.'

Harding hurried over to the car. Rachel ran after him, delighted with her little triumph. 'You have to take me to the Public

Information Office,' she insisted. 'It's only a few minutes away. You have to. I've got to get a cable off. Don't you see, I've got a head's start on the lot of them?'

Reluctantly he dropped her at the Information Office and waited outside until she emerged. 'Done,' she announced with a grin. 'UPI, an hour ahead of anyone else. Victory for Rachel Simson.'

They went with Killin and Emily to the Regence that evening. Of course Killin knew the head waiter and got a table in the right place, just beside the dance floor, along with a bottle of champagne on the house. Shadowy and smokey, buried beneath the south wing of the King David, the Regence was the place you went to if you had something to celebrate and a bit of money to celebrate with. Rachel's small success was the excuse.

'To the newshound and her scoop!' Killin cried, raising his glass.

The floor show involved a fire-eater – 'strong case of halitosis,' said Killin – and a girl who wore a top hat and tails and black stockings, and sang 'Falling in Love Again' in a tubercular *mittel*-European accent. But for all the singer's efforts to turn the place into a pre-war German cabaret, she couldn't make it anything other than what it was – a simulacrum of an English restaurant and bar created in the Holy Land to bring comfort to English hearts.

'They'll be calling for "Lili Marlene" next,' Andrew whispered to Rachel, and of course they did, and the girl sang it three times in three different languages and the audience loved it.

Later, pressed close to each other, he and Rachel shuffled round the exiguous dance floor while the band played 'Body and Soul'. She reached up and whispered in his ear, 'Did I take advantage of you?'

'Rather.' Her smell, whatever it was, a compound of flowers and talc and the rich scent of herself, clouded his mind.

'And am I forgiven?'

'You're forgiven.' But there was something disturbing him, something he couldn't confront while she moved against him like this, her hips against his, her hair against his face. He kissed the soft hollow of her neck, and she turned her face so that their lips met. 'Major Harding,' she whispered, pulling gently away, 'are your intentions—'

'Excuse me!' Someone tapped him on the shoulder. He looked round into the ill-focused gaze of a fellow officer, someone he recognised vaguely.

'What is it?'

'You're Harding, aren't you?' The man's voice was high-pitched, as unsteady as his focus. 'Do you know who you're dancing with, Harding?'

'As a matter of fact, I do—'

'Have you read the putrid tripe she writes in the *Post*? Have you?'

'Fame at last,' Rachel cried.

'She's a bloody Jew-lover, Harding. You're fraternising with the enemy.'

'I'm dancing with a girl, you idiot.'

'You're a bloody traitor, Harding!'

The dancing stumbled to a halt. The music faltered, then picked up again bravely. People nearby looked away while those in the background strained to see. Harding released Rachel and turned to face the man. 'Don't be a silly fool—'

'Fool, am I?' The man stepped back, drew back his fist and swung it wildly at Harding's head. A woman gave a little cry and someone said, 'Oh, too bad!' There was a confused struggle between the two men in the centre of the exiguous dance floor and in the middle of the struggle Harding hit his assailant, once, just below the chest.

The dance floor emptied as the man sank to the floor. Rachel was laughing and crying at the same time, suddenly no longer the hard-bitten journalist but an upset girl. Harding put his arm round her shoulder and led her towards their table. His assailant was rolling on the floor gasping like a stranded fish. Friends went to his assistance. There was a confusion of waiters and guests, apologies and recriminations.

'I think it might be time to leave,' Killin suggested grandly. They gathered up their things and made their way up into the lobby of the hotel, where peace and good manners reigned, where the Nubian stewards stood still as statues, and where an assistant manager caught up with them and tried to offer apologies. 'You may present our bill to the lout who ruined our evening,' Killin replied, with magnificent indignation. As they went out into the night air he drew in a deep breath. 'I feel another verse of the Mandate Blues upon me,' he said.

'I'm sorry,' Rachel said miserably. 'Evening ruined. Again.'

Killin and Emily went on somewhere else, but Rachel wanted to go back to her hostel. She seemed unsettled by the incident, jumping from one thing to another, from recrimination to belligerence. 'I feel so dumb,' she kept saying, 'So goddam stupid.'

'Why on earth?'

'For being upset, for not laughing at the guy. Christ, who needed to cry?'

'You didn't cry.'

'Well maybe I *wept*,' she said with heavy sarcasm. 'But you see what kind of people you've got here, don't you? You realise? What bastards?'

The hostel was in East Jerusalem, Arab Jerusalem where the Anglican Cathedral and Sheik Jarrah Mosque rubbed uneasy shoulders. At the end of the street the ground sloped steeply down towards Wadi El-Joz. They stood on the pavement outside the front door, bathed in the feeble light from a lamp overhead. She held his hand and turned it this way and that as though to catch the light and find out what damage had been done to it.

'He was drunk,' Harding said, almost as though trying to justify the man's behaviour.

'That's when people get to tell the truth.' She reached up and kissed him lightly on the cheek, a gesture that was almost filial. 'I'd best go,' she said. 'I'm sorry. About everything.' But as she moved away he held her wrist.

'Wait a moment,' he said.

She paused, frowning, looking at her wrist and the hand that held it just a fraction too hard. 'What's the matter?'

'You knew about the bomb, didn't you?' he said.

'Don't be stupid'

But he persisted. 'How did you know about the bomb, Rachel? You knew, didn't you? You were waiting for it.'

'Let me go,' she complained. 'You're hurting me.'

He released her wrist. She stood there in front of him, looking up at him in the lamplight. Her expression was hard to read, a blend of defiance and resignation. 'Okay, I knew. I knew that *something* was going to happen, sure. Nothing specific.' She shrugged her shoulders. 'Hell, it's part of the job.'

'People might have been killed.'

'But they weren't. There was a warning and they weren't.' There was a sudden bright anger. 'What did *you* do in the war, Andrew? Didn't you set off bombs or something, blow things to pieces? Airplanes, trucks, I don't know . . . people. You justified it by the fact that you believed in your cause. That's all it is. Neither more nor less admirable. The other side always sees things differently.'

The building loomed silent above them. 'Since when has personal perspective been the basis for a moral judgement?' he asked.

'Christ, we're not going to get into an ethical argument, are we?'

'Well we're in some kind of argument. You can't just assume that all points of view are equal.'

'I don't.' Her face was hard, suddenly rather plain and aggressive. 'I'm afraid I just assume that the British one is wrong.' And she turned away from him and went inside.

★

Dear Lorna,

Today a bomb attack at the railway station. You'll have read about it in the papers. This country is barmy (balmy?) – during the war it was one of the few places you could go to find peace – no blackout, cafés open all hours, lots of things off the ration, all kinds of stuff – and now that peace has broken out almost everywhere else, fighting has begun here. It really isn't open war yet but with all the troops there are here and the various private armies and the fanatics amongst the Jews, it's difficult to see how it won't end up as one. Otherwise it's the usual tedious round of tennis parties, bridge parties, dinner parties . . .

2

'A grandstand view for the Day of Judgement,' Gilbert Sweetfield said. The Sweetfields lived near the American Colony, not far from Rachel's hostel. Their apartment overlooked Wadi El-Joz, the Kidron Valley, and from the roof of the building you got the full view: the walls of the Old City on the right and the Mount of Olives climbing up out of the valley on the left. In the shadows at the bottom of the valley dark trees marked the Garden of Gethsemane. The setting sun painted the summit of the Mount of Olives and the Hills of Moab with rose and peach.

'Isn't it just amazing?' Rachel murmured.

'The Muslim belief is that the last judgement will take place here. The angel of death, Israfil' – Sweetfield's accent was elaborate and, one presumed, impeccable – 'will blow his ram's horn three times and a bridge will be suspended over the valley from the Mount of Olives to the point of the Haram-es-Sharif for the souls to walk across.' With his finger he drew a line in the fading light. 'The bridge will be narrower than a hair, sharper than a sword and darker than night, and at every one of its seven arches the soul will be asked to account for its actions during its life.' He paused and coughed faintly. It may have been a laugh. 'An *uncomfortable* crossing, one would imagine.'

They went down the narrow stairs from the roof. Sweetfield had seemed surprised to find them there at all, affecting to have no more than the vaguest recollection of the tennis party – 'Not my game, old fellow, not my game' – and not really understanding why someone from the military had been invited to dinner, a mere Major, for heaven's sake. And an American reporter. But he knew about the fracas at the Regence all right. 'I understand you've been in a spot of bother, old fellow? Most unfortunate.'

160

'Oliphant was drunk, and really quite offensive.'

'Oh quite. Quite. Unfortunate that British officers should brawl in public, though. Now do come and meet the others.'

In the sitting room there were carpets from Afghanistan and Turkey, brasses from Persia and Syria, oddments and artifacts from the whole of the Middle East. The metal gleamed flatly in the shadows. The bookshelves had works in Arabic and French as well as English. There was *The Arab Awakening* by George Antinous and *The Heart of Arabia* by Philby. A signed copy of Ronald Storrs' *Orientations* lay discreetly open on a low table.

'It's all the stuff Gilbert has collected over the years, you know,' Angela Sweetfield explained. 'Tehran, Baghdad, Beirut, Cairo. He does have an eye for things, doesn't he?' She took Rachel by the arm and led the two of them over to where the other guests were assembled in front of a large, impressionistic painting of the Treasury of Petra. They were inhabitants of a world set far apart from the military and the minor colonial – an Arab civil servant and his wife, a businessman from Beirut whose companion may have been his daughter but turned out to be his mistress, and an economist of some kind from London University. The Arabs displayed that sleek urbanity, that elegant and studied sophistication which characterised the upper-class of the city. The tides of the Levant – French and Greek as well as Arab – flowed in their veins. The women were dark and vivacious, vivid in gold and silk; beside them Rachel seemed brash and hopeful.

'No Jews,' she whispered to Harding.

There was something dangerous about her, something subversive that he couldn't quite define. Lorna would have been at ease here, would have flattered the Arab men and found tastes in common with their women, would have discussed Fleet Street with the editor – she had a cousin on the *Times* – and economics with the LSE man without ever having to claim more than common sense as a qualification. Rachel, it transpired, had majored in political science, whatever that was, and got herself deep into an argument with both of them.

'The trouble is, you guys don't see the morality of it. You don't see what has *happened* to the Jews. And you don't look to the future. The British want friends in the Middle East, they can't ignore the Jews. Arabs and Jews both need a place. Support partition and you gain yourselves real allies for the future—'

Sweetfield was at his most urbane, pouring the wine, signalling for the servant to change the plates, smiling sympathetically at the guests when Rachel's voice cut sharp across the conversation. 'I think perhaps you are being somewhat obtuse, young lady,' he told her at one point. 'As far as HMG is concerned it is precisely the future that gives cause for concern, and that the future is now the Soviet bloc, not the Nazis and their treatment of the Jews.' He coughed faintly. 'However deplorable that may have been. I think that may well be the view of the American government too. When the stakes are down.'

'Did you say *deplorable*?' Rachel cried. Harding closed his eyes. 'Why, you make it sound like the Nazis just broke wind in public. They didn't commit some solecism, Mr Sweetfield, they *massacred* six *million* Jews.'

Sweetfield glared at his wife, as though to admonish her for inviting this awkward guest. 'Not Jews alone, my dear. The Jews weren't the only ones to suffer. Slavs, gypsies, all kinds of people. Do you think we should also take in the gypsies here in Palestine? No, I am afraid that Europe's problems are for Europe to solve. How can Palestine be expected to bear the burden?'

'And, my dear, just look at the way they're trying to get into the country,' the businessman added wearily. He might have been talking of gatecrashers trying to get into an exclusive party. 'All these dreadful refugee boats. So sordid. Why should a small country like ours be expected to receive what's left of European Jewry?'

'Perhaps because they *are* all that's left,' Rachel retorted. 'The United States won't let them in. Britain won't let them in, nobody will let them in. Where else do they go?'

'I believe there's another one of those boats preparing to sail,' someone remarked.

'Why can't they remake their lives in their own countries?'

'*Remake* their lives?' She was shrill with indignation. 'Do you know what's happening in Poland still? Have you read about it? The *Manchester Guardian* estimates that over three hundred and fifty survivors of the camps have been murdered since the war. Polish Jews, survivors of the camps, being killed by Poles *now*.'

'You mustn't believe everything you read in the papers, my dear,' said Sweetfield with a smile.

'Oh, for God's sake . . .' Rachel looked desperately round the table for help. 'Maybe Andrew can explain why they can't rebuild their lives in Europe. He was at Belsen when it was liberated. Did you know that?'

The name brought a silence. One of the women began to talk about a place she had found in the Old City which sold beautiful silks. Angela turned in her chair and called the servant to bring the coffee. The newspaper man asked, 'Are you by any chance Jewish, young lady?'

'Rachel is Episcopalian,' said Angela hastily. 'She just feels passionately about things, don't you my dear? Isn't that the prerogative of the young? And this is a city for passions, isn't it? If you see what I mean. Goodness, was that a play on words?' She rose from her chair and displayed her teeth to the ladies. 'Now perhaps we can leave the gentlemen to their discussion . . .'

The other women left the table; the men half-rising to bow them away. Rachel looked startled. 'What's this, off to the hareem?'

No one laughed. Angela took the girl's arm. 'Shall we, my dear?' The talk about silk had spread and deepened: 'It comes from Cyprus, much of it,' someone said in knowing tones, 'although the best is Syrian. Now this dress . . .'

Grimly Rachel accompanied her hostess out of the room, while Sweetfield fiddled with a bottle of port and glanced up at the male guests with a smirk of condescension.

'Transatlantic enthusiasms can get a little out of hand,' he murmured.

They left the party soon after, walking through the empty streets to the hostel. A cool moon lit their way. 'What do you think?' she asked him.

'About what?'

'Our hosts and their society.'

'Thought you were pretty outspoken.'

'Does that mean rude?'

He shrugged. 'What did you hope to gain by antagonising them?'

'I wanted to stir up their damned complacency. And you've evaded the question.'

He laughed, not knowing how to take her, not grasping the motions of her American mind. 'I think the economist fellow took a fancy to you, you know that? He might not have approved of your politics, but he couldn't take his eyes off you.'

'You think I give a damn about that?'

'I think he has good taste.'

'They talked about the immigrants. The ships . . .'

'Everyone talks about them these days.'

'What do you think about them?'

'I think it's bloody difficult to know what to do.'

'But you've got to do something.'

'*I* have?'

'*One* has. Everyone has.' There was a silence. She had something more to say, he could tell that, something towards which she had been manoeuvring the conversation. They turned a corner into the street where the hostel stood in the shadows, its door shut, the brass name plaque gleaming dully in the light from over the door. 'You could, couldn't you?' she said. 'Your work . . .'

'What do you know about my work?'

'Someone I met. Hell, I meet a whole lot of people. And one of them said that you were involved. Security, or something. I mean, it obviously isn't the Claims Commission or whatever you pretend. Look at that business at the station.'

'So what?'

She pulled the handle beside the main door. A bell sounded somewhere inside. 'So this man thought you might be able to help.'

'Why did he think that?'

The door opened and an Arab face peered out at them through the crack. 'Suhail,' she said apologetically. 'Am I late again? Look, I'm sorry.'

The man grinned. He had uneven, blackened teeth. 'You are American, madame. American's are always on time.'

'Can you just wait one more moment?'

'Of course I can, madame.' The porter disappeared, leaving the door ajar. She turned back to Harding. 'He thought you could help because you were at one of the camps. Because you can understand better than others.'

'And what does this man think I can do?'

'That's what he'd like to talk about. Will you meet him? Just as a favour?'

'So that's it.'

She grinned at him. 'Will you?'

'A bloody plot.'

She raised herself on tiptoe and kissed him on the cheek. 'How about tomorrow afternoon? We can maybe go down to the coast. How about that?'

'And meet this man?'

She nodded. 'And meet this man. Pick me up here. You'll do that? Say, two thirty.' Her expression was bright and ironical, as though laughing at him, as though laughing at herself for her devious little plot.

'You've already arranged it,' he accused her.

'Sure,' she said, pushing the door open. 'Sure I've arranged it. Bring your swimming things.' And then, lithe and elusive, she had slipped through into the building.

3

The general gazed thoughtfully out of the window, across the Valley of Hinnom towards the Old City.

'The ship was originally called *Stella Maris*,' Harding was saying, 'but they've renamed her *Shali'ah*. She's around five hundred tons displacement, so at their current levels of loading they've probably got something over five hundred people on board. It's hardly Board of Trade but they seem to be reckoning one passenger per ton these days.' He slipped his report back in its folder and looked up at the general's back. 'Poles mainly, many of them from Belsen. They were driven there from the East in the last days.'

Did the general react? Did the name send a chill up his spine and make the hair crawl on his scalp? Harding could see only the vague reflection of his face in the window. The general had been at Belsen as well. It had been his men who had liberated the place. He had been there and had seen the mass graves, and it seemed not to have made much impression. 'When you've seen two world wars,' he was fond of saying, 'it's hard to shock you.'

'So where we go from here, Major?' he asked.

Harding shrugged. 'She left La Spezia yesterday. Give her a week. We're trying to find out what their plans are, but there's no information around, nothing better than rumour at any rate. The Jews are frightfully well-organised in that way. As tight as clams. As you know, sir.'

The general nodded, as though the view outside the windows had just confirmed his worst suspicions. 'What you appear to be saying is that we just sit and wait.'

'That's more or less the picture, sir. Of course the Air Force is mounting round-the-clock patrols, but the weather is right against them at the moment and the ship appears to be keeping strict radio silence. They're becoming very professional.'

The general snorted. 'First the station bombing and then this. They're saving it up for the visit of the damned Anglo-American Committee, aren't they? Professional! They're a bunch of schemers and they're saving it all up for when the nosey-parkers are here, and then they can spread egg all over our faces. You'll have to make a report to the Security Committee, you know that. You'll have to give them something.'

'Of course, sir. Whatever we know.' There was a silence. The general stood motionless, staring out of the window, his hands clasped behind his back. 'Will that be all, sir?' Harding asked.

The question was ignored. 'Lovely country, bloody people, that's what I always say, Andrew. Good enough if you're single – polo, bit of duck shooting, that kind of thing' – he looked round with a bright smile – 'but it can be difficult for a married man, can't it?'

'We've all of us got used to it over the years.'

'But you'd like to get back home? To the wife and daughter?'

There was a silence in the office. The clacking of a typewriter sounded through the wall from the room next door. Somewhere a filing cabinet slammed shut. 'I'm quite happy for the moment,' Harding replied evasively.

The general stroked his moustache. He came over and perched on the corner of the desk, arms folded to show that all this was just an informal chat, between comrades-in-arms. 'You've got a distinguished war record, Andrew, most distinguished. And you're one of my best staff officers. You know that?'

'Thank you, sir.'

'No thanks to me. The merit's yours. You were damned useful in Germany and you're damned useful here, for what it's worth. It's difficult when it all comes to an end, isn't it? Difficult just to go back home and put your slippers on.'

'Sounds dreadful to me.'

'And yet that's what we were all looking forward to, wasn't it?'

'I suppose it was, sir.'

'Land fit for heroes and all that tripe.'

'Yes, sir.'

The general nodded benignly. 'I heard about the fracas at the Regence the other evening. Not good, that kind of thing. Striking a brother officer.'

Harding bridled. 'It was entirely Oliphant's fault. He swung a punch at me—'

166

'Oh quite, quite.' The general's hands dampened down flames in front of him. 'Bloody fool anyway, and had a little too much to drink as well. Still, it's not too wise to go brawling in front of a bunch of civilians, is it? Jews and Arabs and Lord knows what, all watching two members of the ruling race clouting one another? Not very seemly. Charges could be laid against the pair of you, you know, although there'd be nothing to gain as I see it.'

'I really had little option, sir.'

The general nodded. 'But discipline is important at times like this, isn't it? Everyone cooped up behind barbed wire, bombs going off, kidnappings, all that kind of thing. Not good for morale.'

'No, sir.'

'Not what an army's for, of course, keeping the peace in this way, never knowing who to call your friend. But someone's got to keep the beggars apart. Gather the whole thing was over a girl, that right?'

'Not in the usual sense, sir. Not jealousy or anything. He insulted my guest and when I argued he swung a punch at me. At least he tried to.'

The general nodded. 'And you swung one back. Rather more efficiently.'

'That's about it.'

'Was it the tennis lady, by any chance? Journalist, isn't she? American, I understand. Friend of Agronsky's.'

'An employee of Agronsky's, sir. She's got a column on the *Post*. Writes for various press agencies as well.'

'Is she the kind of person who ought to be the friend of a British Officer?'

'I don't see why not. She's perfectly legal, earning an honest living—'

'Is that what journalists do? I never realised.' The general chuckled at his joke. 'Not a Jew, is she?'

'No sir. Episcopalian as a matter of fact.'

There was a sensation of relief. 'That's all right, then. Almost Church of England, isn't it?' The general nodded thoughtfully, then seemed to come to some kind of decision. 'I'm posting Oliphant away, Andrew. You're too valuable to me, so it had to be him. Anyway, I've heard that he's been mixed up in something none too pretty. You heard that?'

'Something, sir.'

'British League, or something. Political. Probably a load of rubbish, but there you are. I hope it doesn't create bad blood

167

between you, but I have no choice really.' The man grunted. 'That's it,' he said. 'That's all I wanted to say.'

It had been raining earlier but as Harding left the King David the cloud was beginning to break and a thin sunshine was coming through. He drove the Riley round to the hostel and there was Rachel waiting for him on the pavement outside, wearing a white blouse and a divided skirt and leather sandals with some kind of oriental design on them, the kind you bought in the *suks* in the Old City. She called out 'Hi there!' and climbed into the car and reached across to give him a swift kiss, then looked at him in that direct way she had, with a bright smile and a faint air of challenge. 'Are you still game?'

'Don't be silly.' A very English word, silly. He felt very English with her in the car beside him. She was bright and sharp, something new from the New World, something naïve and dangerous. 'So where are we going?' he asked.

'Down to the coast. Towards Netanya.'

'And then?'

She laughed. 'That'll do for now.' They might have been going on a treasure hunt or something, an adolescent game. That's how she seemed to treat it: a game.

They drove out along the Jaffa Road, past the public market in Mehane Yehuda and the Arab quarter of Romema, out onto the uplands of Judaea, as bare as bone. He watched her out of the corner of his eye. 'The Old Man gave me a dressing-down about the fiasco at the Regence.'

She laughed. 'Like being called before the college dean, was it?'

'The other fellow's being posted home.'

'I guess he's the lucky one.'

'I was almost offered the choice.'

She fell silent, as though trying to work out the significance of that.

'But you didn't bite?'

'No.' They drove down through the limestone gorge that gave access to the coastal plain, the Plain of Sharon which was, he explained to break the silence, a tautology, *sharon* meaning plain in Hebrew. The Plain of Plain, then. The road passed the monastery at Latrun and the barbed wire and Nissen huts of the detention camp, and she lit a cigarette and opened the window to blow the smoke out. He glanced at her, and contemplated . . . what? Duty? Betrayal? Escape? Where, he wondered, did loyalty lie?

168

Lydda, Petah Tiqwa. Dark green citrus groves ran by on either side of the road. There were men and women at work between the trees, spraying insecticide or something. The sun was out now, the sun which stirred the orange blossom, nurtured the fruit, brought the people out to the fields and the beaches, exposed refugee ships to the eyes of searching aircraft. Rachel Simson smoked and looked out at the view. In the few weeks he had known her she seemed to have grown up, not physically of course but mentally: grown in confidence in the way that men in the desert war had grown in confidence once they had seen action. 'I hope to God you know what you're doing,' he said, and she shrugged and said nothing.

They drove along the coast road beyond the town of Netanya, past the occasional Arab village and small clusters of pre-fabs that were the settlements of the Jews. Orange groves stretched back into the hills. Occasionally they glimpsed the sea glittering in the brilliant sunshine beyond the dunes to the left. He turned off the road where she told him to, at a beach restaurant called the Dolphin, a tawdry place of blistered concrete and rusted iron which claimed MOST SPECIAL FISH MEAL SINCE HAIFA. The forecourt of the place was deserted. The sign was faded and battered and there were no customers to challenge its boast.

'Is this it?'

'This is it.'

Somehow it reminded Harding of the places on the south coast of England. There was the same atmosphere of desolation, the same withering salt air, the same background sound of the sea, the same sense of impermanence.

'Where is he?'

'He'll come.'

They climbed out of the car and went in through the glass doors. The owner greeted them in Hebrew as they approached the bar, then scowled when he realised his mistake. 'English?'

'American,' Rachel said quickly.

'American is better. You are press?' His accent was heavily German. One wondered, as one always wondered, what his story was, how he had escaped. 'What do you know of the Committee?' he asked. 'Will they support us or will they support the British?'

Harding made some anodyne reply, something about honest brokers, a concept which evoked a bitter laugh. 'Who is ever honest about Eretz Yisra'el?' the man asked.

They ordered two beers and took the drinks out onto the terrace where a few metal tables and chairs rusted in the salt wind.

The sea boomed along the beach, dragging its claws in the sand as it retreated, as though desperate not to let go. The colour of the water was of an indeterminate grey-blue, neither one thing nor the other: neither quite the sour grey of the English Channel, nor the brilliant azure of the Mediterranean in summer. It was almost as though it was caught in between the seasons, uncertain which way to jump. 'The ship is out there someplace,' she said.

He shrugged. He had almost forgotten. He was almost a man with a girl, out sight-seeing. Almost. 'There's a lot of coastline.'

'Can't you feel its presence? Like the Flying Dutchman.' She shivered at the idea. 'A thousand lost souls.'

'Is that what you'll write? Actually it's five hundred.'

'You've got a literal mind.' She was silent for a while, watching droplets of condensation run down the outside of her glass. 'And if they catch them they'll pack them off to some detention camp in Cyprus, and they'll be behind barbed wire again, just like at Belsen.'

'Do we have to talk about it again?'

'Why can't they just let them be? Why do they have to spend so much energy keeping them out of their own home?'

'They have obligations to the people who live here.'

'And who has obligations to the Jews?' She turned to him. 'In Christ's name, these people have just come out of the concentration camps, Andrew. You've seen them there. You've *seen* them. Their whole population has been decimated. Do you know the meaning of that word, decimated? Do you?'

'Yes, I do—'

'It used to mean to kill one tenth. *One-tenth*. Well Adolf Hitler and the Nazis have turned the word right on its head. They murdered *nine-tenths* and left one-tenth *alive*. They've not only destroyed a culture, they've re-written the fucking dictionary!' Her eyes were glistening, like a child's fighting tears.

'I know,' he said. 'I know all that, we all know all that. That's the whole problem.'

'So why don't you do something about it?'

'That's why I'm here, for God's sake. To try and do something about it.'

They were silent. The wind battered about them and they were silent up there on the bare terrace, alone with anger and suspicion, and something more, a faint stir of fear.

'Look,' she said suddenly, 'I'm sorry. Okay? I was talking like a spoiled kid and now I'm eating crow.'

'You're doing *what*?'

170

She smiled. 'Don't the English say that? I'm apologising, humbling myself, saying, can we please be friends again? I know you don't want a lecture from a brash Yank. Okay, I'll go along with that. You were there at Belsen. Okay. So, back to first base and pretend it never happened. There's another Americanism. Christ, you make me feel as though I don't really speak English at all. Can we do that? Just forget it? I'm nervous, see? I'm nervous and when I get nervous I shoot my mouth off.' She looked round at the empty terrace and the windows of the deserted restaurant. 'Christ, where *is* this guy? Where's he got to?'

He came a few minutes later. There was the sound of a motorbike in the forecourt, and then they could see a figure coming through the restaurant towards the windows which gave onto the terrace. He was a young man with cropped hair and a nondescript face, the kind of face you might see behind a desk in a government office. He wore a moustache, perhaps to make himself look older. He came through onto the terrace and nodded at Rachel and held his hand out to Harding. 'My name is Ben-Oz,' he announced.

Harding had a sudden sense of the absurd. 'Sounds like a wizard.'

The man frowned. 'Sorry?'

'It doesn't matter.'

Ben-Oz shrugged. 'My name, you mean? It means Son of Strength. May I sit? I must apologise for being late. There is a roadblock.' His English was excellent, but tainted by some accent, Polish maybe.

'There was no roadblock when we came along.'

'They put them up without warning. Maybe you haven't noticed.' His voice was laden with sarcasm. 'I was suspicious when I saw it. Suspicious of you, I mean. May I see your identity card, please?'

Harding handed it over.

'Of course it could be forged.'

'Why should it be forged?'

'Maybe you are a policeman.' Rachel opened her mouth to speak and Ben-Oz grinned suddenly. 'A joke,' he said. 'A joke.' He gave the card back. 'Now, can we get down to business? I understand that you know about our ship?'

'The *Shali'ah*.'

'Exactly. It carries one thousand refugees—'

'One thousand?' Harding glanced at Rachel.

'One thousand, more or less. You are surprised?'

'That's two passengers per ton.'

'Well done, Mr Harding. It is two passengers per ton, more or less.' Ben-Oz gave the impression that he was pleased with the phrase. 'More or less,' he repeated. 'You see, we are desperate, Mr Harding. These people have been taken to the gates of hell, and then snatched back at the last minute. We are desperate, they are desperate. The British would try to send them back to where they've come from, can you imagine that?' The man shook his head, as though he couldn't either. 'What no one seems to understand, Mr Harding, is that Adolf Hitler has won. Does that surprise you? You thought you were the victors, didn't you? Well, you're wrong. Adolf Hitler is the victor. He has destroyed a whole people. European Jewry is no more. There is no place for these people anywhere in the world but here in the land of Israel.'

There was an awkward silence, almost as though Ben-Oz had suddenly realised that he was delivering his lecture to the wrong audience. 'And we need your help,' he said quietly. 'Nothing more. We can pay you, if that is what you want, but I do not think you are the kind of man who would take bribes. The trouble is, I don't know what kind of man you *are*. We have a term in Hebrew: *hasidei umot ha'olam*, the righteous of the nations. Maybe you are one of those?'

Harding said angrily, 'For God's sake don't put a moral interpretation on it.'

'Andrew just wants to help,' Rachel added.

Ben-Oz smiled. His lips were thin and colourless. 'My mission is twofold,' he said portentously. 'It is to create a Jewish state, and to create a Jewish proletariat. What is your mission, Mister Harding?'

'I don't think I have a mission. Englishmen don't have such things.'

'What about the war against the Nazis.'

'It wasn't a war against the Nazis. It was a war against the Germans, the usual bloody European war. It just got out of hand. Everything else – the Japanese, the concentration camps, the atom bomb – all that kind of thing was just an aberration.'

'That is what you think?'

'It's what my people think. It's what the British government thinks. That's why they don't seem to be able to make up their minds what to do here. They can only see Palestine as a bit of the Empire that's giving trouble.'

'The British can't see beyond their noses,' Rachel muttered.

'They don't understand the Jews, you see,' Harding said. 'Not outside Golders Green, anyway. They like the Arabs because the English have always had a soft spot for the exotic and they think the Arabs are exotic. But the Jews are beyond their comprehension.'

Ben-Oz smiled. 'Are you a Christian, Mister Harding?'

'I suppose so.'

'You suppose so. I am a Jew, plain enough, despite the fact that I am atheist. Yet you *suppose* you are a Christian.'

'Isn't Jewishness race as well as a belief? Isn't that the difference?'

'Is it? There are Arab Jews as well as European ones. Did you know that? Arab and Indian and Ethiopian. What has race got to do with that? And there are Jews who have no religion at all except the survival of their culture and their people. Can you understand that, Mister Harding? Can a Christian appreciate that?'

There was irony in the man's tone. The word *Christian* rang with accusation. Harding was looking at Ben-Oz, but he didn't really see him. Instead he saw Lorna dismissing problems of morality and ethics in weary tones; and heard Rachel's voice, sharp and accusatory, thrusting them in front of him. He thought of the pile of limbs and torsos being bulldozed across the screen of the cinema in Ben Yehuda Street, being bulldozed across the screen of his own memory. He smelt again that stench that had come across the dull German plain one sunny morning last spring, and the vision that had greeted him when he got there, the lines of Jews like shades in Hades, neither weeping, nor moaning, just staring.

'Tell me what you want,' he said.

Ben-Oz smiled. 'We just want to know what you know,' he said. 'About the movements of the *Shali'ah*. Nothing more.'

When Ben-Oz left they waited, as he had instructed, for fifteen minutes before moving. Perhaps he still didn't trust them completely.

'Are you brave enough to swim?' Harding asked as they walked to the car.

'I brought my things.'

They continued north along the coast road. They didn't talk about the meeting, they didn't talk about much really, just the day and the view and the details of the countryside.

Whose idea was it to go to Caesarea? Afterwards he wondered, but at the time it just seemed an obvious choice to turn off the road where a battered sign pointed the way to *Kaisaryie* and a second sign, in both English and Hebrew characters, announced *Sedot Yam*. A dusty track led between eucalyptus trees and prickly pear cacti until it finally opened out in a sandy space where there was a custodian's hut, and beyond it a ditch and then the decayed and overgrown crusader walls of the ancient city. A notice of the Department of Antiquities announced the *Ruins of Caesarea (lst–13th.c.)* but no one seemed particularly interested. The custodian's hut was deserted and locked.

They left the car and went through the remains of the main gate into the ruins. The ground was broken and uneven, as though all the turmoil of the past lay just below the surface. Building stones and bits of marble poked through the skin of earth like bones out of a multiple compound fracture. In the midst of it all, the shell of a church emerged from the scrub. Down by the small harbour a white-washed mosque and a dozen houses had been built amongst the wreckage of the place. Beyond them the breakers thundered against the ruined mole, sending curtains of spray up into the air. The view out to sea was blurred by the Khamseen, the horizon drawn down to no more than a few miles away. Rachel looked disconsolately round at the litter of decay. 'Let's go see the village,' she suggested. 'At least there's some life there.'

As they approached the houses a couple of old women peered suspiciously at them before scuttling away out of sight and leaving a young boy, no more than twelve, to deal with the strangers. He was barefoot and wore a ragged *galabiyah* but he had the air of an important official.

'Christian?' he called.

'Christian,' Rachel agreed.

'You want I guide.' It wasn't a question. He pointed portentously to his left arm where he wore a band with some kind of badge on it. 'Come.' Dutifully they followed him to the edge of the little harbour where granite pillars lay like drowned corpses in the water. The boy climbed onto one of them as though to command his audience's attention. Rachel smiled and held Harding's hand tightly, as though to prevent herself from laughing. A small group of younger children had materialised from the houses to watch the performance.

'Harbour,' said the boy, pointing. His arm swept round in an arc like the barrel of a rifle. 'Rocks, Fort, House-of-Herod, Christian church of Paul. Paul holy Christ. Over there' – he pointed south – 'Theatre-of-Girls. Over there' – the arm swept round and pointed beyond the church and the car park – 'the Horse-Place.'

That seemed to be the limit of his knowledge. The overgrown ruins lay beneath the sky and offered no clue as to whether he was right or not, while the children giggled as though they knew that it was all rubbish.

'Theatre-of-Girls,' said Rachel. 'Imagine *that* in Philadelphia.' She searched in her bag and found some piastres for the boy. 'Thank you very much. *Shukran*.' The boy grabbed the coins; then he reached within the folds of his *galabiyah* and produced a small blackened disc of metal. 'Souvenir?'

'What is it?'

'Herod treasure.'

Rachel and Andrew peered at the thing and saw designs in its worn surface and the vague trace of letters. Was that a crude palm tree on one side, and a head on the other? 'Roman, I expect,' Andrew said. 'But I'm no expert.'

'Bound,' the boy announced.

'*One pound?*'

'Herod treasure,' the boy repeated. The children giggled, as though they knew its real worth.

'Is it real?' she asked Andrew.

'Why shouldn't it be? There must be millions of the things here.'

She turned to the child. 'Five piastres.'

'Bound.'

'Ten piastres.'

'Bound.'

She laughed. 'I thought they were meant to dicker.'

'He's probably learned this technique from the Jews.'

'What's that mean?'

'Herod treasure,' repeated the boy. 'Bound.'

'Fifteen piastres. No more.' As though to emphasise the finality of her decision she turned away and began to walk towards House-of-Herod.

'Herod treasure,' the boy called after her. 'Fifty biastre.'

Rachel turned, searched in her bag and held out some coins. 'Twenty. That's all I've got.' The boy examined the offering. Then he grabbed the piastres and left the little, blackened disc of metal in their place. The bargain, if bargain it was, had been struck.

'Now I show Theatre-of-Girls.'

'There's no more money,' Rachel protested. 'You've taken everything.'

'No more money,' the guide agreed. 'I like Christian.'

And so in procession, led by a barefoot boy in a striped *galabiyah* and trailed by a gaggle of younger children, they made their way over the uneven ground of the ruined city towards Theatre-of-Girls. 'Whatever can it be?' Rachel wondered aloud.

'Theatre-of-Girls,' their guide replied, as though it was self-evident. They reached a bank of overgrown masonry and the boy clambered up a slope of rubble to the top. He turned and beckoned Rachel and Andrew to join him. A few sharp words of Arabic kept the other children at the bottom.

'Behold,' the boy announced solemnly. They stood beside him amidst the rubble of the parapet. A breeze blew in off the sea, carrying with it the smell of salt and weed. Laid out before them, amidst the dunes just inland from a small beach, was the semi-circular bowl of a ruined classical theatre.

'Theatre-of-Girls,' exclaimed Rachel in delight.

'Theatre-of-Girls,' the boy repeated. '*Masrah-el-banat.* Theatre-of-Girls.'

'Why do you call it that?'

The boy shrugged vacantly, perhaps not understanding the question, perhaps because that was just its name, and names were without reason. 'Theatre-of-Girls,' he said again.

'Maybe they used to have dancing girls,' Harding suggested. 'Nautch girls. Salome and all that.'

Beyond the theatre was the fencing of a Jewish settlement. Barbed wire and huts and a watch-tower gave the place the look of an army camp. People in khaki were walking along the paths. There was something relentless about the place, an air of austerity and regimentation which stood in sharp relief to the anarchy of the ruins and the squalor of the Arab houses down by the harbour. A sentry in the tower raised binoculars to watch the figures that had appeared on the ancient crusader walls.

'*Yehud,*' the boy said. He hacked volubly, gathered phlegm into his mouth, and spat into the bushes. '*Yehud,*' he repeated, and then, as though the view was too much to bear, he turned and slid back down the slope to the children at the bottom. Rachel turned to Harding with a bitter little smile. She might have been about to make a comment, but instead she merely shrugged, picked up her bag and scrambled down the far slope towards the theatre.

176

Harding followed her down to the ruins. They passed through a narrow passage-way into the central space, the *orchestra*. Rachel stood on the flat paving at the very focus of the theatre and flung her arms out as though acknowledging the applause of an audience up there on the great curve of seats. 'Theatre-of-Girls!' she cried. 'I should be Salome.' She turned and swept towards him with arms outstretched, before slipping from his grasp and setting off up the tiers of seats, shamelessly hitching up her skirt to climb, calling for him to race her.

'The royal box!' she cried, gaining a platform in the centre of the curve of seats just before he did. 'Herod himself must have sat here while the music played and the girls danced and Herodias whispered wicked things in his ear.'

It was warm and windy on the bare limestone. The sea boomed against the mole of the old harbour and against the small headland in front of the theatre. They stood together hand in hand and looked out across the *orchestra* and the uneven ground where the stage had once been, out across dunes and the waves beyond, out to the blurred horizon, as though perhaps some kind of performance was about to begin far out there. Gulls cried in the wind.

'That ship is out there someplace. Can't you feel its presence?' She was silent for a while. He was conscious of her pressed close against him, the smell of her hair and the live warmth of her body. The hand which clasped his was soft and smooth, like the hand of a child. 'What will you do, Andrew? Will you do what Ben-Oz asked?'

'I don't know. I just don't know.'

'What if the British stop them?'

'You know very well. They'll take them into Haifa probably, and put them in the detention camp at Athlit.'

'It'll be no better than Belsen.'

'That's just bloody stupid, and you know it.'

She was angry, with herself as much as anything. 'Why do they have to keep them out of their own home?'

'Because that little Arab boy has different ideas about whose home it is. Come on, let's go and swim.' He bent and kissed her hair. 'Or aren't you brave enough?'

She laughed, and the mood was broken. 'I'm used to the ocean,' she asserted. 'We used to vacation at Cape May. I'm brave enough for anything.'

They walked down through the low dunes to the beach. There were white blooms of sea daffodil tucked against the marram grass,

177

and on the sand bits of driftwood that had been thrown up by the weather of the last few days. The sea was a patchwork of grey and blue, rimed with foam.

Rachel pulled things from her bag and wrestled with modesty beneath her towel for a moment, then flung the towel aside and ran like a sprinter for the sea. 'Come on!' she cried. The waves rolled towards her in wide, white breakers and their sound drowned her voice so that when she turned and shouted to him he just saw her mouth opened, a black O which may have been calling for him to come, may have been shouting for help. Then she turned and dived into the waves, and the foam broke over her and ran glistening down her back. When she emerged from the water she turned back, laughing and beckoning. 'It's lovely once you're in!' he heard faintly.

He ducked behind a fallen pillar to change and followed her into the sea. The water was cold, the wind was cold, and the sunshine was a pale yellow, a mere colour against the grey of the sea and cloud without any power of warmth. For a while they crashed around in the waves like children and when finally they retreated from the water she was white and shivering.

'You'll catch your death.'

'When you've swum at Cape May you grow used to it.'

'Let me rub you down.'

So she stood still in the sand amongst the flotsam and their scraps of clothing, while he tried to drive some warmth into her. Her hair was plastered to her skull and her shoulders were rough with goose pimples. For all her assertions she was shivering. 'Change out of that costume,' he ordered her. 'I'll hold the towel for you.'

She laughed. 'Theatre-of-Girls? I'm not falling for that one. You look the other way.'

He did as he was told, and when she allowed him to turn she was back in her skirt and blouse; but her hair still hung in wet rats' tails and her lips were still blue. There was something disturbingly moving about the sight, something of the refugee about her, something of the homeless and the destitute. 'You're lovely,' he told her, but, stooping to gather her sodden bathing costume, she denied it.

'Aggressive,' she said. 'Aggressive little American girl with a chip on her shoulder. Come on. We ought to be getting back. You know we never saw the Horse-Place? What could it be?'

'It's the hippodrome. Just an open space. Nothing on Theatre-of-Girls.'

'Another time, maybe.'

'Perhaps.'

So they drove back, past the café called The Dolphin with its battered sign, back towards Latrun and the gorge of Bab el-Wad, and the Holy City.

4

There was a roadblock at Latrun, metal stanchions and coils of barbed wire across the tarmac. They drew to a halt. Policemen, civilian ones in dark blue and military ones in khaki with their familiar red caps, saluted and scrutinised their documents and peered inside the boot of the car, while Rachel sat in the front staring stolidly ahead through the windscreen as though smarting under some kind of insult. Finally the police waved them on. The road began to climb up through the deep gorge of the Judaean hills and Harding felt a sensation of freedom lost, an acute sense of the restrictions of life and circumstance closing in on him like a vice.

When the road finally left the narrow gorge for the limestone uplands, the sun was setting in a blaze of orange. The shadowy bulk of an Arab village was silhouetted above them. On the road in front a battered, blue EGGED bus ground along spewing black exhaust fumes behind it. Harding hooted to try and get past, but the road curved sharply and he couldn't see more than a few yards. He wrestled with more than the steering-wheel: he wrestled with conscience, with loyalty, with a dozen abstracts which were all less than the raw fact of this girl beside him in the car.

She spoke quietly. 'Do you know, I hate this city at times? It never leaves you alone.' They were amongst the first buildings now. He glanced across at her almost as though to detect the lie if it came.

'You're Jewish, aren't you?'

She stared ahead. 'Why do you say that?'

'Isn't it obvious? How else would you have the confidence of a man like Ben-Oz? And then some of the things you said. That last one especially.'

'The last one?'

'About hating the city, yet never being able to get away. That's Jewish.'

'Why the hell is it Jewish?'

'Only Jews have that love-hate for the place. The British think it's quaint or fascinating or dull or dangerous or whatever, but the Jews love it and hate it.'

She shrugged. The bus in front finally pulled into the bus station and they could get out of the exhaust fumes. 'Okay, so I'm Jewish,' she admitted. 'There's a lot of it about. Why should you worry?'

'I'm not worried. Just wanted to know, that's all.'

'But I'm American too.'

'In Philadelphia, maybe.' He slowed to let some pedestrians cross the road. Someone hooted from behind. 'You haven't been very open with me, have you?'

She sighed. 'I didn't *say* I was Jewish, because I'm *not* really Jewish, not in the States anyway. And I know what some of you British think of the Jews out here. Look at that guy in the Régence. Anyway I've been Rachel Simson all my life. My father moved the family from New York and changed the family name from Shimshon before I was born. So . . .' She spoke quickly and nervously, as though all this had been there all the time and it only wanted a breach in the dam to let it out. 'He wanted to assimilate, you see. I went to a church school like a good little *shiksa* and all that kind of thing, and we almost forgot about what we came from. Being Jewish was the last thing my parents wanted to be reminded of. They were modern and progressive and hated synagogue and the Hasids in their fur hats and ringlets and all that kind of stuff you get in Borough Park, and they just wanted out. You know what I mean? Got married and ran away to Philly where they could pretend to be nice, civitised *goyyim*. As God's my witness all that is true.'

'And you?'

'I guess I'd have gone along with that if it hadn't been for the war. I mean, I never really thought about it. Who cares? I went to Sunday School and learned about baby Jesus and all that because all the other kids did, and I was nothing in particular at high school and nothing in particular at Bryn Mawr. A good old-fashioned Bryn Mawr liberal, maybe. And then the war came and the rumours about the camps, and I saw the newsreels and it dawned on me that it wasn't really up to me at all, any more than it was up to those millions who died. How many of them didn't really want to be Jewish, I wondered? Europe had been full of Jews that just wanted to get on with their lives and maybe even play at being gentiles a bit, but *they* had no choice so why should I?' She looked round with a bright and sarcastic expression on her face. 'No choice, don't you see? That's the great gift that Adolf Hitler gave to the Jewish people.'

They passed the main police station with its sand-bags and barbed wire and floodlights, and Rachel Simson, or Rahel Shimshon or whoever she was, was suddenly close to tears. 'God, I feel a fool,' she said. She shook her head, as though to shake the tears from her eyes. 'I just decided to I come out here to have a look. Just to have a look. No *Aliyah* or anything. I wanted to see what was happening and write about it, and I thought that would be enough. Now I see that more is needed. A new country demands help.'

'A new country? Is that what it is?'

'Of course it's a new country. Or it will be, whatever the British think or do. A Jewish state.'

'There are those who would disagree.'

'Idiots,' she said dismissively. 'The usual experts who can't see beyond their own prejudices. It'll be a Jewish state because it already is one. *Fait accompli.*'

'And will you be part of it?'

She was silent as they slowed for the traffic. The Old City seemed to be under siege by an invasion force of the twentieth century. Military jeeps and Arab buses and cars and vans all milled round Allenby Square as though preparing to breach the ancient walls. 'My trouble is, I don't feel part of anything,' she said. 'That's the American disease.'

He hooted for a donkey cart to get out of the way, then turned left along the north wall, towards the American Colony and her hostel. She looked across at him. 'So now you have unearthed the family skeleton you're going to banish me to the ghetto, is that it?'

He didn't answer. Oh, he knew what he ought to do, clearly enough, but duty, in this world of phoney peace, was a concept that became ever more confused. During the war it had been clear enough. Then he had known who his friends were and recognised his enemies clearly enough. In peace neither seemed very certain.

'Let's stop,' she said suddenly. 'Stop here for a moment.'

'Aren't you well?'

'Stupid. Just stop. I want to talk.'

So he pulled into the kerb near the Damascus Gate and put the brake on and turned to face her. 'Talk about what?'

A tide of Arabs was spilling out through the gate, pushing past a couple of market stalls, spreading out into the new city after a day's work in the old. Policemen were on duty, and an armoured car was parked further down the road near the Arab bus station. The line of the wall and the road outside it might have been an international boundary between two countries – the old and the new, the future and the past. Outlined against the sky like a row of teeth the crenellations of the gate gave the scene an absurd, theatrical mood, the sensation that some oriental play was shortly to take place on the stage in front of it, something out of The Thousand and One Nights perhaps.

'Talk about what?' he repeated. She asked for a cigarette and he found a packet in the glove compartment of the car. A match flared quickly in the shadows. She held his hands to steady the flame as she bent towards it, and for a moment the sharp smell of tobacco smoke mingled with the warm scent of her hair and the extraneous smells of the city coming in through the windows – the ordure, the crushed vegetables, the traffic fumes.

'Talk about what?'

'Okay, okay,' she said. 'Give me a moment.' She inhaled deeply and blew smoke out of the window, then turned to Harding with a wry smile. 'I'm nervous, you see. Nervous with you, I mean.' She put up her hand and touched the lapel of his jacket as she had the last time, as though she might, literally, be about to brush something off it. Then she looked away. 'I've blown it, haven't I? Really frightened you off.' She drew on the cigarette again and spoke towards the windscreen and the passing crowd and the buses and the trucks, as though she might find more sympathy there. 'I love you, Andrew Harding, that's the problem. And saying that's going to make you back off even faster. But I love you. I think right from the start, from the moment when you came across with Dennis Killin amongst all those damned British at the Club and I thought, hey, this one's different. I don't know why. I just thought that, seeing you. Christ, I hate this. I'm getting incoherent.' She looked back at him and she was half laughing and her eyes were glistening. She put up her hand again, but this time to his cheek. 'And then you asked me to the movies, and I thought, wow, it's happening – this is it. And then you said, more or less, forget it. And I tried. Believe me, I tried. I sound like something out of high school, don't I? I thought I could concentrate on being a writer, and I've not done badly, have I? But all the time I'm thinking, when am I going to see Andrew Harding again, the English bastard who doesn't give a damn? When am I going to see him? And then I got Emily to arrange the tennis, and it all seemed to go all right, you know, the Regence and everything, except for that bloody drunk, and now all this has happened and I've blown it.' She shook her head and let her hand drop and just sat there waiting. 'There. Hard-bitten reporter confesses all. You think I'm a stupid little girl, don't you? Just a child, dabbling in something that doesn't concern her, not understanding how dangerous it may be. But *you* make me like this. In Christ's name, I'm meant to be an educated woman who's travelled halfway round the world, and I just sound plain stupid.'

Stoopid. He could imagine Lorna's expression: a mingling of amusement and cynicism. Above them the crenellations of the old gate cut sharp as dragons' teeth against a sky of fading gold. The gate was called by the Arabs Bab el Amud, which is the Gate of the Pillar, the pillar being the marker from which they used to measure the distance to Damascus. They sat there in his Riley at the beginning of the road to Damascus while Lorna smiled at him from the shadows, a smile of contempt.

'I don't care,' Rachel continued. 'I've got to tell you the truth, and if the truth's embarrassing, so I'll be embarrassed and maybe you'll be embarrassed. And I don't care that you're married. I don't care if you just go with me for a while and then dump me and go back to England and forget all about me. I don't care, Andrew, truly I don't. I won't give any trouble.'

He put out his hand and touched her chin and turned her towards him. If he had known whether to believe her or not it would have been easy. What intrigued him was the uncertainty, the sensation that he was about to cross some kind of border and the country beyond was uncertain. The potent face – American, Jewish, Gentile, he wasn't certain how to place it – looked at him with an expression of entreaty. 'You are an English bastard and I love you,' she said. 'Promise.'

At that moment there was a tap on the window of the car. Rachel gave a little cry and jerked round. An Arab face peered in at them, laughing. 'Have a good time English,' the Arab called.

'We'd better go,' Harding said vaguely. 'We'd better go.'

'Go where?'

He didn't offer her an answer. Perhaps even then he wasn't really sure. He started the engine again and pulled the car back into the stream of traffic and turned away from the noise and

184

chaos of the Damascus Gate while Rachel sat motionless beside him as though to move would be to break the pattern of what was happening, fracture the subtle tissues of contigency, of cause and effect. He stared through the windscreen and seemed to search the road as though he had never been there before, as thought the Hinnom Valley down which they drove, and the Jaffa Gate, and the absurd windmill which Jewish pioneers had built in the last century, and the great block of the King David Hotel on the hill behind it, were an unknown to him.

The car climbed up the road into the bourgeois calm of the German Colony and the two of them had finally crossed the border, moved right into the territory of betrayal. It was as though they were stepping into a new country.

. He parked the car outside the house. Rachel sat in the passenger's seat and only moved when he held the door open for her. She climbed out onto the pavement and looked round at the shadowy street, with the houses crouched behind their walls almost like cottages in a village.

'Is this your place?'

'Dennis' and mine. Joint tenants.'

She smiled. In the small front garden the canary palm rustled in the breeze, a dry, sardonic sound. He led her up the path and opened the door onto a dark and silent hallway. It was Daoud's day off and Silver was most probably with his study group. 'Dennis must be out as well,' he said. 'It's never this quiet when he's here.'

'He's with Emily.' She followed him in and closed the door behind her. 'She told me.' They went upstairs to his room. He opened the shutters and the evening air, cool and fragrant with the scent of jasmine, drifted in. Over the nearby roofs he could see the flush of light from the city centre. When he turned she was standing beside the bed, holding the photograph that always stood on his bedside table, the snap of Lorna and Helen. She examined it for a moment, then shrugged. 'They're very beautiful.'

He noticed that the hair on her arm was quite dark. Was that from her Jewish blood? What tide of genes flowed beneath her skin, what ebb and flow of miscegenation during two millenia of the Diaspora? What ideas and loves and hates? No, she clearly wasn't as pretty as Lorna, but then she had something that Lorna didn't have – it was something physical yes, partly the curve of that particular mouth and the cast of those particular eyes, but it was also a quality you could not measure by shape and form and colour, a strange impression of independence about her, the sensation that she was entirely herself. Beauty, that was it. He'd never have admitted it in England. Beauty. In England, if they'd met on a train or somewhere he'd have placed her with ease, and by placing her dismissed her: American, with a chip on her shoulder like all of them. A bit pushy, a bit loose, a bit childish. And he'd have been wrong, quite wrong. And he never would have seen the beauty.

Downstairs a door opened. 'What's that?'

He listened as footsteps came up the stairs. 'Silver, probably.'

'Oh God, what do we do?'

The man's voice came through the door. 'Andrew? You in?'

'I'm asleep.'

'Sorry.' Footsteps sounded down the corridor and they heard Silver's door slam. Rachel smiled, returning the photograph to the table, placing it carefully face downwards. 'I'm being as honest as I can, Andrew,' she said 'Don't you see that? As honest as I can.'

'I know you are.' He stumbled with an image he had of his wife. It was an image that owed more to his imagination than it did to any real moment in their lives — a distillate of her cool manner and her delicate selfishness and the slim lines of her body. It was the image he slept with, the image that consoled him. It did for him things which Lorna herself never did.

'So will you be honest with me?'

'Honest?'

'Tell me what you feel. It won't change things. I just want to know.'

He leant against the window sill and looked at her. 'I want you,' he said. 'Rahel Shimshon or Rachel Simson or whoever you are. Now, at this moment and in this place I want you as much as I've ever wanted anyone else.' It was a childish sentiment perhaps, but then in a sense he was still at war and there is nothing more childish than war — it absolves you from consequences and responsibilities, and that is the epitome of childhood.

She watched him, head on one side. 'That's very equivocal.'

'It's honest.'

'Is it? And tomorrow, or the day after, or the day after that when they post you back to England? Will you still be honest?'

'Shall we face that when it happens?'

She laughed a bitter, ironical laugh which he thought of as very Jewish. 'How often the future is held in mortgage for the present.'

'What do you mean by that?'

She shook her head. 'Forget it. I asked for all this. There's no way I want to back out now.'

186

Nothing more was said. There was neither remorse nor endearment, neither avowal nor denial. There was just the silence of complicity. They undressed there and then in front of the open window, turned away from each other as though clinging to the last vestiges of modesty, and then turning to each other shamelessly when they were quite naked. She was small and lithe against him, somehow smaller than he imagined she would be. She shivered and he caught the scent of her body, like a breath of her own personality reflected even in the material things of the flesh, an alien and unfamiliar presence.

It was a disturbing discovery to find her quick and practised. She kissed him in a way that Lorna never had, and said things into his ear which he had never heard before, and all the time he thought of loyalty and betrayal, and what he had done and what he was doing now; and then she knelt astride him and looked down on him lying there and he could see her smiling in the darkness, the gleam of her teeth, the whiteness of her eyes. She opened herself for him with her fingers and leant forward over him so that her hair made a tent round his face.

'Is it safe?' he whispered.

She laughed softly. Her breath was warm on his face and tainted with the smell of cigarette smoke. Her voice was no longer the voice of a half-child playing about with things she barely understood. 'It's the most dangerous thing in the world,' she answered him. She moved her hips against him and her small breasts swung gently. 'The most dangerous thing in the world.'

Afterwards she wrapped herself in his dressing gown – a silk one he had bought in Cairo – and went to wash. She left him lying on the bed, still bathed in the scent which a few minutes ago had been hers alone and was now a thing shared. It was this blending of scents that struck him. More than a blending of bodies or a blending of fluids or whatever it was that sex involved, it was this blending of her animal smell with his that seemed to be the very quick of the whole thing.

She came back from the bathroom fully dressed. She was grinning. 'I just met your friend coming out of the bathroom. He looked like he'd seen a ghost. Said "good evening".' She giggled. 'What the hell else do you say to a ghost?'

'He's very pious,' Andrew said. 'Have you heard Dennis' joke? If "joyous" means full of joy, what does "pious" mean?'

She laughed. 'Do you think he was offended?'

'I don't really care. Do you have to go?'

She was gathering up her things, her shoulder bag, looking for her shoes where she had kicked them underneath the bed. 'Andrew, I'm staying in a hostel run by the American Episcopal Church. They have rules and regulations, all in capital letters. If they found out I spent the night with a man they'd throw me out quicker than you can say *goy*. Now hurry or I'll have to wake the porter up.'

He dressed and crept downstairs with her. The Riley was outside in the street. As he opened the door of the car he wondered whether he should glance beneath the vehicle as everyone had been told to, but of course he didn't. The real dangers lay elsewhere now.

'Hurry up,' she said. 'It's a quarter of twelve.'

He climbed in beside her and started the engine.

'What's going to happen to us?' he asked.

She shook her head and turned to look out of the window at the dark streets, at the shuttered houses going past. There was the usual single lamp glowing over the gate of the hostel but the place looked shuttered and barred. 'I'll have to wake the porter up,' she murmured. And then she turned to Andrew and put her hand up to touch his cheek. 'Whatever happens someone is bound to be hurt, aren't they?' she said. 'So we've got to be very sure.' She leant over and kissed him, and climbed out of the car. 'Give me a ring Thursday,' she called. 'Now you'd better go before you have the police breathing down your neck. I'm sure you're not meant to be driving round at this time.'

As he pulled away from the kerb he looked in the mirror. She was standing on the edge of the pavement watching him. She stayed there motionless, getting smaller and smaller in the frame of the mirror, until he turned at the end of the street beneath the walls of the Old City. Behind was the Kidron Valley and the Garden of Gethsemene; ahead was Herod's Gate.

5

A café in Tel-Aviv, in Ben Yehuda Street, next door to a bookshop crammed with books in English, French and Hebrew. No German, although German was first language for a good percentage of the population. German had connotations, implications, echoes. German sounded across the dull plains of central Europe and through the birch trees and the barbed wire like a loud and murderous wind. German was tainted. As they passed by the window of the bookshop they saw Ben-Oz leafing through a French novel as though considering whether to buy it or not. 'He's there,' Rachel said. She seemed caught up in the tension of the moment, glancing pointedly in the opposite direction as though looking for someone on the other side of the street.

'What did you expect?'

The café had tables out underneath the trees but Rachel and Andrew ignored these and went through the fly curtain into the shadowy interior. They chose a table in the far corner beneath a large wall mirror. In the reflection of the darkened room their figures were little more than silhouettes against the glare from the doorway.

'What do you think?' she asked.

'About what?' Andrew sat on the bench against the wall so that he could see the whole room. There was an air of unreality about this rendezvous, just as there was about the city itself. Jerusalem he could take, with its Middle-Eastern squalor, its narrow alleys, its markets strewing decaying vegetables across the pavement, its sounds and smells. He recognised it from Cairo, from Damascus, from Nicosia, from a dozen other places he had known in the last few years. There was the stamp of Islam and the stamp of the Ottomans on the city. There were dust and flies and ordure.

There was a sense of the past leaning on the present with its weight of guilt and agony. But Tel-Aviv was different. Tel-Aviv had no past. It was neither Muslim nor Jewish. It was more like a film set, jerry-built on the dunes out of ferro-concrete and rusting iron, and peopled by a cast of strangers. No one actually belonged here. The place seemed a sham, a fabrication, something got up for appearance's sake, just like this café with its vaguely Viennese air, its pastries underneath the glass counter, its waiters in long aprons, its mirrors with their ornate frames.

'About this man.'

'You should know. You arranged it all. You tell me.'

She smiled distractedly. 'I don't know. I told you, I don't know.'

'You know them.'

'I don't *know* them. I've met them from time to time. Contacts, nothing more.' She spread her hands out on the table, palms uppermost. 'Look, you can always call it off. If you're unhappy.'

'What's happiness got to do with it?'

He looked round the place. There were posters on the wall, some in English, others in the arcane Hebrew script which he could read but barely understand. The strange letters seemed to belong more to the world of hasidism and the cabal than to the foundation of a new and modern state, yet the Habima Theatre Company was putting on a production in Hebrew of *Heartbreak House* and the Philharmonic Orchestra was giving a series of concerts of Stravinsky (next Wednesday it was the *The Firebird* and the C Major Symphony). So which was the truth? The mystic or the realistic? Imagination, or the hard facts of reality?

A few minutes later Ben-Oz came in, wandering vaguely into the café as though indifferent to what he might find there. Surprisingly the moustache, which had been such a feature of his face at the first meeting, had gone. Harding wondered if it had been false, a carnival decoration glued in place with spirit gum. He glanced at Rachel and suddenly found himself having to control a fit of giggles. He could see it in her eyes too, almost a plea for help. Don't smile, she seemed to be saying. Take it seriously, this is serious, don't laugh.

'May I?' Ben-Oz asked, pulling an empty chair up to their table. Without the moustache he seemed curiously innocent and slightly absurd, a child playing with fire.

'Of course you may.'

Ben-Oz looked over his shoulder and signalled for the waiter to bring a drink. When it came it turned out to be a fizzy concoction of soda water and artifical colouring. *Gazoz*, it was called. He took an appreciative sip then put the glass down on the table and looked up at Harding. 'What do they know?' he asked. His skin was pale and his eyes were watery, as though he had been awake too long, spent too many hours in smoke-filled rooms. He could have been twenty-five or forty-five so indeterminate were his features. Harding imagined him in some alternative life working in a library, going home in the evenings to a pokey flat in the Jewish quarter of whatever city it had been, Lodz or Krakow or somewhere, attending earnest meetings on Zionism and Socialism, taking an interest in music and politics, disliking the trappings of his religion, talking, arguing, debating, always expressing a point of view that was slightly at variance with the company. Something like that. And instead, here he was in Palestine fighting a curious and desperate little war for a country that didn't exist and a people who had almost been destroyed. Part of Hitler's victory.

'What do they know?' he repeated.

'They're looking for her.' Harding found himself using the third person, just like Ben-Oz. *They*, not *we*. 'There are air patrols from the Canal Zone and from Cyprus. They'll find her.'

'But they haven't yet?'

'The weather's been against them.'

The man nodded with satisfaction. 'That is good.'

'But they will eventually.'

'That is where you come in.'

'Me?'

'You, Mr Harding.'

He felt something, a little stirring of anxiety. 'But I've already done what we agreed. Information. That's what we discussed and that's what I've given you. What I'm giving you now.'

'That is right. Exactly right. Information, more or less. Only this time it is to go the other way. From you to your colleagues.'

'What information? What the hell are you on about?'

'*On* about?'

'Talking about. What are you talking about?'

'*On* about,' Ben-Oz repeated with apparent satisfaction. 'I like *on* about.'

'Oh for God's sake!'

'God's sake is it? For God's sake?' The man chuckled. 'Maybe it is, Mister Harding, maybe it is. Although where God has been in the last few years I don't really know.'

'Get to the point, man.'

'The point Mister Harding, is that you must tell the Security Committee that you know where the ship will come ashore.'

'I must do *what*?' He looked from Ben-Oz to Rachel. He felt a kind of panic, the sensation of a trap closing behind him. 'What the hell do you mean?'

Ben-Oz shrugged. 'You can invent a source, can't you? You can claim that it comes from within the *Mossad le Aliyah Bet*.'

'There are no informers within the *Mossad*.'

'There are now.' Unexpectedly the man grinned. 'More or less. What you will do is this. You will put a tap on a telephone. That is what you say, isn't it? You will tap a telephone. I have the number here.' He passed a slip of paper across. 'It has all been arranged. You will have the security forces listen in to this number, and they will hear what we want them to hear. Simple.'

'Don't be daft.'

'A phone call, that is all. You can arrange that.'

'Not at this notice, for God's sake. There's a procedure to follow.'

'Oh, come, Mister Harding. You know as well as I that the police are always listening in to telephones.'

'But I'm not the police.'

'Aren't you?'

'You know I'm not. GSI, General Staff, Intelligence. You know bloody well. We have to work through the police or Defence Security.'

'You can manage it.'

'And when I am shown to be wrong? What happens then?'

Ben-Oz shrugged. It seemed as nothing. 'Your source is shown to be fallible, that is all. And one thousand victims of Bergen-Belsen will have reached safety.' The man's hands lay on the top of the table, as though he had put them there to show that there was no trickery. Harding noticed that his little finger nail was long, as long as a woman's, like a talon. 'When is the next meeting of the Security Committee?' Ben-Oz asked.

'The day after tomorrow.'

'The day after tomorrow will be fine.'

'This is ridiculous.'

Ben-Oz smiled. 'Here is the number,' he said.

'I'm sorry,' she said afterwards. 'Hell, Andrew, I'm sorry. You can get out of it, just tell them to get lost. I'll tell them to get lost.'

'But it's not that simple, is it? It never is that simple.'

They were lying on his bed in the heat of the afternoon. The windows were open to the sky and the sound of cicadas shrieked in his ears. She touched him softly. 'I'm sorry Andrew,' she repeated, but all the sorrow that she had expressed since their meeting with Ben-Oz couldn't change the facts.

'I must go,' he said. 'I've got to set something up. I know a fellow in the Defence Security Office. But how the hell I just give him a tip out of the blue—'

'You tell him you got it from me. You've got a girlfriend who's a journalist and she heard on the grapevine . . . you know the kind of thing.'

He looked down at her pityingly. 'Do you really imagine it's as simple as that?'

'Have you got a better idea?'

The meeting was on the top floor of the King David. A long table like a gleaming coffin lay down the centre of the room and the view, *that* view, lay beyond the windows. The air was tainted with cigarette smoke and the heavy smell of importance and failure.

'What about the Navy?' the general asked, glaring down the length of the table past Assistant High Commissioner and head of the Defence Security Office and Inspector General of Police, past lesser men such as Gilbert Sweetfield and Andrew Harding. The navy man coughed uncomfortably. 'We're very stretched to cover such a large sea area, sir,' he said. 'Of course we're doing all we can, but they're always up to something. Diversions, mid-sea transhipments, all that kind of thing. One of our destroyers chased a Greek caique halfway to Rhodes . . .' His voice trailed away feebly.

Harding looked away over the head of the naval officer, out through the window at the view of the Old City with the great grey dome floating over the holiest place in the world. He wondered how long it would be before his turn came.

'And the Air Force?' The general had finished with the navy and was glaring down the table at the group captain. The airman looked uncomfortable. The sailor brightened visibly.

'As the Committee is aware, we've been flying patrols from Cyprus and the Canal Zone, but this time the weather has really played into their hands. Visibility has been down to a few miles at times. The Khamseen, I'm afraid.' The airman spread his hands helplessly. 'The last contact was two hundred miles south of Cyprus.'

'Doesn't radar help?' the general asked. 'I thought you could see in the dark with the damn thing.'

'You might be able to spot a ship, sir, but I'm afraid you can't read its passenger list.'

There was a murmur of amusement at the table.

'It really is most important that this ship is stopped,' Sweetfield said impatiently. 'HMG is adamant about it. The Jews *cannot* just jump the queue. And we've got this blessed Anglo-American Committee hanging round our necks.'

The general turned on Harding. 'Major Harding? I gather GSI has some rather better news for us.'

The members of the Committee watched and waited. Harding shuffled his papers, like a card-sharper about to deal something from the bottom of the pack. 'There's this,' he said, holding up a sheet of typewritten flimsy.

'What is it?'

'The transcript from a phone tap.'

The head of the Political Branch of the CID raised his eyebrows. 'I thought that there was meant to be liaison over telephone interceptions—'

'Let the Major speak, please.'

Harding nodded. 'The phone belongs to a suspected *Palmach* commander. I'd rather the name was kept secret for the moment. The caller is unknown. As you'll see he appears to be talking about the *Shali'ah*. Although the ship isn't mentioned by name, I don't think there can be much doubt.'

'And what's he say, this fellow?'

Harding began to pass copies of the transcript down the table. 'The conversation was, of course, in Hebrew. This is a translation. As you may see, it's clear enough where the ship is going to come ashore. The caller talks about "the kibbutz" a couple of times without giving a name, but then lets it slip out at the end. Bat Yam, he says.'

'Where the devil's that?' Sweetfield demanded.

The senior policeman said, 'South of Jaffa. It means "Daughter of the Sea".' He was proud of his knowledge of Hebrew.

'They'll run her aground during the night and get the refugees off and into the settlement before daybreak,' Harding went on. 'That's what we presume is the plan, anyway. It seems that they'll attempt a landing tonight.'

The general was beaming round the table. 'Gentlemen, at last we seem to have a head start on them.' He nodded to Harding. 'Thank you, Major. Thank you very much indeed.'

★

194

The day seemed infinitely long, the events inconsequential. He read reports and wrote comments on a document entitled *Internal Security Duties, Notes for Officers*. He tried to ring Rachel just before lunch but there was no trace of her either at the hostel or at the UPI office. 'I didn't see her at all,' the porter at the hostel said.

'At all?'

'She wasn't here last night. Is that the Major? I am Suhail.' There was a faint giggle on the far end of the line. 'I thought perhaps she might be with you . . .'

'She wasn't,' Harding retorted sharply.

At the *Palestine Post* a telephonist said that she thought Rachel had been in earlier, but couldn't be sure. He swore damnation on her and went down to meet Killin in the bar and they had lunch together in the grill room. Killin was his usual ebullient self, telling jokes, laughing at the Nubian stewards, upbraiding the assistant manager for running a house of ill-repute. 'You look as though you've just lost a fiver and found sixpence,' he said to Harding. 'Have you heard the latest? This'll buck you up. Apparently there was this rabbi and this imam sitting next to each other in the Regence. After a while they begin to talk. "My synagogue's the biggest in Palestine," the rabbi says. "That's nothing," says the imam. "My mosque's the biggest in the Middle East." "Well, I've never even seen a pig," says the rabbi. "That's nothing," replies the imam. "I've never even spoken the word." By this time the rabbi's getting a bit pissed off. "Well, my whole family was killed at Auschwitz," he says. "Beat that." "That's nothing," answers the imam. "I've got four wives."' Killin's laughter sounded round the grill room, halting waiters in their tracks and stilling the rattle of cutlery. 'I've got four wives,' he repeated.

'I got it Dennis,' Harding said. 'I got it the first time.'

'You *are* in a mood, aren't you? What's happened? Rachel in the family way or something?'

She wasn't back at the hostel in the evening, either, but she had left a message with the porter. 'Is that the Major again?' the man asked. 'The lady telephoned me to tell you that she has a job to do. Is that right? A story, she said.' The porter giggled. 'She is always telling stories, isn't she?'

Harding was woken early next morning by the telephone. When he got down to the hall Silver was standing there with the receiver in his hand: 'It's your office.' There was accusation in his voice, as though having an office which worked at five-thirty in the morning was no less a sin than bringing girls home and taking them to his bedroom. Harding grabbed the receiver.

'Major Harding?' a female voice asked. 'It's that ship, sir.'

'Ship? What ship?'

'That refugee ship. The one we've been waiting for. It's just come through on the teleprinter. You know, the Shally-Ar.' Shally-Ar. The girl made it sound like a music hall song. 'It seems it's got through.'

'Damn.'

'It's gone aground somewhere south of Atlit, sir,' the voice was saying.

'It's done *what*? In God's name what's it doing there?'

'Was it meant to be anywhere else, sir?'

'Yes, it bloody well was.'

'Well, that's where it is,' the girl said indignantly. 'I've got the message in front of me. The Third Infantry Brigade has got there, but they're not having much joy. Apparently there's one of those Jewish settlements nearby and the settlers are making things difficult. They were out in force when the ship arrived. The Navy's been informed.'

'Where is it exactly?'

'Just north of Hadera. Caesarea, apparently. One of those ruins. The settlement's called Sedot Yam.'

Caesarea. The sea boomed in his mind. Spray flung up from the rocks and the old stones and the broken pillars. Gulls circled in the wind and Rachel ran down the sand and into the waves.

'Who the devil was that at this hour?' Dennis called from upstairs. 'Not Rachel?'

'The office.'

'Claims Commission works all round the clock,' he said with heavy sarcasm.

'Oh, shut up. What time did you get back last night anyway?'

Dennis appeared at the top of the stairs, his face wearing a predatory smile. 'Late, my friend. The late worm catches the bird, and in this case the bird is called Emily.' He whistled softly. 'Things are hotting up, old man. Thighs like hams, pussy like a black cat with its throat cut.'

'Spare us the details, Dennis.'

'It's the details that are interesting. How have you been making out? Silver tells me you've been a naughty boy.'

Harding ignored him. He phoned the hostel again, but the porter said that she still wasn't in. Perhaps she already knew.

Perhaps she was at the Information Office cabling one of her bloody stories. Maybe she was even trying to get to Caesarea. The name Caesarea went round in his mind, sibilant, seductive, curious in its echoes of other words, other phrases. Seize her ear, he heard. Seize her here. As he put the phone down Silver suddenly reappeared at the door to the kitchen. Harding had barely seen the man over the last few days, just glimpses of him shutting the door of his room, or slipping out of the front door off to one of his confounded study groups. He seemed evasive and embarrassed, but this time there was some kind of determination in his expression. 'I didn't expect it of you, Andrew,' he said accusingly. 'Dennis, yes, but not you.'

Harding paused, thinking of other things. 'What the hell are you talking about?'

'That girl. That girl who was at the picnic. Rachel something.'

'What the devil's it got to do with you?'

Suddenly Silver was white with indignation. 'You're married. You've got a child.'

'That's my business, isn't it?'

'It's your wife's as well.'

'Oh, for God's sake shut up.' Harding pushed past, but Silver found the courage to grab at his arm.

'Don't trust her, Andrew. She's . . .' He hesitated, frowning, struggling for words. 'You know she laughed at you?'

'Laughed at me? What the hell do you mean?'

'When she was here with you that night. I met her in the corridor. She said something about Samson and Delilah.'

'It's her name, you silly idiot. Shimshon, Samson.'

'She's betraying you, Andrew.'

Harding shook himself free and ran upstairs. 'Don't be a silly bugger,' he shouted. 'Just mind your own business.'

He dressed quickly and drove round to the King David. The place was coiled round with barbed wire, sandbagged against bomb blast, guarded by paratroopers of the Sixth Airborne. There were some early-risers in the foyer lounge, members of that damned Committee. An American accent called for waffles and coffee, and made him think of Rachel. Over by the Winter Garden a British trade unionist and a Labour peer stood looking at the view of the Old City as though they were wondering how a thing like that fitted in with socialist dogma. Gilbert Sweetfield was dancing attendance.

Harding turned for the lifts. There were others going up with him, two staff officers going on duty and a middle-aged couple who were obviously guests of the hotel. The guests got out first into the carpeted plush of the second floor and the men in uniform went on up, to step out of the cocoon of the lift into the bleak green of the military headquarters on the top floor. A notice on the wall warned that only authorised personnel had right of entry. At the desk a sergeant MP was self-consciously examining the passes of people he saw every day of his working life. The talk in the entrance area was already about the ship. 'At the very moment when the bloody Commission comes poking its nose in,' someone complained.

Along the corridor, beyond where the teleprinters chuttered and radios squabbled throughout the night, Harding found his sergeant ready with a situation report.

'I've warned them you may be coming down, sir. They didn't seem wild about seeing you as a matter of fact. Said it was in the hands of the local military command now. There's a car ready with a driver.'

Caesarea. He tried to recall something she had said but the thought eluded him, as swift and smooth as a fish, swift and smooth as her legs evading his grasp as they splashed in the water. He handed the report back. 'Forget the driver.'

He took the staff car himself and drove down to the coast, down past Latrun and Ramla, past the RAF airfield at Lydda and onwards, leaving the concrete sprawl of Tel-Aviv away to the left and joining the coast road at Netanya. There was military traffic on the road, trucks and armoured cars going in the same direction as he. They wore the divisional sign of the First Infantry on their tailgates.

Just north of Hadera a roadblock had been set up and a line of civilian vehicles had pulled off the road to be examined. There were lorries and buses full of young Jews jeering and shouting slogans at the military vehicles going past. The soldiers in the back of the lorries jerked two fingers towards them. At the roadblock there was a deliberate lack of hurry to let any civilians through. Each bus was being emptied, every identity card checked. Some vehicles were being turned back.

'One of them bleeding ships run aground,' a corporal called out when Harding slowed down. 'Full o' bleeding yids.'

Harding edged the car through the chicane of steel stanchions. The road beyond was almost deserted. He turned off at the sign saying *Kaisaryie*. The car-park outside the crusader walls, deserted the day before, was now choked with military vehicles, so he pulled off the road some way back and walked the last hundred yards. In the park soldiers of a Scottish regiment were already supervising the loading of a group of refugees into one of the buses. At least the soldiers weren't wearing helmets. You judged the situation by little signs like that. The refugees were women and children mainly, bedraggled and wet, shivering under grey army blankets. One or two of them were moaning but no one protested. One imagined that they were used to this, being pushed here and there by soldiers, herded onto trains, herded onto buses, shut up behind barbed wire. The soldiers were keeping up a facetious banter all the while – 'Last bus to Paisley, bairns half price,' that kind of thing – but the comments seemed to be more for their own benefit than their charges. What would Scots humour mean to the women and children of Bergen-Belsen?

A subaltern glanced with scant interest at Harding's pass and offered what little information he had. 'Apparently the ship's stuck on a rock just offshore. Do you know the place? It's one of those Roman ruins. There are a few Arab houses and—'

'I know the place.'

'Oh, fine.' He turned to one of his men. 'Go easy with the kids, MacLeish.'

'The little bugger's just bit me, sor.'

'Well bite him back then, but do it *gently*.' The subaltern turned back to Harding. 'We got a bit of a warning from the Navy that the ship was approaching so we managed to get into place fairly quickly. Problem is, there's one of those Jewish collectives just over there. It seems the ship was trying to beach in front of it and the Navy managed to head her off a bit. Anyway now there's a tiff with the settlers. We've rounded up a whole crowd of them and we're holding that part of the perimeter to stop any more getting through. It seems okay at the moment, but you know what these things are like . . .'

Behind him his signaller was talking into the radio. The machine wittered and jabbered in the bright sunlight, a mad commentary on the life of the Mandate, while the loading of the civilians went on, the dull shuffle of feet punctuated by the comments of the soldiers. 'Mind yerself, missus . . . standing room only on the top deck . . . all aboard for the mystery tour.'

'What's best, Lieutenant?' Harding asked. 'I want to see how things are shaping up.'

The soldier pointed to the gate which led into the ruined city. 'You can get up there if you want to get a view of the whole place. My company commander's there somewhere. Maybe he can put you in the picture. I'm afraid I've got my hands full here.'

Harding found the Scots captain up amongst the weeds and the broken masonry of the gatehouse. He was a harassed National Serviceman, without the lieutenant's languid manner, without the casual fatalism of the professional soldier. His accent was strongly Scottish. 'Who the hell are you?' he demanded, and then when Harding had introduced himself, added with an air of belligerence: 'Pity your boys didn't put up a better show and stop 'em before they got here.'

'Hardly my boys.'

'Well, your colleagues, anyway. It's going to be a right mess now, I can tell you. That commission will be down here as soon as they can find the transport and we'll be all over the front pages of the world's press.' He led the way up broken stairs to the top of an ancient tower, where, he assured Harding, you could get a view of the whole fucking cock-up. The breeze buffeted the little platform. As the man had said, you could see everything: the broken ground of the ruined city, then the small harbour and Arab village, and beyond that the ancient mole and the breakers of the open sea. That was where the ship was.

Shali'ah, messenger. She lay at an awkward angle with her bows on a spit of sand and the sea breaking round her. The hull was streaked with rust and people, a mass of people crowding down the companionway and clambering down rope ladders to the boats which waited for them. One or two figures jumped. You could see them detach from the taffrail and plummet down into the chaos below where the boats rose and fell on the waves like flotsam. A Royal Navy destroyer lay further offshore and its own launches were there amongst the boats. Two cables were strung from the bows of the ship, one to the mole and the other to the beach where Rachel and he had swum just days before. Figures were struggling through the waves to safety using the cables as hand rails. They reached the shore to find themselves in the hands of British soldiers.

'What a fucking mess,' said the captain, shaking his head. 'See what I mean?' He handed binoculars to Harding. 'Of course it was completely deliberate. Ran the bloody thing aground on purpose, otherwise we'd have taken her in tow into Haifa and disembarked the bastards in our own good time. What kind of captaincy is that, I ask you?' He waved his hand at the chaos, as though navigation alone were to blame. Above the sound of the sea they could hear the cries of people, like gulls in the distance.

'Why did the Navy miss her?'

The Scotsman shrugged. 'You know better than me. I'm just a soldier trying to do my job.'

'What's the plan now?'

'To get them off as soon as possible and get them into the camp at Atlit. The Navy's thinking about trying to tow her off, but they're waiting for a tug from Haifa.'

'There's nearly a thousand of them.' Through the binoculars Harding could see that some of the refugees were trying to swim, small heads bobbing amongst the foam. They were on the south side of the ship, swimming away from the boats, away from the ancient town; away.

'How do you know all that?'

Harding ignored the question. 'Is there room in Atlit?'

'Not my problem.'

'It's someone's.'

'Someone else's. They'll probably only keep them a short while anyway, then ship them off to Cyprus.'

One of the swimming heads disappeared. Harding tried to count but the binoculars were unsteady in his hands. Three . . . four . . . five . . . There had been six, surely there had been six a moment ago. The waves made it difficult to see. Maybe the sixth was just out of sight. None of the five looked back. There was no sixth; not any longer, anyway.

Harding swept the binoculars back to the beached ship and the flotilla of small boats. Men and women leapt into his vision, some holding babies, some with children clutched beneath their arms. They hung and clambered and jumped and fell, like souls falling into perdition. He dropped the binoculars from his eyes and the scene dissolved into the distance. It was easier like that.

'We've rounded up some people from the settlement,' the company commander said. Perhaps he was trying to restore friendly relations by offering this piece of information. He pointed over towards the Roman theatre. Deserted the day before, now it had found an audience and a cast: men in khaki stood ranged round the tiers of seating while beneath them in the *orchestra* was a crowd of civilians.

Harding handed the binoculars back. 'I think I'll take a closer look. Your CO should be expecting me.'

6

He made his way down the shattered stairs and out into the ruins. Now that it was occupied by the military Caesarea had taken on a curiously modern aspect, as though it was a village in the front line somewhere, first pulverised by shelling and now occupied by the advancing army. One expected to see a party of sappers going over the ground with a mine detector, marking safe passages, clearing obstructions, that kind of thing. Amongst the Arab houses down at the harbour groups of refugees were being kept under guard like prisoners from some recent engagement. The only things missing were the bodies.

He walked towards the village. The roaring of the surf and the shouting of the people were all around him now, strange, insensate cries on the wind. Women and children were being urged to their feet and marched back towards the car-park and the buses. One or two struggled up with bundles or cardboard boxes containing, presumably, all that remained of a lifetime's possessions. Some of the younger ones shouted, but the majority were just frightened and confused.

Were these Rachel's people? The question seemed absurdly theoretical, divorced from the depressing reality of the refugees' emaciation and confusion and, he discovered with hideous remembrance when the wind gusted towards him, their smell. The fact was that they were no one's people. What had Rachel called them – a thousand lost souls? It seemed true enough. They belonged neither here nor in Europe. The Nazis had actually succeeded, more than they had ever understood, not by killing but merely by dispossessing.

He found the battalion commander in a walled garden beside one of the houses, House-of-Herod perhaps. He was surrounded by a group of officers and NCOs. 'No time now, Harding,' the man said when Harding appeared. 'We don't need Intelligence any longer.'

'I'm sure you don't, sir.'

'Don't be impertinent. You know what I mean. We need logistics – lorries and men.'

'Have you any idea of their numbers yet?'

'Your lot said five-fifty.' The colonel's tone was accusing. 'Well, we've just been talking with their so-called Captain – they've got over nine hundred on board.'

'That's almost two passengers per ton,' Harding said. 'They've never loaded like that.'

'They bloody well have now.'

'Have you taken any of the leaders?'

The colonel appeared not to hear. He scribbled something on a message pad and handed it to a signaller. Harding waited. The officer glanced round, as though surprised to find him still there. 'They're still on board,' he snapped. 'The Navy's trying to reason with them.'

'They're armed?'

'Of course they're armed, Harding. They're terrorists, aren't they? You ought to know about that.'

'Have they said who they are?'

'Moses and Joshua, I expect. Now will you kindly—'

There was the sudden sound of gunfire from the direction of the kibbutz – two shots. The colonel sighed. 'Oh God in heaven, what now?' Some of the refugees looked round vaguely, but most of them took no notice at all. 'Small arms fire from the settlement, sir,' someone called. The soldiers of the Headquarters Company had taken up defensive positions behind a low wall, slamming their rifle bolts forward in readiness as though they were expecting a full scale attack at any moment.

'Get me C Company,' the colonel said to his signaller. He snapped his fingers impatiently. 'Come on, man! Get me C Company. Find out what the bloody hell's going on. Last thing we want is shooting. And try to get brigade on the phone again. We must have more support here.'

The signaller began to mutter into his microphone.

'It's strict *Palmach* policy not to engage British troops,' Harding said.

The colonel looked at him pityingly. 'Thank you very much, Major. I'll remember that when the first of my men gets killed. Now please let me get on with my job.'

Harding slipped away from the pushing and shoving and the mess of boats and humanity in the little harbour, and walked towards the southern wall of the old city. A large banner was now draped from the bridge of the beached ship. There were Hebrew letters crudely painted on what looked like a piece of sailcloth, but the message was also in English, presumably for the benefit of any press cameras there might be around: LET MY PEOPLE GO.

Soldiers had taken up positions on the ruined wall overlooking the theatre. He scrambled up beside them and looked out towards the theatre. Theatre-of-Girls. Three days ago it had been deserted. Now there were soldiers up on the highest row of seats peering nervously over the parapet towards the kibbutz from where, presumably, the sound of firing had come.

He clambered down the far slope and across the open ground. There were grim-faced Jocks guarding the passage-way that led into the *orchestra*. 'You'd best keep your head down, sor,' a sergeant warned him. 'There's been one o' they Jew bastards shooting from their camp.'

'Anyone hurt?'

'I don't think they were really trying. Not yet. But you never know with they bastards.' At the end of the passage beyond the sergeant was the bright open space of the *orchestra*, the dancing-place where Rachel had pirouetted, where she had swept towards him almost mockingly and then eluded his grasp and run away up the terraces of stone seats. He remembered the skirt hitched up, the bare legs, and, deep in the shadows, a tantalising glimpse of white. Now the scene had changed profoundly: watched over by a dozen soldiers there were about thirty civilians sitting amongst the withered grass, men and women, none older than about twenty-five, all dressed indifferently in khaki shorts and shirts. Some were talking amongst themselves. One of them appeared to be having an argument with one of the guards. All of them exuded an air of self-righteous enthusiasm. They might have been some kind of scout group, caught trespassing or something.

'Are they from the kibbutz?'

'From the camp, aye. They were trying to get a line from the ship when we arrived.' The sergeant added with a certain grim satisfaction, 'we've beaten the fockers this time.' He turned and yelled to a figure at the top of the theatre. 'What's going on over there now, Jimmy?'

'Bugger all, sarge,' came the reply. 'Quiet as focking mice. Don't trust 'em a focking inch.'

The sergeant laughed and turned back to Harding. 'Company

commander's over there somewhere trying to talk sense into their heads. Don't envy him a bit.' He glanced sideways at Harding. 'You don't have a fag on you by any chance, do you sir? If you don't mind my cadging.'

It was then that Harding saw Rachel.

'Cigarette, sir? I'm dying for a smoke.'

She was sitting cross-legged on the edge of the group of prisoners with her chin in her hands. Her hair hung forward and partly obscured her face, but there was no doubt it was her. Rachel Simson.

'Have you sir?' the sergeant repeated.

Distractedly Harding patted his battledress pockets and fished out a battered packet. 'Here, have them.'

'The whole lot? That's very decent of you, sir.'

'It's nothing.' He stepped back into the shadow of a wall, almost off balance.

'You all right, sir?' The sergeant eyed him through a cloud of smoke from his match.

'I'm fine, fine.'

She sat cross-legged with her head hanging almost between her bare knees and from what he could see of her face she looked tired and frightened. But it was her. No doubt, no mistake, no hallucination, no illusion. Rachel Simson. Rahel Shimshon.

'They're tricky buggers, them Jews,' the sergeant was saying. 'Ungrateful too. Look what we did to the Krauts, and this kind of thing's all the thanks we get.'

'What's going to happen to these people?'

She sat cross-legged with her thighs splayed open, those same thighs that had opened for him in the shadows of his room. How long ago? Absurdly he glanced at his watch to make the calculation. Mere hours, and yet the memory seemed so remote both in time and place as to inhabit an entirely separate universe.

The sergeant was still talking. 'We're waiting for orders,' he was saying, 'always waiting for fockin' orders. But if that bastard starts shooting again . . .'

Then suddenly, as though there had been a signal amongst them, the prisoners rose to their feet. 'What the fock?' The sergeant spat his cigarette out and turned towards the crowd of prisoners. 'Sit down, yer buggers!' he yelled. 'If ye move my men'll shoot. D'ye hear?'

Up on the terraces the Jocks shifted their rifles to the ready. The prisoners looked at him and at the other soldiers round about the theatre. There was a single, collective expression of hatred.

'We have no guns,' a voice called. It bore a middle-European accent of some kind. 'We are unarmed.'

'Then sit down and shut up!' the sergeant retorted. ''Cause we've got focking great bazookas.'

None of the settlers moved. There was the clatter of bolts being shot home, a sinister sound in the morning sunshine. In the background was the sound of the sea and the gulls, while here, amongst the whitened stones of the ancient theatre, a death rattle sounded in the throats of a dozen rifles.

The same accented voice shouted again. It was impossible to see where it came from. It was disembodied, as though nothing less than the single voice of the group of settlers. 'Let my people go!' it cried. It was a signal of some kind. At the words the group of prisoners exploded, flew apart as though driven by some centrifugal force, scattered towards the seats, towards the passage-ways which led out of the orchestra, towards the broken ground where the stage had once been and the actors had once performed for Herod the Great. A shot rang out and stone exploded somewhere nearby. A bullet sang off into the distance.

'Ye bastard fockers!' screamed the sergeant.

One of the girls, but it wasn't Rachel, stumbled and fell screaming into the dirt. A couple of the men were struggling with soldiers, trying to wrestle their rifles away from them, trying to distract them while the others ran. A Scot kicked his assailant in the crotch and hit him with the rifle butt, shouting, 'If ye want my focking weapon, ye can have my focking weapon!'

And Harding ran too. He sprinted into the open and went up the terracing after Rachel. The figure ahead of him didn't look back, didn't pause, dodged one of the Scottish soldiers running towards her round the curve of seats, clambered over the broken masonry at the top of the auditorium and disappeared down the slope at the other side.

'I'll get her!' Harding called to the soldier. 'You take those chaps down there.'

He reached the top. She was clambering down the broken abutments at the back of the theatre and for an instant she paused before the drop. Ahead of her was a stretch of level ground and the track leading to the gate of the kibbutz. She jumped, stumbled, got up and began to run towards the gate.

At that moment a soldier appeared ahead of her to block her way. He levelled his rifle. 'Stop, bitch!' he called.

Harding shouted. What he shouted he never knew. Words

never formulated themselves in his mind. It was just a scream of mingled anger and panic, an animal sound that distracted the soldier for an instant. By the time the man looked back to his target Rachel had dodged across the track and vanished into a plantation of bananas on the other side. Harding leapt to the ground. 'I'll go after her,' he cried. 'You'd best go back and join your company.'

The soldier stared at him. 'Go, man!' Harding repeated. 'Go back to your company.' He ran across the track and dived into the plantation like a swimmer plunging into a raging sea. Ragged leaves slapped into his face. He went down between the rows of plants and caught a glimpse of her figure veering to the left. 'Rachel!' he called. She jumped over a ditch into a thicket of reeds. Thorns snagged his face as he followed. He stumbled over some half-buried masonry and fell into a shallow trench beyond and as he picked himself up he could hear her blundering through the vegetation a short way in front. The tops of oleander bushes lay just ahead and about two hundred yards over to the left there was a row of eucalyptus trees which he guessed was the line of the road. He plunged forward again and pushed his way through the oleanders and out into the open.

Below him the ground sloped sharply down into a wide, grassy space. The space was over two hundred yards long and about fifty wide, stretching down to the left towards the line of eucalyptus trees, banked all the way round like a race track.

'Rachel!' he called again. Her momentum had taken her down to the bottom of the bank and she was out in the open now, running towards the great curve at the end of the track. She stopped and turned. She was breathing hard and her face was streaked with sweat and grime. Her shirt was stained and torn. She looked up at him with her hand held to shield her eyes against the glare, and she called something which he couldn't hear. Then she sank down to the ground, sitting with her elbows on her knees, waiting.

'The Horse-Place,' he said as he approached. 'The hippodrome of Caesarea, which was the greatest Roman city of Palestine, the capital city of Herod the Great, the place where Paul faced Festus and preached to Herod Agrippa, the home of the bishop Eusebius, and one of the last strongholds of the crusaders in the Holy Land. This is the Horse-Place!'

She sat with her head between her knees and didn't move. He walked along the top of the bank and slid down beside her.

'So we've seen the Horse-Place after all.'

Her expression was sullen. There was spittle at the corner of her mouth. 'Are they killing people? Are they killing people?'

'Don't be bloody stupid.'

'They were firing.'

'That's what happens when people play with guns.'

She asked, 'What do you want?' and he grabbed her chin and forced her to look directly at him.

'What do *I* want?' he repeated incredulously. 'I could ask what *you* want.' She didn't offer any reply. 'Look' – he pointed – 'the road is over there where you can see the trees. My car is parked there somewhere. I'm going to take you to it and get you out of here.'

Without waiting for her reply he grabbed her wrist. She came reluctantly, like a schoolgirl caught out in some stupid misdemeanour. 'My place is here,' she said, but the protest was half-hearted, as though she had just said it for the form, to salve her conscience. When they reached the road he dumped her on the ground behind a clump of prickly pear cacti.

'You don't move, d'you hear? You bloody well wait there until I come back.'

She shrugged. Her expression was one of dull resignation, as though the schoolgirl prank had come to an end and there was only childish self-respect to salvage. He left her and climbed up onto the road and looked cautiously round. His Humber was parked a little way down the road towards the ruins, towards the car-park where the military vehicles were manoeuvring. As he approached it, a jeep drove by followed by a ten-tonner full of soldiers, paratroopers this time, with their red berets. They stared dully out of the back at him, indifferent to the antics of officers, indifferent to most of what happened in the Holy Land. He reached the car and started the engine, waited while another lorry roared past and then backed out into the road, struggling with the heavy steering of the Humber. The rear wheels scrabbled amongst the loose earth before they found a grip. He managed to pull the car round and drive the few yards back to where he had left her.

He wondered whether he would still find her there. A part of him hoped not. He didn't really know anything any more, either what he was doing now or what he was going to do in the immediate future. He felt like a novice playing chess, thinking of nothing more than the current move, not planning ahead, not considering the consequences of his actions, not thinking of very much in particular except of the figure of Rachel standing beside him in the auditorium of the old theatre, or running into the sea and calling for him to follow, or kneeling astride him and shifting her hips in that slow circular movement which had seemed so practised.

Another lorry drew to a halt alongside him and a soldier leant out of the window. 'Any news of the skylark, sir?'

Harding gestured ahead. 'Can't miss it.' He watched the lorry continue down the road, then went to find Rachel. She was sitting where he had left her, staring sightlessly at the ground, her face ragged with exhaustion.

'Come on, get in.'

'They've got my papers,' she said dully. 'They took our documents.'

'Christ alive! What in God's name—'

'Don't shout at me.'

'You'll have to hide in the back. Maybe it'd be better in the boot—'

'Not the trunk.' She shook her head decisively, as though it was more important a decision than any other. 'Not in the trunk.'

'Then get in the back and lie on the floor. There's a rug on the back seat. Pull it over you and keep your bloody head down.'

'Where are we going?'

'I've not got the slightest idea.'

He glanced up and down the road to check that it was empty, then dragged her to the car and pulled the door open. She half climbed, half fell inside. He pushed a foot further in, slammed the door and ran round to the other side. We'll laugh about this, he thought, as he climbed in behind the wheel. One day we'll remember it and find it screamingly funny. He put the car into gear and pulled away. He had to swerve to avoid another lorry and then he was turning onto the main Haifa to Tel-Aviv road, heading towards Netanya, exactly the way they had driven a few days before. And just before Hadera there was the roadblock.

He glanced over his shoulder. She was down below the back of the seat. All he could see was part of the rug. 'There's a roadblock. Don't move.'

The car slid to a halt. On the other side of the road a large American car was stopped, a bright red Ford Mercury. Harding recognised one of the passengers as a member of the Commission that was staying at the King David, the trade unionist. There was an argument going on around it, arms being waved, military policemen shaking their heads. Gilbert Sweetfield was there expostulating.

An MP came over and Harding wound down the window to proffer his identity card. The policeman saluted and actually apologised for what he was doing as he took the card. 'You been at Caesarea, sir?' He put the stress in the wrong place so that the name came out *seize-area*. 'I'm afraid we're checking everything that moves at the moment. If you don't mind I'll have a look in the boot, sir. We're under very strict orders. You never know where these yids can get themselves.'

'Of course.' Harding climbed out. He was perfectly calm. He smiled at the MP and fiddled with the handle of the boot and found that it was locked, and then had to go and get the keys from the ignition. He didn't hurry at all. The thought of being caught with her inside the car seemed curiously remote, like the idea of dying. It could happen, but not to him. He opened the boot and revealed a jack and a bag of tools and a folded sheet of canvas which had once been part of a tent. The MP nodded, as though he'd known it all along. 'Thank you, sir.' He saluted smartly. He was one of those gleaming ramrod types. As Harding climbed back in and started the engine the man was already pacing towards a battered lorry driven by an Arab in a *keffiyeh*. The argument around the red Ford was still going on. The trade unionist was saying something about his rights. Sweetfield was gazing pointedly at the heavens, as though rights were the kind of thing only amateurs talked about.

The German Colony lay quiet in the sunshine. There were no vehicles and no pedestrians in the silent backwater. Harding parked the car outside the house and climbed out to open the back door. When he pulled the rug aside he discovered that Rachel was asleep. He shook her. She lay awkwardly over the transmission tunnel with her head pillowed on her arms. Her hair was tangled with bits of twig. One leg was tucked up to support her body; the other was half extended so that it pushed against the door. There were sparse hairs on her shins where she had forgotten, or hadn't bothered, to shave. The pale flesh and the white sock rolled down over the ankle had something of the schoolgirl about it, something foolish and poignant.

He shook her again and she stirred vaguely. 'For God's sake wake up, Rachel. Look, I'm going to check if anyone's at home. When I come back you be ready for a quick exit.'

The house was silent. The green slatted shutters cast an aqueous light into shadowy rooms. The kitchen bore that precise smell of ammonia and Arab coffee and drains which Harding knew would stay with him always, wherever he might be, to bring to mind this moment, this place.

Back outside he found that Rachel had more or less woken up. She was crouched in the back of the car, gazing at the world with the ill-focused stare of exhaustion. Glancing furtively up and down the street he put his arm round her shoulders and pulled her out onto the pavement. 'What's going to happen?' she asked vaguely as they stumbled up the path to the front door. He got her inside and closed the door, and she leant against him like a drunk. 'What's going to happen to me?' she repeated.

'You're going to have a bath and then a damn good sleep,' he said.

'That's not what I meant.'

'It's what I said, though.'

He hurried her upstairs and ran the water. The pipes shuddered and grunted and emitted the usual grudging trickle. 'Get undressed,' he called, but when he went back to his room he found her still sitting on the bed staring vacantly at the wall. 'Get undressed.'

She looked round as though for a way out. 'I've got to go. I've got friends.'

'You're not going anywhere. The police will be looking for you all over. The army has got your ID card and they'll be looking for you everywhere.'

'I can't stay here.' She looked up at him with swollen, red eyes and shook her head. 'This is an Arab area. I can't stay here.'

'For the moment there's nowhere else you bloody well *can* stay. When you've rested a bit, then we'll decide what to do.'

She considered him for a moment, with an expression of ironical curiosity he had come to recognise. 'Why are you doing this for me?'

'What did you expect?'

She shrugged and began to unbutton her shirt, quite unconcerned at his watching her. 'I don't know. Anger, even violence. I don't know. British indignation, maybe.' She tossed the shirt aside and smiled up at him wearily. 'Do you want to watch?'

He felt a disturbing blend of emotion at the sight of her sitting there on the bed. There was anger and there was desire, and a strange sensation of protectiveness. He remembered her body in the half-light, a pale, suave thing that moved with methodical expertise, a succubus. And now she sat there in the bleak light of daytime wearing a crumpled skirt and a plain, pink brassière, looking pallid and dull. Yet his flesh stirred at the sight knowing that, in some sense, she had been his and maybe was still. He had never felt before this focus on one person.

'I'll go. Just hurry up and get cleaned up and get to bed.'

He went down and rang the office to tell them that he was on his way back, that he had been delayed. When he got back up to his room he found her clothes lying in a crumpled heap on the floor beside the bed. She was in the bathroom. He picked her things up and took them down to the wash-room off the kitchen, where there was a mangle and a sink with a washboard and a boiler which dated from the days when the house had been occupied by Germans. *Siemens* announced the plate on the side. What's stiff and hot and marked with siemens? – Killin's joke.

For a moment Harding stood in the room with the bundle of clothes in his hand, thinking of her upstairs in the bath, sitting in the shallow water stark naked. He lifted the bundle to his face and her smell assaulted him, a rancid stench of sweat which was underlain with that scent that he had first come to know only a few nights before, the animal smell of her body. He tossed the clothes onto the washboard and went out into the garden at the back of the house, trying to get his thoughts together, trying to conquer memory and desire, trying to rid dull duty and duller morality of the heady spice of betrayal. He listened to her moving around upstairs and he contemplated her as an enemy of his country, a Jewess who had different allegiences and diverse loyalties, and found that he couldn't. There was just Rachel: everything else appeared irrelevant.

He gave her ten minutes and then went back to his room. She was standing there beside the bed wearing his dressing-gown, the one he had bought in Cairo. The thing was vastly too big for her. She was hitching the sleeves up and trying to tie it round her waist so that it didn't trail on the floor. Her hair was wrapped up into a towel. 'Where are my things?'

'I took them away when you were in the bath.'

'Well give me them.'

'They need washing.'

'They can be washed later. Give me them.'

'Are you thinking of going?'

'Sure I am. You've been real sweet and everything, but it would be stupid of me to stay here—'

'It'd be stupid of you to go anywhere else.' He suddenly felt angry, felt like knocking some sense into her silly head, in fact. He even stepped towards her with some vague intention of that kind, but when he was halfway there the dressing-gown came unfastened – whether by design or accident he couldn't tell – and for a moment, before she had time to grab the thing round her, she stood there naked for him. Her skin was flushed from the hot water, her breasts were small and oval, the shape, exactly, of the lemons which grew in the Plain of Sharon. And the small tuft of hair between her legs seemed as fragile as a flower.

'I'm sorry,' she said fiddling with the cord. 'I'm sorry for the whole fucking mess.'

He swallowed something. 'You were working for them all the time, weren't you? The journalist thing was just a front. You were working for them all the bloody time and you just led me on. From the bloody beginning.'

She shook her head. 'You won't understand, will you? The trouble with you British is that you see only one motive for anything, one explanation, one reason. But it's not like that.'

'You should have told me.'

'I didn't see how it could hurt you. You need never have known . . .'

'That's just naïve.'

She looked defiant. 'I guess so. That's us Americans, isn't it? Naïve. Unused to the subtleties of the real world like you good old British are.'

'Oh, for God's sake—'

'I figured that I could do some good for my people without you knowing, without anyone knowing. And I screwed up. That's it. That's all. And I'm sorry.' She had finally succeeded in tying the cord of the dressing-gown. She looked up at him with an air of defiance. 'Now you've got me what are you going to do?'

IV

1

She came out of the library and paused on the pavement for a bus to pass, then crossed the road quickly and entered the cold and scented gloom of the Church of Saint Edward the Confessor. A sanctuary light gleamed red at the far end of the nave like a single, mad eye. Christ hung crucified in the shadows. She stood for a while in the nave and said a prayer, almost in the manner of someone throwing a stone into a well to find out its depth, to find out if there was even water there at all. After waiting in the silence for a few minutes (could she hear the ripples?) she went back out into the evening light of the city and took a taxi home, thinking of her forthcoming visit to Jerusalem, wondering whether she could afford to take an extra week and stay on after the conference, wondering whether the library would give her leave or not, wondering other things beneath those immediate ones, the inexorable fact of ageing stirring her memory with images that she could not control, pictures of the past that moved beneath her present like a hidden current beneath the surface.

The house seemed desolate, the more so because it wasn't deserted, because Paul was there shut inside his room, shut inside his adolescence, barely in contact with the adult world.

'We're out this evening.'

'So what?'

'So I'm telling you, darling. Will you be okay?'

'Why not?'

She picked up some letters from the doormat and went to shower and get changed, memory stirring, images shifting her mind like leaves shifting in the wind stirred into new patterns that were only ever rearrangements of the old pattern, the immutable facts of the past.

While she was drying herself, Eric rang to say that he would be delayed at work and could she go on without him? Of course she could. She had gone on for most of her life without him, so why should a mere dinner party prove a problem? She rang for another taxi and sat down to do her make-up. Claws, she thought, watching her hands in the mirror. Who had called her fingers claws?

The taxi-driver rang the doorbell just as she was doing her eye-shadow. 'Coming!' she called, and wondered why couldn't Paul answer the blessed door, why he couldn't be useful in some way. She finished the rest of the make-up in unseemly haste, leaving the lipstick to do in the cab. Claws. Who had it been? She grabbed her coat – 'Paul darling, I'm going. Can you find yourself something in the fridge? We might be late, so don't wait up. Be good' – and ran downstairs to the hall and remembered just as she opened the door: Michael. Twenty years ago.

'It goes faster and faster,' her mother had once told her, and Helen hadn't really believed her, at least hadn't felt it then in the way she felt it now. 'You think you've got all the time in the world, but you haven't.' And in one of her rare flights of poetry, Lorna had added: 'It's like a boulder rolling down a hill towards a cliff. It starts slowly enough, so slowly you don't notice it at first. But then it begins to gather pace. Faster and faster it goes. Faster and faster, and then – crash! All over.'

It? 'What is the *it* in the question: what time is it?' One of Eric's little jokes. Life, of course. The problem with her mother was that it *had* gone crash – but it wasn't all over.

Dinner with Gemma and Howard. Helen moved between two circles, the faded and rather earnest academic one which was her own, and the circle in which Eric lived, where journalists and bankers and politicians met in occasionally uneasy juxtaposition. She felt even less a part of that. In this world of Eric's there were few real businessmen because he had an old-fashioned disregard for men in trade. Eric adopted old-fashioned attitudes as others will revive a way of dressing or a type of pop music. In his case it was Keynesian economics and Fabian socialism and, for all his professed egalitarianism, an air of ineffable (some said insufferable) superiority over people who were actually *seen* to be making money.

These particular friends were with the Foreign Office, or at least Gemma was. All that really meant was that she spent much of her time in Brussels – 'arguing over the price of sprouts' as Eric put it — and most of the rest of it in an aeroplane, but there was always the possibility of returning to the Far East and becoming once again the real diplomat that she had been when she had met Howard. She greeted Helen at the front door with a kiss and a cry of disappointment. 'Are you on your own? Where's Eric? Come on in. Howard's stuck in the kitchen with some kind of new sauce he's discovered.'

Gemma's house was cool and elegant, always changing with taste and fashion, subtly different from a home. They went through to the sitting room with Helen apologising that Eric had some kind of telephone deal to make with someone in New York, and Gemma insisting that it didn't matter at all, not at all. 'We've got an old friend of ours here whom you *must* meet. Complete surprise.' They went through to the sitting room. 'By the way, when are you off?'

'Off where?'

'That conference.'

'Jerusalem? Not till November.'

'Lucky you. Swap you bloody Brussels in November any day.'

Helen hesitated in the doorway. A figure had risen from an armchair to greet her as they came into the room. 'Oh, go on in, Helen,' Gemma said brightly behind her. 'Don't stand on ceremony. Helen says Eric's going to be late, Howard. A phone call from the States or something . . .'

Howard's voice came from the kitchen where he was preparing one of his famous Thai recipes: 'Bugger him!' And the other guest smiled that particular, knowing smile.

'Michael. How strange.'

Gemma looked from one to the other with something like disappointment. 'You know each other already? What a surprise.'

'Oh, yes,' Helen said, 'we know each other,' as though it had been a month ago. 'I was just thinking of you. Just now.'

And so the circles touched again, in a drawing room in London, in that avaricious and acquisitive decade, the nineteen-eighties. Two decades on. We shall all be changed. But changed how? That was what each wondered of the other as the brittle little party ran its course. Michael had remembered her as taller, but she still had that narrow, fragile frame, those sharp features and wide eyes. She even wore the same kind of clothes as she had in the sixties, a full-length skirt with some kind of paisley design and a bolero jacket. The fashion must have come round again, as fashions do. 'You look wonderful,' he assured her, but the truth was subtly otherwise: she looked just the same. Both of them looked just the same. There were changes of course, but none of real substance. We are not our skin of grime. There were lines round the eyes and across the foreheads, there was a greying of Michael's hair at the temples and a certain looseness of the flesh at Helen's neck, and she had done something different with that errant cloud of hair – cut it shorter, crimped it, made it look deliberately chaotic and thus somehow under control, and probably dyed it at the temples to hide the incipient grey – but underneath they were the same two people, surely.

'I heard you married,' she said. 'Do you have children?'

'They're with their mother in Argentina.'

'Oh.' She hesitated. The expression, the drawing together of her eyebrows, the narrowing of the mouth, was so familiar that he almost cried out. 'Is that . . . difficult?'

'It was, but not now. We're more or less happily divorced.'

'I'm sorry.'

'There's nothing to be sorry about.'

'The children?'

'Well, yes. The children of course.' He shrugged and looked away almost as though he might try and draw someone else into their conversation. She found herself dreading the possibility, delighted when he turned back to her. 'And you?'

She nodded. 'Eric. He'll be here soon.' She laughed, brushing a strand of hair out of her eyes and reaching for the glass of wine that Gemma offered. 'And two children. Well children, I mean Miriam's grown up now. At university. Reading. Paul's at the difficult age . . .'

Out in the hall the doorbell rang and someone called out: 'Anyone at home?'

'She's not Eric's.' She laughed awkwardly. 'I mean, I married Eric later. We, Miriam and I, were a single parent family before they became all the rage. Then I married Eric, and Paul came along . . .' Why am I telling him this? she wondered. Why not lies, lies by intimation, lies by allusion? Why the truth just like that? She put her glass down as the other guests came in. There was that strained laughter that goes with introductions, a kind of recognition call like animals sniffing each other's backsides. Other people joined their conversation, outsiders intruded.

It was not until they were all sitting down at the table that Eric arrived. He carried with him gracious apologies for all and orchids for Gemma and two bottles of a '75 Pomerol for Howard. He did a round of the table, shaking hands, bending to kiss, touching a shoulder here and an arm there, making gracious apologies which absolved him from all blame – 'These cursed Americans seem to have adopted a different time to us. They must be trying to assert their independence' – and finally took his seat and unfolded his table napkin as though unfolding the corporal in preparation for celebrating mass. Only then did he look across the table to where Helen and Michael sat next to each other. 'So you two already know each other?'

'We used to,' Helen said carefully. It was a curious qualification, implying that you can *unknow* someone.

'And when would that be?' Eric sounded like a barrister. Michael watched the man curiously, trying to gauge his relationship with Helen, trying almost to smell the scents of intimacy which drifted between them across the table. Eric shone like some fine artifact, as though he had been scrubbed and polished. His movements and gestures were almost feminine. He would like cats. He would like well-bound books. He would like the opera. He would hate popular music and television. He would nurture hates and his sense of humour would be like a cold knife. But what was his relationship with Helen? What were the subtle structures of their marriage?

'We were family,' Helen was saying, shrugging, as though at nothing, as though it were an appellation devoid of all potency. 'Michael was my stepbrother.'

'Good Lord.'

'Was, is, I'm not really sure.' She smiled round the table, a detached and ironical smile.

'And I never even knew you had one,' Gemma exclaimed. 'How astonishing that . . .' The conversation drifted into a consideration of coincidence and chance. Helen caught Michael's eye. 'I thought of you earlier this evening,' she said to him. 'Isn't that remarkable?'

'Is it?'

'And here you are.' She laughed and shook her head, as though his appearance had been some kind of relief. She felt an unconscionable happiness, which she tried her best to disguise in ironical amusement. 'It seems so unlikely.'

'Tell me about the last twenty years,' Michael suggested flippantly and Helen smiled and shook her head again. The truth was the last twenty years seemed almost without significance. People had been born, people had died, nothing had changed. 'I'm sorry about Tommy,' she said.

Michael shrugged. 'You heard, did you?'

'Mother . . . couldn't face the funeral. That's what she said, anyway. I wanted to be there in fact. Would have been, but I was away at the time. Work. It must have been Edinburgh.'

'Work?'

'Doctor Helen, remember? I'm Librarian of the School of Bible Studies now, part of the University. Known as SOBS, can you imagine? Sounds like one of our games.'

'BOSS.'

She laughed, and felt the exquisite pain of memory, the word games they used to play. 'Could almost be. The research is secondary these days, I'm afraid. You need a proper job, otherwise you get cut.'

'Tell me about your children. Tell me about Miriam.'

Helen rewarded him with a bright smile. 'She's a scientist. That's unusual, do you know that? Especially for a girl. Apart from a few who want to become doctors these days they all opt for English and Drama, things like that . . .'

'A geneticist,' Gemma put in. 'That's what she says she wants to become. She wants to manipulate people's genes.'

'Sounds more like dress-making,' someone else remarked. And as he sat there amidst dinner party conversation and beneath Eric's curious gaze, Michael tried to imagine her pregnant, her slight figure swollen and awkward. He thought of a child swelling within that narrow belly, breaking out of that damp flock of hair, bringing with it blood and pain. And then he thought of her as memory presented her to his inner eye: in the cottage near Lapithos, and tried to imagine her as she might be now beneath her calf-length skirt and the little velvet jacket: two Helens therefore, the mother and the daughter. And he wondered at the differences of detail, and the differences of significance. 'And how is Lorna?' he asked, trying to steer the conversation onto more neutral ground while understanding with a small rush of amazement that there really was very little that was neutral about his knowledge of her, everything being charged with the hidden currents of sex and familiarity and love. And her exterior, as always, was this balanced façade of composure and moderation – remoteness, even. A classical frontage amongst the new brutalism of the city.

She smiled bleakly. 'She's not well, I'm afraid. She had a stroke last year. It' – a helpless shrug – 'affected her mind.'

'Oh dear, I'm sorry.'

'It's all a bit upsetting . . .'

'It's bad, is it? I'd like to see her again . . .'

'She's not easy . . .'

'Don't forget she was mother to me for ten years . . . sort of.'

'Very sort of at times. I'm afraid she might not even remember you now. She's really not very good.'

One of the other guests was going on about genetics now, explaining how it meant the end of civilisation as we know it or something. Helen looked down at her plate, as though expecting to find help there, and then up at Michael again. 'Maybe you could come down and see her?' she suggested quietly. 'Are you here in London? Perhaps . . .'

'I'm borrowing a colleague's place in Pimlico.'

'Perhaps we could arrange it?'

'Perhaps we could . . .'

'I'll give you a ring. If you're sure.'

'Of course I'm sure.'

2

The station echoed and rang like the inside of a huge steel drum. Michael was waiting on the concourse as they had arranged, with the crowds streaming past him, hurrying for the buses, for the underground, for the taxi rank, breaking round his figure like a stream round a rock. He stood beneath the departure board reading a newspaper, heedless both of the crowds and the letters clattering round above his head. He looked bigger than she remembered him, taller and more solid. And age seemed to show at a distance. When she had been with him at Gemma's dinner party it had been the constancies that she was aware of, the mannerisms, the expressions, the inflexions in his speech, the things that hadn't changed. But at a distance she saw, with something like surprise, that he was a middle-aged man – a slightly daunting one, with a stoop that implied condescension, and a negligent manner that suggested arrogance.

A drunk shuffled past like a piece of flotsam in the stream and she watched Michael look up from his paper and search his pocket for some change; and then he caught sight of her coming towards him through the crowd and he pushed coins into the drunk's hand and came towards her, his smile exactly the smile that she remembered so well, which was neither arrogant nor condescending, but which betokened knowledge.

'I wondered if you'd come,' she said, standing in front of him to be kissed, lifting herself up on one foot to reach his cheek, recalling a similar kiss in an Oxford street twenty years ago.

'Why ever not?'

'Cold feet or something.'

'I always accused you of that, do you remember?'

'Of what?'

'Having cold feet.'

She felt almost embarrassed, glancing round almost as though fearful that someone might have overheard. 'Have you got a ticket? We'd better hurry.'

She lead the way onto the platform. The first carriages were full, people shoving past each other to claim spaces, children bawling, a woman arguing with someone over who had got to a place first, a man trying to manoeuvre a large package over everyone's heads. They struggled past into the calmer water of first class. 'Let's pay the difference,' he suggested.

She settled herself, newspaper folded to the crossword, opposite him. A musical tone sounded through the carriage and a voice came over the public address system to announce the departure time and the route. 'So here we are,' she said, absurdly, while he merely nodded, watching her. 'How do you find England? You've been away all these years. What's it like coming home?'

He shrugged. 'Is it home? I barely understand what's going on half the time.'

'Is it really that different?'

'The people are more or less the same, but everything seems to change around them. They look more and more like refugees in a foreign country, trying to master a new language. What did I read the other day? England is the last colony of the British Empire.'

She smiled distractedly and glanced at the crossword and wondered for a moment what she was doing here sitting opposite this man with the faintly greying hair and the strangely familiar face. Twenty years suddenly seemed a lifetime. It was a lifetime for some, in fact. Miriam, for example. For Paul it was more than a lifetime. Her childhood was, he was fond of pointing out to her, ancient history.

'Are there any ground rules?' Michael asked eventually. 'For this meeting, I mean. Is there anything I shouldn't ask about?'

'Of course. Lots. Twenty years is a long time.' But she realised with a shock that the true answer was quite the opposite − there were no rules, none at all.

'It doesn't seem such a long time.'

'We're both grown up now. We were children then.'

'Does it make much difference?'

Did it? She didn't answer. She felt that curious lightness of being, a sense of the possibilities of life which she had not known since . . . oh, for years. For years. 'I'm a happy woman, Michael,' she said. 'Not like I was when you knew me. I have a stimulating job, a nice flat, a lovely son and daughter.' She hesitated, wondering about the next sentence. 'And a husband who is very understanding.'

'That's wonderful.' Was there irony in his tone? She experienced a sudden panic, as though it were all a mistake, he wasn't Michael at all, merely an imposter who looked like Michael, someone who had taken on the appearance but not the soul, the accidents not the substance, someone who was there to find her out.

'Tell me about yourself,' he said. 'We hardly had a chance to speak at that bloody party.'

'Hardly had a chance? When I rang Gemma the next day she said that they couldn't prise us apart all evening.'

'And Eric? What did he say?'

She ignored the question. 'Look,' she said suddenly, opening her bag and passing a photograph to him. 'Look what I found amongst my things. What do you think?'

He put on spectacles to examine the picture, and smiled at what he saw – Helen squinting against the bright sunlight, Helen in bikini briefs and some kind of cheese-cloth shirt. The young man beside her held one hand up as though to ward off the glare. He was long-haired and wore rather ridiculous side-burns. The contrasts of the scene were too much for the film and it had surrendered in some places: behind the two of them there was only white, where once there had been the rough stones of a wall that was infested with lizards and patrolled by scorpions. 'Do you remember?' she asked, as though testing him. 'Do you remember?'

'Did we have a camera?'

'It was mine. We balanced it on the table and set the timer. Don't you remember?'

He smiled, handing the photo back. 'It seems another world.'

'Does it? You know what's surprised me about growing up? The fact that I haven't. I always thought grown-ups were different, thought in different ways, that kind of thing. But now I see that they don't, or at least I don't. Not underneath, anyway. Maybe I'm defective. I just don't see any difference between now and when we were twenty, not really . . .'

'Except?'

'Except that we don't have as much time left.' She laughed faintly and without humour. 'When I was a child I spoke as a child, I understood as a child, I thought as a child; but when I became woman I put away childish things. One of them is faith in the future. We haven't got much future left, have we? We're both of us near enough fifty and we have to hasten the present or

226

otherwise we'll find that the moment has passed us by.' Distracted by her little speech, she put the photo back. 'Oh, and there's this . . .' She produced another picture. It showed a teenage girl whom Michael didn't recognise. Her features were stronger than Helen's and somewhere on the other side of beauty – a certain business-like good looks. Short, sharp hair and dark lips and a row of small studs round the rim of one ear. She didn't squint against the light, but looked back at the camera with deliberate sternness.

'Miriam,' Helen said, adding apologetically, 'I'm afraid, I don't have one of Paul. He's growing so quickly that photographs of him are out of date almost by the time they're developed.' She watched as he examined the picture, tried to read his thoughts as they had as children. He always used to think of aeroplanes and tanks, she had always thought of knights in armour and fair maidens and equivocal unicorns. It had been an easy game.

'She looks interesting.' He gave it back. 'I don't have pictures of mine.'

'But you've got children? You told me . . .'

'Boys. Two boys.'

'In Argentina.'

The train began to slide forward. The grimy underpinnings of the city moved past the window – cliffs of iron and brickwork, grey and glistening in a feeble sun. The train rattled over the points and the carriage swung abruptly sideways as though it had hit an air pocket. She noticed him glance at her legs, folded as carefully as her newspaper, the knees just visible beneath the edge of her skirt. And, with a sudden rush that was physical in its intensity, she sensed that he was remembering just as she remembered: a dusty room in Lapithos, the daylight coming through the shutters, the little puddle of clothing at her feet. She shifted in her seat, turning herself sideways and looking out of the window. Familiarity lay between them like a gulf. They knew everything about each other, and almost nothing. They understood the quick, but not the callus that grows as one gets older.

'Tell me about Lorna,' he said, and she began to explain, almost as though she was anticipating a question that he might ask: 'We had to put her in the home. We had no choice. She came to live with us after her stroke – dear Eric was very good really – but it wasn't safe to leave her on her own and the flat isn't very big. We tried a nurse during the day, but they changed so often and . . .' She looked at him as though for help. 'It was difficult, very difficult. The question is, how much difficulty must one try to bear? That's the question, isn't it? She began to have rages, the nurses kept changing – who can blame them for heaven's sake? – and it all became too much . . .' Her eyes brightened with tears. She smiled as Michael leaned forward and touched her hand. 'It's all right. I'm not usually like this. Anyway, thank you for coming. I need a bit of support at times. Eric's not very good at that bit.'

'What is he good at?' Michael asked.

For a moment there were the blurred green fields of southern England outside the windows, then a motorway, then more sprawling suburb. 'Oh dear, what a question!' she said. A waiter came along the carriage pushing a trolley, like the bar you get in airlines, the kind of thing that gets wedged in between the seats and stops people getting past to the lavatory. An impatient queue of passengers had gathered behind him even now. He began to argue with one of them: 'Just doin' my job, squire. That's all.'

'Does he know?' Michael asked when the small disturbance had passed.

'Know what?'

'About today.'

'Of course,' she said. 'Of course he knows. We're brother and sister, aren't we? More or less. What harm can there be?' She looked at him, suddenly anxious. Anxiety is fear spread out thin; she had read that somewhere. That was what she felt, fear spread thinly over the even surface of the day. 'What harm can there be?'

'Are you in love with him?'

'In love?' The phrase echoed. Another place, another time, a different crowd – Jerusalem. 'I love him,' she said carefully. '*In* love? Isn't that something different?'

'And Dennis Killin? What happened to him?'

'Good God, I haven't seen him in years.' For a moment she looked away, out of the window, then turned back to him purposefully, as though she had made up her mind about something. 'Look, Michael, I don't want to begin again where we left off. I want to meet you as adult to adult without all that dreadful adolescent *intensity*. Can't we do that? Please.'

'Maybe that dreadful adolescent intensity was called love.'

'Who knows? You can give it any name you like. I think it's different with each person, and each person's different at different times. I think giving one name to it is simplifying it to the point of imbecility.'

'Is that an answer to my question?'

'Maybe.'

'Miriam.' He looked directly at her. 'How old is she, Helen?'

She leant her head back against the seat and closed her eyes, as though she was tired, as though a great weight was pressing down on her lids. She remained quite expressionless for a while, her head back against the headrest, her hands folded in her lap on top of the paper, as though she was waiting. Her neck was where the years showed most. The skin was loose, the sinews showed through. 'She's just twenty,' she answered. 'The twelfth of September.'

He seemed to absorb that piece of information slowly. 'And who's child is she?'

There was a silence. People pushed down the aisle. In the next carriage children screamed at their mother. A station flashed past the windows – a name board you couldn't read and a line of people standing in the rain. The train rattled onwards. She felt familiarity, a sense of possession and being possessed. 'She's mine.' Her voice was quiet. 'Miriam's my child. No one else's.'

The nursing home was a rambling mock-Tudor house surrounded by expansive lawns and gloomy pines. Once it had been Dene Close Preparatory School; now it was the Rest Home of Our Lady of Walsingham, and impregnated with that atmosphere of over-heated cleanliness which nuns impart to such places. Plaster Madonnas, confections of pink and silver and blue, waited in patient ambush at the head of each flight of stairs. Floor polish scented the air. Cleanliness and Godliness had come together in triumphant consummation.

Helen and Michael followed one of the sisters along the corridors. Where once grubby little boys had scampered now only gaunt creatures at the other end of the life span shuffled and hobbled around the place. Suddenly and surprisingly she took hold of his hand. 'It is a bit depressing at times,' she whispered. 'Miriam comes with me when she can, but it's lovely to have some moral support. Eric can't bear the place.'

The sister stopped at the door marked *Mrs Harding*. 'She's quite cheerful today,' she announced. 'Quite aware of what's going on. Of course we have our little problems, but nothing to get too worried about.' She knocked briskly and opened the door. 'Visitors,' she called. 'Your daughter, and' – she hesitated, looking at the two of them curiously, her eyes fastening onto their clasped hands – 'a friend.'

The atmosphere in the room was like a hothouse, warm and damp and tainted with the smell of mould and ammonia. A figure sat in a chair by the empty fireplace and looked up at her visitors suspiciously. She was surrounded by oddments from her past, old photos, bits of furniture that had come from Guerdon House, an entirely useless sewing box, things like that. Prominently displayed on the bedside table were two portrait photos which Michael recognised instantly — one of Helen's father, the young army officer gazing out at the world with an easy insouciance; the other, surprisingly, a shot of his own father, also in uniform, but more stern of expression than his predecessor, as though life were not really a joke after all but something bloody serious. Michael recognised the photographs all right; what he did not recognise was the figure in the chair.

'Who is it?' the figure asked.

'It's me, mother. Helen. And I've brought someone to see you.'

The old woman peered, as though through a fog. 'Andrew,' she said.

'Not Andrew, darling. Michael. You remember Michael.'

She was a mask. She was a carnival mask, a skull-like construction of papier-mâché behind which Lorna Constance was hiding. The golden body at Ladies Mile, eyed by junior officers, ogled by adolescents, guarded ineffectually by Michael's father and ravished by Dennis Killin and others, was shrunk to a fossil. Once it had leaned carelessly forward to reveal to adolescent eyes a single breast couched in a bed of lycra — like a pale lemon nestled in tissue paper. Now it was something shrunken and dried, a bundle of sticks in a floral dress, a pigmented skull with glaucous eyes and a ragged mouth like an old scar. Her meagre hair was pulled back and held by a clasp. Her eyes peered out like terrified animals from a cage.

'Andrew,' she said. And she laughed. 'I knew you'd come back.'

'Michael, mother.' Helen looked anguished as she bent to kiss the hollow cheek. 'It's Michael. You remember Michael. Tommy's son.'

But the old woman — how old? seventy? seventy-five? — was not going to be caught out by tricks like that. 'He can call himself what he likes,' she said, 'but I know . . .'

Helen looked desperate. 'Oh, God, it's going to be one of those days.' She turned to Michael. 'I'm sorry. Do you want to go? You can wait for me outside . . .'

'I'm happy to stay. Unless you think it'd be better . . .'

She shrugged helplessly and went back to her mother, drawing up a chair so that she was sitting close enough to hold her hand. 'We've brought you some things, darling. Look: some of those macaroons you like. And a packet of proper tea, not like the awful stuff they have here . . .'

'Andrew.' Lorna hadn't taken her eyes off him. 'Andrew,' she repeated. Her face was almost devoid of expression, devoid at least of the flexibility of expression. It seemed to wear just one look, which was of a strange, detached hatred, as though she were looking at a photograph and remembering. 'I knew all about you, you know. I knew everything.'

'Tommy's son,' Michael said gamely. 'Don't you remember? And there was Anthony. Michael and Anthony.'

Lorna's mouth moved. Her tongue, pink and wet and curiously youthful, emerged from its lair to run across the lower edge of the scar. There was lipstick there, applied with the vaguely recalled gestures of the past, a smudge of lipstick like a smear of clotted blood. 'Tommy?' she said. 'Tommy? But you're not Tommy. You're Andrew, whatever you may pretend to be. You're Andrew.' She turned to Helen with a sudden look of triumph. 'They blew him to bits, you know that? The bloody Jews blew Andrew to bits. That's his story – you ask him. They blew your father to bits.'

'Yes darling, I know. And it's Michael who's come to see you. Michael. Isn't that kind of him?'

Confusion reigned in Lorna's mind, as it reigns almost everywhere. 'Michael? Who's Michael? Andrew loved me once. Not like the others. They just wanted my body. Except for poor old Tommy. He loved me too. Where is he, anyway? He never comes to see me, never bothers with me at all.'

Helen turned to Michael helplessly. 'I've told her a dozen times about Tommy. She just doesn't understand.'

'Oh, yes, I do. I understand perfectly. I understand what they all wanted, all of them. They wanted me. They loved me. They loved my tits, loved my cunt—'

'Mother!'

There was a sudden moment of clarity in the old woman's mind. 'What's the matter?' she asked. 'One of the sisters listening, is that it?'

Helen giggled, on the edge of tears. 'It's just not the kind of thing you should say, that's all.'

'Not the kind of thing *you* should say. I'm old enough to say precisely what I please. You're jealous. You seem ashamed of it. All you've got is that dreadful queer, what's his name?'

'I don't know what you're saying, dear.'

But Lorna's moment of clarity had not yet dimmed. 'Oh yes

231

you do. Eric, that's him, Eric. All you've got is him, and you're ashamed. But not me, my dear. Not ashamed at all.' She laughed, a high, brittle laugh that was like the crackling of twigs in a fire. 'Andrew. Nothing to be ashamed of. The Jews took him, you know. The bastard Jews took him from me!' And then she quoted, and it was almost oracular, as though someone else was speaking through her thin and shrivelled lips, some deity, some spirit: 'And so they shall quench my coal which is left, and shall not leave my husband neither name nor remainder upon the earth.'

The fire raged and died, just like a conflagration in a pile of twigs. There was that sudden, sharp burst of animation and then the flames smouldered away into nothing – the blank stare, the eyes bulging with glaucoma, the awful groping fingers.

'I'm sorry,' Helen whispered, looking up at Michael and shaking her head. 'God, how dreadful. I'm sorry.' She was crying gently to herself, holding her mother's hands and crying gently and shaking her head as though as to shake the tears out of her eyes; and the old woman never even noticed. 'She's not always as bad as this,' Helen whispered. 'Are you, Mother dear? You're not always so bad.'

Afterwards they walked in the grounds, past the rhododendron bushes and towards an open field that had once been the school cricket pitch. A bulldozer had already been at work cutting trenches across the green. Three men in muddy boots were fiddling with a theodolite and a holding up a surveying rod like an overgrown stick of candy. The space had been ear-marked for an addition to the nursing home. The balance had swung back from the baby boom of the fifties – now, in the eighties, it was better to invest in the old and the dying rather than in the young and the hopeful. A sign explained who the architects were and how wonderful the place would be when it was finished.

'Eric came down with me once,' Helen said, 'and do you know what?' The tears had dried, the emotion had died. She had put the façade back in place. 'He discovered that he had been to school here. Can you imagine? He showed me round the place as it had been – "this is where they used to torture the juniors, and over there they used to stamp you into the mud", all that kind of thing. I think stamping into the mud was rugger.'

'What was the torturing?'

She shrugged 'Making a man of you, I suppose. Eric said that it was the worst time of his life, but then he always says that kind of thing. Maybe it was just uncomfortable, like the Army or something. Anyway, that's why he hates coming down. So he says.'

The surveyors were staking out a line from one side of the space to the other, the line of a wall presumably. At the far end the bulldozer shuddered and slithered in the mud. 'You know she's often talked about your father since she became ill? Isn't that strange?'

'Guilt, maybe?'

She shrugged. 'Who knows? Poor old Tommy. She must have loved him in her own way.' She giggled. She was infected by the tensions of visiting Lorna, her mind jumping from one thing to another, from sadness to happiness and back again in the space of one sentence. 'Do you remember Archie Kesteven? He called your father a "brick". Can you *imagine*? A *brick*: the ultimate accolade. Archie did awfully well in the Falklands, did you see that? Lots of bricks there, all right. Dropped, most of them.' But her laugh was fragile, an echo of her mother's, and the sound soon died away and she was in tears again, speaking softly. 'I hate her. You know that, don't you? I hate her. I've always hated her, as long as I can remember. I fear for myself, for the hatred within me and the judgement that I'll suffer. But I hate her all the same.'

He took her hand. 'Judgement? That seems a little primitive.'

'Oh, but I believe it, you see. In my heart of hearts I believe it. Honour thy father and thy mother, that thy days may be long in the land. I believe it. But she hardly gave me a chance, did she?'

Behind them the taxi drew up in front of the house and hooted briefly to stir someone out of the torpid silence of the afternoon. As they walked back across the lawn she held onto his hand, the thin fingers interlocking with his like a child's grip. 'I even expected her to take you away,' she told him. 'Do you know that? I expected her to take you just as she tried to take everyone else.'

The driver looked over his shoulder as they climbed into the back of the taxi. 'Station, is it?' he asked.

Helen turned to Michael. 'Would you like to see the house again?'

'The house?'

'Guerdon, of course.' A bright smile, the tears drying, the misery being replaced by a sudden surge of delight. 'It's not far and I always like to check the place over when I come down. There'll be a later train.'

Guerdon: a gift; a recompense. He made a gesture which might have been some kind of acceptance. 'Guerdon House,' she told the driver. 'Do you know it? It's beyond Maidenhead. I'll direct you when we get there.'

And so they drove away from the Rest Home of Our Lady of Walsingham, away from the dying present towards Maidenhead and the river, and the past.

3

Helen leant forward to show the driver the way. They stopped in the village to pick the keys up from the woman who looked after the place, then drove on. There were some landmarks Michael half recognised – the church on the edge of the village, a pub where they used to have an occasional drink – but much was unfamiliar. A stretch of woodland had been fenced off and provided with picnic amenities. There was a new roundabout and by-pass, with signs to the motorway; and where once there had been open fields there was now an estate of newly built houses – *Queen Anne Style Executive Accommodation*, a placard announced. Beyond that the *Thames Leisure Centre and Country Club* lay amongst emerald lawns.

Then the taxi turned off the main road and drove down towards the river, and came to a halt in front of the familiar gates. 'Quite a place,' the driver said appreciatively. 'Must be worth a packet.'

The house stood desolate in its circle of trees at the head of the drive. While Helen paid off the taxi Michael stood looking up at the weather-beaten frontage, remembering it larger, more imposing, less the rather ordinary Victorian pile that it seemed now. The ground floor windows were shuttered, as blank as cataracted eyes. The upstairs ones reflected a grey and threatening sky.

'I told the driver to pick us up in an hour,' she said. 'That'll be all right, won't it?'

'I expect so.'

'What do you think of it?'

Traffic sounded in the distance but it did little to intrude. Around the house there was a great silence – just the movement of the trees and the calling of birds. 'The house? Smaller. Like

235

looking through the wrong end of a telescope or something. I can see here us as we used to be, but we seem very far away.'

Helen unlocked the front door and they went in, to a half familiar smell and a strange simulacrum of the past – the hallway as it had been redecorated by Lorna two decades earlier, the shadowy sitting room with its hessian wallpaper, the dining room with it's Regency stripe. The furniture was shrouded, like so many corpses lying round the room. The insidious damp of the river had got a grip once more and there were dark patches on some of the walls. In the conservatory some of the lights had been broken and there was water on the cement floor. Perhaps the fruiting body of dry rot fungus was once again lodged in the Aga. It was a melancholy place.

'It needs living in,' Helen said sorrowfully. 'We come down for weekends, but ever since mother fell ill it's been empty most of the time. It just isn't worth keeping like this.'

The place seemed imbued with the presence of Lorna, gaunt and haggard as she was now or elegant and dissolute as she had been then – the spirit of the woman, abandoning its useless body and haunting this old, damp house to watch with glee the havoc it had wreaked once and would wreak still. Michael echoed the taxi-driver's comment, but he did so to dispel the atmosphere that he felt there: 'It must be worth a fortune with the market as it is.'

'That's what everyone says. They only see Guerdon House in terms of the boom in property prices.'

'And how do you think of it?'

'I think of it like I think of her,' she said, leading the way upstairs. 'I love it and hate it. I want never to see it again, and I fear to lose it.' She shrugged. 'What else do you do with your memories? You may loathe them, but ultimately they're the only thing you've got.'

They went past doors that Michael remembered, over floorboards that creaked evocatively. She opened the door to her bedroom, where once, breathless with excitement and anticipation, he had lain almost chastely with her in the darkness. Now she was a brisk, rather dry, rather reserved middle-aged woman with husband, daughter and son. Now the mattress was bare to the ticking, and the bed-head – blue with white birds painted on it – was faded as though it had been long in the sun. There was a carpet on the floor and curtains round the windows, but there were none of those intimate, female things on the dressing-table that had made it hers, no pictures on the wall. None of that remained. Everything seemed to be packed away as though for departure, as though for a future which would begin when the old woman died.

'Let's go down to the river and have a quick look at the boathouse,' she suggested. 'The taxi should be back by then.'

They went outside and across the overgrown lawns down to where the boathouse crouched, black as a moorhen amongst willow and reed. Water slapped against the wooden piles. Helen fiddled with a padlock and the door creaked open. As they went in shadows seemed to push past them into the daylight, laughing and calling to each other, chasing each other with stories of ghosts and fiends. 'Careful,' she warned, and took his hand as they tiptoed onto the rotten stage. The opening to the river was curtained with willow fronds. An aqueous, chlorotic light came in. The water at their feet was as black and lucid as obsidian, casting intangible reflections up onto the roof.

'Do you remember stealing the punt?' she asked. 'And that fool Adrian. Do you remember?'

But the fleeing shadows had left the place empty – there was no punt there, nothing there at all until their eyes grew accustomed to the dark and they could make out, a foot below the surface, the outline of the vessel's gunwales. 'It must have sunk during the winter,' she said sorrowfully. 'No one has used it for years. Miriam's not into that kind of thing and Paul only seems to think of pop groups and motorbikes. Come on, the taxi should be here any minute.'

They slipped their hands free of one another and went out into the daylight. Clouds had come down and it was starting to rain. There, raising its bulk against the dark sky, was the holm oak they had climbed; but the orchard beyond the wall was no more – in its place could be seen the skeletal forms of half-completed rooves.

'We've had to sell it off for building,' Helen explained. 'No choice really.' She led him back to the house, feeling detached from both past and present, unable to decide whether she was in the company of a stranger or an intimate. In the sitting room she turned on the lights and pulled a dust sheet off one of the chairs to sit down. 'I'm sorry to drag you out of your way like this. I just wanted to see that the place was all right. It's always a bit of a worry.'

'Of course.'

She picked at a piece of thread in the upholstery of the chair and looked round the room as though to find something that was missing or out of place. 'I'm not brave enough to take the plunge and clear everything out. We took some stuff to the house in

London, but otherwise we left everything as it always was. We've not got that much space, you see . . .' She frowned. 'Michael, it wasn't that bad, was it?'

'What?'

She seemed to cast around for an answer. 'This. Coming with me to see her, to see this.'

'Bad? Not at all.'

'That sounds pretty half-hearted.' She glanced at her watch. 'The taxi should be here any minute. I could make tea, if I can find the things.'

'I wouldn't bother.'

'And she thought you were Daddy,' she said unexpectedly. 'Oh my God, how awful it was.' She shook her head as though in disbelief.

'I don't mind, really. Maybe I did some good, who knows?'

She smiled at him almost pityingly and went off to the kitchen, leaving him to wander round the room and make what he could of the place. There were still things there that he half recognised – some porcelain figures of no great worth, some old books on the shelves. There was also a framed photograph of a young man standing in front of a clapboard shed of some kind, holding the hand of a little girl. The girl had large and anxious eyes. The two figures looked out of the uncertain past with smiles respectively faintly mocking and nervous. Dimly he realised that the shed behind the two figures was the boathouse, not creosoted as it was now, but painted white. The little girl was Helen, standing with her father.

He put the picture down as she came in. 'I haven't seen this before.'

'What?'

'This photo.'

'I found it amongst some papers.' She handed him a mug of tea. 'Earl Grey,' she said.

'Reform Bill.'

She smiled. 'Why was it Reform Bill? I don't even remember. Selsey Bill.'

'Portland,' insisted Michael. 'It was *Portland* Bill. Where is he now anyway? Nadir. Sounds like a Pakistani middle-order batsman.'

'Or a dubious Cypriot businessman. It's *A* nadir. You've got to get it exact or it doesn't count. Haven't you seen?'

'Seen what?'

'At the Mermaid Theatre?'

'Adrian Oliver?'

'The very same. Eric and I went a month ago. A one-man show. It's called *Dante*.'

'Alighieri?'

'Gabriel Rossetti.'

'It would be. It just bloody well would be.'

She laughed. 'He paints pictures of the blessed Damozel on stage, and recites poetry, and feeds his wombat, and exhumes poor old Lizzie Siddal to steal the poems that he buried with her, all that kind of thing. It was huge success. For months you couldn't open a colour supplement without finding an article on the blessed Adrian or the bloody Pre-Raphaelites.'

She wandered over to where he had left the photo and picked it up. 'Who was he, do you think? He has haunted me all my life, do you know that? But who *was* he?' Then, glancing at her watch again, she exclaimed, 'It's late, damn it. I'll phone just in case,' and got up and went into the hall while he sat on the edge of one of the shrouded chairs like someone waiting for a significant event to happen, the arrival of a funeral cortège, something like that. A few seconds later Helen came back. 'Dead.'

He started. 'Who's dead?'

'The telephone. There's nothing. The line must be cut.'

He smiled with a kind of relief. 'Haven't you been paying the bills?'

'Mrs Moon is meant to see to things like that.' She went back and tried again, jiggling the cradle as though to coax a spark of life out of the instrument. It did no good. The phone remained obstinately silent. 'Oh dammit! What'll we do?' As though to answer her the sky outside grew darker and the rain began to beat against the windows, a thin thrashing sound like trees gusting in the wind. 'We can't go out in that.'

'Maybe the taxi will come.' He was standing watching her from the doorway to the sitting room. 'Maybe it's just delayed.'

She looked sceptical. 'Do you think so?'

'How should I know? It's possible.'

'Perhaps he's forgotten.' She felt that lightness again, the purity and lightness of caprice.

'We're going to get very wet.'

'Or stay completely dry.' She replaced the telephone on its cradle and went through into the kitchen. 'I'll see if there's something to eat. Are you hungry?'

'Hungry?'

'Supper,' she said.

'What do you mean, *supper*?'

She glanced round. 'The nearest house is God knows how far away. Those bloody maisonettes. Queen Anne villas, or whatever they call themselves. You'd get soaked going to phone.'

'*I'd* get soaked? I like that.'

She laughed. 'Well I'm not even going to try. If the rain doesn't stop and the taxi doesn't come I'm staying. The library's closed tomorrow.'

'But I'm due in the office . . .'

'Tell them you're ill.' She laughed with delight at the idea. 'Ring them tomorrow and tell them the phone wasn't working. You told me you were just kicking your heels here anyway.'

'You—'

'I what?' She raised her eyebrows inquisitively. The girl of twenty years ago watched him, with a look of challenge.

The rain didn't stop and the taxi didn't come. They were marooned on an island in the middle of the storm, in the middle of the water meadows, in the middle of rivulets and streams. The rain poured down in an incessant monotone and beneath it, beneath the dull fact of rain, there was the undercurrent of malice and enmity which water possesses when it is unleashed. Somewhere they heard it dripping – 'Oh God, we'll have to see about that' – elsewhere it trickled and scurried like some malign organism, eating away, dissolving, clinging and pulling. Michael found a pair of boots and an old mackintosh and struggled out in the downpour to get some coal from one of the outhouses while Helen stood in the lighted doorway and laughed at his plight. She found firelighters and newspapers in the cupboard under the stairs. 'Eighth of June 1975,' she read as she emerged with them. 'Where were you then?'

Michael contemplated the years. 'In Argentina. With Beatrice.'

'Who's she with now?'

'I guess she's with her parents. There wasn't another man, not at the time.'

'Was there another woman?' She giggled. 'For *you*, I mean.'

'Yes. It didn't come to anything, but we were happy for a while. That's all you can hope for, I guess.'

'Is it?'

Mercifully the matches that they found in the kitchen were dry enough to strike. She knelt down in front of the fireplace in the sitting-room and constructed a little wigwam of kindling wood and crumpled newspaper, then coaxed a flame from POLLS SAY

240

'YES' TO MARKET. 'Burning up the past,' she murmured. 'Sometimes I wish I could.' She smiled as she watched the flame flicker and grow. 'I was a bitch, wasn't I? It all seems so different from the perspective of middle-age.'

'Is that what we are now – middle-aged? Is it official?'

'Oh, I think so. Paul even gets muddled up over which world war we just missed, the first or the second. Miriam and her kind think we're just fossils. I watch her with her boyfriends and think how silly they are to be so serious about everything, and yet when we were their age it was all life and death for us as well, wasn't it? Adulthood just isn't as intense.'

'It is sometimes.'

The kindling wood caught and blazed. She looked at him over her shoulder. 'Was it intense with Beatrice?' She pronounced the name in the English manner – *Beertriss.*

'It was, for about ten years. That's not bad, is it? Ten years of passion and excitement?'

She eyed him narrowly, looking to see if he was teasing her. 'That's remarkable.'

'Is it?'

She went back to watching the embryo fire.

'Does Eric know we're here?' he asked.

'Of course not.'

'And what would happen if he turned up?'

She laughed. 'But why should he? Eric has never, ever done anything unexpected in his life. The unexpected is vulgar.'

'Is passion vulgar?'

'Very.' She brushed coal dust from her hands and stood up. 'That bloody taxi isn't coming, is it? Let's see what we can find to eat.'

They discovered a can of consommé and a can of baked beans, and, in the scullery which had once held the wine cellar, a single bottle of beer. It was like opening up Dennis Killin's little cottage near Lapithos that summer, finding the debris in the kitchen, airing the place, trying to make some kind of habitation of it. They sat at the card table in the sitting room and laughed over their absurd situation and the refugees' meal they had concocted, and talked about neutral things, about his work for the Institute, and her work at the university, the conference she had organised the year before in London, and the one she was going to this November in Jerusalem. They told each other about friends and acquaintances that they didn't have in common, conjuring characters who were larger than life, finding the incongruous and the absurd in almost everything they did and most things they said. They laughed a lot, and she watched his laughter and felt the pressure of the past, their adult past and their childhood past, holding the present in tension like the two sides of a balance.

'Miriam,' he said softly, choosing his moment. 'Tell me about Miriam.'

The balance rocked gently. The silence in the room was intense, highlighted by the wash of rain outside in the darkness. She answered him obliquely. Her gaze was mellowed by the low light so that it took back some of the softness of youth and appeared little changed from all those years ago. 'I left Oxford and went to live in London. Sometimes Mother was a help, other times she was just bloody about the whole thing. Anyway, eventually I found a job at the School of Bible Studies. I had to keep it quiet that I had a child, or at least I *assumed* I had to keep it quiet because I imagined that I'd be thrown out if they got to know. I didn't dare find out for sure.' She laughed humourlessly. 'Can you imagine? Can't ask, because you may find out there's no longer anything to ask about. So I lived this quiet, sequestered life and I used to wonder who I was, and who Miriam was and it took me a long time before I understood that we weren't anyone in particular, that there's no such thing as identity given, like your face is given or your limbs or your body. Once I discovered that I felt much happier.'

'You could have let me know.'

'You'd gone. Argentina, Brazil, I wasn't really sure where. Anyway, it wasn't long before I met Eric, and he sort of took me on, let me be who the hell I wanted to be and I was happy after a fashion. Miriam was five by then, and I'd published something, and people had got to know about her anyway, and by then it didn't seem to matter at all. And I was happy enough with Eric, and then Paul came and . . .' She shrugged. 'Happy families.' The wind shook the windows. Rain dashed against the glass like a handful of pebbles thrown by some malignant child. She stood up, and for a moment she stood in front of him as though she was about to say something more. Then abruptly she turned away with their plates and went into the kitchen. He followed, watched her putting a kettle on to boil and taking a jar of instant coffee on one of the shelves. Seen from behind there was still that illusion that she was unchanged from twenty years ago: there were none of those small brush strokes of age that gave her face that new dimension which had surprised him when they had met at the dinner party. From behind, except for a broadening of her hips, she was still the girl of twenty-something.

'Do you want some of this stuff if I can get it out?' she asked. The coffee powder was clotted into a brown lump at the bottom and she struggled to dig it out. 'It's a bit past its sell-by date.'

'And now?' he asked.

'Now?'

'Us, here.'

'What about it?'

'Don't you see the problem?'

'Problem? Not really. We're grown-ups now, aren't we?' The very use of the term called the fact into question. She gave up with the coffee and tossed the jar in the bin. 'Dead loss,' she said. 'Let's sort out where we're going to sleep. There's bedding somewhere upstairs, but I'm afraid the sheets won't be aired.'

'What are you doing, Helen?' he asked. 'What's this all about?'

She looked at him with a matter-of-fact expression, as though explaining something to a child. 'It's all about nothing whatever. It just *is*. Why should you look for a meaning? A rainstorm, a modestly haunted old house, two people who once knew each other rather well; what else?' She turned out the lights and he followed her out into the hall and up the stairs. The rain was still falling. Somewhere water was still dripping 'This bloody place . . .' she muttered as she walked along the corridor. He noticed how slender her feet were and how she walked with long strides as though determined to get somewhere. She had always been like that, walking with determination, yet expecting nothing.

A cupboard upstairs yielded bedding. She climbed up on a stepladder to reach the shelves and doled things out to him like a quarter-master handing items to a recruit. 'Blanket, blanket – how many do you want? there's plenty here – pillow, pillow, pillow-case, pillowcase, sheets.' The sheets were threadbare, cold and damp. 'You'd better count them,' she said as she came down. 'Do you want your old room?' She was brisk and organised, following one sentence with another as fast as she could in case thought should come in between. 'I put the water heater on so there might be some hot water for a wash. No toothbrush, I'm afraid. Squalid really, but it is quite fun, isn't it? Like camping. Do you remember we used to camp in the attic? You use the bathroom first, if you want.'

He reached out and took hold of her hand. She watched, not smiling but considering the grip of his hand as though it were

243

something very new and remarkable. 'Let's go back downstairs,' he suggested. 'At least it's warm there.'

Helen opened her mouth to speak, and then closed it again. Instead she just gave a little nod. Carrying some of the bedding they went down to the sitting room. The fire was still smouldering. He took the guard away and put more coal on, while she settled cross-legged on the hearth rug and watched him. She arranged her skirt over her knees and her pose was one of slightly self-conscious expectation, almost as though she was waiting to have her photograph taken.

'Perhaps you were right. It's warmer here.' She smiled. In the uncertain firelight her face seemed sharp and thin, her eyes very large and very dark. Behind them the house creaked and shifted in the darkness, as though uneasy with its new burden.

'Strange, meeting you again so . . . unexpectedly. And that same afternoon I'd thought of you, I told you that. Quite out of the blue. I was just waiting for a taxi, fiddling around. Do you think . . .?' And then she faltered and gave a little half-laugh. 'I'm sorry, I'm becoming inarticulate. I had no idea I would see you that evening and yet I thought of you. That's all. I just wonder whether in some subliminal way I already knew that you were nearby. As soon as you put it into words like that it sounds bloody silly, doesn't it? I remembered how you once called my fingers claws, that was it. Is that what they're like?' She looked down at them as they lay in her lap and held them open as though he might look at them and give her a considered answer. He reached out and took hold of one of them and lifted it up. 'Talons,' he said. 'You never realised how sharp.'

She laughed uncertainly. 'And now this mess. I'm sorry, Michael. I didn't mean to . . .' Her voice trailed away. 'Trap you. I didn't mean to trap you.'

Outside the wind was ransacking the trees, ransacking the branches of the holm oak as though searching for something of value there. Rain dashed against the windows. The sound came through to them in the narrow shadows of the living room, a sound like the roaring of the sea, the roaring of the surf on Aphrodite's beach. Something cried in her mind, something that might have been the memory of gulls, might have been pure derision. She thought of Eric and she thought of Killin and she thought of Adrian. Four men in a lifetime. She thought of the years of abstinence, with Miriam a child. 'Do you know how many men there have been?' she asked. 'Just four. How does that work out in the national averages, I wonder?'

244

'Is that one of our games? Do I guess their names or something?'

She laughed. She got to her feet and knelt in front of him and she no longer seemed like a child who was in control of her world, but an adult who understood quite clearly the uncertainty of things. 'Oh, Michael,' she whispered, touching his face as though to make certain of it, and feeling a roughness that had never been there when they had known each other last, a roughness that was like the whole paradox of ageing, being both a sign of strength and a hint of decay. She felt consumed by a dreadful incoherence, and by a dreadful fear against which his strange familiarity was the only bulwark. She leant towards him so that he was forced to put his arms round her, forced to give her comfort. 'I'm sorry,' she said, as though apologising for everything, the past as well as the present. 'I should never have let you go, should I? I didn't realise, that's the trouble. I knew you too well, I suppose. We never realise, do we? We just assume that there'll be other moments, other ways of putting things right, and there so rarely are. There's nothing more irreversible than the past.'

'And can we reverse it now?'

She pulled away to look at him, to see the lines on his face and wonder what they signified. 'Can we try?'

'What do you want from this, Helen?'

Things were clear now, if there had ever been any doubt. 'I want to understand,' she replied. 'The older I get, the less that I understand. I want you to help me understand.' She looked like a little girl, stubborn in the face of adult refusal. 'Please don't let me down, Michael.'

'What about Eric?'

She shrugged ruefully. 'I'm happy enough with Eric. Eric is just irrelevant, that's the problem. Eric's a palliative, and there comes a point when you have to face the fact that palliatives don't cure.' She seemed to think for a minute and then, as though making up her mind, stood up and began to unbutton her shirt. It was some kind of echo of that scene in the cottage near Lapithos, firelight taking the place of the thin daylight that had come through the shutters and created a pool of light around her. Her figure was touched by ochre, bathed in a kind of gold. She tossed the shirt aside and reached behind to the catch of her brassière, smiling wryly at his expression.

'I'm still nothing much, I'm afraid.' She held the scrap of lace against her chest and looked down on him as she had long before in the shadows of the woodland. Then she threw the brassière after the shirt and stood there in her pants, feeling rather foolish, feeling as though she was playing at some childish game which adults ought to have outgrown.

'Helen,' he said quietly. 'You don't want this.' And he too looked confused, the child again, watching her just as he had that time in the woods.

'Do I look awful? I've even got stretch marks now.'

'Helen . . .'

'Don't you want me any longer? I'm a poor enough specimen, I suppose. Scrawny.' She held out her arms to display herself, the fragile limbs and the loose breasts and the thin and corrugated flesh of her abdomen. There was anguish and delight at having Michael look at her. 'Didn't you always want this? Always?' She felt the weight of the past on her, the unbearable load of memory and desire crushing her. Somewhere in the distance her father called her, a faint voice amongst the noise of the past . . .

4

She woke to a cold dawn, with the fire dead in the grate and Michael asleep on the sofa, curled up beneath a rug. The room around them was sketched in the chiaroscuro tones of a pencil drawing. She got up stiffly with her joints cracking, and pulled her clothes on and went through into the kitchen in cold, stockinged feet. Her mouth was thick and dry. Even to herself her breath smelt tainted. She put a kettle on to boil and stood by the sink staring through the window. The whole garden glistened in the pewter light. Branches had come down in the storm, branches of holm oak lying like broken limbs, with their torn flesh naked and white. In the midst of the lawn a lake of rainwater flung an inverted image of the sky down through the grass – trees, clouds, all hung upside between the margins of the flood.

She felt light-headed with tiredness and emotion, a clear sensation that she was not really here in this drab dawn; or rather she had always been here, from the little girl lost in the mists of memory to the adult lost in the confusions of middle-age: a whole lifetime burning in this single moment. Somewhere too there was her father, his image there for the grasping as surely as this present one she was looking on now. She had dreamed of him during the night, during her fitful sleep at Michael's side. She had dreamed of Andrew and of Tommy and of Killin, and the whole assembly of men in her life and her mother's – Adrian even, and Eric; and of course Michael himself, who was no more substantially there than the others although logic told her it was he who slept beside her on the sofa, he who actually occupied this tangible moment rather than all the others.

The kettle boiled. Her thoughts – impressions, snatches of dreams, snatches of memory – ran on. She had always believed that her thoughts were within her control and yet she knew different now: here she was with her mind freewheeling, not truly out of control but speeding along just as she and Michael had once on their bikes, down to the river, along the towpath and through the fields, the sky vast above them and the world infinite in its possibilities. Childhood. It seemed something more than mere memory – an experience that was going on still, her mind being no different now, merely cluttered up with information, merely bunged full of ideas that were not her own, that came from outside, that were on loan or had been stolen. But she existed, her own, bright self. She was Helen, with a fierce look and a tight mouth and a cloud of errant hair: Helen deciphering a simple postcard; Helen climbing the holm oak; Helen watching a moving aeroplane which glittered with coloured light like a Christmas tree and trailed a plume of water along behind it; Helen amongst the ruins of Paphos and the desolation of Aphrodite's beach. She was the alpha and the omega, the beginning and the end, all that there was.

A footfall behind her. 'Good morning.' He smiled ruefully and came over to kiss her. 'I feel terrible. Daresay I look terrible. I feel as though I've got a bloody hangover.'

She pointed out of the window. 'There are some branches down. Can you see? Maybe they are ones we climbed on. Do you think so?'

He peered through the window. 'Perhaps. Quite a bit of damage. The tree looks completely different, doesn't it? We couldn't have got lost up in there if it had been like that.'

'We weren't lost.'

'Hidden. We were hiding.'

'Were we?'

'It took them hours to find us. Don't you remember? We held our breath while they went calling through the garden. Don't you remember?'

'I just remember being there.'

'And then they went down to the river, to the boathouse and your mother started shouting. And we began to realise that the joke had gone too far.'

'I don't remember that bit at all.'

'She thought we'd drowned.' He looked back at her. 'What are we going to do, Helen?'

She spooned the last out of the tea caddy. 'I'd like to stay here,' she said. 'Just like this.'

'It'd be bloody uncomfortable.'

'You know what I mean.'

'Camping in the attic?'

'If you like.' The kettle came to the boil. They sat at the kitchen table. Michael was watching her over the top of his cup, through the vapour that rose from the tea. She knew that he was about to speak, knew more or less what he was about to say. She tried to postpone the moment. 'Do you remember the trapdoor to the attic? Do you remember? It seemed so threatening, didn't it? What did we expect to find up there?'

'Miriam,' he said quietly, ignoring her attempts. 'Is Miriam my daughter, Helen?'

She considered him thoughtfully. It wasn't love. It was something worse – familiarity, a sense of possession and being possessed, a sense that, if she let herself, she would be entirely his, body and soul. Maybe that was what had frightened her all those years ago.

'I don't know,' she said abruptly. And she got up from the table and took her mug to the sink, while he sat at the table staring across the room through the space she had occupied, staring at the dresser against the far wall.

'Do you mean that?'

'Yes.' She ran water into the sink, stood there running the water over her hands as though they might be dirty. 'I had a cocktail inside me, don't you see? Yours and Killin's. And I just don't know.' She paused, looking down into the sink. There was just the sound of the running water. 'It seems madness, doesn't it? You'd have thought you could tell. But you can't. I used to look at her and wonder, and think one thing and then another . . . and I just don't know. And now, seeing you again . . .' she shrugged helplessly. 'And what difference would it make anyway? There must be some kind of test available – DNA or something – but what good would it do? She's herself. Miriam's no one but herself.'

'Don't the people involved have rights?'

'You? What would it do if she was yours? Gratify your sense of masculine pride? Very *macho*. Did you learn that in Argentina? And what would it do for her to know that her mother was like a bitch on heat with the dogs queuing up to fuck her, and one of them was twice her age and is the biggest bastard I've ever known, and would you mind having a test just to find out whose sperm it happened to be that won the race? In Christ's name, how could I do that?' She shook her head as though to shake the tears from her eyes. 'I *don't* know why, Michael,' she said, in answer to a question that hadn't been asked. 'I still don't know why. And here I am again . . .'

He went over to her and held her shoulders. 'That's not fair on either of us.'

'No, it's not.' She looked round at him with a smile. Her eyes were red. 'Not fair at all.' And she kissed his hand, and that contact seemed as intimate as any they had had. 'No one ever found out,' she said. 'Not my mother, no one. Just you. Of course I never told Dennis. I never even saw him again. He went abroad just as you did and I never contacted him. I've never seen him since. He rang once, years ago, and left a message, but I didn't follow it up.'

'And what happens now?' he asked. 'To us, I mean.'

She shrugged. 'I don't know that either. There's rather a lot I don't know. Do we want an affair?'

'Is that what it would be? An affair?'

'What's the alternative? Smashing up a marriage?'

'Putting it like that . . .'

'Is there another way? Have you finished with that cup? I'll wash it. Then we'd better sort ourselves out . . .'

'Will we ever?'

'I don't know, Michael, I don't know.'

And so they began to tidy up, putting the sitting room back in order and carrying the bedding back upstairs, and just as they were about finished they heard a noise outside, the sound of a car drawing up on the gravel. Michael was coming down the stairs and Helen was at the door to the drawing room. She looked round in something like fright. 'What's that?'

'The postman?'

'Don't be daft. Everything's redirected.'

Car doors slammed and footsteps approached. 'Maybe it's Eric,' he suggested, only half joking.

Helen looked at him in sudden panic. 'You'd better go,' she said urgently. 'For goodness' sake get upstairs out of sight.' But before he could move, if he intended to move, there was a voice outside – 'Christ, it's unlocked. Don't tell me there's been another bloody break-in' – and the front door swung open.

A girl stood silhouetted in the doorway, a figure drawn in two dimensions against the light outside. 'Who the hell—?' Then recognition dawned. 'Christ alive, it's you Mum.' She came through into the hall, a young girl wearing black tights and clumsy black boots and a black PVC raincoat, her hair an artful brush of similar shiny black, her lips purple, her ears studded with pearls like a row of baby-teeth. 'You didn't half give me a shock. We came over to see if there was any damage . . .' She paused, staring past Helen into the shadows of the hall. 'Who in Christ's name is this?'

There was a moment's silence. Helen looked round at Michael and then back at Miriam, from the girl with the hard edge of London about her, the aggressive black clothes and short, sharp hair, to the unkempt man, greying at the temples and wearing a heavy stubble and an expression of faint disquiet. And she fancied that she saw the one reflected in the other like a glimpse of a face seen in a sheet of water, the features subtly transformed by the angle and the light and the inherent transparency of the medium. She breathed out sharply. Did he see it too?

'This is Michael,' she said. 'And this, as you have probably gathered, is my daughter, Miriam.'

And she rehearsed words in her mind and wondered whether she would have the courage actually to say them. For a moment the whole thing teetered in the balance. And then, as though the pond had been disturbed and the sheet of water ruffled by a breeze, the reflections were no longer there. The moment had passed.

'What in Christ's name have you been up to, mum?'

'Up to?'

'You've spent the night here, haven't you? Who the hell *is* this?'

'Michael is my stepbrother,' Helen explained quietly. 'I've told you about him. Well, here he is. We came down to see your grandmother and got caught by the storm.'

'How long have you been doing this?'

'I don't know what you're talking about, darling . . . look, why don't you come inside?' She went through into the living room, assuming that Miriam would follow. But the girl only came as far as the doorway. She had an unwavering expression that contained all the determination and bloody-mindedness of youth, as though demanding an answer and prepared to disbelieve the one she was given. 'Does Eric know?' she demanded. 'Does Eric know what's going on?'

'Not especially. I might have mentioned it, I can't remember. We just came down – brother and sister – to see your grandmother, and we got caught by the storm. The phone doesn't work. We couldn't get a taxi.'

The girl looked round suspiciously. She picked the phone up and held it to her ear, then dumped it back on its cradle. Then she turned to the front door and called to the man who hovered on the step. 'It's all right, Bill. It's family. Can you check round outside or something? See if any tiles have come down, or whatever it is you do.' She pushed past Michael into the drawing room.

'You're really behaving most offensively,' Helen said.

'You can't just pretend these things don't matter, Mum. What's Eric meant to think? What am I meant to think, come to that?''

Helen shrugged. 'We met again just the other day. At Gemma and Howard's . . . Eric was there.'

The girl picked up the cushions from the sofa and tossed them aside, then sat down heavily where mere hours before, the two of them had lain. 'I mean, a night in the house with a strange man.'

'Strange to you, my dear. I know him very well: since I was, goodness knows, eight, I suppose. We were brother and sister. For years, if you see what I mean. You've heard me talk about him. Tommy's son.'

'You mean he's my uncle?'

Michael appeared confused by the sharp flavour of the city that the girl possessed, almost bewildered by the contrast between mother and daughter. 'Step-uncle, I guess,' he said. 'If there is such a thing. Another of your grandmother's victims.'

The girl looked at him with shrewd eyes. 'Constant Tommy, that's what she used to call your father. You must be the one she called a silly bastard.'

'Miriam!'

'Lorna used to call everyone a silly bastard at one time or another,' Michael replied. 'Let me make you some tea or something. Can't offer you much more. We don't seem very well equipped, I'm afraid.'

'We don't?'

He smiled wryly. 'This was my second home, too. We shared a lot here, your mother and I. You know the kind of thing. Climbing trees, camping in the attic, playing doctors and nurses behind the potting shed.'

The anger in the girl's expression was dissipating, suspicion dying. She half laughed. 'I'll bet you did. I climbed the holm oak with that kid from the council estate in the village. You know the one? Mrs Moon's nephew.'

'Darren.'

'Darren. And all I remember about it was wondering whether he could see my knickers.'

'And could he?' asked Michael.

'You bet he could.'

Michael laughed. It was almost done, the deception connived at, the half truths disbursed with subtlety and care, the dose carefully limited and the pill sugared.

'I'll go and put the kettle on,' Helen said. 'There's only tinned milk, I'm afraid. Do you want it without?'

'Please.' Miriam got up. 'Make a mug for Bill as well. I'll get him in. We came over to see if there was any damage. There's stuff down all over the place, telephone poles, trees.'

'Some branches came down,' Helen said as she went through to the kitchen. 'We haven't been out to have a look yet.'

Miriam paused at the door and looked back at Michael, waiting to make sure her mother was out of earshot. 'Fancy you turning up,' she said. 'When did you last see each other?'

'Decades ago. When we were still students. In the sixties. Before you were around.'

'Amazing. Why did you lose touch?' She looked at him critically, as though trying to measure his size in the scheme of things.

He shrugged. 'The divorce. You can imagine it wasn't too easy on us. A messy affair.'

She nodded. 'I bet she was dead straight as a girl, wasn't she? Yet she had me all by herself, did you know that? Imagine. No father, no mention of a father. You know Eric's not my father, don't you? She's told you that bit?'

'I'd worked it out.'

'I'll bet you'd never have imagined it, would you? I mean, all this Bible research and stuff. You'd think she was dead straight.' She looked at him thoughtfully. 'I might have been a virgin birth,' she said. Then she turned and went out to find her boyfriend.

The train roared through the purlieus of West London, past terraced houses, factories, supermarkets, warehouses, everything painted in shades of grey or rust, spotted with rain and punctuated by fluorescent light. People passing along the carriage and glancing down would not have noticed much: a couple sitting opposite one another, talking in a desultory fashion like strangers who have nothing left to say, or people who know each other so well that conversation is not really necessary any longer. You needed to pause for a while to listen before deciding which of the two it was. They looked as though they were coming to the end of a long journey, one that had started far away and had involved a number of changes and much waiting around and little sleep. Perhaps the fact of their appearing to have shared the journey gave them an aspect of intimacy, but you couldn't be sure. As with many journeys the final destination was in doubt.

She shifted uneasily in her seat, looking at him sitting opposite her, grey and unshaven, worn and crumpled, with a faint frown on his face as though he were trying to read her thoughts. I know him, she thought. From top to toe, from childhood to this dreadful adulthood, I know him as intimately as one can know another.

'How are you feeling?' he asked.

It was as though she was at the bar, expected to plead in a trial whose outcome hung in the balance. 'I don't know, Michael. I don't know anything very much any more . . .'

'Except?'

'How do you know there's an "except"?'

'I can tell. I can always tell.'

She smiled wearily. The train ran on, plummeting towards its destination. They were part of its headlong rush. She watched the countryside pass. 'Except I want to be at Guerdon,' she said. 'Not here, not going back to London.'

'Here, there; is there a difference?'

'I want to feel like a child again.'

'A child! Surely the one thing we've got to be is adult.'

The word adultery rang in her ears. She knew all its echoes and nuances, its etymology and its paronyms. 'No guilt,' she said quietly. 'I don't want to feel the guilt.'

They were silent for a while, watching the countryside pass. 'Do you think Miriam guessed?' Michael asked eventually.

Helen shrugged. 'Who knows? I think she can pretend quite happily that there's nothing between us. But she isn't a fool . . .'

'We're safe for the moment, is that it?'

The idea amused her. 'No one's ever safe.'

'And what do we do now? Do we plan? Do we just let things drift? What do we do?'

She shook her head like a petulant child. 'I don't *know* what to do.'

'You must decide. I know what I want.'

'What do you want?' she asked, but she had guessed the answer already.

'I want you.'

At the station they stood beneath the departures board where they had met only the day before. She fiddled distractedly with the front of his jacket, as though smoothing creases out of it. Nearby a newspaper-seller was shouting about the IRA; one of his placards announced TERROR THREAT FROM LIBYA. Indifferent to the warnings the crowds streamed past, hurrying for the buses, for the underground, for the taxi rank.

She gave a bitter little laugh. 'Thanks for coming with me. Moral support, that's what she'd have called it.' Lorna was already in the past, already another part of memory. 'We'll work something out, Michael. I'll ring you, this evening if I can. It won't be difficult.'

'Is that all there is?'

'It's all we've got, isn't it?' She raised herself on tiptoe and kissed him briefly and remotely, cheek to cheek as brother and sister might. Then she turned and walked away towards the entrance to the underground.

Lorna slipped into a coma. Something, some blood vessel or other, broke inside her brain and wreaked havoc amongst the synapses and neurones, that electrical circuitry which, according to the neurologists and the behaviourists but not many other people, makes us what we are. Helen called Michael – 'Eric can't come. He's got some meeting or other' – and they went down together, like the first time. But now she was distracted, looking away from him, thinking of her mother and the decay of things. They were silent for much of the journey, silent in the taxi that took them from the station. There was the sensation of time repeating itself, but in some alternative system where all was not quite the same, where everything appeared warped by what had gone before. At the nursing home they were ushered into a different room from the previous occasion, a room in the clinic where things were surgical white and the staff wore gowns and people spoke in hushed but purposeful voices. This, after all, was what the whole place was about. Death is what life is all about, children; death and going to Jesus if you're good. Bad people? Well that's a bit more complicated. A priest hovered, as though prepared to offer his views on that particular matter if requested.

Lorna lay in a room with flowers in a bowl on the window sill and a reproduction of Piero della Francesca's Resurrection on the wall. She lay on her back with her eyes closed and her rib cage moving faintly beneath the sheet. A plastic tube emerged from her nose and disappeared somewhere beneath the bed, carrying some nameless fluid away almost as though it was carrying away her life force. Pieces of electronic apparatus were more animate than all this, tracing the fluorescent script of brain and heart across a pair of screens, like writing from some distant and barely understood civilisation.

The doctor had brisk, matter-of-fact tones. 'At first she was drifting in and out of consciousness. Now I'm afraid she's in a coma.'

'Is she dying? Is there nothing you can do?'

'You have to face the facts, Mrs Smythe. Quite frankly an operation at this stage . . .'

'How long?' Michael asked.

The doctor hesitated, looking down at the figure on the bed as though for some kind of indication. No sign came. Lorna's chest rose and fell as lightly as a sleeping child's. A sibilant movement of air came from her nostrils. There was nothing more. She seemed to have moved beyond mere age, beyond mere dying, into some kind of limbo. 'It's hard to say with any certainty, Mr Smythe.'

'Constance,' Helen said. A glacial smile from the doctor, and a glance at their clasped hands. She felt the need to explain. 'We're brother and sister.'

'Yes, of course. The trouble is this state can continue rather static for some time. You see, Mr Constance, physically your mother's quite strong—'

'Stepmother,' Helen interrupted, matters of genealogy suddenly seeming absurdly important. 'She's Michael's stepmother. I should have said stepbrother and sister.' She clung to his hand and felt confusion and misery. 'I'm sorry, it doesn't matter. It really doesn't matter.'

Indifferent to such considerations the figure of her mother lay there on the bed and seemed about to take away with her a whole segment of the past. Helen felt a sensation akin to panic. We are our memories, nothing more. And in the claustrophobic room with its electronic apparatus and its dying woman, her own past suddenly seemed an insubstantial thing, at the mercy of mere memory, at the mercy of Lorna's imminent death. A whole dimension of her own childhood was about to be extinguished. She watched the faint rise and fall of the sheet and the impassive face of her mother, and she felt a kind of panic. Where was she now; and where was her own father? In the random shutting down of different bits of her mother's brain memories of him had surely already gone, leaving Helen's own recollections unique, hers alone, and somehow the poorer for that. Where was the woman she had loved and hated; where was that blandly handsome man in the peaked cap who had smiled at the photographer with a curious insouciance and gone to war to become some kind of hero, and then to the Holy Land to become some kind of martyr? Martyr, μαρτυς, a witness. Where was the church they had walked to hand-in-hand, or the car whose engine they had examined together, or the airfield, slick with rain where he had left her for that last time? These things were so far away as to seem to belong to different people, to a different construct of things, a different world drawn in shades of grey and inhabiting some other corner of the universe. Where were those glittering soldiers?

Standing in the over-heated room, with the pine trees beyond the windows looking like funeral mutes, Helen watched a portion of her own existence die. The word *mother* rang in her mind – a word laden with a whole complex of meaning amongst which she could find guilt and hate as well as love – and she clung to memory as though this was the only way to keep a grip on the mundane facts of life.

The priest approached as they came out. He was a thin, austere man, the kind one might imagine in theological dispute with heretics. His smile was bleak. 'Mrs Smythe?'

Helen hesitated, as though she didn't quite recognise the name. 'We're not Catholics,' she said. 'Neither my mother nor I. I don't think she even believed . . .'

'I think perhaps that doesn't matter very much now. Perhaps you would allow me to be with her and say some prayers?'

'A sort of insurance policy?'

He struggled to read her tone, his smile still there, patient in the face of the literal world. 'If you like.'

'Go ahead,' she said almost dismissively. 'Go ahead.'

So the priest went into Lorna's room to do whatever it was they did, and Helen and Michael walked away down the corridor towards the reception area, where the plaster Madonna looked on the customers with her knowing smile. 'What will happen?' she asked vaguely. 'What will happen?' But of course she didn't expect an answer. Words bubbled up to the surface of her mind like the products of some cerebral thesaurus, and a corrupted line, one that any textual critic would have spotted immediately, nagged at her with the insistent voice of a child: I live; yet not I but the past lives in me.

Out in the grounds the new building was under way now, the wall footings rising from the soil almost as though they had been discovered there and the builders were merely uncovering them from the earth. Two men in hard hats wandered round the site with the plans of the future opened out to show where doors and windows and bathrooms would be. They pointed decisively as though they knew what was going to happen.

'I've got to go to Guerdon House,' Helen said. 'The mother superior gave me some of her things to take. Apparently they wanted the room.' She corrected herself. 'They needed it. They *needed* the room.' She looked at him for understanding. 'You can't stay, Michael. Not now. Not with things the way they are now.'

He was angry, as she knew he would be. 'For God's sake, your mother's been like this for years. How has this changed things? I've seen so little of you.'

'It's difficult, isn't it?'

'*Diff,*' he said. He laughed bitterly, and childhood mocked them.

'I've tried to get away as often as I can, you know I've tried. But it's not always that easy. And that pokey little flat you've got . . .' Rancour edged into her voice. Guilt flowed like a caustic fluid, saturating everything, corrupting everything, easing its way into every corner of her life. 'And Eric says what an excellent chap you are. That sort of makes it worse. If he'd only loathe you.'

'Making it worse means it's bad already.'

'You know what I mean.'

'But do *you?*'

'Oh, for God's sake.' She tried to change the subject, talking about Lorna; but of course that wasn't really changing the subject at all. All it did was project them back into memory, and memory was the most dangerous territory of all. 'Please,' she said. 'Please just take me there and leave me alone. For the moment.'

Michael helped her carry her mother's things into the house – the pictures, the sewing box she had never used, the inlaid writing box – *escritoire,* Lorna would insist – a suitcase with her clothes. Then he kissed her cursorily on the cheek and climbed into the car.

'Keep in touch,' he said. She stood at the door and watched him drive away towards the main road, then turned and went inside.

A fire was already lit in the drawing room. Eric was in London, Miriam was at university and Paul at school, but Mrs Moon was there. 'I'm not having you on your own in that great big house, not at a time like this,' she had told Helen. 'I'll stay and look after you for a day or two.' She was in the kitchen, slamming pots and pans around, and now she put her head round the door. 'Do you want me to get some tea for you, dear?'

'I think I'll have a drink actually. I'll get it, don't worry.'

The woman looked faintly disapproving. 'Just as you please, dear. You go easy on that kind of thing, though. You've got to look after yourself.'

Helen smiled and went over to where the bottles stood. She felt the relief of solitude. The tensions of deception and betrayal were abating. She poured herself a whisky and looked round the over-familiar room, and felt the ghosts watching her, ghosts of the present as well as the past, the ghosts of Michael and herself beside the ghosts of Lorna and Tommy and Andrew. Her mother's writing box stood where Michael had left it on the card table. It was a pleasing piece, veneered with rosewood and inlaid with ivory, with a brass plate on the lid that bore the ornate initials of Lorna's great-grandmother. Helen opened it and released a sudden musty smell into the air, almost as though she had released some kind of spirit from the box. She opened it right out so that it sat like a sloping desktop. The leather skiver needed replacing. She ran her fingers round the edges and then inserted a fingernail in the crack and lifted the desk up. There were letters in the space beneath, a random mass of letters and envelopes and old post cards. One of the cards was written by her grandfather. It was dated 1917 and showed – she felt a faint thrill at the sight – the city of Jerusalem from the Mount of Olives. The foreground was occupied by two soldiers of Allenby's army, their rifles at the slope.

My dearest, Having a good time, love William, was the terse message on the back. It was addressed to Helen's grandmother. Most of the other letters were her mother's.

In what, she wondered, does the past consist? Is it substance or accident? Is it mendacious memory or does it lie in the deceptive artifacts that one finds buried in the present? She sat at the card table and began to take the letters out, wondering peripheral things – where had her mother kept them all these years? how had she concealed them? – and then: should she simply consign them to the flames of the fire that Mrs Moon had just lit, the fire before which she and Michael had made love mere weeks before? A holocaust, it would be, a burnt offering of the past, bringing a purity through annihilation. Surely the past, such as it was, was dying. It would be a quicker, less painful end by the sacrifice of those letters. She hefted the letters in her hand, remembering her mother as a young woman, blonde and brown on a Cyprus beach, with the men eyeing her – the whole tribe of men watching, imagining, knowing; and Lorna herself basking in their fantasies just as she basked in the Mediterranean sun, growing hardened by use, tanned by exposure, burnished to a fine hard shine. And the dark stain of melanoma on her mind, the seed of that cancer planted a decade earlier.

Most of the letters were preserved with their envelopes. There was the HMSO inscription and the royal arms on the flap and familiar writing on the front. She rifled through them as though they were cards; fortune-telling cards, maybe.

It was already dusk outside. She began to take the letters out of their envelopes one at a time, putting them more or less in order, glancing through them as she did so, skimming the words, stopping occasionally to read them fully, trying to treat them as a piece of text that she might have come across in a library, something that could not affect her directly.

Another missive from the Unholy Land, she read, *where Jews hate the British and the Arabs, the Arabs hate the Jews and the British, and the British hate themselves for getting into such a frightful mess. Dennis Killin makes things slightly normal by appearing pig-ignorant about the whole thing. Last Sunday he organised a picnic lunch with – can you imagine? – smoked salmon and bottles of wine. Snap-shot enclosed, and notice the sunshine even at this time of year.*

Then another and another, all more or less mundane, each describing the trivialities of garrison life, the parties, the tedium, the incidents – *today a bomb at the railway station . . . yesterday (or was it the day before?) we had a soccer match, headquarters staff against the Secretariat: fat and indolent soldiers against fat and indolent bureaucrats . . . On Wednesday, a sacrificial junior officer amongst the brass, I had dinner at the High Commission.* Others faintly embarrassing, faintly embarrassed, touched on the intimate – *I miss your touch, the taste and smell of you . . . how I long to feel you beside me . . . I keep your photo beside my bed and dream of you at night* – others mentioned the distant and half-apprehended daughter – *she must be quite grown now, no longer a baby, but a little girl. Give her a special kiss from me and tell her that her daddy loves her.*

The earliest one, dated April 1945, came not from Palestine at all but from some Army headquarters in northern Germany and the envelope bore the sticker of the military censor:

Today I went to one of the camps. Belsen. Maybe you have heard about it? The press people have been crawling all over and Pathé news will have done its bit, I'm sure. Jack Springer and I drove down to have a look, rather like tourists I'm afraid to say. There are birch trees and pines and that kind of thing, not unlike parts of the New Forest really. You could smell the place from a mile off. There were notices warning about typhus, and Jack and I had to do a bit of smart talking to get through. It was five days after the arrival of our boys and they haven't even finished burying the bodies. People are still dying by the hundred every day despite everything the medics can do. The doctors mark a red cross on the foreheads of those they think might be saved, just like the great plague. Poor old Jack was as sick as a dag.

Helen put the letter down. She sat motionless, staring out across the shadowy, familiar room and seeing other things there. She felt the past lying all around her, a past that lay just beyond her reach and yet was so close to her that for a moment she fancied she actually *saw* him there, almost an apparition conjured out of the shadows of the room – the man himself holding up something that she recognised well, that stood now in the corner cupboard in the dining room: a German *bierstein*, a thing of cream china and deep blue panels across which shepherds and shepherdesses cavorted. And he even said something: the word *trophy*.

She put the letter back in its envelope and that door on the past closed and left just the dull, familiar room all round her, and a sense of loss.

There were two letters left. She picked up the one that bore his handwriting. It had not been sent through the mail because there was no address on the envelope, just her mother's name. She opened the envelope and took out the single page, and felt an intestine fear, a sensation of disquiet crawling through her bowels. The door on the past was ajar once more. She was close to the quick of things, close to one of those moments of betrayal that she understood so well.

She is called Rachel. What can I say about her that won't be misinterpreted? I love her. I love her more completely than I could have imagined was possible, and yet strangely this does not affect my feelings for you. You won't accept this, and I can understand your rejection of it, but it remains true. My feelings for you, and for Helen as well come to that, are unchanged. I suppose my love for Rachel is therefore something added on top – but that's misleading as well, suggesting icing and cake, or something nauseating like that. It isn't topographical, for heaven's sake. Nor is it confectionery. Nor is it a matter of degree. My love for her isn't greater than my love for you. It is plainly different. I have never before experienced this focus *on one person. Not on her body, not on any particular aspect of her (incidentally, she isn't very pretty) but on the* whole *of her. Completeness, that's what I feel. I feel complete when I'm with her, and I feel that she is completely part of me. I'm afraid I'm becoming inarticulate. I suppose that's always the danger with a letter of this nature. Perhaps I won't actually send it.*

Helen put the letter aside. What was this man? Vain? Stupid? Selfish? Sentimental? Hypocritical? She tried to fit perjorative words to her image of him, to that bland image, hand-tinted like a holy picture, that she carried round in her mind; and she failed. The Andrew Harding whom the epithets fitted was a different person altogether.

She sipped her whisky. The letters lay on the table like fortune-telling cards, but cards played out to read the past rather than the future. *Perhaps I won't actually send it.* She smiled at the self-deceit. She guessed that it had been Dennis, going through her father's things after the bomb, who had found the letter; Dennis who had brought it with him to England, to the grieving widow; Dennis who had handed it over. Had he known what it contained? And was that letter the first that Lorna had known about the woman called Rachel? Perhaps, Helen thought, perhaps even before the letter she had known and not known. You can have your cake and eat it, as she herself had discovered long ago, standing in the wood with Michael, with her pants round her ankles. Self-deceit. It was what distinguished man from the machine.

'What would you like for your tea, dear?'

She started.

'Awfully sorry,' said Mrs Moon from the door. 'Tried to make a bit of noise coming in, if you know what I mean. Just wanted to know what you'd like for your tea?'

'You're very kind. You really shouldn't go to all this trouble. I'm quite happy with this drink.'

'Your *tea*, dear. Your *high* tea.'

'Oh, of course.'

'How about an omelette? That'd be all right?'

'It'd be lovely.'

'Omelette it is then.'

Mrs Moon went, but not before stoking up the fire, not before plumping the cushions and closing the curtains and turning on the table lamps, not before giving Helen a bit of advice, a bit of worldly wisdom. 'Strain your eyes, you will in this light. You looking at Mrs Constance's letters, then are you? Don't you go upsetting yourself. After my Richard went I burned everything, you know that? All his clothes, everything. I said to myself, well Deirdre, that's over and done with and you've got the rest of your life to live. That's what I said.'

'She's not dead yet, Mrs Moon.'

'No, my dear. Of course not. But seeing how things are, I mean. Now I'll just go and do that omelette.'

Helen picked up the one letter that was still unread. This was different from the others. It was an odd man out, a misfit: the writing was not her father's, and the name on the envelope was not her mother's: it was his own. She examined it carefully as one might examine a piece of evidence in a court of law. There was something else, an anachronism that she had noticed from the start: the date of the postmark was 1966 and the stamp bore the profile of the Queen. On the flap was the sender's address and Helen wondered who, seventeen years after his death, might be writing to Andrew Harding from the Jesuit House in Farm Street. She took the letter out.

> Dear Andrew
> I'm writing this to you at the address I remember, which wasn't your house at all but your wife's old home as far as I recall. I hope it finds you there. Anyway the reason for writing is that I caught a glimpse of you when I was in Jerusalem the other day and although I called after you, you obviously didn't hear. I must admit I heard somewhere that you had been caught up in that dreadful King David business, but obviously I was mistaken. The sight of you after all these years brought back many memories of the bad old days – remember Dennis Killin? – and I thought perhaps we might meet up again some time if you are ever in London. You may be surprised (then again you may not!) to learn that since those Jerusalem days I have been ordained to the priesthood (RC variety) which was the kind of thing Dennis always feared. How is he, I wonder? Do you see him still?

Twenty years. Fantasy crowded her mind with a mob of unruly images. She saw the past, her past and her mother's past, dissolve. Shapes flowed and broke and reformed. She saw Killin laughing at her, and Michael weeping over her, and Eric turning from her with disdain, and whether these images were memory or imagination she couldn't tell. The two had become one, the hard rock of memory melting into a strange and caustic magma, the fluid caprices of fantasy crystallising out into something like remembrance. 1966. Miriam shrieked at her and her mother smiled at her and a dozen others cried and laughed at the same time, and her father looked at her with incomprehension.

'There we are, dear. Where do you want me to put it? You feeling all right, dear?' Mrs Moon's voice was far away in the distance, no more than a vague recollection.

'Quite all right, Mrs Moon. Quite all right.'

'I've done you a pot of tea to go with it. That what you like? Or I expect you'd like some wine would you? Do you drink wine with omelette? I expect the French do, don't they? Drink wine with everything. There's that much alcoholism in France, so they say.'

'Don't worry about it, Mrs Moon. It's fine just as it is.'

She ate her supper sitting at the table with the letters spread out around her, and that one, the anachronism, the paradox, lying directly in front of her. *The sight of you after all these years brought back many memories of the bad old days.*

'Do you want anything else, dear?'

'I think I'll go to bed actually.'

'What a good idea. I've turned down your sheets and put the electric blanket on for you. Don't really hold with the things myself, but the old place is so damp, isn't it? Enough to give anyone rheumatism . . .'

Helen pushed her plate aside and gathered up the letters. Then a thought occurred to her and she went over to the desk to retrieve the old photograph album. She went upstairs through the desolate house to her room, taking the pile of papers with her. Sitting up in bed she leafed through the album, past the photos of groups in Cyprus, past the bathing parties and the sailing dinghies, past Lorna in a bikini pulling on a halliard; and stopped at the last picture, the monchrome picnic scene, the parched Palestinian hillside. She sorted through the letters again and found the one that matched. . . . *last Sunday he organised a picnic lunch with, can you imagine? smoked salmon and bottles of wine. Snap-shot enclosed, and notice the sunshine even at this time of year.*

The group in the foreground waved glasses and smiles at the camera and a young Dennis Killin brandished a bottle of wine. The girls wore sling-back sandals with platform soles and summer frocks with square shoulders and one of them held a wide-brimmed hat against the breeze.

Killin is in the floral hat and Silver is the rather supercilious one next to me. The girls by courtesy of a nurses' hostel. Not camp-followers, despite what your father says!

Helen snatched the photo out of its holders and turned it over. On the reverse, pencilled in her father's handwriting, were the names: *Killin – Emily – Mary (Killin's cousin) – Me – Silver (God-botherer) – Rachel (American journalist)*. She turned back to the picture and counted across until her finger rested for a moment beneath the face of the girl called Rachel. The girl squinted against the light as though peering into the future to try and make out what was waiting there; then Helen's finger moved to the young man. *Silver (God-botherer)*.

'David Silver.' Helen said the name out loud and the young man frowned at the camera almost as though he had heard. She shivered. Between the present and the past she felt some kind of gulf, a void of incomprehension and confusion. The chain of cause and effect, the imperative chain of contigency, seemed to have broken.

After a while she put the album and letters aside. She turned off the light and slept, and half woke, and slept again, drifting in and out of sleep and dream and nightmare. And all the time the date 1966 rang in her mind, a date set in the hard fact of recollection, not in the fluid territory of childhood memory where time is dilated and the gaps between events expand into a kind of lifetime. Adult time is quick, like the passage of history – time squeezed out of the press of experience. Memories of her father were so far away as to belong to a different order of existence altogether; but 1966 was only yesterday. In the summer of 1966 she had been with Michael in Cyprus.

Next morning she rang the Jesuit house in Farm Street and asked about Father Silver. There was a pause on the other end, some discussion. 'Who is this speaking, please?'

'I'm the librarian of the School of Bible Studies. I'm sure you know it. Father Devlin is one of our readers.'

'Oh, but of course.' A faint Irish touch to the voice. 'Father Silver is not here, you see. I mean, he is no longer with us. Will this be to do with his work, perhaps? You'll find him at our house in Jerusalem. I mean, you might contact him there. If you wish to.'

It seemed absurdly easy.

6

Lorna died a week later. Helen stayed at Guerdon House to make whatever arrangements were necessary. Miriam kept her company, did things for her that she would never have done in the normal run of things – 'Let me do that, Mummy. There's no need for you to take on everything yourself. Let me get supper, let me phone the solicitor, let me see to the flowers' – but in the event it all seemed disturbingly simple: a telephone call to the local undertaker, a notice in the newspapers, a talk with the rector, an official certificate from a sympathetic registrar and a meeting with the lawyer. All was easy in the disposal of a corpse. Together they made a list and wrote letters to those people who ought to know. Together they chose the coffin from an illustrated catalogue at the undertaker's, much as you might choose a new sink unit for the kitchen. A life had gone and the whole fabric of the present seemed ready to move together so that the space once occupied by Lorna Harding, or Lorna Constance, might never have been.

Michael came down to Guerdon the day before the funeral, looking solemn and adult. 'I've got something for you to see,' she told him when she got him alone that evening. She felt a curious agitation, a sensation that was akin to fear. It involved the muscles and nerves of her chest and stomach, a feeling of breathlessness and tension.

'Are you all right?'

'You sound like Mrs Moon. She asks me if I'm all right every other sentence.'

'But are you?'

'Don't be idiotic, of course I'm all right.' She took him into the dining room where the writing box sat on the sideboard. Eric was on the phone, talking to someone in London, as he always seemed to be. Paul was somewhere upstairs and Miriam was helping Mrs Moon in the kitchen. 'It's her letters,' she said, opening the box. 'I've been reading through her letters. She kept the letters from my father all the time, can you imagine that? In her blessed *escritoire*.' She held them out to him as proof. 'I've been reading through them.'

'Is that allowed?'

She ignored his irony. 'Do you want to see?'

'Not really.'

'Just one of them isn't written by my father. It's written *to* him.'

'So what?'

She felt the knowledge swelling inside her, precisely pressing behind her breastbone like something organic. 'Michael, it was dated 1966. It came from a man who knew him. He saw him *alive*.' She held it out. 'Here.'

He glanced at the page of scrawl, and handed it back with a faint shrug. 'I know.'

'What do you mean, you *know*? Read it.'

'I've read it. Your mother showed it to me, years ago.'

She stared at him. 'She *showed* it to you?'

'I assumed it was some kind of mistake. It obviously *was* some kind of mistake. Someone who looked like your father.'

'When? In Christ's name, *when* did you read it?'

'That day we were here with Adrian. Don't you remember? She showed it to me then.'

Recollection dawned. The house was suddenly peopled by different figures, a generation past: Adrian in the kitchen, Michael and Lorna in the drawing room, Helen herself watching them from the doorway. 'I knew. I knew something had happened between you and mother.' She felt like a child, being kept from learning the truth about life. 'Why did you keep it secret?'

'I didn't, particularly. It just didn't seem worth mentioning.' He got up and went over to the window to look out at the garden, mellow in the evening light. 'The holm oak really took a beating in the storm, didn't it?'

'You're evading the issue.'

'There just isn't an issue to evade,' he replied indifferently. 'Look, we've got to do something Helen, something concrete. We can't just go on like this. . .'

But she ignored him. She was over at the desk, going through the papers as though searching for further evidence. When he turned to speak she was holding out the photograph of the picnic on the Hill of Evil Council. 'Look.' She pointed to one of the figures. 'Do you see him? He's the one. David Silver. Father David Silver. That's the one who saw Daddy twenty years after he was killed.'

'The one who *thought* he did,' Michael said wearily.

Helen shivered. 'I've tried to get in touch with him. I'm going to go and find out.'

'Find out *what*, in heaven's name?'

'He's in Jerusalem. You know I've got this conference there next month? Well, I'm going to find him.'

'Find out *what*?' Michael repeated. Suddenly he sounded just like Eric. There was that same remoteness, the same sense of impatience. Just like a grown-up talking to a child.

'Whether the woman is still alive. Whether my father was still alive in 1966.'

'Don't be absurd.'

'Why should it be absurd? Why?' She looked at him, and felt the whole fabric of her life tremble, her present as well as her past. It was as though all were ephemeral, existence itself a mere fluttering of fragile matter in a great void. 'Why should it be absurd?' she repeated.

The service was held in the local parish church amidst the dying elms and the flourishing yews. Eric and Helen followed the coffin through the lych-gate and up the path to the porch where outdated notices of parish council meetings were posted. Miriam and Paul walked behind, the young boy crushed into a dark suit that was slightly too small for him, Miriam dressed all in black in her usual manner – black sweater, black tights, heavy black shoes like army boots.

'I am the resurrection and the life, saith the Lord,' intoned the rector. Inside the church there was a delegation of sisters from the nursing home, a few forgotten relatives, and a scattering of Lorna's old friends, people whom Helen barely recognised from distant, military days, anxious scanners of the obituary columns of the *Times* and *Telegraph* every one of them. They nodded recognition and tried to compose suitable expressions of condolence and regret as the cortège passed up the aisle. Anthony, balding now, past fifty, had come up from the West Country at Michael's insistence. He had his wife with him, but he had left his children at home, perhaps as a hostage against his return. 'My dear Helen,' he murmured, leaning towards her and delivering a kiss beneath the tasteful veil. 'It's been so many years. I'm so sorry.' Of course he wasn't, but then there wasn't much sincerity about any of the service really. The organ creaked Crimond out into the chill, damp air and almost drowned the voices, so unconvinced did they seem.

> Yea, though I walk in Death's dark vale,
> Yet will I fear none ill.

'Marvel at the convenience of an established religion,' Eric murmured to Michael. 'I can't bear those dreadful municipal crematoria, can you? With the church you just pay your taxes to get your just deserts complete with the comfort of religion. You don't actually have to *believe*. It's a remarkable bargain.'

He went up to the lectern to read. 'Behold, I shew you a mystery,' he announced in his rich and confiding voice, as though he was a conjuror about to perform a particularly fine trick: 'We shall not all sleep, but we shall all be changed, in a moment, in the twinkling of an eye, at the last trump.' And Helen noticed the irrelevant things, the brilliance of his shoes, the exactness of the crease in his trousers; and she wondered how much he knew and how much he guessed and how much he didn't yet dare to put into words, even to himself. She glanced along the pew at Michael but he gave no signal.

'For this corruption must put on incorruption, and this mortal must put on immortality. So when this corruptible shall have put on incorruption, and this mortal shall have put on immortality ...' The coffin stood on trestles in front of the altar and one wondered, one really wondered, whether the body was there inside it, or whether the whole thing was a deception, stage-managed by the men in black, or perhaps by this man in the impeccable suit with the impeccable voice. '... then shall be brought to pass that saying that is written, Death is swallowed up in victory. O Death, where is thy sting? O Grave, where is thy victory?'

And Helen felt the sting of death all right, felt it smarting behind her eyes, the very sting of death like the sting of acid. Sitting there in the church she wept for her mother as she had never, in the whole of her life, wept for her father.

'A brave woman who lost her first husband, Helen's father, in the service of her country ...' suggested the rector in his homily.

'And her second one through pure carelessness,' murmured Eric, once more beside Michael.

'...and who soldiered on to bring up her daughter, at first

270

alone and then as part of a second family which we see gathered together here for the first time for many years. Thus this is, in a sense, a resurrection of its own, Lorna's death bringing together people who have been separated for so long by the tribulations of our mortal concerns. . .'

Then there were some prayers and a hymn, and after that the undertaker's men humped the coffin onto their shoulders and the sorry little congregation trooped out into the churchyard. The grave was an awful brown pit amongst the brilliant green, an affront to the nature of things. They shuffled forward like a crowd approaching the edge of a cliff, anxious not to come too near, but desperate to peer over and see what had happened down there on the rocks at the bottom.

'Man that is born of a woman hath but a short time to live, and is full of misery. He cometh up, and is cut down like a flower.'

Earth rattled down onto the coffin; rain rattled down onto umbrellas. At the gate the mourners hovered nervously, Peter Oldcastle among them looking distinguished and grey, Sir Peter now, stooping over Helen's hand while his wife smiled tightly in the background, remembering how near they had come to disaster all those years ago in the torrid climate of Cyprus. 'You won't remember me . . .'

'Oh, but I do.'

'I was very fond of your mother,' he said, recalling a different Lorna from the one they had just buried, a blonde and tanned Lorna prostrate beneath his hand, stirring to his touch.

'As she was of you. It was very kind of you to be here. Perhaps you'd like to come back to Guerdon House for some tea or something? We're hoping that people will. The long drive down and everything . . .'

And there he was, outside the gate, standing amongst the Rovers and the Jaguars and the ancient Armstrong-Sidley hearse with its garlands of flowers on the roof (one of the wreaths had blown off during the drive to the church and the whole cortège had been forced to pause while the thing was retrieved from the ditch and restored to something like its former glory), there he was, unmistakeable for all that the years had done, massive and bald, and still looking fit and tanned, as though he had just flown in from the Mediterranean; there he was, looking almost as though the past had never happened.

'Excuse me, but I must just go and say hello to someone,' Helen said. 'You will come back, won't you? If you follow the other cars . . .'

Oldcastle watched her walk away through the gate and fancied he saw reflections of Lorna in the way she moved.

'I say,' remarked his wife, 'isn't that the fellow who . . .?'

'Killin,' said Oldcastle sourly as he watched the two of them talking. 'Dennis Killin.'

Helen knew fear and fascination. Age had done nothing to telescope the difference between them. She was still a girl and he was still the man who had taken her and Lorna to Kyrenia, still the man who had bowed his head over her own meagre body in the bedroom of the cottage near Lapithos, the man who grasped something at the quick of her in a way that she had never understood, and never understanding, had always feared. In the drawing room of Guerdon House he smiled at the motley selection of guests that the funeral had dredged out of the detritus of southern England, and she watched him with fear. The expression on his face suggested that, of all the participants, he alone saw the joke.

'How wonderful to see a family reunited,' the rector enthused. Perhaps he sensed, as one learns to do at funerals, that there were undercurrents here that might suck people down. 'Somehow it gives meaning to a funeral.'

'What meaning is that, father?' Killin asked.

The rector was low church. 'Father' unnerved him. 'The hope of resurrection,' he suggested.

'It always sounds a bit of a long shot to me.' Killin shook Eric's hand as though shaking on a deal. 'So you're the lucky fellow who married La Belle Hélène. Delighted to meet you at last. Delighted. Killin's the name, Dennis Killin. A long time ago they used to call me Deadly. You may have heard tell . . .'

'I can't say I have.'

'Water under the bridge, now. This is your son, is it? My word, I see his mother in him.' Paul shook hands self-consciously, as though the ritual had been invented specifically to make him feel awkward. 'Fine figure of a man,' Dennis exclaimed. When he smiled a row of beautiful ivory teeth gleamed out at the world like an advertisement for modern dentistry. His clothes looked smooth and fine and costly and rather tasteless. Against the faded background of the drawing room of Guerdon House he seemed almost grotesquely out of place. 'What are you in, old fellow?

'In?' Eric affected bewilderment. 'A Gieves suit, I believe.'

Killin laughed loudly. 'Do, man. What do you do?'

'Oh. Banking. Merchant banking,' he added just to make it clear.

272

'Very stylish.'

'I hope so.'

'I'm practically retired, of course. Bought a property in the Algarve and now I just get fellows like you to play around with my money.' He took Helen's hand, put his arm round her shoulder, drew her into the conversation. 'Helen and I knew each other long before any of you came on the scene.'

'It was a long time ago. We haven't seen each other for years.' She smiled at Eric as though pleading for understanding, but for Eric there was nothing to understand. Michael, then. She looked round desperately for Michael.

'Dandled her on my knee, I did. When poor old Lorna was in her widows weeds. I knew Andrew, you see.'

Eric frowned. 'Andrew?'

'Helen's father. He and I were close friends.'

'Dennis knew Daddy in Palestine,' Helen explained. 'They shared a house.'

'In the German Colony.' The conversation tip-toed through the minefields of the past. 'I brought him back after the bombing. The King David: surely you know about that. I was the last person to see Andrew alive, you see. I came back with the coffin, returned his personal effects, gave the brave widow a shoulder to weep on, you know the kind of thing.'

And quite suddenly Helen remembered, as though a hidden seed of memory had germinated there in the depths of her mind: a man holding her on his knee; the rough touch of his trousers against her legs and the sharp smell of cigarette smoke; and the way he watched her mother with shrewd and understanding eyes. She remembered: Lorna was sitting across the room reading a letter, frowning faintly. That was all there was: little more than a sensation, a mere blink of the memory.

'Please, Dennis, it's history now,' she said. 'Finished.'

He grinned. 'But it hasn't finished, has it? It never finishes, at least not until you've passed on like poor old Lorna.' He looked round as though for evidence of his assertion – and found it: 'Michael's here as well, I see. That's a turn up for the book, isn't it? And good Lord, isn't that Peter whatsisname? Oldfellow, Oldschooltie, Oldsomething.'

'Castle,' said Helen. 'He's *Sir* Peter now.'

'I'll bet he is. Must go and have a word.' Killin detached himself from them and made his way across the room. Helen went after him, grabbing at his sleeve, feeling like a child again clinging to the adult. 'Dennis, please . . .'

'You got all her former lovers here then?'

'Dennis—'

'And yours, if it comes to that.'

Panic bubbled up within her, the desperation of things running out of control of masses sliding and slipping, of the whole careful construct of her life facing dissolution. 'For God's sake!'

Heads turned. She noticed Gemma frowning in that Foreign Office manner of hers and Eric staring.

Dennis smiled reassuringly and patted Helen's arm. 'Don't worry darling. You know me: I'll be the soul of tact. I'll play the grown-up's game of pretending it all never happened and we're just the very best of friends. Now surely this is Anthony? Goodness me, this is just like Madame Tussauds. Remember me, Anthony? Daresay you don't, or won't. What a thing this is, eh? The vicar was just telling me that there was nothing like a funeral to awaken the hope of resurrection and here I am.'

'I think I'm the only person who's going to miss her,' Miriam told Michael. They had gone into the kitchen to help Mrs Moon.

'I wouldn't put it as harshly as that.'

'You might not; I would.' She poured boiling water into a teapot. Mrs Moon advised her on how long to let it brew – 'They'll want it nice and strong, you see. A bit of a pick-me-up' – and tutted over the way the conversation was going.

'She owned too much of the rest of you,' Miriam said. 'That's the problem. Everyone's happy to see a creditor die. You know that man in there? The bald one? He was her lover. You know that? Yes, I expect you do.'

'My dear, you shouldn't say such things,' Mrs Moon admonished her. 'And she not cold in her grave.'

Miriam ignored the rebuke. 'I bet he's glad to see her gone. You're all glad to see her gone. Mum hated her. I reckon you hated her, wicked stepmother and that kind of thing. Eric thought she was just a pain in the arse and Paul couldn't have given a damn. But I was fond of her. She had more guts than the rest of you put together. I'll take the sandwiches. I doubt anyone will want them but Mum insisted that we have something ready.'

'You're Oldcastle, aren't you? Knew you in Cyprus.'

'Yes, of course.' It wasn't clear from Oldcastle's expression whether he remembered or not. 'Weren't you in the army?'

'Business. Import-export, you know the kind of thing. Friend of Lorna's.'

'Oh, yes.'

Dennis grinned at him. 'You were quite close, weren't you?'

Lady Oldcastle glared. Helen had freed herself from Anthony and his wife and had come over to police the tense little group. She looked round at Michael as though for help, as she never had done in the past, never until that evening just a few weeks ago, before the fire in this very room. The conversation spluttered and snapped, like a firework that has not quite taken, but threatens all the time, threatens damage and destruction.

'We knew them both,' Oldcastle emphasised. 'Both Tommy and Lorna.'

'One better than the other, I guess.'

'I beg your pardon?' Lady Oldcastle said.

'I think perhaps we ought to be going, dear.' Oldcastle took his wife's arm and steered her towards the door. Tact reigned supreme in the mind of a retired ambassador, tact and discretion, and the recognition of disaster looming through the fog of a difficult social occasion. 'Quite a journey home, but so glad we could make it.'

'I thought you were one of Lorna's young men,' Killin said.

Helen grabbed his arm, like a drowning woman. Panic was welling up inside her. 'We don't want to hear, Dennis,' said. She felt it still, that was the terrifying thing, that awful blend of desire and revulsion. She could feel him touching her lips, wiping the rime of wine away and then sucking his finger. She could smell the damp of the little room in the cottage and the intensity of his touch; and she could sense the man feeling her mother, just like that. 'Please shut up,' she whispered. 'Please go. Please leave me alone.'

And then Michael came over, and smiled on the little disturbance and clapped his hand on Dennis' shoulder and moved the man away. The Oldcastles were finding their coats and hovering by the front door. Helen went and opened it for them, thanking them profusely for finding the time to come, and apologising for things that hadn't quite happened.

'Funerals are always emotional affairs,' Oldcastle said.

His wife tugged at his sleeve. 'Come on Peter. You know you don't like driving in the dark.'

In the drawing room Miriam was moving amongst the guests with a plate of sandwiches that no one seemed to want, accepting sympathy and condolence with an ironic smile. 'She's a fine girl,' Killin said as Helen came back.

'I think you ought to go, Dennis,' she said quietly.

'How old is she?'

'You'd best be going,' she repeated. 'It's getting dark.'

'You haven't answered my question.'

'I'm not going to.'

The girl's voice was a clash in the quietness of the room, a generation different, harsh in its vowels, truncated by the glottal stops of the London basin: 'Everyone's ready to go, I reckon.' She looked pointedly at the man standing there talking to her mother. 'D'you want anything else?'

He grinned. 'I'm just on my way. We didn't really get a chance to talk, did we? I was a friend of your grandmother's . . . years ago. And your mother's.'

Miriam smiled back at him, but without humour. 'I'm not stupid, you know. I know perfectly well who you are.'

He seemed to appraise the girl, almost looked her up and down. 'But do you, I wonder?'

'Dennis, please.' Helen's voice was edged with desperation. She felt the burden of fear as something compelling inside her. She wanted to beg. She wanted to get down on her knees before him and plead. And he looked at her as though he understood.

'It's been a long time,' he said. 'But it goes so fast, doesn't it? You wonder where it all goes to.' He touched Helen on the arm and smiled at her. 'I'd best be off. I'd best leave you all in peace.'

'What a nasty piece of work,' Miriam muttered.

Helen followed him out into the hall. Killin didn't pause, didn't even look back, just grabbed his raincoat from the hangers by the door and went out. She watched him crunch his way across the gravel. From behind he might have been no older than he was during that summer in Cyprus, a bulky man with a great domed head and a blunt masculinity about him. The beeches along the drive beyond him and the lowering grey sky overhead and the thin drizzle all seemed so far from Cyprus, so distant from the bleached hillsides of Pentadaktylos, so remote from a dusty, whitewashed room in a tiny cottage. Grey and green against the hard white limestone, damp against dust, the dull facts of the present against the intense fragments of the past. Different spirit, different substance.

He was halfway to his car when she called out to him. 'Dennis!'

He turned. She hurried across to him through the drizzle, while he waited, his smile tinged with irony. 'I wanted to ask . . .' She hesitated, standing in front of him like a suppliant. 'I've been reading her letters, mother's letters. There's one from a man called Silver.'

He gave a sharp, humourless laugh.

'David Silver.'

'I know who you mean.'

'Silver said he saw him. He saw him in nineteen sixty-six.'

'Saw who?'

'My father. Andrew. Silver said he saw him alive, somewhere in Jerusalem. Dennis, you know. You were his friend.'

'In a manner of speaking.'

'Did he die in the King David; did he?'

He put out a finger to brush water from her cheek. It was unclear whether it was rain or tears, but then funerals are places where you are allowed to cry in moderation. He looked at her with something like pity. 'It's been a long time,' he repeated quietly. 'A long, long time.' He opened the car door and climbed in; then just as he was about to close it he looked up at her. 'Miriam's mine, isn't she?'

The drizzle was coming down, harder now. From the house someone called her to come in. 'Yes,' she replied, 'she's yours.'

'I could tell, you see. Apart from her age. I could tell.'

The door slammed and the engine came to life. She stepped back and watched him turn the car and drive away, and before he was even out of sight, before he had even turned onto the road at the end of the drive, there was Michael bringing her out of the rain and Eric admonishing her for getting wet, and other guests saying goodbye and how sorry they were, and how they'd never forget her mother.

Thus the fragments of Lorna's past dispersed into the cold and cheerless afternoon. Car doors slammed, tyres crunched over the gravel as though over a thousand dry bones.

7

A policeman called Savage. Savage by name, savage by nature. He had the tightly-sprung manner you noticed among Physical Training Instructors, men forever looking for something to jump over, something to lift or something to throw. He possessed no graces and few manners and he appeared proud of the fact. As though taking part in some arcane training schedule they went round and round in circles.

'Let's go over it again, shall we, Major?'

'If we must.'

'This girl, this Rachel Simson' – Savage gave the surname particular emphasis, as though to point up its improbabilty – 'you met her at the Club.'

'I met her at the Club.'

'And you got friendly with her, without knowing anything about her—'

'That's usually the way when you first meet someone.'

'Quite. You got friendly with her, and you, er, *dated* her a couple of times.'

'Once.'

Savage's eyebrows rose. He had a prominent brow ridge, and dark eyebrows which met across the top of his nose. This gave him the look of a boxer, a man of reduced intelligence and heightened physical powers. There was nothing wrong with suspecting the latter, but it seemed rather dangerous to assume the former. From the beginning Harding suspected that Savage was a clever man. 'But Mrs Sweetfield—'

'I have told you. Mrs Sweetfield is a gossip. She reads more into things than are actually there. She *thought* we were together. She invited us to dinner together and I drove Rachel back to her hostel afterwards. That is all.'

'But you did take her out on another occasion. To the Regence. There was that incident. And there was talk about you.'

'Gossip.'

'You took her to the cinema.'

'Ages ago.'

'And were seen driving with her. The porter at the' – he glanced at the sheet in front of him – 'at Saint Paul's American Episcopal Hostel, he says that you were together.'

'I've not denied it. For God's sake, anyone would have thought I was a suspect in some crime.'

No reply. There was bait to which you did not rise. 'Tell me about the times you went out with her.'

'In Christ's name, this is an outrage!'

Savage looked impassive. 'Tell me.'

Harding's temper died away. 'Very well. Once, before Easter, I took her to the cinema. The Zion. We saw ... Oh, for crying out loud, I can't remember what we saw. You can find out if you ring the cinema management up. Something with Katharine Hepburn. Bryn Mawr, '28.'

'What's that?'

'It doesn't matter. A joke. And there was a newsreel film about Belsen.'

Savage glanced down at the papers in front of him, then back up with a quick smile. 'You were there, weren't you?'

'I've just told you. Look, this is ridiculous—'

'I mean at Belsen. You were there at Belsen.'

A silence. The inert things in the office – filing cabinets, desk, issue chairs, a framed photograph of Allenby's entry into the Old City in 1917 – all seemed to wait for the answer. 'Does that make me guilty of something?'

'Not guilty of anything, not at all.'

'So?'

'It must have been a very disturbing experience.'

'Yes, very.'

'Changed you, perhaps?'

'I don't think that's for me to say. I feel the same.'

'Wiser?'

Harding shrugged. 'More cynical.'

'More sympathetic to the Jews maybe? I've heard that you have expressed some very pro-Jew sentiments.'

'Who's said that? The Sweetfields again?'

Savage shrugged. 'Just people.'

'And is sympathy for the Jews misplaced?'

'Maybe it is here. Here they aren't exactly the innocent victims, are they?'

'Some are.'

'The illegals, for example?'

'If you like.'

Savage nodded, as though his suspicions had been confirmed. 'Tell me about your date with this girl.'

'I already have.'

'Again. Tell me again.'

Harding sighed. 'We saw the film and then we went for a drink, and then I took her back to her hostel. Then we met up again at a tennis party. That was the day of the station bombing . . .'

'Oh, yes, the station bombing. Did this friend of yours appear to have any knowledge of the attack?'

For a fraction of a second Harding hesitated. 'No.'

'But you took her round to have a look.'

'She insisted on coming. She is a very insistent girl. Maybe you've got to be to be a reporter.'

'But you didn't mind her coming with you?'

'As a matter of fact I did.'

'But still you let her?'

'Maybe it was a mistake.'

Savage raised his eyebrows. 'Maybe it was a mistake,' he repeated. He nodded thoughtfully. 'You are married, Major, aren't you?' he asked.

'You know damn well I am. And my private life has nothing whatever to do with you.'

'Of course not. I am just after the whole picture. The context, so to speak. Now this lady, an *American* lady working in one of the Protestant schools.' He glanced down at the file in front of him. 'The American Episcopal School to be precise – this lady turns out, in fact, to be not a teacher at all, but a journalist – '

'She was making a start, earning a bit of money from articles—'

'And not Christian at all, but Jewish.'

'Of Jewish descent. There's a lot of it about. It's perfectly legal.'

'Oh quite so, Major. Sometimes one wishes . . .' Savage smiled humourlessly. 'But of course personal wish is not the basis for law, not in *civilised* countries, at any rate. So this Rachel Simson, then, is not a Christian and a teacher, but a Jew and a journalist. You take her out once or twice – the last time being just a few days ago – and then, quite by chance she turns up at the incident with this illegal immigration ship, the Shall'eeah.'

'Shali'ah.'

'Whatever. She turns up there and the army takes her into custody along with a couple of dozen other Jews who appear to constitute some kind of reception committee, and by pure chance – that's another pure chance, incidentally – you turn up—'

'It wasn't chance. You know damn well that I'm part of General Staff, Intelligence, directly concerned with illegal immigration.'

'But you're *being* there, at that moment in that place. That's chance, isn't it Major? If it's not chance then it must be planning, and if it's planning then things are looking pretty serious.'

'What the devil are you insinuating?'

'No insinuations. Facts and circumstances, those are what concern a policeman. You are there at this place just at the moment that these . . . er, detainees, shall we call them? . . . stage some kind of break-out. There is a certain amount of chaos, in the course of which you are seen to be pursuing this lady.' Savage smiled at the turn of phrase. 'One Corporal Sinclair of the Highland Light Infantry actually claims that you directed him to rejoin his platoon while you set off after her.'

'The corporal is quite correct.'

'And the question is, did you catch her?'

Harding sighed. He adopted the sigh as a useful expression of boredom and impatience. He doubted if it fooled Savage. 'I have told you, Inspector. I lost her. I chased her into some plantations and she slipped away. I looked around for a while and eventually I gave up. And then I came home for a wash and brush-up. There was nothing much I could do there and anyway it was no longer my pigeon. I just came home.'

'Quite. And you have heard nothing of the lady since.'

'Would you have expected me to? She's on the run, hiding in one of their settlements, I'd guess. It's common enough. You've got her identity card and at the least she'd face deportation if she was arrested. She'd hardly be likely to get on the telephone to someone like me, is she?'

'It seems unlikely.' Savage nodded and looked down at his file for a moment, then up again with a smile. He was conscious of his image, Savage was, conscious of his reputation as the hardened investigator, the man who had trapped crooks in the East End before the war, the man who had trapped blackmarketeers during the war, and now, since his transfer to the Palestine Police, was going to trap the murdering bastards of the Irgun and the Stern Gang and their sympathisers. He smiled, and when he spoke his voice was quiet. 'How do you know we have her ID card, Major?'

Harding paused. He licked his lips, as though they had suddenly grown dry. 'Because the soldier I spoke to, a sergeant if I remember correctly, told me that they had taken all their cards, something about stopping them burning them. They've done that in the past so that we can't separate illegals from settlers.'

Savage sucked his teeth. 'Is that right? Aren't they clever little devils, these Yids? Could you perhaps identify this sergeant?'

'I daresay. He was the CSM, I think.'

Savage wrote something, then looked up. 'Tell me, Major: did you have an intimate relationship with this Rachel Simson? Had you, have you *slept* together?'

'How can that be any of your business?'

'As long as she is on the run anything about her may be my business, Major. The colour of her knickers may be my business. And I am sure that you would wish to help us in the detention of one of your country's enemies.'

'That's rather over-doing it, isn't it?'

'Not in my book, it isn't. He who is not for us is against us. Didn't someone once say that?'

'More or less. Jesus.'

'Well I never. You mean I've just quoted the Good Lord? Isn't that amazing? So, Major Harding, are you for us or against us?'

'That has never been in question.'

'And have you had sex with this Jew woman who is wanted by the Palestine Police?'

'That remains none of your business. And I find your language distasteful.'

'Why? Because you've had her, is that it? Maybe you are a sympathiser yourself. I gather you know quite a bit about these Jews, a bit of their language and so on.'

'I've told you that I sympathise with them. I don't see how anyone with a modicum of humanity can fail to. Certainly nobody who has been in one of the camps.'

'I don't see how anyone with what you refer to as a *modicum* of humanity can support the way they murder people—'

'You are not talking about all the Jewish people. You're talking about *some* of them, the extremists, the revisionists. Look Inspector, I find this conversation rather tiresome, and your insinuations distinctly offensive. I think you had better go.'

Savage nodded thoughtfully, as though he had been thinking

that all the time. 'Just one thing, Major. Have you ever met any of Miss Simson's friends?'

'Yes, of course. The girls who live at the hostel with her. Mary, Emily . . . I don't know their surnames, but I can find out soon enough.'

'I mean other friends. Locals, so to speak. She must have had some, mustn't she? I mean, there she was at this *kibbutz* place. She must have known them. She never mentioned Jew friends, did she?'

'Never. Now, if you don't mind . . .'

'That's funny, because we know she has plenty of contacts. Because of her work, of course. As a journalist.'

'We never talked about—'

'How about these?' Savage reached into his crumpled jacket and produced an envelope. He pulled out some photographs and began to deal them out on the desk. Faces looked up at Harding, a variety of faces in a variety of poses. Some were pictures taken in custody, the subject glaring defiantly straight back at the camera and holding up a card that gave official details. Others were just casual poses of men smiling, smoking, staring into space. One showed two men with their arms round each other's shoulders. Some shots were blurred, as though the camera had been hidden and the subject unaware of being observed.

Harding shook his head at all of them. Savage pointed. 'What about this one?' His finger was resting on a picture of Ben-Oz.

'I may have seen the picture before. An intelligence briefing or something. I don't remember . . .'

'You've not met him? In the company of Miss Simson?'

'No.'

'That's a disappointment.' Savage nodded, as though to emphasise the enormity of his distress. 'Because we have a report of his meeting a man and a woman in some kind of bar in Tel-Aviv. By the description the man and the woman could almost be you and Miss Simson.' The policeman rose to his feet. 'Still, if you say not . . .' Behind him, through the open window, was the Valley of Hinnom and the walls and towers of the Old City. It really was the most stupendous view. 'Oh, you don't mind if I come round with a couple of officers to check over your house, do you Major? You live in what they call the German Colony, don't you?'

'Whatever for?'

'Just for form's sake. When would be convenient? Might now be all right?' Savage smiled. 'Right now?'

★

They clumped through the house with a callous disregard for personal sentiment. Insolent eyes peered into drawers, into cupboards, into desks. A neighbour was watching from a nearby window and Savage sent a constable to ask if he had seen anything. 'A terrorist on the run, that's the story,' he said. Upstairs he had another officer strip Harding's bed. He looked bleakly at the exposed sheets and there was something indecent about his gaze, as though merely by looking he was conjuring scenes of illicit passion.

'This is an outrage, Savage,' Harding said quietly. 'I'll have your guts for this.'

The man smiled. 'Nothing to do with me, I'm afraid. Just following orders. And the only people'll have my guts are those in authority over me. So to speak.' He reached down and picked up the pillows, raising them to his nose to smell. 'Wear ladies' perfume, do you Major?' he asked, glancing over his shoulder.

'Don't talk crap.'

The policeman straightened up, smiling at his little piece of bluff. 'Where else is there?'

'The bathroom.'

But in the bathroom, aside from soap and tins of toothpaste, he found only razors and shaving brushes and masculine things like that. 'The bird has flown,' he remarked.

'There never was a bird.'

'The other rooms?'

'They belong to the men I share with.'

'I'd still like a look, if you don't mind.' But the other rooms yielded nothing to his cynical eyes.

'Don't you have a servant?' he asked.

'He's on leave, with his family in Jaffa.'

'Is he now?' Savage led the way downstairs, with Harding coming after him and a constable taking up the rear. As they reached the hall Killin entered through the front door, Killin swearing and cursing about a copper out at the front, and who the devil were these creeps?

Savage answered with that maddening calmness that these creeps were only police officers doing their job.

'What the blazes do you mean, your job? Your job's bloody criminals and terrorists!'

'Rachel,' Harding explained. 'She's gone missing and they think I'm something to do with it. They think she's part of the Stern Gang or something.'

'The Stern Gang? They must be bloody mad.'

Savage corrected him in the tones of a patient schoolmaster: 'Oh, we never said Stern Gang, Mr Killin. Palmach, perhaps. But then who cares, eh? They're all ungrateful, murdering bastards, aren't they? Aren't they, Major Harding? Perhaps I can have a quick word with you, Mr Killin?'

The interview with Killin led to nothing. Savage emerged with his humourless smile still in place 'It's like playing Patience,' he told Harding, and by his tone he might have been making light conversation. 'Just like playing Patience. You don't have to be particularly clever, not like you fellows in GSI. You just have to know the rules and keep dealing the cards and eventually you win.' He nodded thoughtfully as he opened the door to let his little clutch of CID officers out. 'I'm sure we'll be in touch, Major,' he said. 'I'll be re-dealing the cards, you see. Over and over. Never a moment's peace.'

Killin whistled. 'He's dangerous, that bastard. Very, very dangerous.' They had gone into the garden at the back of the house, beside the palm tree where the rats had been. Killin was sitting in one of the cane chairs with a gin in his hand, but Harding couldn't be still, couldn't stop pacing.

'Of course he's bloody dangerous.'

'I wouldn't trust him an inch, if I were you, Andrew. I could smell Bethnal Green cop shop all over him.'

'Where did you take her?' Harding asked. 'What did you do with her?'

Killin nodded appreciatively. 'But she'll be a match for him. She's a fine girl. I can see your point, old man, see your point.'

'Where did you take her, for God's sake?'

'To the bus station.'

'The bus station! They'll be searching the bloody buses! If they really think she came back with me they'll be going through the buses with a nit comb.'

Killin held up his hands in mock surrender. 'Don't get excited, old fellow. Sit down, have a drink and relax. Rachel knows what she's doing. She's a tough little cookie. She said she knew someone who would hide her there. It's a Jewish area, you know that as well as I do. It's lousy with sympathisers.'

'Did she say anything about me?'

Killin shrugged. 'She said she'd get in touch. She didn't say how.'

'How did she seem?'

The big man repeated Harding's words mockingly. 'How did

she seem? How did she seem? She seemed like she always seems. Tough number. Absolutely reeking of sex. I can see what you see in her.'

'Oh, shut up.' Abruptly Harding went through into the house. He picked up the phone and held it to his ear, then dialled the number of his office. The duty sergeant answered. There was some kind of flap in the offing, the man said, but nothing at the moment. Harding put the phone down and came back out into the garden. Killin had lit a cigarette. He leant back and blew a smoke ring into the air above him.

'We're being tapped,' Harding said.

Killin didn't move. His mouth remained a perfect O and his tongue flipped another ring after the first. He watched it rise gently into the bright air of the garden. 'Surprise me,' he said.

Silver left the house that week. There was a tense confrontation in which he grew rather emotional and accused Harding of betraying his wife, his family, his country, and finally, and this appeared to be the greatest of the three crimes, he himself; David Silver, a sensitive soul in torment who had invested a great deal of his own sensibilities in their friendship.

'I don't know what the blazes you're talking about, David.'

Silver was white with anger. His Adam's apple bobbed frenetically. 'I've had to lie to the police, you know that? That man came round and asked me questions about you and Rachel, and I had to lie to them, tell them that as far as I know your relationship was purely platonic, that I didn't know whether she had spent the night here, all sorts of lies. Don't you understand how this leaves me?'

He went to pack his things and shuffled out of the house, going, so he claimed, where he would be well-received. They discovered later that this meant to the Jesuits. Killin laughed long and loud at that. It merited, he decided, another verse of the Mandate Blues.

> Old Silver got the message
> Old Silver got the news
> Old Silver gone to the Jesuits
> He got the Mandate Blues

But Harding wasn't so sanguine. 'I won't get away with this Dennis,' he said softly. 'Savage is the danger. I won't get away with it.'

★

That was the month of Operation AGATHA, the time when the Security Forces launched their great offensive against Jewish organisations, arresting the leading members of the Yishuv, raiding the Jewish Agency and the headquarters of the Histadruth in the search for incriminating documents, raiding settlements, taking men and women into custody, stirring up resentment and bitterness and the murk of incomprehension. It was the time when the British forces and the Jewish people finally came into open conflict.

'It's a tiresome business,' the General admitted. 'But it's the only way to deal with these extremists. Force them out into the open.' He had called Harding into his office, out of the chaos of the operation, away from the summary reports, the interrogations, the piles of documents, the sudden alarms and excursions. 'Understand you've had a spot of bother with your journalist lady? Turned out to be a Jewess, after all?'

'Yes, sir.'

'Well, I'm sure you're not the first man to be taken in by that kind of thing. You see, they're always going to have divided loyalties, whoever they are. Look at Vivian Herzog. You know the fellow, of course. In the Guards. Look at any number of them.' He paused and eyed Harding. 'Hope my confidence in you wasn't misplaced?'

'No, sir.'

The General nodded. 'I'm sure not. The police are a heavy-handed lot. They live in a different world from us, Andrew; trained to mistrust everyone and anyone. Quite the opposite to an army officer's life. Trust is the whole basis of our world, isn't it? You've got to trust your brother officer, haven't you?'

'Of course, sir.'

'Of course.' The General regarded him thoughtfully. 'Probably a good thing it all blew up, isn't it?'

'Probably, sir.'

'Get on with the job without any distractions. They've probably already got her in detention by now. Anyway, I reckon your best move is just to keep your head down until it all blows over.'

But they didn't get Rachel. He saw the lists of detainees coming in, hundreds and hundreds of them, but her name was not among them and he felt a small stir of pride at that. Down at the detention centre at Latrun he observed anger and bitterness, but he never saw the face of Rachel Simson.

And then, a few days later, she reached out of the shadows to touch him. He was walking along a crowded King George V

Street with Killin when someone barged against them. 'Hey, steady on!' Killin protested. The figure disappeared amongst the crowd. Killin patted his trousers suspiciously. 'Bloody pickpocket? Check your ghoolies, if I were you.'

But it wasn't a pickpocket. If anything it was the reverse. In the momentary confusion, Harding had felt a tiny ball of paper being pushed into his hand. He said nothing to Killin, but slipped the paper into his pocket and waited until he had gained the safety of the lavatory at the Royal before unfolding the little scrap. He knew where it came from surely enough: *I'm sorry*, she had scrawled at the bottom in a childish hand, *evening ruined again*. The message was nothing more than the word *Majestic* and the cipher Gl and a time.

The Majestic was an open air cinema in Rehavia. The seat in question was occupied, but it wasn't her. Harding stood uncertainly in the side aisle while figures flickered across the screen and the shadowy audience roared with laughter. A comedy, then. He'd not even noticed. Behind him a pale sign on the wall said EMERGENCY EXIT. Overhead was the open roof and the night sky: a myriad of stars glittering in the blackness. *He telleth the number of the stars and calleth them by their names*. But it was not a great feat apparently. According to Silver there were only about three thousand stars visible to the naked eye. In one of their discussions he had used that as an illustration of the arcane knowledge contained within the Bible, evidence of understanding beyond mere human knowledge. Killin had called it 'bloody ignorance'.

On the screen Groucho Marx looked up from a corpse and announced, 'Either he's dead, or my watch has stopped,' and the laughter came again, like the laughter of gulls along the sea shore, and that was the moment when someone took his arm behind him. 'Do what you're told,' a man's voice whispered. He was hustled out through the emergency exit and into the alley that ran along the side of the cinema. It was a place of bins and stray cats. A car was waiting at the end with its engine running. He had time to notice military plates before shadowy figures bundled him into the vehicle, gave him a hood to wear, told him to get down on the floor and shut up. 'Don't know why we're taking this risk,' a voice said in perfect English. 'What the hell does a *goy* matter?' The car accelerated out of the alley and swung onto the main road.

They drove through the stifling darkness. At one point they stopped to drag him out of the car and manhandle him round the back. He made some kind of protest when he realised what was happening, but they took no notice, merely shoved his head down and lifted up his legs and tipped him unceremoniously into the boot. The door slammed shut and the car started off again and he lay sweating in the darkness, struggling for air, struggling against nausea, assaulted by the stench of petrol. Later there was another brief halt while voices sounded outside his metal coffin. He heard a burst of laughter and words of agreement, and then the journey continued and time itself became a dimension that he had lost along with all the others.

Finally the car slowed down and turned sharply. It lurched over some kind of obstacle and came to a halt. A door slammed shut, a great metallic sound like the slamming of the doors of hell, and the boot opened and they manhandled him out. Someone snatched off his hood and he found himself in some kind of garage. He was dazed by the sudden light, faint with the heat and the motion of the vehicle. He stared round into hooded faces, anonymous eyes that peered at him through holes. Incongruously his captors were dressed in British army uniforms. 'Don't make a sound,' the English voice said. 'Just do what you're told.'

A door opened onto a short flight of stairs. Two of them hustled him up to the landing at the top. One of his escorts leant forward and opened a door. 'In you go.'

She wasn't there, either. There was a table and two chairs and a threadbare sofa, but Rachel wasn't there. There was just Ben-Oz, sitting at a table in the centre of the room and looking up almost in surprise at the group that had appeared in the doorway in front of him. And for the first time Harding wondered whether this was a trap. With so many Jews being arrested, could this be a reprisal? 'I've survived the war,' he remembered telling her, 'but I'm not so sure that I'm going to survive the peace.'

'The Security Forces have arrested over two thousand of our people,' Ben-Oz said by way of greeting. 'They have given us a difficult time.'

'That was their intention.'

Ben-Oz indicated the empty chair. The masked men said something in Hebrew and retreated. The door closed and someone outside turned the key in the lock.

'When will I see her?' Harding demanded.

Ben-Oz smiled. 'Major Harding, do you realise what is the German translation of "Security Force"? It is *Schutzstaffel*.'

'So?'

'*Schutzstaffel* is SS.'

'I've got there,' Harding retorted angrily. 'I'm not stupid.'

'I just wanted to make the point.'

'There is no point to make. It's rubbish. If you go around trying to equate the British with the Nazis you'll just make idiots of yourselves. When will I see her?'

'They sang the Horst Wessel song when they raided the kibbutz at Givat Brenner.'

'For crying out loud, British soldiers don't even *know* the Horst Wessel song. When will I see her, for Christ's sake?'

'Be patient. Just be patient. We have time to talk a bit. I like to talk with someone from the other side. AGATHA was a disaster, you realise that, don't you? It has thrown us together with the IZL and the Stern Group. It has pushed us into the arms of the extremists. We are under great pressure to do things we would not otherwise do. Kidnap, assassination, all these things are being proposed. Maybe you can help us recover something from the mess.'

'Is that the price of being allowed to see her?'

'That's all you want, isn't it? Your bimbo.'

Harding managed a laugh. 'Bimbo! Where the hell did you get that from?'

'Isn't it right?'

'It's right in a Raymond Chandler novel. Not much else.'

Ben-Oz looked crestfallen. 'I thought you said bimbo. I thought it was the word.' Abruptly he got up from the table. 'It's not blackmail,' he said, shaking his head as though denying it to himself. 'You don't understand. It's not blackmail. You must consider what I have said.' Then he left the room and Harding was alone.

The single window was shuttered and the atmosphere was unbearably hot, the stifling midsummer heat of the coastal plain. He tried the door, but of course it was locked; he tried the shutters but they were fastened. He guessed he was somewhere in Tel-Aviv, in the hands of the Palmach. But was it the Palmach? He paced round the room in anger and wondered again whether the whole thing was a trap. Could it be the Irgun, who had long made a habit of kidnapping British officers? Membership of these clandestine groups was fluid, people chopping and changing on a whim. Maybe even now Ben-Oz was a member of one of the groups he claimed to despise. And if he was, where did that put Rachel?

He felt a disturbing amalgam of emotion, in which he could distinguish fury and frustration, but also that other thing, the most caustic of all – fear. Not the fear he had known during the war, which had been fear of a threat that you could measure. This was fear of the unknown, a helpless fear, something like, he guessed, the fear of those who had been in the camps.

The wait seemed interminable. His wristwatch told him it was no more than half an hour, but it had felt like hours, alone there in the stifling room, with nothing to do but think. And then there were footsteps outside and a key turned in the lock and the door opened. He looked up almost in terror.

She was standing there. She wore the uniform of the Jews, khaki shirt and khaki shorts and black plimsolls, the least flattering clothes it was possible to imagine. The door slammed shut behind her.

'In Christ's name—'

Small, pugnacious, entirely herself, she looked back at him with a strange blend of affection and anger. 'Is that what it is? It's in Christ's name, is it?'

He almost shouted at her: 'What the hell is going on?' and she raised a forefinger mockingly to her lips. 'We have one hour,' she said softly. 'No more. We have to talk.'

8

'There's the matter of the phone tap,' Savage said. This time he had called Harding to his office at Police Headquarters in the Russian compound. It was a polite request, hedged around with apologies and disclaimers, but for all that it was clear that in Savage's eyes the balance had shifted.

'You don't give up, do you?'

'Didn't I promise? We've got a whole lot of her friends inside now, you know that? Thanks to Aunt AGATHA.'

'You've got a whole lot of people who don't matter a damn.' Through the window Harding could see part of the Russian Cathedral, an edge of white stone, the corner of a green dome; and beyond that the peerless blue of the Jerusalem sky. He thought of Rachel.

'That's your perspective.'

'So what phone tap are you talking about?'

'You know very well, Major Harding. The transcript of an intercepted telephone conversation that you quoted to a meeting of the Security Committee.'

'How the devil do you know about that?'

'That's beside the point.'

'It's not beside the point. The proceedings of that committee are restricted. If there has been a breach of security then I'm bound to report it.'

Savage nodded, as though congratulating him on his act. 'Of course you may report what you like. But there's no record of any such interception in our files.'

'I'd just like to know who passed you that information.'

'And I'd like to know where that phone tap came from.'

There was a silence. Through the open window, above the

noise of traffic on the Jaffa Road, came the sound of a police siren. That was the norm, a background to any conversation in the city. Sirens and the tramp of boots and the battering of doors. 'Let me tell you what I think, Major Harding. I think it was phoney. I think it was a plant, designed to distract everyone from where that bloody refugee ship was going to land. We have no records whatever of that tap because I don't think it ever existed. I think you planted it.'

'That,' said Harding, 'is complete and putrid crap.'

'So where did it come from?'

Harding considered his answer. 'It came from the Defence Security Office,' he answered finally.

Savage was silent, scepticism written all over his face. 'MI5,' he said sourly.

'Precisely.'

'I can put in a request for confirmation.'

'You can. And you might get an answer. Then again, you might not.'

He went out into the sunshine, through the coils of barbed wire, past the sandbags and guards with their Lee Enfields. He turned left down the Jaffa Road towards Allenby Square and the Old City. Almost nowhere was without memories of Rachel now. This was where they had parked the car that evening after first meeting Ben-Oz, where she had made her confession of love. Could he still believe it? Recalling how she lay down on the threadbare couch in that room in the Palmach safe house, could he ever doubt it? He walked along towards the Damascus Gate, oblivious to the roar of traffic, oblivious to the shouts and the calls, oblivious to street vendors and beggars. Time: that was all he possessed. It would take Savage time to get anything out of the Defence Security Office. The man would have to battle with bureaucracy and inter-departmental jealousy, with the traditional mistrust of the military for the police, and MI5's suspicion of the CID. But Savage would do it. He was like a terrier at a rabbit hole, wagging his tail and digging away and yelping with delight. And now, for the first time, Harding had caught a glimpse of the handler standing behind the terrier, someone moving in the shadows, edging him forward. *There's the matter of the phone tap.* It was someone on the Security Committee.

He bought something to eat off a street vendor at the Damascus Gate and then strolled through into the confusion of the *suk* inside the old walls. Bearded Arab faces urged him to buy anything from aubergines to crucifixes, food for body and soul. He smiled and shook his head, and went on down the *suk*, more of a tunnel than an alleyway, lined with one-room shops, hung about with references to what had happened here, or what might have happened somewhere about here: the murder of an innocent man.

'English Officer,' a voice called out. 'You buy holy object. Rosary beads, crucifix, Virgin Mary, face of Christ. Olive wood from Garden of Gethsemane.'

A foot patrol of the Argyll and Sutherland Highlanders pushed their way past, muttering Scots damnation. A sign on the wall marked Station VII, where Jesus fell for the second time, where now, almost two thousand years later there was a blind beggar crumpled against the wall. Harding pushed a coin into the man's palm and won the blessings of Allah. He walked on between the shops, turning the corner into the exiguous space in front of the Church of the Holy Sepulchre.

'Genuine crucifix, blessed by archbishop,' a stallholder cried.

Inside the church there was the smell incense and ancient stones, and the powerful scent of the irrational. Orthodox priests were celebrating mass in the main body of the church, oblivious to the sparse audience of off-duty soldiers in the company of a chaplain, oblivious to the troubles of the Mandate, conscious only of the ritual sacrifice of a god. This was a religion – dark, ambiguous, haunted. It had nothing to do with church parades, little to do with the church in England where he used to take Helen, little to do with reason and understanding. Harding stood by the Stone of Unction at the foot of the steps that led up to Golgotha and listened for a while, believing and not believing. It was a familiar enough experience. England seemed further away than ever.

He made his way out into the bright sunshine, through the Muristan quarter and out of the Old City by the Jaffa Gate. The King David loomed over the valley like a liner beached on the hillside and he wondered whether all the men and women inside were nothing more than victims of shipwreck. He crossed the road and climbed up the hill, sweating in the sunshine, longing for the mundane attractions of a beer, longing for the normal. In the foyer of the hotel the absurd Nubian stewards stood like contestants in a fancy dress parade. Ceiling fans stirred the air above them. From the bar came the familiar sound of men at drink. 'Over here, Andrew,' someone called. 'Come and have a jar.' They were talking of drinking and of women, of a duck shoot up in the Hulah valley last May, and a polo tournament at the Sport's Club that weekend. They were not talking of loyalty and betrayal, of sin and redemption.

'Done a bunk, has she, Andrew?' one of them asked unexpectedly. It took him a while to understand that the man was referring to Rachel. 'Your little Jewess. Old Oliphant was right, wasn't he?'

'Oliphant is a shit,' he replied.

'A right shit.' There was a gust of nervous laughter in the bar. 'Never trust them, I say,' the man went on. 'Never trust them. With the Arabs you know where you stand. The Arabs cheat you honestly. But with *them* it's for real. Real cheating.'

'Who are you talking about?' Harding asked. 'Never trust whom?'

'Jews.'

There was an uncomfortable silence. 'Jesus was a Jew,' Harding said. He finished his beer, returned his glass to the bar and walked out in silence. And then the noise returned, the same noise as before, the duck shoot in Hulah, the polo tournament, the women and the drinking: '. . . old Oliphant could certainly stow it away. I remember once at Shepheard's, he'd had a few and there was this French totty . . . well, she may have been Italian . . . and . . .'

He stood in the foyer, looking round at the absurd furnishings and wondering what the hell he was doing there, who the devil these people were. Logic told him they were no different than they had ever been, that they were identical to his companions during the war – the same idiots and the same wise men, the same friends and the same fools. But logic let him down because it didn't bring conviction with understanding. He felt as though he had suffered some kind of amnesia and that all that remained to him were snatched recollections without chronology or context: fuel tanks burning on the horizon; the stickiness of blood and the gnawing sense of fear; Corporal Tyler's head lying in his lap, swarming with flies; men running, men shouting, men moaning with pain and fear; and Jack Springer being as sick as a dog into the bushes while faces watched, faces frowning with bewilderment, faces all teeth and nose and hollow eyes – faces like skulls. People and incidents and moments: threads pulled out of the fabric of time.

'Major Harding? A letter for you, sir.'

He focused his eyes and discovered the assistant manager bobbing around in front of him, holding out an envelope. It was the same man who had been there at the Regence that evening when the fracas with Oliphant had occurred.

'A letter?'

'Personal, sir. To Major Harding's hand directly.'

'Who delivered it?'

'A messenger, sir.'

Harding glanced at the thing – there was just his name typed on the front: Major A.H. Harding, DSO, MC – and slipped it into his pocket. Then he thanked the man and wandered out of the building.

That afternoon he opened the letter in the sanctuary of his bedroom. There was something in the envelope beside the single sheet of paper, something small and hard. He shook it and a black disc of metal fell into the palm of his hand. Dimly, through centuries of tarnish, he could make out the vague shape of a palm tree. Herod treasure. The sea boomed in his mind, and gulls cried.

The message itself was typed on a machine with an old, worn ribbon: *Tomorrow morning at 12.45. At the windmill. Be on time.*

He lay on his bed with the shutters closed against the heat, and he wondered. The windmill was obvious: the absurd, incongruous Montefiore windmill that lay in an olive grove just down the hill from the King David. But how much else was? He felt tied up in something he couldn't control, events with a logic behind them that was dictated by the malign and random force of fate. *We must talk*, she had said. *We must talk.* And choice, moral choice – that which distinguishes man from beast – stared him in the face.

9

The taxi drove into the darkness. A signpost flashed into the headlights for an instant: JERUSALEM 40. Rain washed the windscreen and the wipers flapped back and forth, the blades squealing on the glass. The journey seemed quite unreal, a great rush of noise and motion with no points of reference, no landmarks. An abstraction.

And I saw the holy city, new Jerusalem, coming down from God out of heaven, prepared as a bride adorned for her husband.

The road began to climb in the darkness, the headlights picking out trees at the roadside and the rusted hulks of vehicles that had lain there ever since the war of 1948.

And the city was pure gold, like unto clear glass.

A truck swept past in the opposite direction, bright with lights, trailing a plume of spray.

O Jerusalem, Jerusalem, thou that killest the prophets and stoneth them which are sent unto thee.

Helen sat in the back of the taxi, the sudden lights flashing across her face like a strobe, her expression frozen into impassivity.

This is almost the view from my window. The building with the dome is where Jesus' Temple used to be, where He drove out the traders and stall-holders.

A hotel in the west of the city, the modern quarter where shopping precincts and banks jostle with skyscrapers and office blocks; a hotel as devoid of local character as an airport, with ethnic references laid on like badges – a fountain in the foyer in the shape of a menorah and a star of David embossed in the ceiling. The walls were decorated with mosaics in the style of Chagall: *En-Gedi* showed rabbis with expressions of innocent surprise emerging from florid vegetation; *Masada* had scowling zealots floating over desert rocks and pools of blood.

Beside the menorah fountain, where a noticeboard announced the International Conference of Bible Studies, a small scrum of guests had gathered round the table to register. The call of fraternity was loud in the land, cries from Chicago and Philadelphia, from Manchester and Melbourne and Marburg. 'Why, Shlomo, you rootless cosmopolitan!' someone exclaimed, 'I wondered whether I'd find you here.' There were name tags along with room keys and programmes. At seven o'clock there would be a reception for members of the conference in the *King Herod Cocktail Lounge*; dinner afterwards would be in the *Queen of Sheba Restaurant*. The restaurant was, of course, kosher. Helen claimed her key and made her way out of the crowd towards the lifts.

Her room was over-heated and the windows wouldn't open properly. She fiddled with the heating control and called for room service and felt lonely; an experience which had pleased her as a young woman but frightened her now. The view out of the window was of modern tower blocks and a sky washed with light from the street lamps. It looked like the light from a great conflagration. Guerdon House, and Michael and Eric and the children seemed more than a thousand miles away, they seemed separated by nature as well as mere distance.

The reception was a dispiriting affair, a thing in which false joviality substituted for humour, and acquaintance did service for friendship. There were clerics in black and grey, Jews wearing kippas, Protestant ladies in long navy skirts and white blouses. The talk was of other meetings, other conferences, people known and heard of, acquaintance and rivalry, and what excitements there might be in the coming week. 'I believe we get to see the Temple Scroll.'

'There's a lecture by Yadin, did you see that?'

'I've decided for the Israel Museum tomorrow afternoon. I mean, I've been before, but the alternative's Masada and Qumran and they *always* lay on Masada and Qumran. Who wants to see chunks of bare rock? We have enough of those back home.'

'A Jewish theme park, that's what the place has become.'

She met one or two people she knew vaguely and a third with whom she had corresponded. 'So you're Helen Harding,' he said as though in some kind of approval. 'Why, what a pleasure this is. I remember your Pauline exegesis, don't I? Are you still working in that field?'

She shook her head and wondered about escape. 'I had to get a

298

real job. Marriage, I'm afraid. Marriage and children. Not necess-
arily in that order.'

He read it as a joke and laughed loudly. 'Of course,' he said,
'my own interest is apocalyptic . . .'

Next morning she rose early. In the conference room (*The King
Solomon Hall*) technicians were checking over the sound system in
preparation for the keynote speech which was entitled, so the
poster proclaimed, *Jesus the Jew*. Except for the staff at the reception
desk the foyer was deserted. She walked out, past the menorah
fountain, past the mural of the crossing of the Red Sea, out
through the plate glass doors and into a bright Jerusalem morning.

She walked. The city awoke slowly and buzzed round her, a
simulacrum of any western city, a place of noise and crowds and
traffic; and she walked. She wondered in what sense this place was
the Jerusalem her father had known, or she herself had known all
those years ago when Tommy and Lorna were still alive. She
walked past the very spot where once she had held up the floral-
frocked group from the wives club at Episkopi to ask her mother
tiresome questions about love, but she didn't recognise the place.
She even walked past the café where Andrew Harding had sat
with Rachel Simson after taking her to the Zion Cinema, but she
couldn't have known that. She walked as far as the King David
Hotel, sitting still on the edge of the new city and facing across
the Valley of Gehenna, looking towards the walls of the Old City
on the opposite slope.

*This is almost the view from my window. The building with the dome
is where Jesus' Temple used to be . . .*

There was still a borderline there. It was no longer one of
concrete and barbed wire as it had been on her first visit to the
city, but it was palpable nevertheless: a border between the new
and the old, a barrier compounded of incomprehension and
misunderstanding. The golden dome floated above the walls,
unearthly in its loveliness. But it was a place of blood and sacrifice,
of death and anguish. How many lives, animal and human, had
been destroyed there? *O Pray for the peace of Jerusalem: they shall
prosper that love thee.* Traffic streamed past the Jaffa Gate. Words
echoed in Helen's mind as she stood there on the hillside looking
down on the scene, a blizzard of words roaring in her ears: *If I
forget thee, O Jerusalem: let my right hand forget her cunning. If I do not
remember thee, let my tongue cleave to the roof of my mouth.*

Who was he who haunted her like this? He had always been
there, changing and shifting with her age and her mood, but

always there, a presence locked in the Jerusalem of her mind, person and place subtly merged so that one became the other, and the whole a paradigm of fatherhood. Who was he? *And lo, I am with you always, even unto the end of the world.*

She walked down the hill towards the Jaffa Gate, dodging through the traffic, crossing the borderline in that determined manner of hers, with long, purposeful strides as though she knew where she was going. Scaffolding had been put up just inside the gate and Arab workmen were already at work repointing the ancient stones. Nearby there was a stall selling *felafel*. She went through the gap in the walls and into the tight alleys of the Old City, finding her way more by memory that by the occasional sign, turning left into the Muristan just by the church of Saint John the Baptist. A foot patrol of the Israeli army came by, three boys barely older than Paul, toting their assault rifles almost as though they were toys. She passed them by and emerged into the narrow space outside the Church of the Holy Sepulchre.

It was still early and the souvenir sellers were only just getting their stalls ready outside the entrance to the church. One of them held up a crucifix. 'Genuine olive wood from Gethsemane,' he called to her. 'Genuine crucifix, genuine rosary beads.' She smiled distractedly and went past into the courtyard towards the dark maw of the entrance.

'You want guide?' a shadowy figure asked.

'No, thank you.'

The interior of the church was a strange, dark womb, alight with a thousand candles and haunted by the perfume of incense. She climbed steps to her right and stood alone in the chapel of Golgotha, staring down through plate glass onto a grey lump of rock while the first tourists muttered in the shadows below.

There was a post hole in the middle of the rock. That was all. A lump of dusty rock, as grey as an elephant's back, with a hole in it. What of it? Could it really have been there amongst the gilded lamps, owned severally by Orthodox and Catholic and Armenian and Copt? Could it really have been there amongst the clouds of incense and the passing tourists? Guide books fluttered, shutters clicked. From this paltry rock had a man known as Christ stepped off into hell? Had all this, now wedged amongst the alleyways of the Old City, once been a grim place just outside the walls, but near enough the gate and the road so that people passing in and out of the city might see and take warning? Gallows Hill? Could it have been here?

She knew all the arguments, of course, knew about the

300

excavations, knew that she, not the chaplain at the Garden Tomb all those years ago, had been right. In her mind's eye she saw the neo-Gothic crucifix in the Church of Saint Edward the Confessor opposite the library, the figure of Christ pinned to a board like a museum specimen, and she found herself murmuring the words of the Jesus Prayer – 'Lord Jesus Christ, Son of God, have mercy on me, a sinner' – almost as though she would be heard, almost as though he was listening. 'Lord Jesus, Son of God, have mercy on me, a sinner.' The first half is said on an inbreath, the second half, the supplication, on the outbreath. But was anyone listening?

She waited for a moment and then went back down the steps to the level of the main church and out into the morning light. Now, for the first time, she had to consult the map she had brought from the hotel.

The Jesuit House was a recent building tucked just inside the walls near the New Gate. There was a porter on the door and a hallway beyond with polished tiles and that atmosphere of sterile cleanliness that she recognised from other religious institutions. There were devotional pictures on the wall showing Saint Francis Xavier and Saint Francis Borgia and a framed photograph of Pope Paul praying at the Coenaculum during his visit to the city in 1964. She refused the offer of a seat, but stood waiting until a grey figure came down the corridor and approached her.

'Mrs Smythe?' He was an austere man in clerical dress, his cheeks lined, his grey hair as thin and insubstantial as wisps of smoke. It seemed impossible that he could be the same as that callow youth who had stood before a camera on the Hill of Evil Council next to Dennis Killin and amongst those laughing girls. 'I am Father Silver. David Silver.'

He appeared confused by the presence of this woman in front of him. There was all the celibate's suspicion of the opposite sex. His nose seemed to twitch, as though searching for the acrid scent of hysteria. 'I'm afraid I didn't quite follow the message that you left with our porter.'

'I'm at the Bible conference,' she said. 'One of the delegates.'

'Ah.' There was a faint air of relief. 'I was hoping to attend some of the lectures myself: I was particularly interest in hearing Vermes on Jesus and Judaism.' The question hung in the air, unasked and unanswered. A couple of priests went out, calling a greeting to him. 'But wasn't there something about a letter, a letter of mine? I write fairly often in the *Tablet*. A Letter from Jerusalem, they call it. They wanted "epistle", but I thought that a trifle presumptuous.' He chuckled at his little joke, standing there in the middle of the hall, with his hands clasped in front of him almost as though he was at prayer, waiting.

'It was a private letter,' Helen said.

'Private letter?' He shook his head, as though he never wrote the things.

'One you wrote to my father more than twenty years ago.'

'Twenty years? Oh, my goodness. We were both younger then . . .' he stumbled in the face of solecism, 'or rather, I was much younger then. You, I imagine, were just a child.'

She smiled. 'I was already a graduate student.'

'One would not have guessed.' The gallantry did not come easily to him. 'Your father, you say . . .'

'My father was Andrew Harding.'

There was a silence. 'Ah.' He seemed to be considering the proposition, trying to sense its truth. 'Perhaps . . . perhaps we can go somewhere more suitable.' He opened a door onto the kind of room that the religious reserve for such things as female visitors, a bare and comfortless room on which Saint Ignatius Loyola gazed with disapproval. There was a plain table and four uncomfortable chairs. He indicated that she might sit, and then he took his place opposite her, almost as though they were settling down to play a game of some kind.

'Andrew Harding, you say?'

'Exactly.'

'So you are . . .'

'Helen.'

'Helen.' He paused. 'He showed me pictures of you. It must have been you.' He shook his head, as though ready to deny the fact. 'Imagine. A little girl.'

'It was a long time ago.'

'Oh, yes. The world has changed since then. We have all changed.'

'This is the letter I'm referring to.' She took it from her bag and handed it across the table to him. He fiddled with reading glasses. 'What terrible writing,' he muttered as he peered at it.

'You remember, do you?'

'Andrew? Of course I do. Oh, yes. We, ah, shared a house.' He tapped the page. 'As I seem to say here. Only for a month or so, mind you. There was some kind of misunderstanding.' He hesitated, for a moment, choosing his words with care. 'Perhaps it was not quite the place for me. But I was fond of your father. He showed me considerable kindness at a time when I was struggling

302

to find my way. He was not a religious man, at least not in the conventional sense, and yet he was a great help.'

'This letter, though. Do you remember it?'

He looked up at her. 'It must have been a mistake, mustn't it? If I recall correctly Mrs Harding wrote back to me. She must have remarried because she wasn't Harding then, was she?'

'Constance.'

'Was that it? Is she still alive?'

'She died a month ago. I found the letter amongst her things.'

'I'm sorry. Perhaps I could say a mass for her? Would that be . . .?'

'She wasn't any kind of Christian.'

'All the same, I will do it if you wish. It would seem the least . . .'

'She wrote back to you?'

'Ah, yes. If my memory does not deceive me, she wrote to me and said that Andrew was dead as I had originally supposed. So I must have been mistaken, mustn't I?' He handed the letter back. 'Sad. He was a man of many gifts.'

'*Were* you mistaken, though?'

He looked surprised. 'Is there any other possibility?'

'You said you saw him. You called out to him. It says so in the letter.'

'The man, whoever it was, was getting on a bus. As far as I recall he was getting on a bus.' He shook his head. 'But I must have been mistaken.'

'Was he alone?'

'Ah, how would I know that? I wouldn't have recognised a companion, would I?'

She took the photograph out of her bag and held it out to him, pointing to one of the faces. 'Would you have recognised this woman?'

'Good Lord, that picnic! How time flies. Please let me see.' He peered at the picture, and muttered something about having once had a copy himself, but who knew where it had got to?

'Would you have recognised her?' Helen repeated.

'Oh yes,' he admitted. 'I would have recognised her.'

'Rachel.'

He looked up. 'Look, Mrs Smythe, all this was a long time ago. What was it our Lord said? Let the dead bury their dead. They already have their deserts, and how can our interest change things?'

'I just want to know, that's all. I want to try and recover a bit of my past. Rachel was his mistress. I know she was. I know all that. There was a letter from my father to my mother explaining about her.'

'I didn't realise that your mother knew, poor woman.' He shook his head, as though at the folly of people caught in the trap of carnality. 'And how do you imagine I can help you?'

'What was he like, Father Silver? What was my father like?' There was an edge of desperation in her voice, as though if she no longer asked the memory of him would vanish altogether. By mere concern, mere persistence, she might somehow keep him alive.

'He was a young man, my dear. A young man whose head was turned by a pretty girl. There's nothing surprising about that. Other than that, what can I say? He was different from the run-of-the-mill British officer. There was a great deal of insensitivity in those days and he was not guilty of that. He was a man who thought a lot. I think he was very disturbed.'

'Disturbed by what?

'By what was happening around him. Around him and to him. The two things were inextricable.'

'Was he in love with Rachel?'

Silver smiled a tired, ironical smile. 'How can I answer that? The love of God I am meant to have some knowledge of; the love of a man for a woman is another thing altogether. I believe they were' – he paused – 'intimate. That is all I can say. Does that constitute love? And perhaps having said that I have said enough.' He pushed his chair back from the table and rose to go. 'Anyway, I hope I have been of some help, Mrs Smythe.'

'Wait.'

He looked at her with something like concern. 'Please.'

'Do you know anything about Rachel? Do you know her name, her surname? She was American, wasn't she? Was she a Jew?'

'Yes, I believe she was a Jew. We talked about it once. She introduced herself to me and made a play on her name. I think she was making fun of me. "I'm not Delilah," she said. "I'm Shimshon." That was her name, you see: Rachel Shimshon. *Shimshon* is Samson, of course. She was one of those Jews trying to find her roots. The country is full of them, poor lost orphans. It was full of them then, it is full of them now. Maybe I was one such.' He nodded and turned to leave.

'And do you believe that my father was alive in 1966, Father Silver? Do you?'

The old priest paused, with his hand on the door. 'I have already said, Mrs Smythe, I must have been mistaken.'

She felt her grip slipping, her grasp on whatever hope this constituted. She made the metaphor real and reached out to grab his wrist. 'Father Silver,' she said, 'I need your help.'

He shook his head. 'I'm afraid I haven't any help to offer, Mrs Smythe.'

'You weren't mistaken, were you?' He stood there by the door looking down on his wrist and the thin fingers of the woman who held it. 'You weren't mistaken, were you. I have reason to believe that my father is alive.'

'No, my dear, you do not have *reason* to believe he is alive, you have a *hope* that he is alive. It is a very different thing.'

Tears had begun. One part of her, a sane part, watched them flow and felt angry at their presence, but mere anger couldn't stem them. 'But I need him to be alive,' she said softly. The tears coursed down her cheeks silently, like an admonishment; and Father Silver looked almost frightened at this display of emotion, as though emotion were a thing that played no part in his own austere life.

'My dear woman,' he said, 'please let me go.'

'What about Rachel, then. Do you know about her? Tell me?'

'I know nothing.'

'You do, Father Silver. You do.'

There was a silence. The past, whatever constituted the past, lay between them like a gulf. He spoke reluctantly. 'She's alive,' he said at last. 'I believe she lives in one of the settlements on Lake Tiberias. Kibbutz Migdal.' He looked at Helen with a disconcerting expression of sorrow, as though she had made some kind of confession and contrary to all expectation he had found himself unable to grant her absolution. 'A journalist. I've seen her from time to time on television. Now please let me go,' he said.

The thing was underway now and there was no stopping it. She felt caught up in the momentum of something that existed outside her, a flow of time, a tide of history perhaps. She abandoned the conference and hired a car at an agency near the hotel. The hire contract warned her that she should not drive on rough roads, that she should avoid areas of public disturbance, that anything that might happen was her fault and her fault alone. She could agree with that.

The road led around the Mount of Olives to the village of El-

Azariye. She knew, of course. She knew why it was so named and what had happened there. She knew all about Lazarus, raised from the dead after four days – the theories and the arguments, she knew them all. *Lord, by this time he stinketh.*

The road went down, down into the bowels of the earth in great plunging curves, past the Good Samaritan Inn with 'Bedouin, Camel, Holy Objects, Photographs', past a sign saying *Sea Level* and a Bedouin camp smelling, even from a speeding car, of burnt rubber and rotting fish; down past desert rocks dusted with a sudden green after the rain, down into the great trench which was the lowest point on Earth.

The Dead Sea lay over to the right, like a great ingot of beaten pewter pressed into the desert. There was little traffic. The plain of salt and scrub lay prostrate, as though weighed down by the very weight of atmosphere above it. Beyond the saturnine gleam of the sea were the hills of Moab where Moses died and from where Joshua son of Nun came down with the Children of Israel to claim the Promised Land. A battered roadside sign announced JERICHO – THE OLDEST CITY IN THE WORLD but the place was not a city: it was nothing more than a scattering of buildings and a line of palm trees beneath a brown escarpment, a nomad's camp that had become frozen into a kind of permanence. All around was a plain which Joshua would surely have recognised, a wide and vacant plain which exuded emptiness as though emptiness can be a positive attribute. Nothing had changed here, she felt, or ever would.

Armed soliders were hitch-hiking back to Jerusalem. She slowed for an army roadblock but the huddled figure in the hut just waved her on. Beyond the barrier was an abandoned camp with the faded blue signs of UNRWA, the UN Relief Works Agency. The windows of the barracks were all smashed.

The road turned left, away from ALLENBY BRIDGE and PLACE OF THE BAPTISM. It skirted the town, passed the tell of ancient Jericho, and led north up the river Jordan, heading for Galilee and Kibbutz Migdal.

10

The Sea of Galilee was pressed into the landscape like a coin lying in a lined and ancient palm. It glittered in the sunlight. It was the antithesis of the Dead Sea: it was silver against lead, sweet against salt, life against death. There were speedboats scouring its surface and modern hotels standing amongst the trees along its shores. There was change and variety, where the Dead Sea was immutable and implacable.

Kibbutz Migdal lay on the western shore, to the north of the town of Tiberias. The settlement was encircled by a perimeter fence, with a guard house and a steel watch tower and a red and white barrier at the entrance. Beyond the fence there were lawns and trees and, over to the left, rows of small houses lying amongst gardens.

As she drew to a halt some kind of recognition stirred in Helen's mind, some chain of memory and experience. She knew the slant of light and the sudden intensity of shade, the houses silent in the warm morning, the distant sounds that did nothing to intrude on the still present. She remembered: a Cyprus hillside; the call of children in the distance; a vehicle grinding up a slope far away; lizards slanting silently across low stone walls.

Expecting someone to come out and demand to see her papers or something, she waited at the barrier; but the pole was pointing towards the sky like a bandaged, bloodied finger and the guard house and tower were both empty, symbols of battles that had been fought and won.

She put the car into gear and drove on towards the eucalyptus trees at the water's edge where there was a car park. The nearest building was an alien, modern construction of grey steel and smoked glass, with a revolving door that led into the sharp embrace of air-conditioning. There was a dribbling fountain and the mindless murmur of piped music. A display case was full of the kind of expensive junk that you find in hotels and airports – silk scarves, jewellery, handbags and leather belts. A sign in four languages announced that everything was hand crafted by members of the National Kibbutz Movement. The prices were in dollars, lots of dollars.

As she approached a white-haired man looked up from behind a reception desk and uttered a cursory *shalom*.

'Do you speak English?' she asked. 'I'm looking for someone, a member of the kibbutz.'

'Guest house,' the man said. He slid a glossy pamphlet across the desk. Sailing and windsurfing and water-skiing were all available. There were cultural tours of the surrounding countryside and the experience of seeing community life at first hand. Since its foundation by Czech Jews in 1938, Kibbutz Migdal had played a leading part in the formation of Eretz Yisrael.

'I'm looking for someone.' She said the name – 'Rachel Simson' – and the sound rang loudly in her mind, echoing through the years of memory, dying away among the display cases and the piece of sculpture that looked as though it was made out of spare tractor parts, and the fountain dribbling water of the Sea of Galilee onto papyrus reeds and fern fronds.

The man shrugged. 'Secretary office,' he said with scant interest.

'Do you know her? Do you know Rachel Simson? Do you know her?'

'Secretary office,' he said once more and turned back to what he had been doing.

The office was a plain, functional building with breeze-block walls and a tar-paper roof: it might have been the adjutant's office of some army barracks. Inside a girl was hammering at a keyboard while a man in a shirtsleeves and khaki shorts argued on the telephone. He was overweight and balding and florid with perspiration. A ceiling fan above his head brought him no cool, only stirred the air around him in a desultory fashion, shifting the chaos of papers on his desk as though it was unable to overcome the lassitude of the day. The office smelt faintly of sweat.

'Rachel Simson,' Helen asked when the man finally slammed the phone down on the desk in disgust. 'Where can I find Rachel Simson?'

'One moment.' He began to leaf through the papers. 'You English?' He didn't look up.

'I'm English. I'm looking for Rachel Simson. Or maybe it's Shimshon. I believe she lives here.'

'You don't want to sell me tractor spares?'

'I don't want to sell you tractor spares,' she agreed.

He laughed and glanced at her. 'Because you couldn't do a worse job than that bastard there.' He went back to searching through the papers. 'I've a goddam quotation here somewhere. Delivery dates, everything, and then the jerk goes on about shipping delays and a strike in Marseilles and all manner of crap . . . Rachel, you say? What do you want her for? You from the TV?'

'No, I'm not from the TV. It's a personal matter.'

He looked at her closely for the first time. 'Thought it might be that damn programme she did. But it's not.'

'No.'

He shrugged, as though the matter couldn't be helped. 'I guess she's around somewhere.' He waved a hand. 'Try the apartments out thataway. Spends most of her time in the garden these days. Fifth on the left down the path towards the community building. Shimshon. Hasn't been Simson for years.' Triumphantly he grabbed up a sheet of paper. 'Here it is! I swear I'll kill that guy.'

She left him shouting abuse down the telephone – '*Shalom* my arse,' he was saying to the tractor dealer. 'This is *war*' – but as she stepped out into the sun he clamped a fat hand over the telephone mouthpiece and called out something to her. She only half-heard the words, and amongst the mixture of Hebrew and English that he had been yelling down the phone she couldn't formulate them into any kind of sense. Something to do with possession. Who did he say possessed what? Puzzling at his words, faintly disturbed by them, she went round the back of the building as he had indicated.

The houses behind the office had something of the look of holiday apartments about them, the kind of box-like constructions you find on the Spanish coast. They lay amongst pine trees, each built of identical materials to an identical plan each with a small verandah at the front, each painted the same faded ochre, each with a water tank and a solar panel on the roof: only the flowers in the diminutive gardens were different, bushes of hibiscus vying with bouganvillea and jacaranda. Crickets rasped in the shrubs and somewhere a radio was blaring pop music.

Helen hesitated on the path between the houses. She had a sensation of unease, as though something was wrong in the regimented lines of the houses and the weeded paths, as though something didn't fit in with the bright spring morning, with the sunlight glittering off the lake and children calling in the distance. What was it that the man in the office had called out? A warning of some kind? She tried to reconstruct the words out of her memory, but they wouldn't make sense. *It doesn't matter.* Was that it?

A heavily-built girl walked past, staring at Helen curiously as though visitors had no right to be there. She wore shorts and a singlet. Her breasts moved volubly beneath the thin cotton as she slopped along. Her feet were as broad as a man's in their battered leather sandals, the toes spatulate and grimy. Absurdly Helen wondered whether those were typical Jewish feet, wondered whether Rachel Simson would have feet like that, the toenails thick and horny, the heels prominent and pale like the heels of an African woman; the feet of a woman who goes barefoot most of her life, who works in the fields. The girl passed by and Helen went on down the path, counting the gates as she went, pausing outside the fifth on the left.

A woman was in the garden, kneeling at a flower bed. She wore jeans and sandals, and her feet weren't thick and horny at all, but slender and neat, almost like a child's, the soles pale pink and innocent. Her hair – all that Helen could see of her head – was iron grey and cut quite short. She was working away at the hard soil with a trowel and when Helen called '*shalom*' she barely paused, merely called something over her shoulder.

'I'm sorry, I don't speak Hebrew.'

The woman clambered to her feet, muttering something unintelligible. At first glance she appeared almost frail, but her arms were sinewy and her face had a toughness about it that was almost masculine. Her eyes were as bright as a child's. 'You want something?'

Helen hesitated. Time, the intransigent dimension, seemed to mock her. The years had abraded the woman's features so that she no longer appeared like the young girl in the photograph, the girl wearing a floral dress and holding her hat against the breeze. Now hard, sharp edges had taken the place of what might have been delicacy and softness.

'I'm just visiting. I saw you working . . .'

'Working!' The woman gave a sharp laugh. 'I've seen work compared with which this would be a rest cure. The guest house is over there. They do tours—'

'I wanted to look round by myself.'

The woman shrugged. 'Go ahead. It's free.'

310

'Have you been here long?' Helen asked. 'You're American, aren't you?'

'*Was*. Been here forty years.' The woman made a dismissive gesture. 'This was tents and huts, then. Watchtower and Stockade, like the Old West. Now . . .' She shrugged, looking round at the measured gardens and the smug rows of houses. The communal building at the end of the path looked like a supermarket. 'Now the voice of the turtle is heard in the land and we've gotten fat and indolent. You know what we produce now? We produce microprocessor switching systems. They're intended to control glasshouse irrigation, but you know what their biggest use is?'

Helen didn't.

'Household security systems. We export to California, can you imagine? That's what we've come to.'

Helen smiled, trying to read the lines on the woman's face, the grey and carelessly cut hair, the narrow lips and hard, blue eyes. 'I'm Helen,' she said.

'Hi, Helen. Good to meet you.' The woman held out her hand across the boundary of the wooden gate. 'Rachel. Here I'm Rach-el' – she pronounced the fricative – 'but once upon a time it was Rachel. Are you from England, Helen? I guess you must be, with that accent . . .'

'I'm Helen Harding.'

Time, that most exigent of dimensions, stopped. Even the sounds of the day – the insect noise, the radio blaring from a nearby house, children calling in the distance – even these sounds seemed momentarily stilled. The woman's eyes shifted, looking for something in the narrow space around her and, not finding it, came reluctantly back to Helen as the only option available. For a while that flicker of her eyes seemed to be the only movement in the whole, soft Galilean morning. The woman frowned, as though assessing the moment. 'I guess you'd better come in,' she said finally.

The inside of her house was spare and functional. The front room had a sofa and an armchair. The walls were lined with books. An oil painting on the wall showed a desert scene in blue and red. A personal computer stood blankly on a table beneath the window.

'Please find somewhere to sit,' Rachel said. 'A coffee or something, can I offer you a coffee?' She had a small kitchen at the back, little more than a cupboard equipped with a sink and cooking plate and fridge. She fiddled around there while Helen sat dumbly on the sofa and examined the books on the shelves. She noticed *The Arab Awakening* and *Orientations* and *Orientalism*. She read the spines and let her mind go, trying not to think what she might say, what it all might mean, this encounter forty years later when the past was dead and finished. *The Seat of Pilate* she saw. *The Revolt. Mandate Memories.*

Rachel came over with a plastic tray and two coffee cups. 'Turkish okay?'

'Turkish is fine.' Helen took the little porcelain cup and sipped at the gritty edge of the coffee, and watched Rachel across the gulf and tried to see the young girl behind the worn mask, a brash young girl, full of hope.

'Helen Harding,' Rachel repeated, almost as though savouring the name.

'Smythe now. Married with two children.'

'Is that right?'

'And you?'

Rachel shook her head. 'Never married.'

'You knew my father.'

'Oh, sure I knew your father.' She laughed. It was an odd, bitter sound, like the noise a museum piece might make, something mechanical and worn out. 'But how, Miss Helen Harding, do you know me?'

'A letter. He left a letter for my mother, a letter about you. Dennis Killin must have brought it back to England with him. I read it when I was going through her things after she died.'

'So she's dead, is she?'

'She's dead.'

Rachel considered that piece of news, her mouth moving, her tongue feeling her lips, almost as though she were tasting it. 'And you know Killin?'

'I knew Killin. I knew him well. But he never told me much. He seemed reluctant, evasive.'

'It was forty years ago, my dear. They were different people, a different world. It wasn't me; it wasn't him.'

'I just want to know what happened.'

Rachel laughed sourly. 'And you expect me to be able to tell you?'

'You must know.'

'Or have you come to pass judgement?'

'Not judgement, no.'

But Rachel nodded, as though she knew better. 'I guess that's it. You're just like all the rest of the British, with their disapproval, their condescension.'

'I'm his daughter, that's all—'

'And you've come to find out whether he was really the hero he might have been, or the traitor they hoped he'd become. Or maybe, just maybe, a man struggling with conscience and loyalty. They're pretty damned difficult adversaries if you're prepared to take them on. Few enough of his colleagues seemed brave enough to try. Killin was about the only other one, I guess.'

She paused, and the telephone stepped into the silence, almost as though it were following some kind of cue, a stage direction. The woman got up to answer it, speaking at first in English – 'Yes, who is it? . . . Yes, of course it's me' – and then lapsing into Hebrew. Something, a certain tone, a hint of evasion and obliqueness about the woman's responses, gave Helen the idea that she was the subject of the call. But the idea was absurd. Who knew she was here?

'I'm sorry if I've intruded,' she said when the call was finished. 'I want to understand, that's all. I lost my father when I was six years old and I've never really understood why. I just want to understand.' Why should she feel helpless in the face of this woman, absurdly, childishly helpless? Anger bubbled up within her, anger against her own weakness as much as anything, but also another and more disturbing thing – anger at the fact that she couldn't like the woman, that she could only see Rachel Simson as she had become, hardened and awkward; and she couldn't like her. Or had she always been like that? Did one change? Had Michael changed? The thought occurred to her that maybe this was what her father had fallen for all those years ago, this sharp and acerbic woman with a chip on her shoulder. 'Did you love him?' she asked.

There was a silence. The woman shrugged, as though the question was of no consequence. 'Perhaps I still love him. Memory can't change, can it? If I loved him then, I love him still.'

'And what about him? What did he feel?'

'The question's unfair.'

'Didn't you talk? For God's sake, he had a family back in England. You must have *talked* about it.' Anger rose within her like bile rising in her throat, anger and insistent pressure of tears, a vicious circle of anger and misery, the one pursuing the other, spiralling within her mind, threatening her self-control. She cried out: 'He must have *said* something to you! You must have had some idea of his feelings!'

Rachel Simson stared at her, as though from a great distance, as though from forty years away. 'This country was almost at war,' she said. 'Can you understand that? I was in hiding and the only way we could meet was in secret. Can you understand that? He had been helping us, and that constituted some kind of treason, I guess. They were after him—'

'Who? Who was after him?'

'The police, my dear, the police. Can't you understand that either? Sure, we talked about it, but what he *felt* I can't say. I know only what he *said*. In circumstances like that, I'm not sure how far the one thing matches the other—'

'And what did he say?'

She laughed. 'He told me the story of Abraham and Isaac. Christ, I really didn't *need* the story of Abraham and Isaac at that moment, but that's what he told me. We sat there together in that stuffy little room and he told me about a jealous god, who demanded sacrifice . . .'

'Of a child.'

'Of a child,' Rachel repeated.

And Helen saw things clearly, saw her father climbing the steps of a silver aircraft, saw the lights and saw the rain, saw the choice that lay ahead of him. 'That was me,' she cried. 'You sit there forty years later and you treat the whole thing as though it's dead and buried, but that child was me.'

The woman seemed to consider the possibility. 'Maybe it was, maybe it wasn't. You mustn't jump to conclusions, Miss Harding. In this particular equation there were two children.'

'Two?'

'I was pregnant.'

Something shifted inside Helen's chest, something organic. The whole of the past, her past, a careful construct of fantasy and fact, seemed to tremble and dissolve and recrystallise into something that was a caricature of what she had known. 'Pregnant?' she whispered.

'Sure,' the woman called Rachel said. 'Pregnant. By Andrew. It happens, you know. All too often it happens. So maybe' – she shrugged – 'who knows? Maybe he was saying to me that either way there was going to be a sacrifice . . .'

'And that he would have to choose which child?'

Rachel nodded. There was silence in the claustrophobic little room and mockery in her expression. It was warm and airless, the atmosphere clinging like damp. Helen wanted to be outside, away from this woman, away from the malign power of memory. 'And did he choose?' she asked quietly.

The woman laughed, a brittle laugh, a laugh entirely appropriate to her dry, emaciated form. 'He chose. Sure he chose.'

'How?' She would know, and it would be over. It seemed a matter of the utmost urgency, this question of choice all those years ago, when Lorna was a young woman and Helen was a girl. She sat waiting for an answer and the woman looked back at her with something like derision.

'I was waiting for him, at the windmill. Sounds very rustic that, doesn't it? Almost out of Thomas Hardy. You know the windmill, don't you, the only damn windmill in Zion? I'd sent him a note to meet me there. At a quarter of one. There are certain things you never forget. A quarter of one exactly.'

'Why then?'

Rachel looked at the younger woman with something like pity. 'Because I knew what was going to happen. I knew about the bomb.'

Time cannot be measured on a linear scale, like distance or weight. That is not its nature. The Montefiore windmill, an absurd monument to Zionist ideals, stands in an olive grove on the edge of the Valley of Gehenna, the valley where once children were sacrificed to the god Moloch. Forty years, or yesterday, it stands in the heat of midsummer, its stones white and hot, while all about it in the olive trees the cicadas shriek. And a young girl waits in the shade of the trees and watches the hotel that stands higher up the hill, and glances at her watch and expects the familiar figure, khaki clad, to come down through the garden and clamber over the wall into the olive grove. She has waited for forty years now.

'And what happened?'

'You know what happened.'

'Did he die?' Helen asked. 'Did he die in the King David?' It seemed absurd, an idiotic question, a child's question, the question of the little girl with her cloud of blond hair and her rather pinched, rather stubborn expression clutching a postcard to herself and trying to interpret the carefully looped handwriting. 'Did he die?' she repeated and the woman called Rachel laughed faintly, a sour laugh that came across the forty years like the breath from a newly opened tomb.

'Sure he died,' she said. 'What in God's name do you think happened? Of course he died. He died on the day he made his choice.'

★

Sunlight glittered on the lake. This was the Sea of Galilee where miracles happened. She walked across the lawn towards the water's edge, where two park benches stood in the shade of the trees, where an old man was sitting and gazing across the shifting surface of the water towards the heights of Golan, which had once been the country of the Gaderenes. Helen sat on the other bench.

She understood now what the man in the office had called out after her. She could resolve his words from the confusions of memory, like cleaning a pane and seeing something clearly beyond it for the first time. She understood both what he had said in that moment as she left his office, and a greater thing, something that had worried her for years, for most of her life perhaps, ever since the entry into her world of that tall, shining officer with his solemn shining face, and the brisk, efficient lady with him: whether there was a pattern in things, whether there was any sense at all.

She's my mother, that's what the man in the office of the kibbutz had said. *She's my mother*.

And Helen felt the randomness of things, the pure indifference of nature and existence. There is no pattern, she thought, looking out across the water; there is no pattern, no God walking the lake, no miraculous draught of fishes. The storm has not been stilled: it rages still.

11

'Andrew?' Killin called, 'come and have a jar!'

Harding looked in at the door to the bar. Killin was perched on one of the stools, brandishing a glass of beer. 'What's going on?' Harding asked. 'Everyone seems in a tizz.'

Killin made a face. 'One of the Arabs went berserk in the kitchens or something. Tried to shoot the chef. I feel like shooting the chef sometimes. What'll you have?'

'Not now.' Harding gave a little wave and turned away. In the lobby there was still confusion, still a senseless milling of people. He glanced at his watch.

At that moment there was a sharp explosion outside. The noise in the lobby increased. People were calling to each other and running out of the main doors to look. In the bar men were leaning out of the windows. 'What the devil's going on?' a voice called.

Harding crossed the corridor into the quiet of the reading room. There was no one there, no commotion and no disturbance. He found a chair and sat down, leaning back against the headrest and closing his eyes. For those few minutes, constrained by time, constrained by choice, he felt free.

12.20.

As a child, when something dreadful was about to happen, he used to look at his watch and will the hands to stop; but however hard he tried, the hands always continued their inexorable movement. He used to wonder whether time moved the clock, or the clock moved time; which was cause and which was effect? When he grew up a bit the question seemed absurd, but as he sat there in the reading room of the King David the question returned to haunt him, transformed, as so often, into a slightly different problem, one that seemed to have no answer: do we act because we will it, or do we will it in order to give reason to the act? Is there any choice that is truly free? *Take now thy son, thine only son Isaac, whom thou lovest, and get thee into the land of Moriah.*

12.25.

And offer him there for a burnt offering upon one of the mountains which I will tell thee of. Rachel knew, that much was certain. She knew that something was due to happen at the King David just after midday. She knew, just as she had known about the bomb at the railway station. Hence the note, hence the time, hence the urgency. And she would be waiting now in the olive grove beside the Montefiore windmill; waiting for him to go out on the terrace and come down through the gardens. A stroll. A stroll at half–past twelve of a hot July day, with chaos in the public rooms of the King David Hotel.

12.30.

Outside the building a siren sounded, the steady note of the All Clear. Events seemed random and without sense, people milling round without purpose or thought, people coming and going, people arguing, people running to look, or running away to hide. The door from the lounge opened for an instant. A face looked in, then vanished.

12.35.

Choice. The scales were loaded, the balance tipped gently this way and that. *And Isaac said, Behold the fire and the wood; but where is the lamb for a burnt offering?* Harding got up from his chair and went back into the corridor. It was deserted. Even the bar appeared deserted. But the lobby was crowded still. Someone ran into the manager's office nearby, and quite distinctly Harding heard the words that he uttered: 'In the basement. Bombs in the basement.'

It was obvious, so obvious that no one could see it. Harding turned left and walked away from the noise towards the end of the corridor where stairs led down to the door of the Regence Café. He tried the handle. The place looked closed but the door swung open. The Regence lay silent in the shadows. The tiny dance floor where he had shuffled round with Rachel, where he had hit Oliphant, was empty. How long ago had it been? Weeks? Months? Time seemed malleable. The stools and the leather chairs were deserted. Some of the tables were lying on their sides almost as though that absurd struggle with Oliphant had only just taken place. *My son. God will provide himself a lamb.* It was obvious. The pillars in the centre of the room supported the whole of the south wing of the building, the whole of the Secretariat; and against the pillars stood six milk churns.

12.37.

Harding stood in the shadows of the Regence Café and watched, thinking of Lorna and Helen, thinking of Rachel, thinking of a child as yet unborn. Time, that most exigent of dimensions, stopped.